$4,15$

INTERBORO

DATE DUE

MM°K			

5R

Promise Me Tomorrow

*Also by Lori Wick
in Large Print:*

Whispers of Moonlight

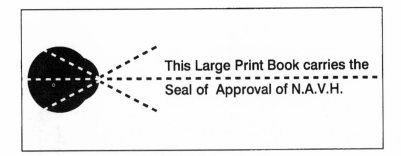

This Large Print Book carries the
Seal of Approval of N.A.V.H.

Promise Me Tomorrow

Lori Wick

Thorndike Press • Thorndike, Maine

Published in 1998 by arrangement with Harvest House Publishers.

Thorndike Large Print ® Christian Fiction Series.

The tree indicium is a trademark of Thorndike Press.

The text of this Large Print edition is unabridged.
Other aspects of the book may vary from the original edition.

Set in 16 pt. Plantin by Warren S. Doersam.

Printed in the United States on permanent paper.

Library of Congress Cataloging in Publication Data

Wick, Lori.
    Promise me tomorrow / Lori Wick.
      p. cm.
    ISBN 0-7862-1404-X (lg. print : hc : alk. paper)
    1. Frontier and pioneer life — Rocky Mountains Region — Fiction. 2. Man–woman relationships — Rocky Mountains Region — Fiction. 3. Rocky Mountains Region — History — Fiction. 4. Orphans — Fiction. 5. Large type books. I. Title.
    [PS3573.I237P76   1998]
    813′.54—dc21   98-10561

*This book is dedicated to my
aunt, Doris Wallace.
To know you are loved as I am
is a wondrous thing.
Thank you for your encouragement
and caring.
My world is a richer place
because of you.*

Acknowledgments

Life is such a wonderful adventure, and daily made sweeter by the ones who fill my world. I praise God for the following people and wish to share my feelings on this page.

Matthew, is there a mother more blessed than I am? I don't think so. Thank you for the warm, wonderful son you are. Thank you for laughing at all my jokes, sitting through haircuts, and for just being you. Your smile comes from your heart and always melts mine. I love you.

Abigail, my ray of sunshine. I begged God not to make me raise myself; I'm so glad He didn't listen. You are precious beyond words. Thank you for those toothless smiles and endless days of fun. God bless you, my darling.

My mini church family, what a time we have! I pray that we will continue to grow together and hold one another accountable for years to come. Thank you for your love, faithfulness, and example to me.

Bob, 17 books! Who would have guessed? Certainly not me. Thank you for being here for all of them.

1

Manitou, Colorado
April 10, 1897

Katherine Alexa Taggart, "Rusty" to family and friends alike, gently took the little girl's hand within her own and smiled as she was watched with worshipful eyes.

"We're going to be late if we don't hurry," she urged the child. Even when rushed, Rusty moved with grace and poise. She wasn't a tall girl, just a hair over five feet, and her frame was on the slim side. Her hair, a dark shade of her nickname, hung rich and full down her back. At times it seemed too heavy for her slender neck.

"Oh, Rusty, there you are," her aunt, Sammy O'Brien, said as soon as she saw her in the hallway outside the girls' bedroom. "Is

Tara ready for bed?"

"Yes, ma'am. I knew we'd be running late, so I told her a story while she was in the bathtub."

"Good thinking. Come along, Tara," Sammy bade kindly. The little girl tugged on Rusty's hand, who bent to hug her and to give as well as receive a kiss. She watched as the little girl skipped off to bed for the night. Rusty peeked into the large room that held 30 beds with almost as many orphan girls. A few called greetings to her and many waved. Rusty waved in return and blew a few kisses before turning away.

She was tired enough to seek her own sleep but thought it might help to have a little dinner. Knowing she was finished for the day, she made her way downstairs, past the kitchen and huge dining room and toward the private living quarters that she shared with her aunt, uncle, and three cousins, Eileen, Nolan, and Renny O'Brien. Surprisingly, her Uncle Paddy was already there.

"The boys must have settled in rather swiftly tonight," she commented.

"Yes, they did. I told them Grandpa O'Brien is coming to visit next month and that now would be an excellent time to work on their best behavior."

Paddy spoke of his own father, Cormac

O'Brien, who lived and worked as a mine surveyor in Georgetown. Paddy and Sammy had met in Georgetown, and although some years separated them, they had attended the same one-room schoolhouse. Eventually the couple began dating and were married when Sammy turned 18. They now ran the Fountain Creek Orphanage for Children, living on the premises as a matter of course.

The orphanage was a huge two-story structure that had dormitory rooms for at least 60 children and enough smaller bedrooms to hold 15 staff members. The private living quarters, sporting a small kitchen, dining area, and parlor, along with two bedrooms, were downstairs at the rear of the mansion. Rusty shared the larger of these two rooms with her three cousins, while Paddy and Sammy occupied the other. There was room for Rusty in one of the upstairs staff rooms, but most of the time everyone preferred the living arrangements the way they were. Rusty's hands now joined Paddy's, and the two of them set the table. Eileen, the oldest of the children at 14, came to help as well.

"How was school today?" her cousin asked her.

"It was okay." She sounded rather down

as she placed forks and knives on the table. "I missed one of my spelling words."

"Which one was it?" her father wanted to know.

The young teen hesitated. "Gramps would howl if he knew." She sighed dramatically. "It was Ireland."

Paddy laughed in delight. "We won't tell," he assured her, but he continued to chuckle.

"It's not funny, Papa." Eileen's tone was aggrieved. "I don't know what I could have been thinking."

He was still laughing when Sammy bustled in.

"Well, this sounds fun," she commented as she lent her hands to the work. She took a casserole from the warming drawer in the oven and placed it on the table. Rusty quickly set a bowl of applesauce next to it.

"It is fun," Paddy replied after he greeted her with a kiss, "but I'm afraid Eileen wouldn't appreciate my telling."

"Telling what?" 11-year-old Nolan asked as he came in. He was the middle of the O'Brien children. His brother, Renny, who was 10, followed just behind him.

"A private joke," his cousin supplied for him, crossing her eyes in his direction. Nolan crossed his eyes right back and asked, "What are we having tonight?" He was willing to let the joke go as long as he could eat.

"Cheese and mushroom casserole," his mother informed him. "Are your hands and face washed?"

The young boy nodded.

"And you, Renny?"

"Yes, Mother," he answered as he took his place at the table.

"I think Renny has the right idea," Paddy commented, and the rest of the family joined him by finding their respective seats. There wasn't an abundance of room, but they all fit. A moment after they were seated, and without needing instruction, every head bowed as Paddy thanked God for the food.

"Father in heaven, You have blessed us so greatly and we thank You. So many people go without food, but our plates will be full tonight. Thank You for each person around this table and for the wonderful children sleeping upstairs. We ask You to find homes for every one and to bless our care of them until that time. In Your holy name I pray. Amen."

Dishes were passed and plates were filled in the minutes that followed, and for a time everyone worked in silence. Renny had a little trouble with his knife, so his mother helped him cut the bread efficiently. The

11

family was eating in no time at all. At an age when he was often hungry, Nolan finished before the rest of the family, putting his fork aside and finishing off the milk in his glass. He then looked to his sister.

"Hey, Eileen," he said conversationally, "did you tell Papa that you spelled Ireland wrong today?"

Eileen could do nothing but groan, her forehead dropping into her hand. Paddy sailed off into laughter again.

"Did I tell you I received a letter from Chase today?"

"I don't think so." Sammy sat on the edge of their bed, Paddy already under the covers. She was working on her nails with a long file and now looked at him. "I hope nothing is wrong."

"No, not at all. He wanted to know how things were going and if he could help with anything. He reminded me that he helped take children to their new homes about two years ago. He didn't come right out and say it, but I can tell he'd like to be asked again."

When Sammy looked at him, his eyes were on the ceiling. "You're thinking, aren't you, Paddy?"

"Yes, I am," he admitted. "I know Rusty can handle the 'people end' of placement. In fact, I think she's better than some of the others who have been doing it far longer, but this placement is in Kurth. I worry about the travel and her safety." He paused and said gently, "She's been very sheltered, you know."

"Yes, and I'm glad she has been, but I know what you mean."

For a moment husband and wife stared at each other.

"I can't remember," Sammy continued. "Did Chase take the children on his own or did he escort one of our women?"

"Let's see," Paddy replied thoughtfully. "He escorted one group and then took children on his own one other time — two little boys it was."

"So you think he would be open to taking Rusty and the Parks children?"

"Yes, I do."

Sammy nodded. "What did Rusty say when you told her she'd be taking them? Was she excited?"

"I didn't tell her. I was about to call her into the office when Lane brought me the mail. After reading Chase's letter, I thought this might be a better plan."

"Well, it won't make any difference to Rusty; she'll be thrilled no matter what."

"It's settled then," Paddy declared. "I'll

13

tell Rusty in the morning and get a letter off to Chase."

They said nothing more on the subject, but husband and wife both thought about it. Sammy climbed into bed and moved close to share a kiss with her husband. As her head settled on the pillow, she wondered what Rusty would make of Chase McCandles. On the other side of the bed, Paddy was wondering if it was really wise to put Chase at Rusty Taggart's mercy.

"Do you remember the people who were here, the man and woman who talked with you?" Sammy asked Lizzy and Thomas Parks.

Thomas nodded in the affirmative, but Lizzy looked uncertain. In truth, Thomas was the younger of this brother-sister team, but he had more confidence because he remembered less of the horrendous situation from which they'd been rescued.

"The woman had black hair and gave you each an apple," Rusty supplied. "Do you remember that?"

Lizzy nodded, but the smile that went all the way to Thomas' eyes at the mention of the apple did not come to Lizzy's face.

"Their names are Mr. and Mrs. Davidson, and they want you to come live with them,"

Sammy said gently. "They want you to come and be their little boy and girl."

"For all time?" Thomas asked.

"That's right. They live on a ranch and have horses and cows. Mr. Davidson just wrote and said to remind you that they have a dog and a cat who just had kittens."

Sammy fell quiet for a moment, giving the children time to take things in, but Rusty plunged on.

"I'll be going with you," she said enthusiastically.

"Oh, Aunt Rusty." This was the first Lizzy had spoken. "You'll be staying with us!"

Rusty looked uncertainly at the pleasure in the little girl's eyes and then to her aunt, knowing she should have remained quiet. But Sammy's look was patient and her voice gentle as she addressed the children again.

"Aunt Rusty will be going with you, Lizzy, and she'll stay with you for a few days, but she won't stay for always. I will tell you that if you're too frightened to stay with Mr. and Mrs. Davidson, you may come home with Rusty."

Sammy and Paddy didn't give this option to all the children they placed, but Lizzy's case was different. Lizzy still remembered being locked in a room for days and fed only when someone remembered.

"How does that sound?" Sammy asked.

"I want to go," Thomas replied eagerly. "I want to see the kittens."

"And you shall," Sammy assured him. "How about you, Lizzy? Do you want to see the kittens?"

She nodded shyly, a small smile on her face.

"Will we ride the train?" Thomas had to know.

"Yes," Rusty returned. "Won't it be fun? We'll ride the train from here to Colorado Springs, where we'll be met by Mr. Mc-Candles. He's going to escort us for the rest of the train ride and then to the Davidsons. They live on a ranch in Kurth. We'll even be riding horses or taking a wagon. Doesn't that sound grand?"

Rusty's enthusiasm was contagious, and even Lizzy's eyes began to show some interest.

"Now —" Sammy's voice brought them back to business, but you couldn't help but hear the satisfaction in her tone. She and Rusty had just prayed together about this meeting, and her heart was very light over how well it had gone. "You will both go with Aunt Rusty and start to gather your things. You'll be here through the weekend and part of next week, and then you and Aunt Rusty will leave on Thursday. How does that sound?"

"Can I take my slate?" Lizzy asked uncertainly. She loved school and her teacher, Miss Linley, and somehow her little heart knew she would not see that lady again. Taking the slate that she used every day in school was very important to her.

"*May* I take my slate," Sammy automatically corrected. "And yes, you certainly may. In fact, if I know Aunt Rusty the way I think I know her, she'll have it right handy on the train with her so you can play games on the way."

Rusty's huge smile told them they would do just that, and knowing they would be welcome, both children put their arms around her. Watching them, Sammy felt something catch in her throat. This was not a job where one could wear her heart on her sleeve, but Sammy knew of no one who had a better way with children than her niece. To a child, she was nearly worshiped by the little ones in the orphanage. It probably helped that she was lovely to look at, but it was more than that. Rusty's manner was so genuine, her touch so light and gentle. When she spoke, she looked each child right in the eye. Added to all of this was the fun. Rusty was never without a game or a funny face, and the children were naturally drawn to her.

The Parks children gave Sammy a hug as well, and Rusty took them to find a spare case in the attic. Sammy stayed in place. Fetching a case was such an ordinary task, but Sammy didn't need to be with them to know that they would soon be shrieking with laughter if Rusty had her way.

2

Colorado Springs

Barring delays, the second half of the letter read, Katherine and the children should be in the Colorado Springs train station at noon on Thursday. I don't believe you've met our niece, Katherine Taggart, so look for a petite redhead. The children, a girl and a boy, are eight and five years of age respectively and are both dark in coloring. Katherine has all the details and paperwork and is very proficient, but she has not traveled extensively for placements.

If the children stay and seem settled, Katherine will travel to Boulder. She has done this many times, so if you can see to it that she transfers safely at Colorado Springs, we would appreciate it. Knowing you're with her puts our hearts at rest.

Your letter couldn't have come at a more perfect time. I only hope the notice for this trip is not too short. If there is a conflict with the timing, I'll go with Katherine myself. If I don't hear from you, I'll assume all is well and that you will be awaiting Katherine and the children on Thursday. Thank you, Chase. Come visit as soon as you can.

God bless you,
Padriac O'Brien

Chase McCandles read the letter carefully one more time, laid it on his desk, and reached for his calendar. Thursday would work fine. He had business out of town at the beginning of the next month, but if this trip took several days or even a week, he didn't think it would interfere at all.

He made a few notes and then stood, leaving the office that sat off of the spacious drawing room. From there he walked toward and through the front foyer, down a short hallway, and finally into the breakfast room. It was empty. He had hoped to find his son, Quintin, and Quintin's nanny, Mrs. Harding. Chase had more work to do, so rather than run about looking for them, he returned to his office, not even noticing the beautiful surroundings.

The mansion he lived in, known around town as Briarly, was huge. If Chase McCandles had had anything to do with it, it would have been functional and no more, but because it had belonged to his parents and had also been the delight of his mother's heart, the layout and lovely furnishings made the home a place of warmth and comfort. Chase didn't see it that way, however. He'd been living in it so long that he was often guilty of taking it for granted.

On the way back to his office, he spotted a maid polishing the shelves in the library that sat across the drawing room, exactly opposite the office. He stepped to the double French doors and stopped.

"Kimberly?" he called to her in his quiet way.

"Yes, sir?"

"When you see Mrs. Harding, will you tell her I wish to see my son?"

"Of course, sir. You'll be in your office?"

"All morning."

Kimberly nodded in obedience, but Chase had turned away, his mind already back to the business of the day.

"Are your hands clean?" Mrs. Harding looked down at her small charge, who, upon hearing her question, held his hands up for inspection.

"Are we eating now?" he asked. Mrs. Harding liked clean hands all of the time, but she didn't usually check them unless it was time for Quintin to eat or see his father; he hoped it was the first.

"No, your father wants to see you."

This news was not greeted with a smile of anticipation; indeed, Quintin felt little. Each day he was summoned to the office and given a short rundown of his father's schedule, most of which he didn't understand. Often his father told him that he was going on a trip. Out of respect, Quintin never asked where he was going or when he would return, but sometimes his father would volunteer the information.

"Come along," Mrs. Harding said in her brisk way. Quintin followed, his little face composed. The double doors to the office were open, and Quintin knew the routine. Sensing that Mrs. Harding was backing away, he stopped on the threshold and waited for his father to notice. The older of the two McCandles had his head bent over some papers in front of him, and there was a stack of files at his elbow. Nearly 60 seconds passed before he looked up and noticed his son.

"Come in, Quintin," he said immediately, his voice pleasant but businesslike. The brown-eyed, brown-haired child came forward and would have stopped at the front of the large wooden desk, but his father turned his chair to the side, and Quintin knew that he was to go and stand before his father's knees.

"I have to go on a trip. I leave Thursday," Chase wasted no time in saying.

Quintin stared at him in silence.

"I'll be gone for a few days, maybe a week. You'll be a good boy for Mrs. Harding?"

"Yes, sir."

"Good job," Chase said as he laid a brief hand on Quintin's shoulder. It was their only physical contact. "You can run and play now."

"Yes, sir," Quintin answered respectfully and turned away, but he certainly did not run; it wasn't allowed in the house. As for playing, he'd already had the playtime Mrs. Harding allotted for the morning.

Manitou

"Are you all set for the morning?" Paddy asked Rusty, an arm around her shoulders.

"I think so. How long do you want me to stay?"

Paddy thought a moment, his face intent, and then with an arm still around her, turned her about and took her into his office.

"I think I should read something to you." Paddy had gone around the desk and taken a seat. Rusty seated herself in front of the desk.

"This is the last letter I received from Mr. Davidson," he began. "He writes, 'Is it foolishness to want something so much? We have said goodbye to so many babies but never really known any of them. If Lizzy and Thomas come and don't want to stay, it will be the most painful thing of all. I will have been forced to watch my wife with them. I will see their faces and smell their skin but then have to watch them walk away. There are times when I ask myself how I can do it, but I must have hope and I must trust in God. We love those children as if we'd had them from birth. I pray only that they'll give us a chance.' "

Paddy raised his head. Rusty's hands had come to her mouth, and her eyes were closed. She kept them closed, and a moment later her uncle began to pray.

"Father in heaven, we thank You for the gift You have given to Rusty, this gift with children. They love her and are loved in return. Please bless the Davidsons. We thank You for bringing them to us. We wish we had a hundred more couples just like them. I know they will love Lizzy and Thomas, if only Lizzy will let herself be loved. Give Rusty great wisdom, Lord, help her to know how long to stay. I know the Davidsons would keep her a month, but that is not prudent. I know she will be wise, Lord. Help her to turn to Chase if she needs advice, and give him wisdom as well. We thank You for all You have planned, Lord Jesus. Bless us all this day and in the days to come. Amen."

"Amen," Rusty echoed. She looked up at her uncle and was quiet for a few moments. When she spoke again, she said, "I dreamed about Mr. McCandles last night. Why do you suppose I did that?"

"Because you haven't met him, and that's always a little uncomfortable."

"Is there anything I should know?"

"There's nothing you should be worrying about, if that's what you mean. He's not the effervescent type, but he's kind, and I know that no harm will come to you in his care. You might not find him overly talkative at first, but if you need help, you need only ask."

Rusty nodded. It was enough. In truth, it

didn't matter to her whom they sent to escort her, just as long as she was able to do the job expected. Lizzy and Thomas were both so sweet, but they couldn't help but be nervous and excited. She was a little excited herself. Kurth was farther than she'd ever been assigned to go. Children who were placed that far from Manitou were harder to check on, and Rusty didn't want anything to go wrong.

After making certain that her uncle was finished with her, Rusty made her way from the office. She didn't have night duty, and she knew all the children would be asleep, but she still climbed the stairs. She went first to the girls' room and made her way to Lizzy's bed. The little girl's hair was dark against the white pillow slip. Without disturbing her, Rusty knelt by the bed and prayed silently.

Father in heaven, what a wonderful little girl You created in Lizzy Parks. She is so special. I love her smile, and I love the shy way she looks at me. Help the Davidsons know how to make her feel loved. Help them to move slowly so that she will not be alarmed. She has looked nervous since she was given the news last week, and I know she's very frightened, but the time has come. As You well know, we head out in the morning. Every-

thing Lizzy has known will change. She won't have me, and she won't have Miss Linley, but she'll have You, Lord. Please remind her of this every mile of the way.

Thank you for Uncle Paddy, Father. Thank You that he knew enough to ask for wisdom on my behalf. I need this so badly. I can't handle this with my heart. Help me to know what to do and be brave enough to carry it out.

Rusty rose to her feet then and bent to smooth Lizzy's hair. The little girl stirred but did not waken. Rusty made her way to the door and down to the boys' room. Someone on the night staff was taking one of the boys to relieve himself, but Rusty slipped quietly by to where she knew Thomas was located. Again she knelt and prayed.

Thomas makes my heart glad, Lord. He is so full of life and joy. Thank You that he is too young to remember everything Lizzy still knows. Thank You that he loves his sister and that Lizzy feels comforted when he's near. It's not hard to understand why the Davidsons fell in love with these children, or why they are anxious, but please help them to go slowly. Help Thomas not to . . .

Rusty stopped. She had almost asked God not to let Thomas adjust too swiftly, but was that really fair?

I'm trying to tell You what to do, Lord, and

I'm out of line. I'm afraid that Thomas will love the Davidsons and Lizzy will want to come back here, and we'll all be miserable. Help me to leave this with You.

Rusty once again came to her feet. She touched the dark hair on Thomas' head just as she had Lizzy's and slipped quietly out the door, her heart still giving the situation to God and asking for Him to work a wondrous act on behalf of the children. She was so intent on her prayer that she almost walked past her cousin.

"Rusty," Renny whispered when she didn't see him.

"Oh, Renny, I'm sorry. I didn't expect to see you up here."

"Mother wants to see you."

"All right."

Rusty accompanied him downstairs and found Sammy in the kitchen.

"Renny said you wanted to see me."

"Yes. Before you go I need those reports you filled out."

"I gave them to Paddy."

"Good. I also want to see how you're doing. Are you excited, nervous, or both?"

"I think both. I was just praying for the kids and for myself as well. It's so easy to become anxious about this."

Sammy nodded. "I well remember some

of my early placements. The hardest ones are when you arrive at the home and all is not what you thought it was going to be."

"I've thought of that," Rusty admitted, "but I don't have that impression from the Davidsons."

"No, I don't either. If Lizzy will stay, I think this will be what we prayed for and more."

"I think you're right."

Rusty gave Sammy a hand with the finishing touches on the kitchen and then moved to the small sitting room. Sammy began to put the children to bed. Rusty made herself comfortable in one of the stuffed chairs, but her body moved much more slowly than her mind. She wondered what the next few days would bring. She also wondered once again what Chase McCandles was like and then reminded herself that she didn't have long to wait. The train pulled out for Colorado Springs at 9:10 the next morning.

3

Colorado Springs

His bag in one hand, Chase moved around the large depot, his eyes scanning the crowd for a redhead. He didn't think he could have missed Miss Taggart and the children, but they were a little late. He circled the station again, his bag in one hand, his eyes searching. It was then that he spotted her, or at least the woman he thought might be her. But why did it appear as though she was coming from town?

Chase didn't think they had planned to come in the night before, but the woman and children he was watching definitely came from the direction of town. Indeed, the children had small sticks of candy in their hands.

Chase watched a few minutes longer and

then decided it must be them. Paddy had described the woman as a petite redhead, and there was no missing that hair and diminutive size. They came directly onto the platform, and as Chase watched, Rusty read the train schedule and then began to search the crowd herself. He approached immediately.

"Miss Taggart?"

"Yes," Rusty craned her head upward and smiled, her voice as bubbly as ever. "I'm Katherine Taggart. People call me Rusty. You must be Mr. McCandles. I hope we didn't keep you. The train was early, and we decided to walk into town. The children have never been here in Colorado Springs, and it was such a fun adventure."

Chase didn't say another word. At the moment he felt incapable of speech. He had been warned in Paddy's letter about her size and the color of her hair, but her uncle had said nothing about her eyes. He had never met anyone whose eyes were the color of the violets that grew each summer in his yard. No, that wasn't it; they were darker than violet. Purple — she had purple-colored eyes that sparkled when she talked. Chase, who usually took little notice of people's appearance, thought they were beautiful.

"You are Mr. McCandles, are you not?" Her now uncertain voice broke through the riot of his thoughts. "Mr. Chase McCandles?"

"Yes," Chase recovered himself and put out his hand. "It's a pleasure to meet you, Miss Taggart."

She beamed at him and shook his hand.

"Children." She spoke formally to gain their attention. "Lizzy and Thomas Parks, please meet Mr. McCandles. He'll be escorting us to Kurth."

Chase looked at the children, realizing he had forgotten their presence. He watched now as Thomas' little hand came out, but Lizzy kept her head down.

"It's good to meet you, Thomas."

"Thank you, sir."

"And this is Lizzy?"

Thomas nodded, but Lizzy still didn't look up. Chase opened his mouth to say something more, but their train was called.

"Fountain, Makepeace, Kurth, and Pueblo — now leaving on Track 14."

"Oh, that's us!" Rusty said to the children. "Hand me your bag now; there you go. Come this way."

She directed them proficiently, and Chase was reminded of what the letter said about her not having traveled far. Something wasn't right. She simply didn't seem to be in need of an escort. For an instant he thought his presence might be unnecessary. After all, she seemed capable and very comfortable on her own, but then he noticed something else. Although he was not given to watching people, he couldn't help but see that she was attracting attention. She wasn't doing anything to accomplish this; she was just walking gracefully with the children on either side of her, but male heads were turning from every direction.

Knowing you're with her puts our hearts at rest. Just one line from Paddy O'Brien's letter came leaping back to Chase's mind. This was what his friend was talking about.

"Was there a particular place you wanted to sit, Mr. McCandles?" Rusty had stopped outside the train and turned to her escort. She was used to taking care of things on her own. If she wasn't careful, she would forget he was there to help.

Hearing her voice, Chase forced his mind back to the task of the moment.

"Anywhere you and the children will be comfortable," he told her honestly, and then realized she was carrying two bags.

"Here, let me have those." Chase took them from her hand holding all three handles, his own and both of hers, in one large hand.

"Thank you," she said simply and led the way on board. She walked down the aisle, the children just behind her, and chose two seats that faced each other.

"I think this will do," she said with that huge smile back in place. "You sit here, Thomas," she motioned, directing him to the window seat, "and Lizzy, you take this seat with me. Would you like the window?"

She nodded shyly, and Rusty stroked her hair when she passed in front of her to sit down.

Chase suddenly found Rusty's eyes centered on him. "I'm sorry, Mr. McCandles. I didn't check whether or not you wanted the window seat."

"The aisle is fine," he assured her and raised the bags to store overhead.

Rusty slipped into the seat next to Lizzy and leaned to look out the window with the children.

"What is that man doing?" Thomas wanted to know.

"Please don't point, Thomas. He's carrying trunks to go on the train."

"We don't have that much," Lizzy said worriedly as she watched the wheeled cart filled with steamer trunks.

"No, we travel light." Rusty kept her voice light as well. It was a bit alarming how few possessions the children had. Well, if the Davidsons' presentation to Paddy could be trusted, the children would never go without. Mr. Davidson was a successful rancher and well-respected in the town of Kurth.

From her periphery Rusty caught Chase's movements as he sat down, and she turned to speak to him. However, her eyes drifted past him, and she started when she noticed several men turned in their seats, staring at her. Sitting together in three seats, they were all young, well-dressed and groomed, but they were staring as if they'd just come from the hills. Rusty was tempted to look behind her, but their seat was the last in the car.

Chase, who had been watching Rusty himself, knew in a moment that something had startled her. He watched as she turned her head to the window, but her eyes moved over the children with alarm. Chase turned slowly. He was larger and older than the young men looking their direction, and when they saw him turn, they shifted in their seats to face forward. One took another chance peek, but Chase was still looking at him and he turned back swiftly. When Chase looked back to Rusty, he could see that she'd witnessed the whole scene.

"Thank you for escorting us, Mr. McCandles," she said softly, her eyes on his for just a moment. "I wouldn't want anything to happen to the children."

Chase nodded, but his mind drifted back to the letter once again. *Knowing you're with her puts our hearts at rest.* She had thought the men might harm the children; her fear had been for them. Chase's heart sighed. This one was definitely in need of protection.

"Are we nearly there?" Thomas asked excitedly, his eyes rarely leaving the train window.

Rusty nodded her head and smiled at his delight, but as she did so, Lizzy's hand went to her stomach. The little girl had grown more fearful with every mile.

"I think we need the slate," Rusty announced.

"Where is it?" Lizzy asked, having just remembered it and hoping that they hadn't left it in Manitou.

"I think it's in my bag."

"I'll get it for you," Chase offered in the deep, quiet voice to which she was becoming accustomed. Rusty watched him. His care of and kindness for them could not be faulted, but it was as Paddy had said, he was not talkative.

"This bag?" Chase held a satchel out for Rusty's inspection.

"It's that other one."

He retrieved the needed bag without comment or show of impatience and even remained standing, his feet spread slightly for balance, waiting for her to find the slate so he could return the case to the overhead rack.

"Thank you, Mr. McCandles," she told him with a smile and got his usual nod of the head. Even though she knew he was quiet, Rusty hoped she had not done anything to upset their escort, but until these children were comfortably settled in the Davidson home, she did not have time to find out.

"Okay," she said lightly, turning to the children, "I'm going to draw a picture, and you must guess what it is. I want you to be specific."

"What's specific?" Lizzy wanted to know, the familiar look of concern lowering her brow.

"It means you must be exact. If I draw a bird, you must say what type of bird, not just a bird."

"Like a robin?" Thomas clarified.

"Exactly," she replied, smiling at him.

Watching her, Chase felt amazed for at

least the dozenth time. She was wonderful with the children. With a moment's notice she had a game or a story for them, and they looked at her as if their every dream had come true. She touched them often and always looked them in the eye when she spoke to them. For the first time in his life, Chase wondered if he looked Quintin in the eye when he talked to him.

"I know what it is," Thomas cried. "It's the clock in the hall from the orphanage."

"Very good," she praised him. "Shall I do another, or do you want to try one?"

"I want to." Thomas didn't need to think twice. Rusty passed him the slate and chalk and waited with Lizzy. Thomas' little lip was tucked between his teeth as he concentrated on the slate. At last he presented a picture. Now it was time for Rusty and Lizzy to bite their own lips in concentration.

"An eagle?" Rusty ventured.

"Nope," he said smugly, and Rusty looked again. Lizzy's face was just as uncertain, so Thomas turned it for Chase.

"Do you know?"

Chase now saw why the ladies had been in the dark, but he thought he might have it.

"Is it a horse?" Chase guessed.

"What kind of horse?" Aunt Rusty had

said to be specific, and he was taking her at her word.

"A wild stallion?"

Thomas looked at him in admiration. "That's right."

"Let me see." Lizzy reached for the slate. "Oh, yeah. I see it now."

"Oh, yes," Rusty agreed as she looked on. "I see it too." Her gaze swung to their escort, and she gave him a big smile. "I'm impressed, Mr. McCandles," she complimented him.

Chase didn't comment, but his eyes lit with amusement and the corners of his mouth turned up a tad. For the first time since meeting him, Rusty thought him quite good-looking. With his dark hair and eyes, something she always found attractive, he took on a whole new look when he smiled, and a handsome one at that.

"The train is slowing," Lizzy said, moving closer to Rusty to take her hand.

"So it is." Rusty put an arm around the girl. "I think we must be very close."

"It didn't take very long," she returned, sounding slightly betrayed.

It had actually taken quite a while, but Rusty still said, "Well, we still have to get to their ranch, Lizzy. That could take a little time."

"Do you have the directions with you?" Chase asked.

"Yes. Would you like to see them?"

"Please."

Rusty started to stand but, as before, Chase detained her and stood himself. They went through the process of choosing the right bag again, but the train was coming into the station, so after the map was in his hand, Chase simply left the bag at their feet.

"Does it look clear to you?" Rusty watched as he studied the paper.

"Yes. I think we're going to want a wagon, not just horses."

Rusty nodded. "My uncle anticipated that possibility and sent money for it."

"I'll rent the wagon," Chase said almost absently.

"It could be several days," Rusty began, but cut off when Chase's eyes came up to meet hers.

"I'll take care of it," he said. His voice was as quiet and mild as ever, but Rusty didn't argue; he was looking at her too intently.

Talks very little, good-looking — especially when he smiles — and likes to have his own way. Rusty ticked these attributes off in her head. Her uncle said she had nothing to worry about where this man was concerned, but clearly there was more to Chase McCandles than a nicely dressed escort. Rusty found herself wishing that Paddy had been a little more informative.

4

Kurth

The station at Kurth was much smaller than the one at Colorado Springs, but several people disembarked — Chase, Rusty, and the children among them. The children stayed very close to Rusty once they were outside the train, and Rusty, feeling as though she was embarking on a new adventure, looked around for only a moment and then began to stride down the boardwalk into town.

Chase stayed with her, the bags in his hands, but he knew a moment of amusement. The petite Miss Taggart looked as if a challenge had been thrown at her feet, and she was not going to let it get away.

They had been walking for just a few minutes when she came to a sudden halt. The children looked up at her as she stared down the street. "We forgot Mr. McCandles."

"He's behind us," Thomas told her.

Rusty turned and found him stopped just a few feet to the rear. There was not just amusement in those eyes now; his smile was huge.

"I forgot you," she said. Her eyes had grown with her oversight, especially when she saw the way he'd taken care of their bags.

"I'm right here," he assured her kindly.

"I didn't mean to do that."

"It's all right. I'm glad you know where the livery is."

"Actually, I don't," she admitted.

Chase blinked. "Where were you headed?"

Rusty shrugged. "Kurth is not that large. I was certain that if I just started out I'd come across it."

The thought of her doing this on her own gave him pause, but as long as he was dogging her heels, he thought this was probably the best method.

"How would you find it?" she asked, remembering that Paddy said he was there to help.

"Probably the same way."

Rusty smiled as if she'd been given a compliment, turned back around and continued down the street. Chase had all he could do

43

not to laugh. With only a brief glance at him, the children followed right behind. He had the impression that they would be willing to follow her off a cliff.

Rusty led the way into the business area of town, her head moving from side to side. The children's heads were moving as well, but their interest was in the town itself. Kurth was a pleasant town with seemingly all the amenities.

"Can we go in there?" Lizzy surprised both adults by asking. Rusty looked to see that the little girl had spotted some wares in a dry goods store. Hanging on a small mannequin was a little girl's dress.

"I don't think we have time, Lizzy, but isn't it pretty?"

"Yes." Her voice was dreamy, and Chase was surprised when he found himself wishing it would have been appropriate to buy the dress for her.

"I don't like dresses," Thomas commented, looking disgruntled that they had stopped at all.

"Well, we won't make you wear one," Rusty told him simply and started off down the street. Just 20 steps later they spotted the livery. It was across the street, and this time Rusty remembered to look for Chase before she barreled her way over. He was silently bringing up the rear, bags still in hand. Rusty looked to be in complete control of things until they discovered the livery was empty. The doors were open, but no one was in attendance. It didn't take as long to remember Chase this time. She turned to him immediately, but he was looking at a sign posted high on the door.

"Back at 2:30," he read, and Rusty followed his gaze.

"What time is it now?" she asked.

He consulted his pocket watch. "It's 2:20."

Rusty nodded and glanced around. Just inside the door was a long bench. "We'll just sit here and wait, children. Are you both warm enough?"

"Yes, Aunt Rusty" was their answer, and she could see that they were both starting to flag.

"Come now." She kept her voice brisk. "I'll sit between you so we can talk."

Fascinated, Chase watched her. He was accustomed to doing things his own way and being in charge. It was rather captivating to have her consult him so seldom and take complete charge of the children. The last woman from the orphanage he'd accompanied had turned to look at him with every question out of the children's mouths. They had placed four boys that time, and the inquiries had been endless. Chase followed Rusty and the children inside, set the bags beside the bench, and stood looking out onto the street.

"All right, Thomas, we'll start with you. I'm certain the Davidsons know about you, but let's make sure you have all the information. Tell me your full name."

"Thomas Joseph Parks."

"And how old are you?"

"Five."

"When is your birthday?"

"I don't know."

"I think it's July 5, but we'll have to check on that."

"July 5."

"That's right. Now to you, Lizzy. Give me your full name."

"Elizabeth May Parks."

"Very good. How old are you?"

"Eight."

"And your birthday."

"December 10."

"Are you going to want them to call you Lizzy or Elizabeth?"

"Lizzy."

"That's fine. We'll be certain that Mr. and Mrs. Davidson know that."

"What's your big name, Aunt Rusty?" Thomas asked.

"Katherine Alexa Taggart," she told him with pleasure.

The little boy's eyes grew.

"Cat."

Rusty turned at that word to find Chase looking down at her. She had not even been aware that he'd been attending.

"My Uncle Robert calls me that," she said softly, not sure if she was supposed to reply.

His eyes moved over her features. "It's overstated."

"Overstated?" she questioned uncertainly.

This time his eyes briefly swept her from head to toe.

"You're more kitten size, I would say."

Their eyes met for the space of several heartbeats, and then Chase's gaze went back to the street. Rusty would have loved to sit and figure out what his comment implied, but Lizzy took that moment to lay her head against Rusty's arm. Rusty still had a job to do.

"I think now would be a good time to clean up a bit," Rusty said as she stood. She dug around in her bag until she found a comb and then gave the children a once-over. She checked their hands and faces, and although not spotless, they were passable. She was wishing for a mirror to work on her own hair when she heard someone speak from the street.

"Excuse me, sir. I'm looking for a woman with two children. Someone at the train station said they had come this way."

Without speaking Chase looked to her. Rusty swiftly put the comb away and moved to the double doorway.

"Are you Miss Taggart?" a man sitting in the seat of a large wagon immediately asked her.

"Yes, I am."

"I'm Douglas Davidson. Did you bring Lizzy and Thomas?"

The question was no more out of his mouth when Thomas peeked around the doorway. Rusty felt something catch in her throat as she watched the man's eyes soften.

"Hello, Thomas. Did you bring your sister?"

Thomas could only stare at him.

"Come, Lizzy," Rusty bade the little girl softly, and although it was said kindly, Lizzy knew better than to disobey. She took the hand that Rusty held out to her and tried to bury herself in the side of Rusty's dress. However, the moment she had the little girl's hand, Rusty moved toward the wagon, her free hand catching Thomas' shoulder and bringing him along as well.

Douglas came down from the wagon, his hat in his hand. He was a large man, cleaned up for town but clearly accustomed to hard work.

"Thomas, Lizzy, do you remember Mr. Davidson?"

Thomas nodded his head yes, but Lizzy's eyes stayed down.

"Come now, Lizzy, our best manners."

The little girl looked up swiftly, dropped her eyes, and nodded.

"How are you?" Douglas asked kindly, and Rusty, seeing that the children were not going to answer, spoke up.

"We're fine."

"How was the train?"

"Exciting," Rusty said truthfully. "We saw so much of the country."

Although Rusty answered, the rancher's eyes were on the children. That he was nearly moved to tears was obvious. She watched as he cast his eyes about to distract himself and knew the exact moment when he spotted Chase still standing behind them. Rusty nearly groaned when she realized she'd forgotten him again.

"Mr. Davidson," Rusty said graciously, wanting to kick herself for yet another breach in manners. "This is Mr. Chase

McCandles. He escorted the children and me today."

Chase came forward and shook Douglas' hand.

"It's a pleasure, Mr. McCandles. I've heard of you. I hope you're planning to join us at the ranch."

"Only if it's convenient. I can stay here in town."

"Please come," Douglas invited warmly. "We have plenty of room, and it would be our pleasure to have you."

"Thank you."

"Can you come out now?" he asked of Chase, but that man only looked to Rusty.

"Yes," Rusty replied right away. "We have our bags right here."

"Please come then." Douglas' smile encompassed them all, but his eyes were on the children. "Come out to the ranch; my wife will be thrilled."

"I know where our bags are," Thomas told him, finally finding his tongue.

"You do? Well, why don't you show me and we'll get them."

Thomas proudly led the way, and although Lizzy didn't let go of Rusty's hand, she turned to follow their progress.

Chase took that moment to say softly, "You forgot me again."

Rusty's eyes were genuinely contrite. "I did, and I'm so sorry."

That he enjoyed catching her out was obvious by the amusement in his eyes. Rusty's chin came into the air, telling him she knew he was having one on her. She might have said something to that effect, but Douglas returned with Thomas, carrying their bags.

"I'm sorry I don't have the other wagon, the one with two seats," Douglas apologized. "The wheel was broke. But I brought a blanket."

"The children and I will be fine in the back," Rusty assured him.

"I'll sit in the back," Chase immediately offered. "You take the seat with Mr. Davidson."

Rusty felt Lizzy's hand squeeze her own, and before Chase could turn away, she gently laid a hand on his sleeve. He looked down at her, and she remembered that he liked to have his own way. However, Rusty was determined to stand her ground.

"I will ride with the children."

Chase opened his mouth to tell her otherwise, but she was already moving to the rear of the wagon. Douglas had put the bags in and jumped up to make sure the blanket was smooth. The children came behind Rusty and she reached to lift them up, but the hands of the men were there ahead of her. Douglas reached for Lizzy and Chase swung Thomas into the back.

Rusty barely contained a small squeak when she suddenly felt herself lifted off her feet. Without so much as a by-your-leave, Chase had lifted her into his arms and set her into the wagon. Turning, she looked down and found his eyes on her again; her own were rather large.

"Thank you," she said breathlessly, but he only continued to look at her. Again she wondered what could be on his mind but thought it the better part of valor to turn and join the children on the blanket. She did so, aware that both men stayed close to see that they were settled, and just a moment later they were underway. The children crowded close to her, and Rusty could feel the tenseness in their bodies. As the wagon pulled from the streets of town and started down a long dusty road to the east, she began to pray.

The Davidson ranch house was like an oasis in the desert. It was tall and white with a large front porch that sported many flower boxes. The children had both lost some of their fear and now crowded to the edge of the buckboard to watch as they approached.

The men had talked for the entire trip, and some of the children's ease had come from listening to them. Rusty's estimation of Chase moved up several notches when he spent the trip asking questions of Douglas that the children might want to know. Would they share a bedroom? How close were their neighbors? And how close was the school? Rusty had watched the children listen and even felt her heart melt at the pleasure on their faces and the looks of excitement they exchanged.

They were in the yard now, and as Rusty watched, a woman came out of the house. Rusty had caught sight of Mrs. Davidson at the orphanage without ever seeing her husband. It wasn't hard to remember her now. She had a head full of black hair and a smile that reached her eyes before it stretched her mouth. Right now both eyes and mouth were smiling as she saw the children in the back.

"Hello," she called to them as she came off the porch. "How was the trip?"

"Fine," her husband answered her, stopping the team. He and Chase came down from the seat together, and Douglas approached the children with a big smile. Lizzy's backward movement was subtle, but he caught it. Rather than reach for the children, he stopped at the wagon side.

"Were you comfortable back here?" he simply asked.

"We leaned on Aunt Rusty," Thomas told him.

"Wasn't it nice that she sat with you?"

Mrs. Davidson came up at that moment and stood beside her spouse. There was something warm and comforting about her. Rusty immediately felt drawn to her.

"Do you remember my wife?" Mr. Davidson asked.

"Hello, Lizzy. Hello, Thomas," she smiled at them. "How was the train?"

"We sat by the window," Thomas informed her.

"You did? That's my favorite place too. Now before you come inside, let me tell you some things." Her tone was kind and authoritative, much like Rusty's, and the children hung on her every word. "You can call me Jessie, and you can call Mr. Davidson, Doug. You don't share a bedroom, but if you want to sleep together, you may. We've tried to make everything comfortable for you, but if you need something and can't find it, you just need to ask." She paused to smile at them again. "Are you ready to come inside?"

Thomas nodded yes and came to his feet to be helped out. Lizzy turned to Rusty.

"Are you coming, Aunt Rusty?"

"I certainly am. You go ahead, and I'll be right behind."

Rusty watched in amazement as Lizzy lifted her arms to leave the wagon. Douglas performed the act as a matter of course and let go of the little girl as soon as she was on the ground. Rusty watched her move away with Thomas and the adults and noticed that she didn't even look back. Chase had moved around the wagon and was watching as well.

"Did you see their faces?" she asked softly. "They already love them. Lizzy has to stay here. No matter what, she and Thomas have to stay."

"The Lord will work it out." Chase's deep voice came to her ears, and she looked at him, her expression telling him she was thankful for the reminder. He helped her from the wagon and then grabbed all the bags. Motioning Rusty to precede him, they followed the others inside.

5

Rusty found the ranch house was as warm and comfortable as the people who lived there. She was no more inside, Chase bringing up the rear, when Jessica Davidson approached, her voice low.

"I'm so sorry, Miss Taggart. I was so excited about the children that I left you sitting in the wagon."

"That's fine. I was so busy watching Lizzy that I didn't even notice."

"She came right with us." Jessie breathed the words, her face full of hope.

"I noticed. Has she even asked about me?"

"No. Right away Doug asked them if they wanted to see the kittens, and they both said yes. He took them out the back door to the barn."

Rusty's heart lifted. They were off to a

wonderful start.

"I'm Rusty, by the way," she said as she held out her hand.

"Jessie," the older woman replied as they shook. "It's so good to have you here."

"Jessie, this is Mr. McCandles."

Chase's hand came out. "Please call me Chase."

"Thank you for bringing Rusty and the children," Jessie told him, her heart in her eyes.

"It was my pleasure. They're wonderful children."

"We think so too. Come upstairs, and I'll show you to your rooms. You have the children's bag?"

"I have it," Chase filled in, following Rusty as Jessie led the way to the stairs.

"They don't have very much, Jessie," Rusty felt the need to explain.

"I figured as much," Jessie responded. They were at the top of the stairs, and she led them down the hall. "I bought some things — not much — I didn't want to overwhelm them. But no matter what happens, I want them to take the clothes we bought."

Rusty nodded. Given similar circumstances, she knew she would feel the same way.

"This will be your room, Rusty. Lizzy is on one side of you, and Thomas is across from her. Your fiancé will be across the hall from you."

Both Rusty and Chase stopped and looked at their hostess. Jessie had moved past them slightly, so it took a moment for her to see that they had both gone very still.

"Is there a problem?" she asked carefully. "Did I misunderstand? Are you already married?"

Rusty blinked, wanting to be as kind as possible in this awkward situation. She was still framing a reply when Chase responded, "As a matter of fact, we are not married, and as engaging as I find Miss Taggart, neither are we engaged."

"Please forgive my assumption," she begged them kindly, but her mind was in a muddle, and she had to work at hiding her confusion and embarrassment. It wasn't anything anyone had said. It was more the way she had witnessed Chase's treatment of Rusty; more specifically, the way he looked at her. Since they had come into the house, he'd been watching her. Jessie realized now that Rusty hadn't even been aware of his scrutiny. With the difference in their height, it was very easy for Chase to subtly watch the petite woman's every move. Rusty, however, would have to tip her head back even to look into his face.

"Did you say this was Miss Taggart's room?" Chase asked as if nothing had gone on.

"Yes," Jessie replied, relieved to hear his voice sound so normal.

"I'll just put your bag inside," he told Rusty, and she thanked him politely. He slipped into her room long enough to do so and then came out to hand the children's bag to Jessie.

"Did you want some help with their things, Jessie?" Rusty asked the older woman, but Jessie shook her head no, her smile tender as she held the satchel in her arms.

"I think I'll put them away myself. That way I'll know what they have." She hesitated. "I'm not certain how this works, Rusty. Do you need to see the children now?"

"No. If they're happy where they are, I'll let them look for me."

"All right. If you'd like to freshen up while I see to the children's clothing, I can meet you both downstairs and offer you something cool to drink."

"That sounds wonderful, thank you."

"Thank you," Chase echoed.

Both Chase and Rusty watched Jessie move down the hall, and then Rusty looked

59

at her traveling companion. She couldn't stop her smile.

"Did I miss a joke?" he asked comfortably, his eyes on hers.

"No," she returned, looking very amused. "I was just thinking how blessed you are that you aren't actually stuck with me for a wife."

"Would that be so bad?" he asked as he smiled in return.

Rusty gave a mock shake of her head. "A wife who keeps forgetting that she actually has a husband." She clicked her tongue. "That wouldn't do at all, Mr. McCandles." With that she tossed him a saucy smile, went into her room, and shut the door.

Chase entered his room as well, thinking how different she was from the women he knew in Colorado Springs. None of them would ever think of bantering with him, but with only a few hours' acquaintance, Rusty Taggart was teasing him. It was a fascination. Indeed, he was so centered on the thought that it was some time before he shut the door, and even longer before he removed his coat, moved to the basin, and had a quick wash.

"They're soft," Thomas told Lizzy, but for just a moment she couldn't move. The kittens were climbing in the straw and even on Thomas, but the kittens, the nice man with them, the barn, indeed, this whole place — Lizzy was afraid that it was all too wonderful to be real.

"Did you want to hold one?" Doug offered a kitten to her, but she shook her head no.

"This one has a purr," Thomas told his sister, and Lizzy leaned close to listen. She smiled a little, and watching her, Doug knew that he would never be the same if she left. He thought he could weep at the prospect, and just as he'd been doing since he found them at the livery, he made his mind move to other things.

"Now this black —" he picked up a kitten, "she has hair almost as pretty as yours, Lizzy."

Lizzy's hand went to her hair. "It's the same color," she said with wonder.

"I think you're right. Maybe you should name this kitten, since you look alike. Can you think of a name?"

Her little brow lowered for just a moment. "Betsy."

"Betsy?"

Lizzy nodded. One time she thought she had heard Aunt Sammy say her mother's name was Betsy, and Lizzy had been partial to the name ever since.

"Betsy's a fine name. I would never have thought of it."

"Should I name this one?" Thomas asked of the kitten in his arms.

"I think you should, Thomas. What do you think, Lizzy?"

"Do, Thomas," she urged him, almost absently taking the black kitten Doug was handing her. "Name that kitten so she won't feel left out."

"Is it a girl?" Thomas looked aggrievedly at Doug.

"I think that one is a boy."

"Oh, good." He didn't bother to hide his feelings on the matter. "I didn't want a girl kitten."

"I wish it was a girl."

"Why, Lizzy?" Thomas frowned at her.

"Because then Betsy would have a sister."

"Brothers are better," Thomas proclaimed and went back to his task of naming the kitten. Lizzy looked at Doug and found his eyes on her.

"I have a sister," he told her. "In fact, I have two sisters and two brothers."

Lizzy's eyes got large. "I just have Thomas, but he doesn't go to school yet."

"Do you like school?"

"I like Miss Linley."

"Your teacher?"

Lizzy nodded.

"The name of the teacher here is Miss Kay. She's very nice."

"Will we go to school?" The worry was on her face again.

Doug wasn't certain how to answer; he opted for honesty. "Only if you stay."

Lizzy nodded. She knew all about this. If she was frightened, she could go back to Manitou with Aunt Rusty.

"Shall we go inside now?" Doug asked, but he made no move to stand. He had sprawled in the hay as soon as they arrived in the barn, and his manner made the children feel like he had all the time in the world.

"Can we take the kittens?"

"I'm afraid not," he told Thomas. "Jessie has rules about such things, but unless I miss my guess, she'll have made cider or lemonade, and that sounds awfully good to me."

"Come on, Thomas," Lizzy said on that note. Not until he mentioned something to drink did she realize how thirsty she was.

"We can come back later?" Thomas had to be certain.

"You certainly may."

Doug came to full height then and watched as both children stood looking up at him.

"You're big," Thomas couldn't help but comment.

"Thomas Parks, that's not polite," his sister scolded. "What would Aunt Rusty say?"

The little boy dropped his head.

"It's all right, Lizzy." Doug's voice was gentle.

Thomas peeked a glance at him, and Doug smiled at both of them.

"Come on now," he encouraged. "I'm thirsty. Let's head to the kitchen."

"That was a wonderful meal," Rusty told her hostess much later that day. "Thank you very much, Jessie."

"You're welcome."

"Thank you, Jessie," Lizzy said as well.

The six of them were sitting on the large front porch. Dinner was over, the sun was dropping in the sky, and the heat of the day was fading fast. Rusty sat in a rocking chair, Thomas at her feet, his little hands stroking the Davidson's dog, Tina. Lizzy was on a little bench by the railing, her eyes working subtly to study their hosts. Chase was on the swing, and Doug and Jessie had chairs. At the moment, Rusty's eyes were leveled on Thomas, who, after noticing her, took a few seconds to catch her meaning.

"Thank you for dinner," he told the

woman with the black hair and smiled when she gave him a wink. Thomas was completely unaware of the way the men had to cover their grins. They both remembered those days as little ones. Food was to be eaten, not talked about, and once you ate you moved on to other things. In Thomas' case, that was paying attention to the black lab that lay at his side.

Having gotten the response she was looking for, Rusty let her eyes roam the land again. There were a few other homes visible, but they sat much in the distance. Cows could be heard, but for the most part, they were just little dots roaming the acres of fenced-off land. It was a serene place, and once again Rusty asked God to help these children stay. Thoughts of them caused her to turn and study each of them.

The evening had gone very well, but the children were accustomed to an early bedtime, and Rusty could see they were beginning to flag. She was certain they would adjust to whatever time schedule the Davidsons followed, but until she left them in their care, the children were her responsibility.

"Lizzy, Thomas," she began in a tone they knew well. "It's been a long day."

"Must we, Aunt Rusty?" Lizzy surprised her by asking.

"Not this moment, but soon."

Lizzy looked content, her eyes shifting to the distance.

"Do you see that building, Lizzy?" Doug asked. He'd been watching her.

The little girl nodded.

"That's the schoolhouse."

Lizzy bit her lip.

"The children will be there tomorrow during the day, but in the afternoon they'll have all gone home. I think we should go and visit."

Lizzy's eyes flew to Rusty.

"Well, now," Rusty said gently. "Doesn't that sound like fun? Do you think we should all go?" Rusty inquired of her charge. "Or do you want to go with Doug on your own?"

"All of us."

"We'll plan on it. Be certain to thank Doug for offering."

Lizzy looked back at that man. "Thank you, Doug."

"It's my pleasure. We'll have a fun day on the range, ride horses and such, and in the afternoon we'll all go to the school."

"We're going to ride horses?" Thomas had heard only that portion of the plan.

"Of course. You can't live on a ranch and not do that."

This was enough to make him leave the

dog. He approached Doug, and standing by his chair, his little body leaning close, Thomas asked, "Big horses?"

"Some are quite large, others are smaller, but I suppose when you're five they all seem pretty big."

"Are they nice?"

"The one you'll ride is very nice."

"And Lizzy too?"

"Lizzy too. Her horse will be nice for her also."

While this conversation went on, Rusty caught Jessie's eye. With just a few movements Jessie understood her meaning, and when Doug and Thomas had exhausted the subject of horses, Jessie stood.

It's time to head up to bed now," she told the children. They stood and moved automatically toward her. Doug also rose to accompany them.

"Aren't you coming, Aunt Rusty?" Lizzy stopped when Rusty kept her seat.

"I think Doug and Jessie want to tuck you in."

"What if we can't find our things?"

"Jessie put everything away, so she'll know just where they are."

Lizzy still looked uncertain.

"I'll tell you what," Rusty suggested, knowing that a compromise was needed. "If you need me, you can ask Doug or Jessie to come for me. If not, I'll see you in the morning."

"You'll be here?"

"Yes I will," Rusty told her and tenderly stroked her little cheek. "Kiss me now, and unless you call for me, I'll see you in the morning. My room is right next to yours."

Lizzy's thin arms went around her neck and hugged her fiercely. Thomas was next, hugging and kissing Rusty and rubbing his nose against hers. She crossed her eyes and made him laugh, and then both children turned to Doug and Jessie, who were waiting by the door.

"Children," Rusty said softly. Both did an immediate about-face.

"Goodnight, Mr. McCandles," they chorused.

"Goodnight, Lizzy; goodnight, Thomas," he told them with a smile.

A moment later they were gone.

From where he was sitting, Chase heard Rusty sigh.

"It's going well," he commented.

"I think so too. It's going to be hard to know how long to stay."

"You're afraid that if you leave too soon, Lizzy will want to come with you?"

"Exactly. I want to see her settled, but I

can't move in here."

"Maybe the next time she asks if you're going to be here, you ought to give her a specific day that you're planning to leave."

She looked at him with such surprise that he had to hide a smile. "That's a wonderful idea." Her voice should have insulted him, but he found it amusing.

"I'm so pleased that I come in handy in some areas."

Rusty's hand went to her mouth, but her eyes were still brimming with laughter.

"I've been just awful to you," she said on a small laugh. "You must think me the rudest woman in the state."

"Not just the state — the whole nation," he told her gravely.

Rusty couldn't hold her laughter. Chase listened to the sound. It was not light, soft, or feminine like the woman herself. It was loud and boisterous and spoke of pure delight. Watching her, Chase wasn't at all surprised that the children adored her.

6

"I have a new nightgown," a little girl's voice intruded into Rusty's dreams. The redhead's eyes opened slowly. Sitting beside her on the bed were the Parks children. Both wore new night apparel and both looked as if they could burst with pride.

"Where did you get those?" she asked sleepily.

"Jessie had them for us." Lizzy's eyes were brimming with excitement. "They were waiting for us right in our rooms last night."

"And I have boots," Thomas added.

"Well, now," Rusty replied, still trying to wake up. "How wonderful."

"Remember, Aunt Rusty, we're going to ride today."

"I remember," she said as she stifled a

yawn. The day before must have been more taxing than she'd thought. She was certainly tired today.

"Do you want to sleep some more, Aunt Rusty?" Lizzy asked in a concerned voice.

Rusty blinked at her. Part of her thought she still was sleeping.

"Come on, Thomas," his sister decided. "Aunt Rusty needs to sleep some more."

Rusty smiled at them, thinking it was already too late, but she was wrong. They weren't out the door two minutes when she fell right back to sleep.

"Good morning," Jessie spoke to the children as soon as they shut Rusty's door. She had just come from downstairs and was pleased to see them in the hallway.

"Good morning," Thomas said, but Lizzy looked shy.

"Are you hungry?" Jessie asked, coming forward to bend down in front of them.

"I'm hungry," Thomas informed her.

"Why don't you come and eat?"

When the children hesitated, she asked, "Did you want to wait for Aunt Rusty?"

"She's going to sleep some more," Lizzy volunteered, having decided this was important.

"How nice for her. You children are so considerate."

Lizzy was pleased with the compliment, even though she didn't understand exactly what it meant.

"Do you like pancakes with berry syrup?"

Lizzy and Thomas looked at each other and then back at Jessie. Both nodded.

"Well, come on," Mrs. Davidson urged and stood.

Still they hesitated. "Do we need to dress?" Lizzy finally managed.

"This morning there isn't time. The cakes are hot and ready to eat."

This time Lizzy couldn't help herself. She beamed up at this woman who was like a dream come to life. Jessie turned to lead the way, and Thomas took her hand, but Lizzy's feet didn't touch the floor all the way to the kitchen.

Chase sat in his room, his Bible open to the book of Acts, but he wasn't reading. His mind was still on the evening before when Doug and Jessie had tucked the children in and returned to the porch. When it looked as if the children would not be up again or need Rusty, they began to question the orphanage worker.

They had known some of the details of

Lizzy and Thomas' life, but not all. They hadn't realized that this was their second placement; the first had been undertaken by a family member. After Betsy Parks died, her aunt had given the children, then one and three years old, to a family in Matheson. The family had adored the baby until he began to be an active two-year-old. By then Lizzy had turned five. When they weren't forcing her to scrub the floor and do the dishes, she was locked in a room with her brother, having to listen to his hungry cries for food.

Not until the couple in the house got into a drunken brawl did the authorities become aware of the children and do something. They were delivered to the Fountain Creek Orphanage for Children. That had been two years ago. Chase could still hear Rusty's quiet voice as she explained the situation. Jessie's hand had been over her eyes, and Doug, a very tenderhearted man, had done nothing to stem the tears that poured down his face. With Doug and the children's faces still in mind, Chase began to pray.

It's no wonder Lizzy is afraid, Lord. She's been so neglected and hurt. At the orphanage she was fed and cared for, but she has no guarantees of that here. Help her to see what a wonderful place this is. Help her young heart to trust You, as well as Miss Taggart, not to leave her anyplace where she would come to harm.

Chase felt his heart lighten. He had told Rusty that the Lord would work it out, but the more he got to know Lizzy and Thomas, the more he wanted this for them. It was easy to see how Rusty could be anxious. However, Chase had to take his own advice and trust.

He did read his Bible for a time and even left it open to the place where he stopped, but his stomach was growling, and he thought he'd heard the children in the hall. Already dressed and shaved for the day, he slipped into his jacket and ventured into the hallway and downstairs.

Rusty felt wonderfully rested and rather hungry and wondered what time it was as she left her room. She thought the children had been in to see her but wasn't sure if she had dreamed that or not. Once downstairs she navigated her way toward the kitchen, but on the way she spotted the grandfather clock in the parlor. Rusty abruptly stopped. It said 9:20. That couldn't be right. She heard footsteps behind her and turned. Chase was standing there as if he'd just come in from the front porch.

"That clock says it's 9:20. That's not right, is it?"

Chase brought a gold pocket watch out of his vest.

"I have 9:25, but mine might be a little fast."

Rusty's mouth opened. "I can't believe I slept that long."

"You worked hard yesterday."

"Not that hard," she argued with him. "What would Paddy say? I'm *supposed* to be working."

"Well, I think if he could see how well the children are doing, he would highly approve of your actions."

"Have you seen them this morning?" Rusty forgot all about herself.

"Indeed, I have. I watched them giggle their way through breakfast — Doug and Jessie saw to that — and then get dressed so they could ride the horses."

"That's where they are now?"

"Yes. Jessie told me to come for her when you wanted breakfast."

"Oh, no," Rusty protested. "I don't want to disturb them. I'll just fend for myself."

Chase nodded. "I know she left coffee on."

"Thank you," Rusty said and turned toward the kitchen.

Chase followed her, and they found that Jessie had left more than coffee for the late riser. Staying warm on the stove was a plate of pancakes. The butter and syrup were still in the center of the table, and Chase, who'd been made to feel very much at ease with the Davidsons, even opened the oven and found some slices of ham. Just five minutes later Rusty felt as though she'd sat down to a feast.

Chase poured coffee for both of them and then joined her at the table.

"Have you decided what day you want us to leave?"

"I think we should head back first thing Monday. I didn't look at the train schedule, but maybe Doug and Jessie know when the early train leaves."

"I have a schedule," he said quietly. He watched as she sat back and studied him.

"Your life is very planned, isn't it, Mr. McCandles?"

"Yes."

"Do you ever long for a break in routine?"

"No."

He wanted to laugh at her expression, which told him she wondered if he came from another planet.

"Have you always been, shall we say, impetuous?" he wished to know in return.

Rusty nodded, her face still thoughtful. "There are times when it lands me in trouble."

I can believe that, Chase thought. Aloud,

he said only, "Have you learned from some of your mistakes?"

"Yes and no," she shrugged a little. "You see, trouble is nothing I ever plan. It just sort of happens."

It was so much a statement that an impetuous person would make, Chase couldn't stop his smile. Seeing it, Rusty heard herself.

"I just realized what I said."

Chase felt free to laugh now. It was all too true. She was capricious. He was certain she would call it fun, but Chase didn't think he could handle that much *fun* in his life. His assets would dwindle to nothing, and his business dealings would crumble around his feet.

The conversation might have remained on that subject, but Lizzy chose that moment to rush into the room.

"You're up, oh, Aunt Rusty, you're up! You've got to see Thomas. He's riding a horse!"

"I'll come right now," she told her with enthusiasm to match. "Did you ride too?" she asked as she rose.

"Not yet. I was scared."

"Well, come on." Rusty had her by the hand now. "I've got to see this wonderful thing."

They rushed out, Chase forgotten yet

again. This time he didn't mind. This time he needed a few moments on his own. As Rusty rose, Chase had been on the verge of telling her to sit back down and eat. She'd barely touched her food. But he had stopped in time, reminding himself that she was not a child, and that he must not treat her as one.

He thought about the things he'd witnessed on the trip so far and slowly shook his head. Letting her lead this operation was taking some tremendous willpower. With a prayer for help to remember all that he'd just resolved, he stood and followed Rusty and Lizzy to the paddock.

"I hope we're not disturbing you, Miss Kay," Doug offered as he led the way into the schoolhouse that afternoon at 4:00, very pleased to see the teacher still in attendance. "We wanted to visit the school after the children left."

"I'm so pleased that you felt free to come, Mr. Davidson. Please come right in." She watched the small band enter. "You have guests with you." Miss Kay knew that the Davidsons were trying to adopt, but she didn't want the children to know that. She smiled at all of them.

"Miss Kay," Doug led the way halfway up

the center aisle. "This is Miss Taggart and Mr. McCandles. And this is Lizzy Parks and her brother, Thomas Parks."

"It's good to meet all of you," Miss Kay said warmly to the adults. She then turned to give the children her attention. "Was it Lizzy?"

That little girl nodded.

"Let me guess," she said slowly. "You must be about eight years old."

Lizzy bit her lip, but her smile came through.

"Was I right?"

Again she was answered with a nod.

"And you're Thomas?"

"Thomas Parks."

"Well, Thomas Parks, I think you must be five or six. Am I right?"

"I'm five. I don't go to school yet. Lizzy goes for both of us."

Miss Kay smiled in delight. "Lizzy must be very smart."

Thomas nodded, his face very serious. "She can read."

The teacher looked suitably impressed and turned back to Lizzy, who was trying not to look too pleased.

"Would you like to look around the room with me, Lizzy? I can show you where things are, and you can tell me the different things you have at your school."

"I have a slate," the little girl admitted. Miss Kay's heart melted when she realized what it had cost her to say even that much.

"That's wonderful. Did you bring it with you?"

"It's at the ranch house."

"That's fine. Let's begin up here by the blackboard."

Miss Kay led Lizzy away, and Thomas followed in their wake. It gave Rusty a chance to speak with Jessie.

"How are you?" the younger woman asked.

"Nervous. I want them to like it so much."

Rusty well understood; she had been reading that in the other woman's eyes for the last 24 hours.

"We're going to leave on Monday," Rusty filled in. "If Lizzy doesn't ask me about that by bedtime, I'll go in to her room and tell her."

"And if she wants to leave with you?"

Doug had come close to hear as well. Rusty could still hear the letter Paddy read to her, the one that broke her heart, but she had to be honest.

"Then I'll take them both back with me," she said softly, "and placement will be reviewed. I feel you'll have these children, Jessie, and I know this is a hard way to go about it, but it might not work out right away. There have been cases where the new parents needed to come and live near the orphanage for a time, say a few days or a week. Yours might be just such a case."

"That's a good thing to remember, Jess," her husband said gently, putting an arm around her. "Just because they leave doesn't mean we can't eventually have them."

Jessie nodded, her face still hopeful. She thanked Rusty with a hand to her arm and then went to join the children and Miss Kay. Doug accompanied her. Rusty stayed in the background, Chase not far from her side, for the remainder of the visit. Not until they were leaving did she need to once again call to the children very softly. They spun swiftly and faced the teacher.

"Goodbye, Miss Kay. Thank you," Lizzy said.

"Thank you," Thomas managed just after her.

Silently watching the whole scene, Chase felt an odd swelling of pride in his chest. The children were wonderful, but Miss Taggart was the one who fascinated him. Etiquette and manners came so naturally to her, and her expectations from the children were met without complaint or hesitation. Someone,

quite possibly Rusty, had spent hours training these children. He was very impressed,
so impressed that he nearly forgot his own
manners and started to leave the schoolhouse
without thanking Miss Kay. He remembered
just before he stepped out the door.

Miss Kay watched him leave, not knowing
when she'd last met such a man. Chase
didn't notice her admiration, however; he
was still thinking about Rusty Taggart.

7

"I'm going to do the dishes tonight," Rusty announced to the occupants of the table as soon as dinner was over.

"You're our guest," Doug protested, but Rusty held her hand up.

"Be that as it may, I want to help."

Jessie was about to put in her own protest, but Doug saw what Rusty was doing and caught his wife's eye.

"Maybe Lizzy and Thomas would like to go for a walk," Doug offered. "We might see some calves if we head out through the pasture."

"Can we?" the children asked of Rusty.

"May we," she corrected, "and that is up to Doug and Jessie."

The children looked to the adults, and Thomas even went to Jessie's side.

"I've never seen cabs."

"Calves," Jessie corrected him gently. "Shall we go and see if we can find some?"

The children rose, Lizzy not holding back at all.

"Can we interest you, Chase?" Doug offered.

"Thank you, but I saw some calves on my walk today, so I think I'll stay here and help Miss Taggart."

The four took their leave, the children nearly jumping with excitement, and Rusty went to work stacking dishes, silver, and glasses on the counter. Chase took his jacket off, hung it on the back of a chair, and rolled up his sleeves. It was on the tip of Rusty's tongue to ask him if he'd ever washed a dish in his life, but she refrained. She didn't count on her expression giving her away.

"Yes, I've washed dishes before."

"I didn't ask that," she swiftly pointed out, her purple eyes growing in mock innocence.

"But you wanted to," he teased her.

Now she had to smile. "True."

"Are you washing or drying?"

"It doesn't make any difference."

"Some of those pots are pretty big; I'd better wash."

Rusty picked up the large dish towel, and said, "I'm stronger than I look."

Chase put a hand around her forearm. His fingers overlapped by quite a bit. "I'll believe that when I see it," he commented.

"You have big hands."

"That's true, but there's just not that much of you."

She couldn't argue with him on that point, so she gave him a pointed look and then shifted her eyes to the dishpan.

"I take it you think we've talked enough."

"I didn't say that," she defended again, a smile in place, but this time they went to work in earnest. For a time there was little conversation. Chase was as good as his word and worked swiftly and proficiently. He had clearly done this type of work before. Rusty dried things, putting the dishes away when she could find the correct space and leaving the rest on the freshly washed table. At one point Chase turned to ask Rusty something and found her staring off into space.

"Are you all right?"

"Yes," she answered immediately and took the plate he offered her, but in truth she didn't know what she was. As they'd worked, there had been a few times when Rusty found herself distracted by Chase's close proximity to her. Her reaction to this man surprised her. She hadn't found him talkative, but now that he knew her better, he was quite verbal.

He even teased her a little.

"Miss Taggart?"

Rusty started at the calling of her name. She jumped a little and looked at Chase. He was studying her closely, his face concerned.

"Are you certain you're all right?"

"I think so," Rusty answered and tried not to be embarrassed. "Maybe I'm just a little tired."

"I can finish these," he told her. "Go and sit on the front porch. Rest awhile."

"We're almost finished," she said and went back to drying, but Chase would not be put off.

"Have I said something?" he asked.

"No," Rusty told him, and this time the earnest widening of her eyes convinced him. "I assure you, no."

"Maybe I shouldn't have suggested that we leave here Monday. We'll stay if you think the children need more time. I didn't mean to pressure you."

"Mr. McCandles," she said sincerely. "That was a wonderful suggestion. I'm very comfortable leaving here Monday, even if the children return with us. Thank you for being concerned, but I am fine."

Chase continued to look at her, clearly hesitant to let the matter drop, but Rusty took a bowl from the wooden drying rack, rubbed it with her cloth, and went on as if all was well. She wasn't trying to deceive Chase, but neither was she ready to talk about what she'd been feeling.

A moment later, Chase knew he would have to let it go as well. Her expression told him he would get nothing more. He began a conversation on general topics, and it was then that Rusty knew what was bothering her.

He always called her Miss Taggart. Rusty suddenly knew that she wanted to get to know this man better, but it seemed he preferred they remain on a more professional level. Rusty attended to the things Chase was saying to her but with only half of her heart. The other half was dealing with the fact that he didn't appear to want their relationship to grow personal and why, when she'd only known the man for two days, that bothered her so much.

"She's looking right at us," Lizzy exclaimed, her hand taking hold of Jessie's without forethought. "I think she likes us."

"I think so too," Jessie agreed with her, not feeling a need to point out to the little girl that the she was a he.

"I wish I could touch one," Thomas admitted.

"Maybe you can," Doug told him, and, pulling a handful of grass, coaxed the young bull to the fence. However, it did not come too close, and the moment Thomas started to move toward the bull calf, it bawled like a baby and darted away. The little boy's look of disappointment was keen. Doug swung him up into his arms.

"It's all right," he said, looking into Thomas's dark eyes. "There'll be another time."

"Tomorrow?"

"Possibly."

"Is Aunt Rusty going to be here tomorrow?" Lizzy asked.

"Why don't you ask her when we go back to the house?" Jessie suggested and began to pray.

Lizzy seemed content with that, so they didn't hurry back. In fact, they'd been gone more than an hour when they finally gained the porch and found Chase and Rusty sitting in the same chairs as the night before.

At first there was no talk of anyone going anywhere — the children were too excited about the cows to talk about anything else — but soon after, Jessie informed them it was bedtime. The children came forward to kiss Rusty, and Lizzy tentatively posed her question.

"Will you be here tomorrow, Aunt Rusty?"

"Yes, Lizzy. I'll be here until Monday."

"What day is this?"

"This is Friday. So I'll be here all day tomorrow and all day Sunday, and then I'll leave first thing Monday morning."

The little girl thought a moment and then said, "Will we go with you?"

"If you want to, Lizzy." Her voice was gentle as her hand stroked the small, dark head. "You may come back to the orphanage with me if you want to."

Lizzy needed to think about this, so she said nothing. Thomas, on the other hand, wanted his Aunt Rusty to know how he felt.

"I want to stay."

"I'm glad you told me, Thomas. We'll keep talking about it and do what's best for everyone."

"I want Lizzy to stay too."

"Of course you do," Rusty answered, making herself ignore the anxious couple waiting by the door. "You'll either both stay or both go back with me, and I don't want you to worry about it. Everything will be fine." Rusty turned back to Lizzy.

"I'll tell you what, Lizzy, in the morning you and I will find someplace where we can talk. You can tell me how you're feeling about things. How would that be?"

Lizzy nodded.

"I don't want you to worry about this to-night. I want you to go up, climb into that new nightgown, and sleep very well the whole night. Can you do that?"

"I don't think I can stay." Lizzy's voice quavered, but Rusty's was calm.

"That's fine. I'm glad you told me, but it's been a big day, and we will wait for morning before we talk about it."

Lizzy nodded, her face already losing its anxiety. Both children kissed her goodnight and went on their way. Rusty seemed completely normal on the outside, but Chase knew better; she had not told the children to bid him goodnight.

"You're upset," he said after a few minutes of quiet.

"I am a little." Her voice was soft, and her eyes were on the horizon. "I've been prepared to do whatever Lizzy needed, but I thought she would give it more time."

"So you think we should still leave Monday?"

"Yes, I do, and I still appreciate your suggesting it. There are only so many decisions that an eight-year-old should be expected to make, but Lizzy's case is different. I can't leave her here if she'll be terrified and miserable."

"So you think she might be?"

Rusty turned her head and looked at him for the first time. "No, I don't," she admitted. "I think she'll miss me and others at home. I think there will be some tears, but I know in my heart that this is the home for those children; they'll be happier than they've ever been in their lives. However, my aunt told her she didn't have to stay unless she wanted to, and I must abide by that."

"You're doing the right thing," Chase told her, not because he wanted to ease her mind, but because it was true. Sammy O'Brien had wisely laid down the guidelines, and Rusty had only to carry them out.

Rusty continued to look at him. It was nice to know that someone thought she was on the right track. She heard movement inside just then and steeled herself for the Davidsons' return. She was certain that Jessie would be upset. She was wrong.

"We want you to know," Doug began as soon as they'd taken seats on the porch, "that we understand your position completely, Rusty. We know you have to take the children if Lizzy wants to go, but we also want you to know that we're praying she changes her mind. We're asking God to work a miracle in her little heart and to help her to see that this is where she belongs."

"Then we're praying for the same thing," Rusty told them, thinking how good God was to them all. "I won't say that her announcement didn't upset me, but I've been praying for that very miracle since you left."

"Thank you," Jessie said to her, now looking close to tears.

"How did it go upstairs?"

"Very well," Doug told them, giving his wife a moment to compose herself. "They were as pleased as last night about their new nightclothing, and I even got a hug from Lizzy. She thanked me for taking her to school."

"I didn't get a hug," Jessie added, "but both gave me shy smiles when I kissed them and said I love you."

Rusty's chest rose with a sigh. "That's wonderful. I'll talk to Lizzy in the morning. Something tells me she'll have changed her mind."

"That might happen more than once in the next two days," Chase inserted.

"I think you're probably right," Doug agreed. "But we're still going to pray, and like you said, Rusty, just because they leave doesn't mean it's over."

It was so good to see the Davidsons treating this with a practical view. Rusty's decision would not have changed had they been unreasonable, but it would have made things all the more uncomfortable.

The sun finally dropped until it was too dark to remain on the porch. Jessie asked everyone in for coffee, and they ended up around the table in the kitchen playing cards. Although the children were still on everyone's mind, the subject of their staying was dropped for the evening, giving a tranquil end to an already wonderful day.

8

"I want to stay," Lizzy told Rusty, and surprisingly enough, it was the first time she had said it. Saturday and most of Sunday had flown by, and in those days Chase and Rusty had watched a miracle transpire. Lizzy Parks had fallen in love with the Davidsons. She spoke as soon as someone talked to her — no more lowered head or eyes — and she went willingly into Doug and Jessie's arms the many times they reached for her.

It was now Sunday night, and Rusty was conducting her final interview. She had already spoken to Thomas, who had not changed his mind about staying. As planned, Rusty had spoken with Lizzy on Saturday morning, and the little girl had still been headed back to Manitou. Telling her she would not try to talk her out of her decision,

Rusty now asked Lizzy what her final word was. Eyes shining with peace, Lizzy told her she would stay on the ranch.

"I'll miss you, Lizzy." Rusty felt she could be honest. "But I know how much you're going to love it here."

"They like us," she told Rusty. "And Jessie said that we can visit you sometime."

"Of course you can. How fun that will be. And think of the school, Lizzy. Miss Kay was so nice."

"She was. I'll have my own desk."

Rusty drew her into her arms and held her close. With another 53 children waiting for her in Manitou, it didn't make sense that she would miss this one little girl, but it was true. She moved back and looked her in the eye.

"Shall we go tell the others?"

Lizzy nodded, and they ventured onto the front porch. Betsy, the tiny black kitten, padded toward them, and Lizzy lifted her into her arms. Her face rather set against the emotions she felt inside, Rusty slipped into a chair and pulled Lizzy and the kitten near to her.

"Lizzy has something she wants to tell you," Rusty said gently. It was a blessing that Lizzy wasted no time. The little girl looked at Doug and then at Jessie.

"I want to stay."

There was no stopping the tears. Jessie's hand came to her face, and Doug shut his eyes against the onslaught of emotions. Lizzy's eyes flew to Rusty's.

"Do you remember," Rusty began gently, "that day when Aunt Sammy handed you your slate and said you were going to school?"

"I cried."

"That's right, you did. It's like that for Doug and Jessie. They're so happy you're staying that they can't do anything but cry."

Lizzy nodded and turned back to look at Jessie. Jessie gave her a watery smile, and Lizzy returned it.

"Come here, Lizzy," she said softly, and a moment later she was in Jessie's arms.

"I'm staying too," Thomas exclaimed, having sat very quietly through this exchange.

"Of course you are!" Doug told him boisterously and scooped him into his arms. "Of course you are. I'm going to need help with the calves, and the kittens would miss you so much if you left. *And*, before you know it, you'll be in school too."

"Will I have a slate?"

"Yes, you will. Your very own."

Thomas looked over at his sister. Lizzy was looking right back. The adults looked on as the two exchanged a smile of pure delight. Doug felt his throat clog all over again. He turned his face and laid his cheek against Thomas' hair. It was all too wonderful to be real.

As much as he wanted to hold this child for hours on end, it was a relief when Jessie announced just a short time later that it was bedtime. Doug carried both children on his back amid much laughter, and after they left, Rusty felt too emotional to speak. Her eyes slid shut against a rush of tears.

You did it, Father, You worked a miracle in her heart. Thank You, Lord; thank You from the bottom of my heart.

Watching her from his seat, Chase remained quiet. His own prayers were much along the same vein.

"I think the children and I should go with you to the train."

"Are you certain, Jessie?" Rusty questioned, concern lowering her brow. She and Doug had returned from seeing the children to bed, and she had wasted no time in telling Rusty what was on her mind.

"Yes. I've thought a lot about it, and Doug agrees." She paused for just a moment. "I have this horrible image of Doug taking the two of you off tomorrow and the children and me here on the porch watching you go. I'm so afraid that one of them will turn to me and say they want to go too. And here I'll be watching the dust of the wagon with nothing I can do about it.

"The train is more final. Doug and I will be together as we watch you leave. The children, Lizzy specifically, may have second thoughts, but the four of us can stay in town and make a day of it. We can take the children to the bank and set up savings accounts in their names, like we've always dreamed of doing. Then we'll stop at the schoolhouse on the way home and talk with Miss Kay about the best time for Lizzy to start. I don't want to bribe the children, but I honestly think it's better this way."

Rusty found herself looking at Chase. "How can I argue with that?"

"I don't think you can," he told Rusty, complimenting Jessie at the same time. "It's an excellent idea."

"I never got that train schedule from you, Mr. McCandles," Rusty suddenly recalled. "What time do we need to leave?"

"The morning train pulls out at 8:25."

"All right. I think we should be on it. Will that work for you?" Rusty asked, turning to her hosts.

"Certainly," Doug assured her. "Whenever you need to leave."

Conversation turned to the final preparations. Rusty had documents on the children's births that she brought down from her room, as well as some papers from the orphanage for Doug and Jessie to sign. It was not late when Doug asked her if all was settled, but as soon as Rusty rechecked everything, she took herself off to bed, her heart still overflowing with thanks. Tired as she was, she did not fall right to sleep, but that was all right. The job was complete, and she knew nothing but peace. She took the next minutes to pray for each and every child still at the orphanage in Manitou. She got through the girls but fell asleep somewhere between Bradley Coffers and Jimmy Kettlesen.

Chase thought she might cry, but it didn't happen. She was quiet while they found their seats and stowed their bags, but she did not cry. Even after the train pulled away and she waved to the children from the window, her eyes were dry. She had not exhibited signs of being the weepy type, but for some reason Chase still expected tears.

Even having seen otherwise, he still asked, "Are you all right?"

"Yes." Her voice was soft, her eyes focused straight ahead. It helped that the children were so pleased and Lizzy only bit her lip once. It also helped to see that glow in Jessie Davidson's eyes."

"They did look happy."

It was the last thing either of them said for several minutes. The past days were starting to blur. So much had been seen and talked about; it was almost too much to take in. Rusty decided that she didn't want to try. She turned to her seat companion and found him sitting quietly.

"Would you think me rude if I read for a time?"

"Not at all," he told her kindly. "I have some papers I should go over. Is your book in your bag?"

"Yes."

He fetched her handbag, which she decided to keep at her feet, as well as his own portfolio of papers, and both settled down to read. Almost 45 minutes passed in silence, whereupon Rusty's stomach growled. She started a little and looked at Chase. The man was smiling.

"I think I forgot to eat breakfast," she told him.

Chase only nodded. He had noticed how centered she was on the children at the breakfast table, leaving her own plate untouched, but remembered his resolve not to treat her as a child.

"Didn't Jessie send some food?"

"Oh, yes," Rusty brightened. "I'd forgotten." Digging in her bag, she found the parcel of food and offered some to Chase. He declined. In the process Rusty noticed that he had put the papers away.

"All done with your work?" she asked before biting into a roll that Jessie had stuffed with beef and cheese.

"Yes. It's nothing too urgent."

"I've never asked you, Mr. McCandles — what type of business are you involved in?"

"Mostly land investments and developments."

"Anything in particular?"

"It's a wide range," he told her, wondering if she knew he was a benefactor to the orphanage. "I own property in several cities in the state, but most are in Colorado Springs."

"And do you always carry papers with you?"

"No, but I have a meeting coming up and thought I might need to go over them."

"Whom will you meet with?"

"A rancher in Pueblo."

"Pueblo?" Rusty's face showed her distress. "Why, we were almost there. You could have gone right to your meeting."

Chase felt himself blink. In his opinion she

was not safe on her own, but he couldn't tell her that. Indeed, when they arrived at Springs he would have to send her on alone — something that made him very uncomfortable.

"I hope my staying until today didn't completely mess things up."

"Not at all." He stared down at her, finding her profile suddenly very distracting.

"Are you certain you don't care for something to eat? Jessie sent plenty."

"I'm certain. Thank you."

"I thought you were staring at my sandwich," she told him with a small shrug and smile.

Chase was again reminded of her innocence. "No, I ate plenty of breakfast. Jessie's a good cook," Chase said to take his mind off leaving her on her own in Colorado Springs. Still, it bothered him.

"Yes she is," Rusty agreed with him. But Chase barely heard her.

"You're taking the train to Boulder when we arrive, is that right?" He couldn't let the matter drop.

"Yes. I'll be home tonight."

"Your parents' home?"

"Yes." Her smile was soft. "I haven't seen them since Christmas."

"Do you have siblings?"

"Three. Two sisters and a brother."

"Let me guess — you're the baby?"

Rusty smiled. "No, I'm the oldest. How about you?"

"I'm an only child."

Rusty turned to him. "Are your parents still living?"

"My mother is. She used to live in Springs, but she moved to Texas about six years ago when she remarried."

Although listening, Rusty put the lunch away, her movements all very proper and neat. They reminded Chase of her way with the children. The thought made him smile. Rusty chose that moment to look back at him.

For the space of several heartbeats, Rusty was taken with his face. He was smiling at her, his eyes kind, and Rusty couldn't look away. Chase looked right back but didn't comment. Still she studied him.

"Did I miss something?" he asked, his voice kind so she didn't feel ashamed to be gawking at him.

"I was just thinking about your father."

"My father?" His brows rose.

Rusty nodded. "I think he must have been very nice-looking," she told him, her eyes young and honest.

It took a moment for Chase to understand

that he'd been complimented, but such things were so foreign to him that he had no idea what to say.

"Would it bother you if I went back to my book now, Mr. McCandles?" she asked softly.

"Not at all." Chase's voice was equally soft.

Rusty picked it up and immediately turned to the correct page. Chase watched her for a minute and then shifted his attention to the others in the train car. His mind, however, was still wholly centered on the woman beside him.

9

Makepeace

The train pulled into the station at Makepeace just a short time later. Since Chase and Rusty had been riding for little more than an hour, neither one felt compelled to stand and stretch their legs. As the train moved to get back underway, their thoughts went to the homes to which each was heading. However, they didn't reckon with mechanical trouble. Seconds after a loud metallic pop ricocheted off the depot, the train shuddered to a stop. The conductor came through announcing that there would be a delay and asking all passengers to disembark and take their carry-on baggage with them. Chase and Rusty naturally complied, gathering their bags and heading for the door. It was a small station and platform, and they were joined by two dozen other passengers, a few with children, others alone, and all carrying their baggage.

"Shouldn't be long folks, but feel free to mill around town," the conductor stuck his head off the train and called to them. "We'll blow the whistle several times to let you know."

"Shall we walk into town?" Chase asked, after having taken Rusty's bag from her hand.

"I think I'd like that. I've never been to Makepeace."

The two started off. Rusty tipped her head back slightly, loving the feel of the sun on her face and thinking she should probably find her poke bonnet. Before she could decide if she should fish it out of her satchel, they were at the edge of the boardwalk in town and often in the shade.

"It's a little like Kurth, isn't it?" commented Rusty.

"I think you're right. The layout is similar. I always find you can learn a lot about a town by looking at its general store. Shall we give it a try?" Chase had gestured with his head, and Rusty looked up to see *Ganzer's Emporium.* It was just two doors down, so Rusty nodded and they continued, passing a coffinmaker and a land office before stopping at *Ganzer's* front door.

Chase held the door, and as soon as Rusty stepped in, she smiled. Mr. McCandles had been right. Not only was it a unique store with everything very orderly and clean, it was huge.

"Shall we split up, Mr. McCandles, and compare notes in, say, 30 minutes?"

Chase made no attempt to stop his smile. He should have known she would find this an adventure to be explored and conquered.

"I think that's a fine idea. Thirty minutes, back here by the door?"

Rusty nodded, turned, and began to move away, but her companion's voice stopped her.

"Miss Taggart?"

Rusty turned.

"If you hear the train whistle and can't find me, go ahead to the station, but don't board without me."

"What if we miss the train?"

"We'll try to catch a later one."

Already knowing what the answer must be, she said, "You still have the schedule, don't you?"

Chase tapped his coat pocket, and Rusty smiled hugely. She turned and started toward the back of the store with the intention of working her way out to the front. She didn't get far. The first things she discovered were the toys. They captured her attention at once. A clown on a stick, a box that played music when the crank was turned, skates with wheels and also with blades for ice, books, stuffed animals, little toy trucks and trains. She handled nearly every toy, imagining the fun the children would have at the orphanage, and in the process, completely forgot about the time. Chase found her more than 30 minutes later, working the funny clown on the stick, her face intent, and to his eyes, very young.

"That looks fun," he said kindly.

"Yes. I think the children would love it," Rusty replied, replacing it with reluctance, "but I would need at least 20 of them to make it fair, so I don't think I'll even try." She finally looked at him. "I take it there wasn't much to interest you."

"Why do you say that?"

"Because you're early."

"It's been almost 40 minutes." His voice was very soft and gentle, but Rusty blinked at him.

"Has it really?"

Chase nodded, just barely holding his smile. "Did you even get out of this aisle?"

"No." Her look was so comical that her

companion chuckled.

"I hate to interrupt, but maybe we should check on the train situation."

"Of course," Rusty agreed, but inside she squirmed with embarrassment. *He's a busy man, Rusty. He doesn't have all day to waste getting you home.* That the whole reason they were stranded in Makepeace was not her fault did not occur to her until she silently accompanied Mr. McCandles from the store and back to the train station. Nothing had changed; their train was still having trouble. Still, the thought of wasting Mr. McCandles' time made Rusty feel even worse. Chase chose that moment to look down at her and mistook her rather strained expression for fatigue. She didn't seem the type to tire easily, but leaving the children had been emotional for her, he was sure, and could easily explain why she might be tired.

"I have an idea. Why don't we take our bags to the hotel, ask the desk manager to hold them, and have a little lunch?" Chase suggested.

It was on the tip of Rusty's tongue to say she'd already eaten, but she remembered at the last moment that her companion had not.

"That sounds fine," she agreed warmly and gladly fell into step as Chase started off. Just 15 minutes later they were comfortably seated at a table, hot coffee in thick mugs before them. Menus had been handed to them, and Rusty decided she could do with a piece of berry pie. She told Mr. McCandles when he asked her.

"No lunch?" her companion confirmed.

"No. I ate one of the sandwiches Jessie sent."

"That's right."

"What will you have?"

"The beef sounds good."

And indeed it was. Because it was still a little early, the hotel dining room was not yet busy, so their order came quickly. They talked about a variety of things, Chase asking Rusty many questions about the orphanage. She loved her work, so it was easy to share with him. The meal passed swiftly.

Chase declined dessert himself. After he'd finished his last cup of coffee, he paid for the food and said to Rusty, "I think I'll walk back and check on the train. Do you want to wait here?"

"I don't mind waiting here, but if they're ready for us, you'll have to come all the way back for me."

Chase shook his head. "They haven't blown the whistle at all, and even if they are ready, the walk will do me good. Would you like your bag so you can read?"

"Yes, please."

He walked to the hotel desk to get it for her, and Rusty thought, not for the first time, that he really was remarkably kind. Chase delivered her bag back to her just minutes later and took his leave. Rusty retrieved *The Red Badge of Courage* from her bag, and was immersed just paragraphs later.

"I'm not sure I can promise you we'll move things out today at all," the man told Chase, whose brows rose in surprise.

"What happened?"

"One of the drive arms broke. Sheared clean through. Still trying to track down the smith. He's out on one of the ranches."

"But what of other trains?"

"What other trains?"

"The ones on the schedule."

"We're the schedule, twice a day, if we don't break down." The man shrugged.

Chase thanked the man cordially, but swiftly left the platform and went directly back to the hotel desk. He booked two rooms for the night before joining Rusty.

"What did they say?" she asked as soon as he took the chair across from her.

"That we might not get out today."

"Oh, Mr. McCandles, I'm so sorry. What

does this do to your business plans?"

Chase shook his head. "It's not me I'm worried about. You had hoped to be with your family tonight."

Rusty shrugged. "It's not that urgent. As soon as the children were placed, my time off started. My family wasn't sure what day I would arrive. It's really no trouble."

But neither one was convinced. Chase thought Rusty wanted to get home more than she was letting on, and Rusty thought Mr. McCandles was only being polite concerning the urgency of his business dealings.

"I've booked two rooms for us here at the hotel," Chase continued.

"But what if the train is able to leave?"

"We'll still hear the whistle, but the conductor did not sound hopeful. This way, we won't be stuck sitting up all night if they can't get the repairs done." Chase explained what the conductor had said and then asked Rusty if she wanted to go to her room for a time.

"I guess maybe I will," Rusty replied, thankful that at the orphanage, where things could change with each movement of the clock, she was learning to take what came. She stood, and Chase picked up her bag. With the manners she so enjoyed from him, he escorted her up the stairs, opened the door for her, set her bag down, checked the lock on the window, looked into the closet, and handed her the key.

"I'm in room 15 if you need me."

"Thank you for everything, Mr. McCandles. Did you," Rusty hesitated, "that is, do I need to go down and pay for the room?"

"I took care of it," he assured her gently.

"I have money for travel expenses," she reminded him.

"I wanted to take care of it."

"You took care of the wagon in Kurth too."

"No, Doug came for us, and we didn't need to rent one."

"Oh, that's right."

"So, we're all set?" he asked, watching her carefully.

Rusty wasn't sure they were, but she let the matter drop with a small nod of her head. Her uncle had anticipated every need and sent a wise amount of cash so she could see to emergencies, but he must not have communicated that to her traveling companion.

Rusty saw Chase to the door and thanked him once again. She shut the portal, made sure it was locked, and leaned against it. A quick survey of the room told her it was neat and clean, but her mind wandered elsewhere as she wondered just how long they should be stranded. It was not her own inconvenience that worried her, but Mr. McCandles'. There could be another way to get to Colorado Springs, one that she hadn't thought of. She sat down on the edge of the bed with plans to do just that.

10

Rusty woke with a start. She hadn't remembered lying back on the bed, but she must have. She had no idea how much time had passed, but something had woken her. The whistle! She'd heard the train whistle.

Glad that she hadn't bothered to unpack her bag, Rusty grabbed it, picked up her key, and let herself out the door. She went straight to number 15 and knocked, but there was no answer. She knocked again, a little harder this time, and even called softly, but Mr. McCandles was not in. Figuring he'd gone on to the train station, Rusty moved down the stairs to the hotel desk.

"Is there a problem, ma'am?" the proprietor wished to know.

"No, sir. I'm one of the train passengers, and they said they would blow the whistle, so I won't be needing my room." Rusty placed the key in front of him on the counter.

"The whistle, ma'am?"

"Yes. I was asleep, so I don't know if it was the first one or the last. I'd better hurry," she added with a smile.

"Jared," the man called to another man at the counter, "did you hear the train whistle?"

"Not me."

The first man looked back at Rusty. "I didn't hear it either, ma'am."

"Oh."

Rusty looked so perplexed that he offered a suggestion. "Maybe you should leave your bag with me and then check, or better yet, I'll send someone to check for you."

"Do you normally hear the whistle clearly?"

"Yes."

Rusty looked undecided for a moment; she'd been so certain of the sound. "I will leave my bag with you," she said at last, "and my key. If the train is ready I'll rush back and get the satchel."

"All right. I'll have it right here behind the counter for you."

"Has Mr. McCandles turned his key in? He's in number 15."

The man checked the box. "No, ma'am, no key."

"All right. Thank you."

Much as Rusty wanted to believe the whistle hadn't sounded, she still felt her heart beat a little faster as she left the hotel and started toward the train station. Things looked calm enough. Maybe she had dreamed the sound of the whistle. With a stride as long as she could manage, Rusty covered the distance rather swiftly, only to see long before she reached the platform that things were just as she'd left them. The train was still being worked on, and the platform was nearly empty. Rusty nearly shook her head. She *had* dreamed that whistle. With a wry smile at her own antics, she turned and bumped into someone who must have been standing directly behind her.

"Excuse me," Rusty spoke, stepping back. She tipped her head to see a large, bearded man in front of her, his eyes fierce as they glowered out at her from under bushy brows. Rusty tried a small smile, but the man was so harsh-looking that she decided against speaking again. With subtle movements she scooted around him and back toward the hotel. It was a good reminder. She was a stranger in this town, not a local orphanage worker or the daughter of the school administrator. She had best get back to the hotel and stay there.

Chase finished the small errand he'd set out to do and headed back through the hotel lobby toward the stairs. If the train couldn't leave, he'd found a nice spot for him and Rusty to have dinner that night. It was a small place with simple decor and would make a nice change from the hotel.

"Mr. McCandles?" The desk manager's voice stopped him.

Chase turned and approached.

"Did the lady find you?"

"Miss Taggart?"

"Yes, the one in the other room you reserved. She thought she heard the whistle and went to check on the train."

"No, I haven't seen her. You say she's left the hotel and not returned?"

"That's right. Her key's still in the box."

"Thank you. Should she come back and miss me again, please ask her to wait here at the hotel."

"I'll do that, sir."

His heart pounding a bit harder in his chest, Chase went back through the elaborate double doors and onto the street. He made a beeline for the train station, wondering what had made Rusty think she heard the whistle. Makepeace wasn't that big. He was sure the train whistle could be heard all over town.

There was no sign of her at the station. Chase wandered around for a time and then started slowly back to the hotel, watching for her all the way. Makepeace was quiet and peaceful from all indications, but if that was the case, then why was Chase's heartrate increasing with nearly every step? He prayed, working to trust the Lord for Rusty's safety as well as use his head, and all the while hoping that she was already safely back at the hotel.

Rusty's intentions were good. She had started to go swiftly back to the hotel, but she hadn't reckoned with the interesting things she would see in town. Partway to the hotel she had got it into her head to see if Makepeace had an orphanage. It would be such fun to visit. She inquired at the reading room, and was disappointed to discover that the town did not have a place for orphans. But she quickly became fascinated by the lovely window displays of the shops. Before she knew it, she had dawdled almost an hour away. When she suddenly realized how long she'd been gone, she felt a twinge of guilt. She knew the hotel was a block over, so rather than go around, she opted to cut between the buildings. There was a small path between a shoe store and the hat shop, so Rusty took it. The hotel would be in sight as soon as she came around the corner. What she didn't plan on was a group of young men gathered at the rear of the building. Rusty spotted them and stopped short, but they had already seen her.

Chase gained his room, shut the door, and just stood in the middle of the rug. Rusty hadn't come back, and he certainly wasn't going to find her in here, but he had to gather his thoughts. He didn't know Rusty very well, but it wasn't hard to figure that she must have become sidetracked. She must have gone to check on the train but then decided to do something else. After all, they hadn't made any plans to meet; neither had they promised to stay in their rooms. She must have felt free to have a look around town if she wanted.

Chase asked himself why that was so little comfort. The likelihood of her being harmed was not great, but there was a chance, and for this reason he couldn't rest until he'd checked on her. Should he look around town or simply sit in the lobby and watch for her? Feeling restless and uncertain, he moved to the window. His heart jolted in his chest when he saw a bright red head. It didn't take long for him to identify the owner. Not even bothering to lock his door, Chase made for the hall, raced down the stairs, and gained the outside, his stride just short of a run.

"Well, hello," one of the young men greeted Rusty as they all turned in a group.

Knowing that just about anything would encourage them, Rusty nodded with a regal air and began to move past them, keeping her right shoulder close to the building. She didn't get far. One of them stepped in front of her, and she came to a stop.

"Excuse me." Rusty's voice was soft but determined. "I would like to pass."

"What's your hurry?"

Rusty's chin rose in the air. She made a move to step around him but suddenly found someone at her shoulder.

"We don't see hair like this too often." The man in front of her was speaking again.

Rusty felt someone else move in behind her and thought it the better part of valor to put her own back against the building. Rusty's gaze encompassed the group. She saw that there were four of them, all standing too close and staring down at her as if they'd never seen a woman. They were all young and well-dressed, probably Rusty's own age, but Rusty was too frightened to say much.

Rusty's cheeks paled, causing her eyes to look huge and vulnerable.

"Please don't stand so close," she whispered. "You're scaring me."

To her utter surprise they all backed up a few inches.

"I have to get back to the hotel."

"You don't live here?" one asked, moving close again.

Rusty only shook her head no and slid along the wall. Her heart sank with dread when they all moved with her. *They're not going to let me pass, Lord. What shall I say? What should I do?*

"There you are."

All five heads turned at the sound of a deep, male voice.

The men changed positions, and Rusty's eyes locked with those of Chase McCandles. She began to shake from head to toe.

"I lost track of you," Chase said congenially as he approached, looking for all the world as if he were on a Sunday stroll. "Hello, gentlemen," Chase nodded to the group and received nods in return. Even the tallest one had to look up at him. Chase's eyes met theirs before he looked back to Rusty.

"I had to run an errand. You must have had one too."

"I was checking on the train," Rusty got out in a small voice.

The men had moved to face Chase, but they were still at Rusty's sides.

Chase nodded. "What did you learn?"

"It's not going yet."

Chase nodded, his eyes more watchful than they appeared. "We'd better head back to the hotel then."

Rusty nodded but couldn't move. She felt frozen in place, her heart beating like that of a snared bird. In truth, Mr. McCandles' voice was sterner than she'd ever heard it, and right now he scared her a little too. Rusty's legs were trembling so badly that she didn't know if they would hold her.

"Come to me, Katherine." His voice held a note of command. It was just enough to propel Rusty away from the wall. As she approached, Chase held out his arm, and Rusty put her hand in the crook of his elbow.

"Good day, gentlemen," he spoke over the top of her head as he started back the way he had come.

Rusty couldn't have told anyone when they left the dirt of the alley and stepped onto the boardwalk. She kept her hand firmly tucked into Mr. McCandles' arm and tried not to cry. She looked straight ahead and told herself that if she could just get to her room, she could let down. It was with near panic that she realized her escort was not taking her to her room. Chase walked into the hotel and started toward the lobby. Rusty's low voice came to him in a panic.

"Oh, please, Mr. McCandles. Please let me go to my room. I beg of you. Please allow me to go to my room."

The hand that had been on his arm was suddenly taken in Chase's right hand. His left hand went to her back as he bent low to speak with her but continued to walk.

"I can't talk with you if I take you to your room. There's a small parlor at the back of the lobby. We'll talk in there."

To Chase's disappointment there was a man in the parlor, but that didn't stop him. He put Rusty in a chair that would allow her to have her back to the room. He took a chair that would let him see her face. As the other man stood to leave, Chase glanced up long enough to give him a grateful glance. When the door was shut again, Chase turned back to Rusty. Her eyes were on the wall, wide and staring.

"Are you all right?"

"Yes, just a little scared." Rusty's hand came to her mouth. She was trembling violently.

"What did they say to you?"

"Just that they liked my hair." Rusty looked at him. "They stood so close, and they wouldn't let me pass. I thought I heard the whistle, and you weren't in your room. I thought I would make us miss the train. I'm sorry, Mr. McCandles. I'm so very sorry."

"It's all right." Her tears were too much for Chase. Without permission he took her hand. "Don't worry about it anymore, Katherine. It's all over."

Rusty didn't even hear him. "I must have fallen asleep. I was trying to figure out a way to get you home, and I was so sure I heard the whistle. It was so loud that it woke me. I'm sorry. I'm so sorry."

"It's all right," he repeated. "I should have told you I was leaving the hotel. Don't worry about it anymore."

Rusty took a deep breath and tried to do just that. Her gaze traveled to the wall again. There was so much to be thankful for. She'd been frightened and not hurt. Mr. McCandles had come when she needed him most. If she could only concentrate on these things, the Lord would comfort her.

"I think I'll go to my room now," she said, but then looked at Chase. "In all of this, have we missed the train whistle?"

"No, and with as late in the day as it is

now, I would want us to stay and take a train tomorrow anyway. Will you be comfortable and feel safe in your room tonight?"

"Yes."

"Good. I think we should eat in about an hour. Does that work for you?"

"I'm not sure I'll be too hungry."

"Would you rather have something in your room?"

Rusty thought about it, but shook her head. "No. That might give me too much time to think. Does that make sense to you?"

"Completely."

Rusty stood and Chase with her. She started toward the door but stopped.

"I didn't thank you. You came just when I needed you, and I forgot to say thank you." Tears that she could no longer stem flooded her eyes. Again Chase was very moved but thought it was best if he stayed quiet. He was right. Rusty composed herself and moved out the door. Chase retrieved her key and bag and saw her to her room, telling her he would be in his room if she needed him and that he would call for her in one hour's time.

11

Rusty was ready when Chase knocked on her door that evening and followed him quietly down the hallway. He had not had a chance to tell her they were dining out of the hotel, but Rusty said nothing as he led the way toward the door. Indeed, she was so quiet that Chase began to be concerned.

"Were you able to rest for a time?" he asked as they started down the street.

"Yes, thank you."

Chase would have given much for more of a response. He prayed even as they walked that he would be able to draw her out over dinner. For the time, however, he left her to walk quietly beside him.

Grandma's Kitchen had a homey feel to it. It was small and clean, and the tables in the middle of the room as well as the booths were decorated in all colors of checkered cloths and various flowers. A man showed them to a private booth and handed out menus.

"Do you think you can manage anything?" Chase asked without even opening his menu.

"I think so. It's a little chilly this evening, so anything hot sounds good."

Chase didn't find it cold at all but said, "This seems like a place that would have great soup. Shall I ask what they're serving?"

"Oh, yes, please."

Chase signaled the waiter back long enough to order coffee and find out that the soup was bean and ham.

"Sound tempting?" he asked with a smile.

"Yes, a nice big bowl."

Chase placed the order and then watched his dinner companion as she stared into space. He thought he could almost read her thoughts and wished she would talk to him. He could have greatly assured her. In fact, he was determined not to let her out of his sight, even to the extent of taking her all the way home to Boulder. When he watched pain cloud her eyes, he knew he had to speak.

"Is this afternoon still heavy on your mind, Katherine?"

She turned as if just realizing he was there. "No, not really. I've thought about it, of course, but other than giving me a rough scare, there was really no harm done."

Chase had a hard time believing her. Her very posture still showed upset and pain. He had watched her in action for days with the children, and she was not the same. The bubbly young woman, ready to take the world by storm, was gone. Something was very wrong, and it wasn't hard to guess what. In hopes that she would open up to him, he began to gently question her, hoping to see her relax.

"Do you have anything special planned when you get home?"

"Nothing specific. Probably just lots of visiting with family and friends — maybe some shopping."

"How long will you be home?"

"About a week."

Their food was delivered a short while later, and for a time they were silent. In the small parlor at the hotel, Rusty had said something about trying to get him home. Chase was curious about that, as well as how she got into the alley in the first place, but she was still so quiet and distant that he didn't feel free to ask.

"I think I needed that," Rusty said as she sat back with a sigh, most of her soup and rolls gone. "Left to myself, I don't think I would have eaten anything. Thank you, Mr. McCandles."

"You're welcome. Does dessert sound good?"

"No, thank you, but an early night does. Do you know for certain if we'll get out in the morning?"

"Yes. The repairs are coming along. Other parts were damaged, so it's going to take most of the night to straighten things out."

Rusty nodded. She desperately wanted to get home to Boulder. She felt she was thinking well about the incident today, putting it into perspective and not letting her emotions run wild, but she had a terrible ache inside to see her family, one that she could only attribute to the upset of today.

"Shall we head back to the hotel?"

"Yes, please. It's been a long day, and I'm quite tired."

Chase did not try to engage her in conversation but simply walked her back to her room, made sure her door was secure, and told her he would be in his own room if she needed him. She did not. She dressed for bed as soon as his footsteps disappeared down the hall, and within seconds of settling the covers around her, she was asleep.

Chase was still concerned. He had called

for Rusty at 8:00, even though he already had their tickets, and other than showing surprise that they were now riding in the first-class dining car, she was just as quiet and pale as she'd been the night before. Chase had no desire to badger her, but something told him she was not telling all. He prayed about questioning her and found his opportunity just after the train left the Makepeace station and a waiter came to take their breakfast orders. Rusty wanted only coffee.

"Are you sure?" Chase questioned her when they were once again alone.

"Yes. I'm not hungry."

"Katherine —" Chase's voice was gentle, but he also felt determined. "I don't feel as though you have been completely candid with me. What did those men say to you that has you so upset? I think you might feel better if you speak of it."

"Oh, Mr. McCandles, I'm sorry," Rusty said contritely. "I'm really not upset about that anymore, but I've been the most awful traveling companion." She paused for a moment and then admitted, "To be honest with you, I'm not feeling all that well. My head hurts terribly."

"Oh, Katherine," Chase said compassionately, "I wish you had said something. We

131

might have consulted a doctor and gotten something for you."

"That's all right. I find I just want to sleep."

"Why don't you?"

Rusty hesitated, strongly tempted. She had never ridden in a first-class train car before, and the elegance was stunning. The fabric on her seat was a soft velvet, the cushion was thickly padded, and she had it all to herself. Chase sat across a small table from her, and at their backs were walls that went to the ceiling, forming a booth. It was remarkably private. If only she wasn't so cold.

"Just lay your head back in the corner," Chase said softly. "No one will be bothered in the least."

Rusty would have nodded, but it hurt too much. She did lay her head in the corner and let her eyes stare out the window at the passing scape. It didn't last long. Her lids grew heavy, and before five minutes had passed she was sound asleep. But the sleep didn't last long either. Inside of 15 minutes she was awake again, feeling chilled to the bone as she stared across the table at Chase's empty seat with fever-bright eyes. He returned just a moment later, and Rusty took a moment to focus on him.

"Is it cold to you, Mr. McCandles?"

"I'll get you a blanket," Chase said without answering her. He signaled to a porter in the wide aisle and then looked back at Rusty. Her face was white save for two poppy-red spots of color in her cheeks. Chase consulted his watch, did a mental calculation, and prayed that there would be no delays at Fountain before they went on to Colorado Springs. A moment later the porter came with the blanket. Chase took it and stood up. He bent over Rusty, tucked it closely around her, and then sat beside her. With one hand he pulled the shade on their window, and with the other, he dropped the curtain over their booth. He heard Rusty sigh in the semi-darkness.

"You have a fever, Katherine," he said when he heard her teeth chatter. "Just lean on me, and we'll try to get you warm."

Rusty had no strength or will to even speak as Chase put an arm around her and pulled her close to his side.

"We'll be in Fountain in about ten minutes and Colorado Springs a half an hour after that."

"I have to get my ticket home," she managed, but Chase didn't comment. She wouldn't be going any farther once they arrived, but with her last statement her head had fallen limply against his chest, and he had no chance to answer.

Colorado Springs

Chase kept Rusty's elbow firmly clamped in his hand as they disembarked the train. What little color had been in her face was now completely drained away, and she looked like a little shadow with red hair. She stayed on her feet, however, as they crossed the platform, and then Chase lifted her into a waiting hack.

The ride passed in a fog for Rusty. She couldn't have told anyone where she was, if her life had depended on it. She never remembered her head hurting like it did now. All she wanted to do was lie down and sleep, but the carriage kept moving and she was still so cold. She felt a little warmer when Chase scooped her into his arms to carry her somewhere, but he kept moving and she couldn't fall asleep.

Without permission Chase carried her over the threshold and into his home. Waiting inside was his housekeeper, Mrs. Whitley.

"The guest chamber, sir?"

"No, the big bedroom."

Mrs. Whitley took the stairs on swift feet, Chase following close behind her. Rusty was aware of being carried but couldn't figure out where she was. She was tired, and Lizzy and Thomas kept flashing through her mind. When had she said goodbye to them? Were they all right?

Her feet touched the ground, but she barely noticed; feeling thoroughly disoriented, she was trying to remember if she'd sent word to her aunt and uncle. Whom could she ask? She felt strong hands steady her and looked up to see Chase McCandles standing above her, his eyes keen with worry.

"Mr. McCandles, did I send word to Sammy and Paddy?"

It took him a moment. "About Lizzy and Thomas?"

"Yes."

"The Davidsons were going to take care of that."

"Oh, yes." Her brow lowered in concentration. "Jessie and Doug. How are they?"

"I think they're fine. You, on the other hand, need some rest."

Rusty looked up at him again. He was so large and comforting, but there was something she had forgotten to do. Maybe if she could get some paper and write, it would come to her.

"I need some paper," she began and started to move away from Chase to search the room. There was sure to be a desk some-where.

He put an arm around her waist and brought her right back.

"Mrs. Whitley is going to help you get ready for bed."

"Oh, how nice." The paper was forgotten. "I'm so tired."

"Let me know when she's settled in," he said to someone beyond her. Rusty turned to see a woman standing near the door.

"Is this your bag, dear?" the woman asked in a motherly fashion.

Rusty didn't want to nod her head, so she whispered a small yes.

"I'll just find something for you, shall I?"

Rusty stood still as her bag was searched. She recognized the nightgown Mrs. Whitley produced.

"The dressing room is just in here, dear." Mrs. Whitley walked around the bed and opened a door. "Why don't you come in here and slip out of your things?"

She preceded Rusty into the room and laid the nightgown on the little bench that sat inside the door, but Rusty was slow in com-ing. Mrs. Whitley slipped out as she came into the dressing room.

"Your bed is all turned down," Mrs. Whitley said softly as she came back to the door and saw that Rusty had done nothing but pick up her nightgown. She stood holding it.

Melinda Whitley knew from experience when someone needed help and when she should be left alone. If she were to leave this young woman alone much longer, she might collapse. Without permission she began to ease Rusty's dress from her shoulders. The younger woman did not protest. Melinda worked silently and efficiently, and in little time at all Rusty was ensconced in the night garment. This done, Mrs. Whitley put a gentle hand on Rusty's back and guided her to the bed. Once she was beneath the covers, Mrs. Whitley stood over her and spoke.

"I believe Mr. McCandles would like to see you, dear. Do you mind if he joins us for a moment?"

"No, ma'am," Rusty whispered.

Rusty watched as the door opened. Chase entered and immediately came toward her. Mrs. Whitley returned to the bed as well and stood at the end. More concerned with Rusty than with propriety, Chase sat right down on the edge of the mattress.

"Are you comfortable?"

"Yes. Is this your home, Mr. McCandles?"

"Yes. This is Briarly."

"So I'm in Colorado Springs?"

"Yes, safe in my home. No one will disturb you. I want you to sleep as long as you like."

"Thank you."

As though having permission was all she needed, Rusty's eyes closed. Before Chase could even move from the mattress, her breathing evened out and her features relaxed. Chase stood and walked quietly from the room. Mrs. Whitley followed him and shut Rusty's door.

"We were held up in Makepeace yesterday," Chase explained to his housekeeper, "and I think she was coming down with something even last night. I didn't realize she was ill until we were back on the train this morning."

"Her skin is so warm." The older woman's voice was compassionate. "Has she been sick to her stomach?"

"I don't think so. Will you be able to keep things quiet today?"

"Yes, sir. I'll let everyone know and open her door again so I can hear her if she needs something."

"Thank you. Don't hesitate to come for me if I can help."

"Certainly, sir."

The two were standing in the wide, room-size landing at the top of the stairs. Their voices remained hushed, although Rusty's door was closed. They parted soon after that, Chase to his office to work on his mail, and Mrs. Whitley taking the next level of stairs to the staff bedrooms in an upper wing in an effort to warn all servants that they must be quiet. Briarly was a huge home, but if she had to walk every inch of it to ensure quiet, that was just what she would do.

Rusty slept all day. Mrs. Whitley came and went, but Rusty heard none of it. It was after 4:00 when she woke, finally warm, and re-membered where she was. Her head still hurt, but she thought the worst of it might be over.

I can't remember when I've ever had such a headache, she thought to herself, but then realized it hurt to think too much. She was lying comfortably, thinking she might drop off again, when Mrs. Whitley came in.

"You're awake," the older lady said softly. "How are you feeling?"

"Still rather weak, I'm afraid."

Mrs. Whitley smiled and moved to the table next to Rusty's bed. "I brought you some tea about 20 minutes ago. The pot is still quite hot. Would you like some?"

"I am thirsty."

Mrs. Whitley went right to work, pouring and adding sugar and a dash of warm milk.

"We'll have you fixed up in no time," she said before passing a cup of tea to Rusty and making sure she could manage it.

It was warm and sweet, and Rusty's sigh was heartfelt. "Thank you. I'm embarrassed to tell you that I don't remember your name."

"Of course you don't, dear. I'm Mrs. Whitley, and Mr. McCandles tells me you're Miss Taggart."

"Everyone calls me Rusty."

The housekeeper beamed. "Because of your hair. It's really quite lovely, you know."

Rusty smiled kindly, but she was already growing tired again.

"Now, how about some food, Miss Taggart? Can I tempt you?"

"I don't think I can manage it, Mrs. Whitley, but thank you."

Mrs. Whitley took the cup from Rusty's hand as she reached to put it back down. She had only drunk about half of it. One look at Rusty's face told her that she was fading again. Mr. McCandles had asked to be summoned when Rusty was awake, but by the time she gained his office and he came upstairs, their guest would be sleeping again, so she didn't even try. And she was right. Rusty was asleep just minutes later, and this time she slept the remainder of the day and the entire night.

12

Rusty woke slowly, her body a little achy, but within moments she knew the headache was gone. She stretched a little, but even that was an effort. She felt as lethargic as a spoiled cat, but then she spotted him, and some of the sluggishness disappeared. Rusty looked over at her open door to see a little boy. She pushed herself higher against her pillow to see him more clearly.

Small and on the thin side, he regarded her seriously with his dark eyes. His hair was dark and straight. He was wearing knee pants with suspenders and a long-sleeved shirt. Rusty guessed him to be about five years old. She also had the impression that he would run if she spoke to him, but she had to try.

"Good morning," she said softly.

He stared at her. Rusty pushed a little

higher onto her pillow, bringing her covers up for warmth.

"Would you like to come in?"

With that he ran. Rusty put a hand over her mouth to cover her laugh. His eyes had gotten so huge, one would have thought she had suggested he write on the wall. Rusty lay thinking about him for a moment. It wasn't long until he returned.

"You're back," Rusty said kindly to the little boy. "Come in." This time her tone was just firm enough. The little boy came forward. Rusty spoke when he stood by the bed.

"My name is Katherine Alexa Taggart. Will you tell me yours?"

He stared at her, his face open, his eyes curious, but no words came from his mouth.

"Do you know," Rusty began again, "that I work with children? I love children — all ages and sizes. How old are you?"

"Four," he said softly.

"You are very grown up for four. Do you like to read books and look at the pictures?"

He nodded very solemnly.

"Do you have a favorite?"

He nodded again, and Rusty smiled at him. It was the smile that always worked its magic. It wasn't anything she tried to do, but even with her hair all over and her face still pale, Rusty's smile went right to her eyes and into the heart of her receiver.

"Well, Quintin, dear, there you are," Mrs. Whitley called as she came into the room. "Mrs. Harding is looking for you, dear."

"Quintin!" Rusty's eyes grew huge with excitement. "Is that your name?"

Again the nod.

"Will you tell me your whole name?"

He didn't respond.

"I'll start it for you, Quintin . . ."

"Quintin James McCandles."

"How wonderful," Rusty said and meant it. Mr. McCandles had a son! "Now tell me, Quintin James McCandles, what do you like to do best?"

The little boy leaned against the bed now, and Rusty secretly smiled at the way he was relaxing. The almost instant rapport was just what she'd hoped for.

"I like birds," he told her. "Mrs. Harding lets me see birds."

"Where do you see them?" Rusty asked. Mrs. Whitley stood quietly by the bed, but this little boy had melted Rusty's heart and she could not let him get away.

"We have woods. We go there."

"Do you have a favorite type of bird?"

He was on the verge of answering when a brisk female voice called from the hall.

"Quintin, come to me at once."

"Goodbye," the little boy said softly and immediately turned to go.

Rusty waved at him with a few fingers and smiled. The owner of the voice from the hall never made an appearance, but Quintin was gone nonetheless.

"How did you sleep, dear?" Mrs. Whitley asked. If she was at all put-out over having to wait, Rusty saw no sign of it.

"I slept well. I'm still a bit weak, but the headache is gone."

"I'm so glad. Are you up to some breakfast?"

Rusty was opening her mouth to reply when someone knocked. Both women turned to see Chase McCandles on the threshold. He entered, wearing black slacks and shoes and a crisp white shirt. Taking in Rusty's pale features at a glance, emotions flooded through Chase, but he pushed them neatly into place. And because they were at Briarly, he proceeded in his usual way, which was to take complete charge.

"Good morning, Katherine. Have you told Mrs. Whitley what you want for breakfast?"

"I'm not hungry right now, thank you."

"Very well. I want you to take it easy today. *All* day," he added firmly. "You can take your meals here in the room. Mrs. Whitley will see to it."

Upon this statement he turned for the door. He left without another word, and Mrs. Whitley, her face expressionless, followed in his wake. Rusty bit her lip as she looked at the now empty doorway.

Rusty, girl, you need to get yourself home today. You've worn out your welcome here. It won't be easy, but just get to the train and you can sleep all the way home. Her decision made, Rusty carefully pushed the covers aside. She was still weak. *I probably just need food,* she thought to herself. At any rate, it was time to go home.

Chase's office did not give him a view of the stairs, but he'd just remembered a book he needed from the library. As he was crossing the drawing room to find it, he saw Rusty as she came down the stairs. She was dressed, although her hair wasn't brushed, but there was even less color to her face than there had been earlier. The book forgotten, Chase arrived in the large foyer at the same time she reached the bottom of the stairs.

"Oh, Mr. McCandles," she began softly, "there you are. I think I should leave. I know you're upset with me, and I understand with the trouble you've had to go to. I think I should go ahead and eat something and catch the train today. It's still early, and I could be home tonight."

"Katherine," Chase began, his voice very gentle, but she was not through.

"I appreciate all you've done, Mr. McCandles, but if you'll just show me where the kitchen is, I'll eat and pack, and then only bother you one more time for a ride to the train station."

"Did I tell you I sent a telegram to your parents?" Chase said suddenly.

Rusty stared at him.

"I also sent word to Paddy at the orphanage," Chase continued conversationally. "I apologize for not telling you. I wanted to let everyone know that the children were settled at the Davidsons', but that we'd run into a delay." He paused to see how she was taking his words. He had her attention, but she still looked uncertain. "I told your parents I would personally see you home on Friday, but if you want to go now, I'll take you. I'm sorry I made you feel as if you've been a bother. Nothing could be further from the truth."

Rusty opened her mouth to speak, but no words came out. Maybe she wasn't as strong as she thought. She suddenly felt tired all over again. Even from the several feet that separated them, Chase could see the way she shook. This was all his fault. His heart clenched that his hospitality had been so poor. Moving carefully, he pulled an ornate chair away from the foyer wall so she could reach it. She sank down onto it gratefully.

"I'm so sorry, Katherine. I'm sorry I made you feel unwelcome."

She looked up at him. "Nobody calls me Katherine."

"I've been called a lot of things in my time, but never a nobody."

It was just the light remark she needed. Laughing just a little, she glanced around the huge foyer.

Chase watched her for a moment. "What would you like to do now?" he asked her.

"Just sit, I think. Is it cold to you?"

"Not really, but the vestibule is always drafty."

Rusty turned to look toward the front door. It was some ways away, beyond an elaborate archway. She had never seen the like.

"Why don't you come into the drawing room?" Chase offered. "The morning sun comes through the bay window. I think you'll find it much more comfortable."

Rusty rose but not without effort. She wondered if once she got home she would have to spend the week in bed. Actually, with this delay she was no longer certain she still had a week.

Chase led Rusty through a doorway right off the wide foyer. The young redhead was not prepared for the room she entered. It was huge and absolutely beautiful. She would have exclaimed over it in her usual exuberant manner, but for the moment she just wanted to stay on her feet.

"Here you go," Chase encouraged. His tone was normal, but he was very worried. "Why don't you get comfortable here?" He directed her to a large, overstuffed chair. Chase noticed she was still trembling.

"I think you need a quilt," he said as she sank into the cushions. Mrs. Whitley, who had been hovering in the background since she had seen Rusty in the foyer, came forward, a thick comforter in her hand. She had grabbed it from a closet under the stairs when she heard Rusty asking Chase if it was cold.

"Here we go." Chase tucked the throw around his houseguest.

"Did you say you'd written to my parents?" Rusty asked, her face anxious. "You told them I was all right?"

"Absolutely."

"Thank you, Mr. McCandles."

"You're very welcome. Now, would you like something hot to drink?"

Relief covered her face. "That sounds good."

"Coffee? Tea?"

Rusty looked uncertain.

"Hot cocoa?"

Again the look of relief. "Yes, please, but I don't need anyone to wait on me, Mr. McCandles. I can go to the kitchen and prepare it."

Chase sat on the ottoman at her feet, effectively blocking her into the chair. He bent his long legs and casually put his forearms on his knees. Rusty would have to crawl over him to leave, and he knew she wouldn't do that.

"Mrs. Whitley will get it for you," Chase said simply. Mrs. Whitley had left the room the minute Rusty had said "yes, please," and if Chase knew his staff like he thought he did, the housekeeper would be back in less than ten minutes with not just a steaming cup of cocoa, but some toast and muffins as well.

"Are you feeling warmer?"

"Yes. Your home is lovely."

"Thank you." He watched as she looked around the room. She was still so pale, her eyes looking larger than ever in her now-thin face. Before either of them could speak again, Mrs. Whitley returned.

"Now then," she began as she usually did, coming in with a tray to place next to Rusty's chair. Seeing her intention, Chase rose to move a small table over. Mrs. Whitley put the tray on top of it, her smile in place.

"I took the liberty of fixing you a little something to eat, Miss Taggart. Under this napkin is buttered toast, and this plate has some muffins. This dish is a ham souffle, just baked this morning. If you can't eat any of it, don't worry. Cook is planning a splendid lunch."

"Mrs. Whitley, this is so nice." Rusty's voice was soft with surprise. "I really didn't expect you to wait on me."

"You're a guest at Briarly, Miss Taggart," she said simply. "It's our pleasure."

"Thank you," Rusty said graciously.

Mrs. Whitley beamed at her and went on her way. Rusty picked up the cup of hot chocolate, noting that the housekeeper had also left a teapot, presumably with more cocoa. She took a sip and looked at Chase, who had once again taken his seat on the ottoman.

"I didn't know I was going to be treated as a princess."

Her words had the oddest effect on Chase's chest. He felt something squeeze around his heart as he looked at her, knowing how ill she'd been on the train and then thinking of her surrounded by those men. *I have to get this girl home safely, Lord,* Chase prayed, thinking the cause of his emotion was fear. *Until I see her home safe with her family, I won't be able to rest.*

"What day did you say we'll be leaving?"

"Friday morning. Does that work for you?"

"Yes, but I'm thinking about your schedule. Didn't you tell me you have to go to Pueblo?"

"I do, but it's not urgent."

"I don't want to hold you up," Rusty said as she reached for a muffin. She offered the plate to Chase.

"I've eaten, thank you."

"What I'm trying to say," she continued, feeling much warmer and consequently better, "is that I can get myself home. I'll just leave tomorrow or Friday, and you can —"

He was already shaking his head. "Please don't ask me to do that," he cut in, his voice soft with suppressed emotion. They were going to have a knock-down-drag-out fight if she insisted on seeing herself home. Chase simply wouldn't have it — not after seeing those men around her and having her so sick.

"I'm sorry I sounded ungrateful, Mr. McCandles. I was just thinking of your business engagements."

"As a matter of fact, Pueblo *can* wait. When I see you to Boulder, I'll stay in town until Monday. I've wanted to look into some property there for some time. So you see, I'll still be conducting business."

He saw instantly that he'd said the right thing. She looked very relieved and even picked up the small dish with the souffle in it. He watched her try a bite.

"Umm, this is good. Did you have some of it, Mr. McCandles?"

"I can't remember," he said honestly.

"Oh, it's so good. Would you like some?"

"No, thank you." He had to hide his laughter. She was so used to taking care of people that she had a hard time eating in front of him.

Misunderstanding his look, Rusty felt embarrassed. She had disrupted his whole morning.

"I'll stop talking now. I've kept you from your work long enough."

"That's not a problem, Katherine. I'm just glad you're feeling better. In fact, it's probably me who should leave you so you can eat. If you need anything I'll be in my office, and if I'm not there, someone on the staff is usually pretty close at hand. Ask for anything you like."

"Thank you," Rusty replied, studying her host. From where she was sitting, he looked very tall as he made his way through the drawing room and into his office, leaving the double doors open as he took a seat behind his desk. His desk looked directly out onto the drawing room, but he kept his eyes on his work. Rusty watched him for just a moment and then let her own eyes wander the wonderful room again.

It was so lovely, decorated in all shades of green and peach. Someone had excellent taste. Probably Mrs. McCandles, but even as the thought came, Rusty somehow knew there wasn't a Mrs. McCandles — at least not now. Mrs. Whitley would not be handling everything if there were. Rusty reminded herself that it was none of her business and went back to her inspection of the room.

The bay window Chase had referred to earlier was the focal point. With floor-to-ceiling panes of glass and a span of at least 12 feet, it let in the sun in a most glorious manner. Most of the furniture was centered around it.

Rusty's chair was one of four in matching fabric. Her chair and one other flanked a long sofa in a leaf green shade. The other two chairs sat with their backs to the window.

Ottomans sat before each overstuffed chair, but before the davenport was a large coffee table, fashioned in a dark wood Rusty guessed to be mahogany. A large fireplace covered one interior wall and numerous bookshelves and plant stands were perfectly placed. Only a room as spacious as this one could get away with so many large pieces.

Throughout her inspection Rusty continued to eat. Until she tasted the muffin, she hadn't realized the extent of her hunger. It also helped that the food was delicious. Eating all she could and drinking two cups of chocolate, she then wanted to laugh at herself when a yawn escaped.

You're just like a baby, Rusty. Give you a little food, and you're ready for a nap.

Rusty's scolding didn't work. Still tired and wrapped in the warm quilt, her stomach nicely filled, she felt her eyes droop. Asking herself why she should fight it, she let her head rest against the back of the chair. She was asleep within ten minutes.

In the office, Chase had forced himself not to look out at Rusty. When he did, she was sound asleep. He had planned to check on her later, but when he saw she was sleeping, he kept his seat. Even so, it was some time before Chase was able to return to his work.

13

"Miss Taggart?" Rusty heard the calling of her name mere moments after she opened her eyes. She looked toward the sound and saw Mrs. Whitley standing nearby. "Does a hot bath sound good to you, dear?"

Rusty smiled at her. "A hot bath sounds heavenly."

"I thought it might. If you'll just come with me."

Rusty rose, noting as she did that the food tray and table were gone. She picked up the quilt that had been lying over her, ignoring Mrs. Whitley's claim that someone would see to it. Rusty folded it neatly and laid it across the arm of the chair. She then turned to follow Briarly's housekeeper.

Mrs. Whitley led the way up one flight of stairs and then a shorter set of stairs that took them up a half level. There were several rooms in this part of the mansion, one of which was an elaborate bathing chamber. Rusty's parents had had an indoor bath for many years, but it didn't compare with the lovely fittings of this room. Neither did her parents' bathroom have its own boiler that produced a hot bath at the turn of a spigot.

"Now then, dear, I'll just start this running for you and explain to you how it works. I'll slip into your room and find fresh clothing for you. The door does not lock, but I assure you no one will bother you since it will be closed."

"Thank you," Rusty said calmly enough, but when the older woman exited, she removed her clothing as swiftly as she could, embarrassed at the thought of being caught standing at the side of the tub in the altogether. The tub wasn't full yet, but Rusty got in nevertheless. She then learned there was no need to hurry. Mrs. Whitley did not rush back. An array of soaps and bathing bubbles occupied a low shelf above the tub. By the time Mrs. Whitley did slip back in with Rusty's things, the young woman was surrounded by suds, her hair lathered, and the water so full of bubbles that she couldn't even see her feet. Adjusting the hot and cold to suit her desire, she spent a delightful hour immersed, the aches floating out of her body with blessed relief.

When Rusty finally left the bathroom, she felt she'd been given a new lease on life. Dressed in her pale lavender day dress with deep violet cording, Rusty went down the half-stairs to the landing with the main bedrooms. There were not many for such a large home, but hers was lovely. She walked across the threshold, not at all surprised to find it in perfect order. Even her clothing, pressed and cleaned, was hung in the wardrobe. She sat on a chair by the fireplace, noting absently that fireplaces seemed to be all over the mansion.

I don't know if I should stay here, Lord. I feel well enough to travel. I know I could go home tomorrow, but what does all of that do to Mr. McCandles' schedule? There being no forthcoming answer, Rusty sat for a time in her room and thought about what she should do. She was still sitting, her hair drying in a riot of curls around her face and down her back, when Chase ran her to earth.

"Wool gathering?" he asked from the doorway.

"No, just glad to feel so much better." She came to her feet. "In fact, I'm trying to decide if I should leave tomorrow or not."

Chase nodded, his face impassive. "Lunch is served. Maybe talking it over and having a little something to eat will help you decide."

"Maybe it will. Thank you," Rusty acknowledged graciously. Having come to the doorway, she preceded him to the landing and down the stairs. Once they were at the bottom, Chase directed her through the first door they came to. The dining room was almost as large as the drawing room. Rusty was again impressed with the lovely furnishings. French doors opened onto a large veranda. The doors were flanked by china cabinets in the same wood as the table. On another wall was a fireplace. A doorway to one side looked as if it led back to the drawing room.

"How is this?" Chase asked as he held a chair for his guest.

"Thank you," she said as she sat, smoothing her skirt as she looked down the length of the table. They were at one end of a solid cherry dining table that sat 20, or rather Chase was at its end. Rusty was around the corner from him. The moment Chase sat down, a salad was placed in front of Rusty. She looked up to thank the young waiter at her elbow and found his eyes on her, his mouth slightly open.

"Thank you," she said softly, but he only stood and stared.

"Did you have a salad for me, Rick?" Chase asked quietly, a note of humor in his voice.

"Oh, yes, sir." Rick moved to do the honors, but it was as if he were in slow motion, his eyes on Rusty as he served Chase. Nothing more was said on the matter. Chase waited for Rick to move from the room and then bowed his head. Rusty followed suit.

"Thank You for this food, Lord. Bless us this day. Amen."

Rusty raised her head, reached for her napkin, and picked up the first of several forks, one thought on her mind: *If this is what lunch is like, I might not have a suitable dress for dinner.*

"I'm sorry about Rick's behavior. He's young."

"I take it you don't have guests often."

"Not that look like you."

Rusty finished the bite of salad in her mouth but didn't reach for more.

"What did you mean by that?"

Chase looked at her. She was not upset, just curious. He decided to be rude and answer her question with a question.

"Do you not find yourself attractive, Katherine?"

Rusty blinked. "What has that got to do with anything?"

"It has everything to do with it. That's the reason Rick stared at you," he informed her calmly. "He's Mrs. Whitley's son, by the way."

Rusty looked over at the door where the young man had disappeared and then back to Chase. He had stopped eating as well and now stared at her. Rusty felt the most incredible rush of emotions. It had almost sounded as though he was complimenting her, but there had been nothing warm or personal about his tone or expression. Rusty wondered why that bothered her. But then understanding hit her.

"Should I apologize to Rick?" Her eyes were rather large.

"For what?" Chase asked in genuine confusion.

"For acting inappropriately."

Chase was stunned. "Katherine, what did I say that made you think your actions were out of order?"

"Well," she responded slowly, her face pale, "you said that I thought myself attractive, and I assumed you found my manner flirtatious."

Chase's eyes closed. How could she have misunderstood? He opened his eyes to try to

160

make amends, but someone had entered behind him. The way Rusty dropped her eyes and put her hands in her lap, he assumed it had to be Rick.

"Am I too early with your entrées, sir?" Rick asked, noticing that they'd barely touched their salads.

"No, Rick, that's all right. Just leave them and the salads too. We'll manage just fine."

"Yes, sir."

Rick worked silently and efficiently, but Rusty didn't witness it. She kept her head down the whole time, chancing a peek up only when she was certain they were alone. With Rick gone she looked back at Chase.

"Should I have said something?"

"No, absolutely not. You've done nothing improper, and if I intimated otherwise, please forgive me."

"But he stared," Rusty began.

"He's 15, Katherine, going on 16. Girls are quite fascinating to him right now. Added to that I would guess that you're not much older than he is. You must be what, 17, 18?"

"Nineteen."

Chase nodded. She was older than he guessed, but that didn't matter. What did matter was that she appeared to be feeling better about the situation.

"You're certain I didn't do anything untoward?"

"Quite certain. Your dress is very becoming on you, and he noticed. That's all that happened."

Rusty nodded, feeling a bit uncomfortable that she had made such a scene. That it was Chase's comment in the first place, and that he had not handled it well, never occurred to her.

They ate for a time in silence, and Rusty had to admit that the food was worth their concentration. A light oil dressing had been sprinkled on her salad, and Rusty knew she'd never had anything like it. It was delicious. The entrée was braised beef, so tender that Rusty didn't need her knife. Asparagus tips as well as carrots sat on the side, as did a small mound of whipped potatoes that tasted as though they'd been seasoned with garlic. Rusty ate with relish, not at all unhappy that Mr. McCandles was quiet for a time. She was well-satisfied when she sat back, but also pleased to see Rick coming with dessert. He had just refilled their coffee cups and given them pieces of pie when Chase took Rusty back to the subject of her leaving.

"Can you tell me why you wish to leave tomorrow?"

Embarrassed, Rusty's head dipped to the side. "I feel as if I've disrupted your whole life and been such a bother. And I really do feel fine. I'm certain I could get myself home —" Rusty stopped when Chase briefly covered her hand with his own. He wanted to remind her that she was not going home on her own — not under any circumstances — but he took another tack.

"If you're really feeling all right, I could really use your help."

"My help?"

"Yes. I have a son," Chase began.

"I met him briefly."

"Did you? Good. His nanny, Mrs. Harding, has a dental appointment tomorrow. It's first thing in the morning, and these appointments usually put her off her feet for several hours, if not the whole day. I know you're eager to see your family, and if you want to leave tomorrow, I'll take you. But if I can take advantage of your being here, it would be a great help." He paused for just a moment. "It's a long day for Quintin to spend on his own, and I fear he'll be rather at loose ends by afternoon."

"And you'd like me to see to him?"

Her voice gave none of her feelings away. Chase had no idea if he'd imposed upon her or not.

"Only if you're up to it," he finished quietly and waited.

"I wouldn't know his schedule."

Chase shook his head. "It doesn't matter. He's only four, well, five next month, but basically he just needs someone to spend time with him and see that he doesn't come to harm."

What about you? The question sprang into Rusty's mind, but it was not her place to ask.

"And then we would leave on Friday as planned?" She saw now that he would come with her no matter what.

"Yes."

"I'd be happy to spend the day with Quintin tomorrow," she said simply.

"Thank you," Chase said sincerely. He had honestly thought they would be leaving in the morning and was pleased that she would be staying another day. Quintin was sure to enjoy her.

They went back to their dessert for a few moments before Chase said, "May I ask you two questions about what happened in Makepeace?"

"Certainly."

"How did you end up behind the building?"

"I was just taking a shortcut. I never dreamed anyone would be back there."

Chase nodded, but he was quiet for a moment.

"You said there were two," Rusty reminded him.

"Oh, yes. You also said something about needing to find a way to get me home. What was that about?"

Rusty's brow lowered in concentration but then she nodded. "That was about the train holdup. I thought it would be helpful if I could find a way for you to get back here so you could go on with your business. That's when I dozed off and thought I heard the train whistle."

Chase nodded and smiled. She really was a remarkably sweet person, but it was also funny.

"Why do I feel as if I'm being laughed at?" Rusty asked, her chin rising slightly in the air.

"You're not. I just wonder if you ever take time off."

"Meaning?"

"You feel a need to take care of everyone, and I wondered if you ever take a day off. It must be exhausting work."

Rusty's mouth dropped open for a moment, but then she closed it with a snap and tried not to smile at Chase's still-amused face. With one more little tilt to her chin, she

165

set her napkin on the table and stood.

"Would you please tell me, Mr. McCandles, who made this lovely meal? I would like to thank her."

Out of propriety, Chase stood, but even as he looked down on Rusty — he was over a foot taller than her small frame — he wanted to laugh. She met his gaze unflinchingly and did not allow the smile in her eyes to go any farther.

"The hallway to the kitchen is through there," he said, indicating the door behind him. "I'm sure Rick or Mrs. Whitley will be on hand to thank."

"Thank you," she replied with a gracious, if not queenlike, nod of her head before she went on her way.

Chase turned to watch her, but Rusty never looked back. He shook his head very slowly, wondering all the while if he'd ever met anyone quite like her.

14

Several hours had passed when Chase found Rusty on the veranda, a book open in her lap. Her eyes were on the window and the greenery outside when she heard his footsteps.

"Why did I think you would be taking a nap just about now?" Chase commented as soon as he had taken a chair opposite her.

"That's a good question. Why *would* you think that?"

"You were pretty sick yesterday," he needlessly reminded her.

Rusty's brows rose. "Now who's taking care of whom, Mr. McCandles?"

Chase laughed at being caught out, but he still speared her with his eyes. "I still think it's a good idea." His voice was very firm.

"You don't quite have all of your color back."

"You do know, don't you, that you like having your own way?"

Chase blinked in surprise, his mouth opening a little.

"I guess you're right," he said, his tone telling Rusty he'd never even thought of it.

Rusty looked amused as she watched him open his mouth to say more, perhaps defend himself, but Mrs. Whitley came to the door just then.

"I'm sorry, sir, but there's a man to see you. He says it's about the crop land you had listed to rent."

"Thank you, Mrs. Whitley. Tell him I'll be right along."

"Very well, sir."

Chase stood and excused himself, but Rusty kept her seat. She wasn't tired enough for a nap, although she did feel a bit lazy. The breeze ruffled the pages of the book in her lap, and she went back to her reading. *A little later,* she told herself, *I'll take a walk around Briarly. That will shake out the webs.*

Chase saw his guest out the door and returned to the foyer to find his housekeeper passing through. She had the book in her hand, the one Rusty had been reading. He asked about her.

"I assume Miss Taggart is lying down."

"No, sir, I don't believe so. She had a glass of cider and then went out the kitchen door. I told her it was chilly, but she declined a wrap."

Chase's brows rose, but he said only, "Thank you."

Mrs. Whitley was not at all surprised to see him turn and stride toward the kitchen. She kept her place, and just seconds later heard the opening and closing of the back door. Only then did she make her way upstairs with an armful of linens, a full smile on her face.

Chase exited the house through the kitchen door and took the long drive toward the stable. He didn't think Rusty had gone inside, so his eyes moved over the smooth acres of grass until he spotted her at the edge of the woods. It was chilly out, so he removed his jacket as he went in order to give it to Rusty. Not wanting to startle her, Chase cleared his throat as he neared, but she didn't turn until he spoke.

"Here," he said quietly as he came up behind her. "Take my coat."

"Now you'll be cold," she commented even as she pulled it around her.

"That's true. Why don't we go into the barn? At least we'll escape the wind in there."

Rusty started to remove the coat to hand it to him, but Chase shifted it back onto her shoulders and guided her with a hand to her back.

"You know you're doing it again, don't you?" Her voice was light.

"What's that?"

"Having your way."

Chase smiled but didn't deny it. Once they stepped into the warm confines of the barn, he asked, "Are you always so stubborn about things that are clearly for your own good?"

"Meaning?" She stood looking up at him.

"Meaning that after we spoke on the veranda, I thought you would take a nap, and now I offer you my coat because it's cold, and you don't want it."

"That's all very simply explained, Mr. McCandles, I assure you," Rusty said, her look tolerant. "I was saving *you* from the cold by not wanting to take your jacket, and as for the nap, I simply didn't need one."

She looked so matter-of-fact that Chase wanted to laugh again. He watched her eyes narrow and knew that he would be in trouble if he did.

"You must be eager to be home," he said suddenly and with great kindness. He thought she still looked a little pale. It made him uncertain about having asked her to work tomorrow. "It's so hard to be sick when you're away from home."

For no apparent reason tears rushed to Rusty's eyes. Seeing them, Chase felt his heart break. He watched as one spilled over and rolled down her cheek. He had to stop himself from taking her in his arms.

"I'm sorry I made you cry," he said quietly.

"You didn't — I mean, not really. But suddenly it seems as though I haven't seen them in years."

Chase nodded. "I think I understand, Katherine. Maybe we should head to Boulder tomorrow so you can see them that much sooner. I can make other arrangements for Quintin."

Rusty shook her head and wiped her cheeks. "I'm looking forward to being with your little boy. Friday is still fine."

Chase stared at her for a moment. She was an amazing person. One minute she was staring at him with huge eyes, wondering if she'd acted inappropriately with Rick. The next minute she was standing up to his teasing, her chin in the air. Now, with tears in her eyes, she was agreeing to remain an extra day and take care of his son. Chase found himself aching to hug her or slip an arm around her but knew that wasn't fair; she was just getting herself back under control. Instead of a hug, the back of Chase's fingers came out and brushed ever so softly against her cheek.

"You missed a tear," he explained and was gratified to see that she didn't recoil or seem offended. "Would you like to see my stable?"

"Yes, please," Rusty said, grateful for the chance to do something else. "Do you have many horses?"

"Six, but just three are for riding. They're all fine animals; I'm rather pleased with them."

Chase led the way between the stalls, and as they went, he let out a low whistle. As if by magic three heads appeared from two stalls. Intelligent eyes watched them approach, and the two in the same box nearly jockeyed for position.

"Oh," Rusty said in delight as they stopped before the first box. "He's beautiful."

Chase slapped the neck of a huge black gelding and caught his nose when he began to root around for sugar.

"This is Shelby." Obvious pleasure filled Chase's voice. "He's on the large side, but he's very gentle."

Rusty put her hand to the soft fuzziness of his muzzle. "He's gorgeous. Have you had him from birth?"

"No, just a few years. I bought him from the Cameron brothers in Wisconsin. Their stables are some of the finest in the Midwest. And these girls, twins actually" — he led the way one box over — "are Rain and Snow. They are wonderful for riding but a little too used to being together. I bought them locally and had them trained for gentleness." The mares rooted at the front of his vest as well.

"And as you can see, I spoil them all with sugar. Now they take me for granted."

Rusty smiled. The mares were as lovely as Shelby, both dark roans with splashes of white under their forelocks.

"How often do you ride?"

"I try to get out at least once a week, but if I'm traveling that's impossible. I have a man who gives them a workout when I can't, so they don't go neglected."

Rusty stood back while he fed them sugar. Chase went on to show her the other horses, first a fat cart pony by the name of Dobbins, and then a matched set of bays, Marley and Flynn, Briarly's carriage horses. Rusty enjoyed seeing them, but Quintin had come to mind, and she was now ready to go back to the house. Chase seemed sensitive to this and suggested they return.

"I haven't seen Quintin around much,"

Rusty commented. "I hope he isn't ill."

"No, but this is Wednesday, and he and Mrs. Harding go to the reading room on Wednesday afternoons."

Rusty nodded but didn't speak. She was dying to ask her host what day of the week he took his son. They continued back to the house, and once inside parted company.

Chase was not around when dinner was served, and Rusty never did run into Quintin, although she assumed he had returned from the library. She ate a solitary meal and then went to her room early, ready for sleep. It was a large house, beautifully decorated, but it didn't feel like a home to her. Someone had started a fire in the fireplace in her room, and it was with great pleasure that she curled up in bed and stared at the bright embers.

In 48 hours I'll be home, she told the Lord when her eyes grew too tired to read. *I'll see my papa and get to hug Mother.* Thinking of the way that hug would feel, Rusty pushed the thought aside, reminding herself that she had already cried that day. She turned the lantern down just minutes later. Sleep claimed her almost immediately.

15

Rusty was on her way back to her room from the bathing chamber when she spotted her young charge. He was headed down the stairs, not having seen her, but he stopped when she softly called to him.

"Good morning, Quintin James McCandles."

"Good morning."

Rusty beckoned to him with one finger. He came directly to her. She loved the navy blue shorts he was wearing, and this time he had a small matching jacket over his pale blue shirt.

"Did you know," she whispered, bending just enough to make it seem like a conspiracy, "that we are going to spend the day together?"

Quintin nodded, his eyes on her face.

"Mrs. Harding told me."

"Well, did you also know that we are going to have *so* much fun?"

Quintin bit his lip and smiled, his little feet moving with excitement.

"Were you going somewhere just now?"

"Mrs Harding told me to go eat breakfast."

"Well, I won't keep you. I'll come down just as soon as I'm ready."

"To eat breakfast?"

"Yes."

He smiled at her again, and Rusty brushed a hand over his hair. She saw the adoration in his eyes and fell just a little more in love with him. He was so sweet, and his skin was like fresh cream. Rusty was on the verge of telling him he could head down when his little stomach growled. She watched in surprise as he looked upset, almost frightened.

"Well, now." Rusty brushed right past it, laughter in her voice. "You must be starving."

Quintin didn't know what to think of her. Mrs. Harding was very strict about noises, even ones you couldn't control. Rusty saw very swiftly that he did not find the situation funny. She put her hand back on his soft hair.

"Go ahead, Quintin, and eat your breakfast," she urged him gently. "I'll be right behind you."

"All right," he said, giving her a tentative smile. Rusty beamed at him and watched his little shoulders relax as he went on his way. Turning to her room, she shut the door and leaned against it, wondering silently what in the world this day would bring.

The breakfast room looked as it always did at this time of the day, except that Mrs. Harding was not present. Only about half the size of the formal dining room, it was cozier, with windows on two walls and four corner cabinets that held lovely dishes and hollowware. Like almost all the other rooms she had been in, there was also a small stone fireplace. Under the front windows was a sideboard, and at the moment it was filled with delectable breakfast foods.

Chase, who sat at the table, a newspaper in his hand, came to his feet and greeted Rusty as soon as she entered. Rusty returned the greeting but then made a beeline for Quintin, who already sat with a full plate in front of him.

"This looks so good," she said as she leaned over his plate.

"Do you want a bite?" His face was alight with excitement.

"Yes!" she declared, and took a bite of the long strip of bacon he held for her. "Oh, my," she said dramatically, not even bothering to wait until she swallowed. "That is delicious. I need to get some of my own."

"I'll help you."

"You will? Thank you."

Quintin came to his feet and took Rusty's hand. The sideboard laden with food was just five steps away, but she allowed her-self to be led. Quintin was on the verge of showing Rusty where the plates were stacked when he glanced back at the table. He stopped when he saw his father's face.

Chase had not taken his seat again. He stood, the now-forgotten newspaper still dangling from his fingertips, and stared at his son. Seeing a look so foreign, Quintin swiftly left the sideboard and slipped back into his chair.

"May I please be excused, sir, for a little time?"

His voice seemed to snap Chase from his trance.

"Of course, Quintin — that will be fine."

Rusty worked hard to keep the emotion from her face. Quintin returned to her side, but his look was subdued. He showed her the plates and then the covered silver dish that held the bacon.

"You are so sweet to help me, Quintin. I think I can manage now. Why don't you go back to your plate? I'll come with mine and sit right next to you."

"Mrs. Harding sits across the table."

"Well, how nice for her." Rusty looked as if this was the best news she had ever received. Quintin smiled at her and did as he was told, slipping back into his chair. Rusty swiftly joined him, careful not to take more than she could eat. For once Chase didn't notice the sparseness of her plate. He was still too busy trying to reckon with the change in his son.

"Did you take some of these eggs, Quintin?" Rusty asked.

"Yes."

"Aren't they good?" Rusty put another forkful in her mouth and looked up to see Chase still standing. Her brow lowered in concern. He had said that she could do things her way, hadn't he? Did it really matter where she sat at the table? She couldn't believe him to be that petty. Chase noticed her look and swiftly took his seat, his eyes going back to his paper, but his mind was preoccupied.

"Who makes this coffee?" Rusty asked of her charge.

"Cook does. She makes the eggs and bacons too."

"Bacon, no *s* on the end," she corrected automatically. "Well, it's some of the best I've ever had." She moved to take a drink of her coffee. "Do you want a taste?"

"Of coffee?" His face suggested that she'd hinted at murder.

"Yes," Rusty said with a laugh. "I use cream and sugar, and they make it very good."

Quintin took the offered cup, sipped, and sipped again. Rusty laughed.

"What did I tell you?"

The entire meal was like that, and Rusty would have been having the time of her life if she hadn't caught occasional looks from Chase. He didn't speak, but she could almost feel his mood. It wasn't disapproval exactly, but Rusty wished she could define it.

"Do you know what we are going to do after breakfast?"

"What?"

"We're going to look at birds."

"On Thursday?"

Rusty looked at him. "Don't tell me all the birds leave town on Thursday?"

"No," he said with a giggle.

"Well, they'd better not because we're

180

going to see them."

"There are nests," Quintin told her excitedly. "I know where some are."

"I can hardly wait. Are you finished, Quintin?"

"Yes, Miss Taggart."

"Very well, let us go to the kitchen, thank Cook and Mrs. Whitley, and then be on our way."

The little boy frowned. "I never do that."

"Do what?"

"Go to the kitchen and thank Cook."

Rusty's brows rose. "Well, we're going to today," she said softly, wondering how any nanny as proper as Quintin's seemed to be could miss this simple courtesy. "This food does not appear by magic. It's a lot of work." With that Rusty stood, and Quintin followed suit. They moved around the table to exit, but for the umpteenth time Rusty caught Chase's eyes on her.

"Quintin, please run ahead. I'll catch up with you."

"All right."

"Did I misunderstand you, Mr. McCandles?" Rusty asked as soon as they were alone.

"Regarding what?"

"Regarding the way I'm to handle things today. You seemed rather disapproving over breakfast. Did we ruin your meal with our chatter?"

"Not in the least," Chase assured her. "I can tell that Quintin likes you very much, and it makes me wonder if he hasn't missed some fun in his life."

Rusty wisely held her peace. Instead, she said, "Well then, I hope he'll have fun with me today."

"He already has."

Rusty thanked him with a small inclination of the head and told him goodbye. Only then did Chase realize he'd been sitting while she stood. He shook his head and gave up all attempts to concentrate on the paper. Was it possible for one small woman to disrupt his thinking and life so completely? Since he had met her, he didn't know if he was coming or going.

I just need to see her home, he told himself not for the first time. *I haven't finished the job I started, and until I do I'm going to be distracted.*

Having taken these few minutes to persuade himself, Chase went upstairs to his room. He had taken some time to read his Bible earlier that morning, but in truth, the last few days had been so busy he knew it wasn't enough. He now longed to read the Scriptures and commit his day to God. He shut the door, thankful that he had nothing pressing this day and could take all the time he needed.

"Do you see it?" Quintin asked. "Do you see the nest?"

"Yes. It's an old one but still in good shape."

The two explorers were in the woods and had been for most of the morning. They were a little bit cold, a bit muddy, and having a wonderful day.

"Do you want me to get it down for you?"

"I'm not supposed to take them out of the tree."

"All right," Rusty said calmly, thinking that if he said that to her one more time, she might scream. Had he been older, she might have come right out and asked him what he *was* allowed to do. It occurred to her suddenly that she had not met Mrs. Harding. What was a woman like who could live by such a strict set of rules? There were rules at the orphanage certainly — they would never survive without them — but they were guidelines only. No one lived or died by them.

"Are you cross?" Quintin asked, and Rusty shook herself.

"No, I'm not. Did you think I was?"

"Your face looked like it might be cross."

Thinking absently that this child had a marvelous vocabulary, Rusty climbed down from the stump she'd been standing on and took Quintin in her arms. She'd been doing that off and on all morning, and he was now returning her hugs.

"I'm not cross at all, but there are times when I don't understand things. However," she said before he could ask what she meant, "I have figured out that I love Quintin McCandles." Rusty smiled into his eyes and pressed a kiss to his forehead. Little arms came around her again, and Rusty's heart felt hugged as well.

"I'm hungry," she declared. "Why don't we see if we can get something to eat?"

"Is it lunchtime?"

"I'm not certain what time it is. Shall we go find out?"

Quintin, who was up for anything Rusty suggested, nodded and took her hand. Rusty began a silly song and taught it to young Mr. McCandles. They moved toward the house, in no great hurry, completely unaware that lunch was on the table waiting for them and had been for quite some time.

Though Quintin and his day-long companion were never far from his mind, Chase actually managed to get quite a bit done in his office. He had written a few letters and sent word to a banker in Boulder, reminding him that he would meet with him Friday morning. A letter arrived from his mother, telling him she and his stepfather would visit that summer. Chase put it aside, wondering what they would think of Katherine Taggart. He knew with little thought on the matter that his mother would like her upon first meeting.

Chase began a letter back to her and then realized he was hungry. He emerged from the office for the first time that day to find the breakfast room empty, clean plates still on the table, with no sign of anyone having enjoyed a meal. He walked to the kitchen in search of answers.

"Mrs. Whitley, have you seen Quintin and Miss Taggart?"

"No, sir, I haven't. I put lunch on, but maybe she didn't understand the time."

Chase consulted his pocket watch. It was nearly 1:30. He told himself not to worry.

"I'll go have a look around. She said they were going to see the birds."

"Probably the woods, sir," Cook put in. "Mrs. Harding always takes Quintin there."

Chase was in the midst of thanking the woman when the kitchen door opened. All eyes turned to see Rusty and Quintin come through the door.

"We're a little bit muddy," she said with a smile. "Should we leave our shoes here?"

"That's fine," Mrs. Whitley replied as she came forward. The kitchen was the staff's domain, and it never occurred to her to check with Mr. McCandles.

"Thank you," Rusty said sincerely and began to help Quintin with his shoes. She spotted a basin and towel in the process and directed Quintin to wash his hands, following suit when he was finished. She noticed that the little boy's eyes were a bit large and figured she was probably breaking every rule in the book.

"Okay now, let me see your face. There's a little mud on your cheek. I got it. How's my face?"

"You have mud on your chin."

She raised the towel.

"Did I get it?"

"Yes."

With that Rusty put the towel down and turned to the group at large. Chase, Mrs. Whitley, and Cook were all staring at her. Rusty took Quintin's hand to reassure him and encompassed them with her smile.

"We're a little hungry, Mrs. Whitley. May we impose upon you for a snack of some type?"

"Certainly you may, Miss Taggart, but if you prefer, lunch is ready when you are."

"Lunch! Did you hear that, Quintin? It's all ready for us. What time is it?" she asked of Chase, who had not said a word during this exchange.

"Almost 1:30," he said calmly.

"No wonder we're hungry," she said, smiling down at Quintin and then looking to the housekeeper. "Do I need to apologize, Mrs. Whitley? Has our tardiness made more work for you?"

"Not at all," the housekeeper returned. "You may eat whenever you care to and take as long as you like."

"What do we say to Cook and Mrs. Whitley, Quintin?"

"Thank you."

"You're welcome," they chorused, and with that, stocking feet and all, Rusty and Quintin made their way from the kitchen. They passed Chase on the way but didn't stop to chat. Rusty didn't know if he would be joining them for lunch or not. He sported the same odd expression that he had that morning, but since Rusty had already checked with him, she felt no need to ask again if all was in order. Beyond that, she was hungry, and for the moment she put everything else aside.

16

After Quintin was bathed, pajamaed, read to, kissed, hugged, and tucked in for the night, Rusty herself fell into bed. Not brushing her hair or even washing her face, the redhead couldn't believe how tired she was. Why this had been more exhausting than a day at the orphanage she didn't know, but her whole body felt like it could melt into the mattress. If only her mind had been as tired . . . Without warning her brain was off and running with events of the day, and it wasn't long before her body was tensing along with it.

Right after lunch they had visited the stable. Rusty had wondered if Mr. McCandles ever took his son riding. The horror in the child's face as they approached the stable, let alone when he saw the horses, gave her the answer. She was not to be put off. They had gone in and had a wonderful time. However, that was not the worst part of the afternoon. The worst had occurred at the lunch table.

Unlike the morning, Chase did not have a newspaper in his hand and could attend to the conversation. He and Rusty had talked some, but when she realized that Quintin had not said a word, she asked him to tell his father what they had done that day. The change in him was frightening.

As if he were a little windup toy, Quintin began to recite their activities from the morning. There was no excitement and no warmth in his voice. He had even risen to stand next to his chair, as though doing a recitation in school. But that wasn't the worst of it. Mr. McCandles had looked as if everything was in order. He clearly expected that very behavior and thanked Quintin quite formally when he was finished. Rusty had felt sick. She had already eaten most of her food, but the rest was left untouched.

She had thought about the incident the rest of the day. It had been a relief to eat a quiet dinner with Quintin and then spend the rest of the evening bathing him and reading to him in his room. She wasn't angry at Mr. McCandles, but neither did she know what to say to him. It was as if he didn't know any better. Was that possible? Rusty couldn't fathom it but had to admit that at 19 she hadn't seen everything. She suddenly noticed that her back was starting to ache and realized she'd been lying like a board: flat on her back and just as stiff. She rolled to her side, curled around the extra pillow on her bed, and prayed.

Rather than thank You for a wonderful day with Quintin, I lie here and complain and fret. He's not growing up the way I did, Lord, or even the way the children are at Fountain Creek, but You're still in control. Quintin is well-fed and cared for, and if You want more for him then You will provide it. Rusty started to ask God to bring a new wife into Mr. McCandles' life but stopped. She didn't know why, but she couldn't bring herself to ask for that . . .

I'm just tired, Lord, and acting silly. Help me to remember that You're sovereign and that You love us all so much, more than we can understand. Thank You for the wonderful time I've had here at Briarly and the extraordinary care from the staff. And thank You heavenly Father, that I'll be in Boulder tomorrow *night. Amen.*

With that, Rusty determined to go to sleep. She lay still until her body relaxed once again, and somewhere between wondering what she would wear home on the train in the morning and whether she would have a chance to tell Quintin goodbye, she fell asleep.

Rusty ate a large breakfast and even read some of the newspaper. She was up earlier than everyone but Mrs. Whitley and Cook, so they served her and even handed her Mr. McCandles' newspaper. She was on her third cup of coffee when Chase entered the room.

"Well, now, you must be eager to be off," he teased her.

"No," she smiled at him. "But I was asleep by 8:30 last night, and I don't need that many hours. Here's your paper." She began to fold and hand it to him.

"You keep it. I'll read it on the train."

"All right. Thank you."

Chase watched as she opened it back up to a specific place and continued to read. Seeing her do this, he knew for the first time that this is what Mrs. Harding and Quintin saw him do every morning. It was rather startling to realize how selfish he usually was. Not that he thought Rusty selfish, but his own actions in the same light were not pleasant to him.

Having finished the article she started,

191

Rusty was just folding the paper away when Quintin entered the room, a trim, gray-haired lady behind him.

"Quintin!" Rusty turned away from the table with a smile, arms wide open. The little boy came into them. "Good morning," she whispered close to his face. "Did you sleep well?"

He nodded, more than content to lie in her arms and look up at her. If Rusty had glanced up at the right time, she would have seen surprise on Mrs. Harding's face, but it wasn't long before the look of surprise turned to one of pleasure. Although not a warm person, she cared deeply for Quintin and had wanted nothing but good care and happiness for him in the hours she'd been absent yesterday. Remembering that she had not been introduced to this guest at Briarly, Mrs. Harding nevertheless slipped into a chair and sat quietly, somehow certain she would not offend.

"Did you eat?" Quintin asked.

"Yes, and it was very good. Try the ham. It's wonderful."

"I always eat bacon."

"Can you get both?" she asked and crossed her eyes, making him laugh.

He slipped from her grasp and went to the sideboard. Chase had been waiting to catch her attention and now made the introduction between Rusty and Quintin's nanny.

"It's a pleasure to meet you, Mrs. Harding."

"As it is you, Miss Taggart. Thank you so much for seeing to Quintin yesterday. You were pleased with his behavior?"

"Absolutely. We had a wonderful time."

"He's done nothing but talk about you since he woke up."

Rusty turned to smile at Quintin, but he was still serving himself.

"Do you need some help, Quintin?" Mrs. Harding asked, and Quintin turned to say yes.

She rose to serve him and then took her own place at the table. It was just as Quintin had said: She sat across from him. Quintin was at his father's left hand, and Mrs. Harding was on the right. This morning Rusty was at the other end of the table, opposite her host. Rusty suddenly felt stifled. She didn't understand how anyone could follow the same routine every day. She knew that at times she was too impulsive, but then again, things were new and fresh to her because she did not let routine dictate her actions. She stopped and confessed her attitude.

I have no right to criticize anyone, Lord. I

don't know who I think I am. I have no place here. You would think I was a queen the way I see myself. Help me to give up my prideful ways, Lord, and love others as You do.

"We have to leave for the train in about 40 minutes." Chase's voice stopped her prayer. "Is that going to work for you?"

"That's fine. I'll just go and put the rest of my things together. It was good to meet you, Mrs. Harding."

"Have a good trip home, Miss Taggart."

"Thank you. Quintin," she turned to the little boy, "will you be around in a little while?"

He naturally turned to his nanny, who said, "I think we can manage to be close at hand."

Rusty watched the older woman smile at him. Quintin returned the smile and turned to nod at Rusty. Chase came to his feet when Rusty rose and exited. He had just sat down when Mrs. Harding saw his folded paper and handed it to him. He thanked her but left it lying by his plate. It was amazing how swiftly he could eat when he wasn't reading. He suddenly found himself finished with breakfast and was on the verge of leaving when he realized he hadn't shared his plans with Quintin.

"I'm going to Boulder, Quintin. I'm going

to see Miss Taggart home. Did I tell you that?"

"Miss Taggart did."

"Very good. I'll see you in a few days."

"Yes, sir."

Since he was already across the table from Quintin, there wasn't even the customary pat on the shoulder. Chase was almost out the door when he thought to check on Mrs. Harding.

"I'm doing well." She was surprised that he had asked but answered calmly enough. "There is little pain today, and Quintin and I will get along fine in your absence."

"Good." Chase thought the word sounded inane, but he was suddenly self-conscious that he'd asked. He nodded and took himself up the stairs to check his own bag, his mind already focusing on the day ahead of him and the business meeting planned for Saturday morning.

"I don't want to insult you or make assumptions," Chase began. He and Rusty were in the carriage on their way to the train station. Rusty turned and looked at him, her eyes bright with curiosity, but he didn't elaborate.

"All right," she said slowly. "I'll keep that in mind."

"Should I pay you for yesterday?"

"Oh, no," she said with a laugh. "It was my pleasure, and besides, you already paid for my room in Makepeace."

"Is that why you did it?" The thought bothered Chase for some reason.

"No," she said again, a smile on her face.

Chase was relieved but didn't admit it. He sat back and once again thought of the scene at the front door when Rusty had said good-bye to his son. With most of the staff looking on, she had gone down on her knees in front of him. She made no attempt to whisper, and with everyone listening had said, "I love you, Quintin McCandles."

Chase had watched in amazement when Quintin threw his small arms around her neck and told her he loved her too. Something had turned over in his chest at that moment, an emotion he could not define. A few seconds later Rusty had come to her feet, waving at everyone and thanking them one last time. It reminded him a little of his wedding send-off with Carla, as they had left Briarly for their honeymoon trip. Chase shook his head to dispel the image and in the process found Rusty watching him.

"Are you all right?" she asked, her voice sweet and concerned.

"Yes, thank you."

She surprised him by laying a hand on his sleeve. "Mr. McCandles, if you don't want to leave your home, I really can get to Boulder on my own."

"That's not it, I assure you, Katherine. My mind was on the way Quintin seems to enjoy you." Which was half true. "You did a wonderful job with him yesterday."

"I'm glad you were pleased." There was so much more she wanted to say, so many things she wanted to ask. She decided on only one.

"Does Quintin have friends with whom he can play?"

"No, I don't believe he does. It's a shame that Briarly's closest neighbors are all older, and then there's Mrs. Harding."

She was only going to ask one question, but with an opening like that, it was impossible not to continue.

"She would rather that Quintin didn't have many playmates?"

"Not exactly, but the reason she left her other posting was because the couple was having so many children. She prefers to work with one, two at the most."

"She's been with Quintin a long time?"

"Since his mother died two months before his second birthday."

Rusty fell silent. In some ways she had

learned more than she desired to know. Quintin McCandles was a convenience. Mrs. Harding was willing to take care of him because he was just one little boy, and his father saw him only when they happened to be in the same room together.

That's not fair, Rusty. You weren't there long enough to know exactly what goes on. But Rusty was not able to convince herself. While it was true that she hadn't seen it all, she thought she had witnessed quite a bit. It was a relief to have the train station come into view — anything to take her mind off of having to leave that little boy.

Boulder

The train station at home was so familiar for Rusty that she started doing it again: forgetting she had a companion. She was off the train, bag in hand, and headed off the platform when she stopped and turned. Sure enough, Chase was just steps behind her, and his face was split with a huge smile. Rusty shook her head.

"I don't know what's the matter with me."

"You're just eager to be home."

"And you're very gracious. Come on, Mr. McCandles. Come and meet my family."

Chase fell into step beside her then, surprised at how swiftly she could move. The train ride had come off without delays, and for most of the way they had sat in silence and read. Chase now realized he wanted to know more about his traveling companion.

"Tell me again how long it's been since you've seen your parents."

"Christmas. They came to the orphanage to have Christmas with all of us, but I haven't been home since last fall."

"And this is where you grew up?"

"Yes. I was born here, and until I began working with Paddy and Sammy, I'd never lived anywhere else."

"And your father is with the school system?"

"Yes. He came to teach when Boulder had only one schoolhouse and needed one teacher. Now we have many schools, and my father is the superintendent over them all. He has a passion for children and their education."

That was not hard for Chase to believe. Rusty's way with children was phenomenal, and he knew she had to have learned it somewhere.

"We still have several blocks to go. Are you up to it?" Rusty asked him with a teasing glance.

"I think so, although you do move faster

than I thought you possibly could."

Rusty laughed. "That comes from chasing 50 children every day.

"Something I know you hate."

Rusty laughed again but didn't answer. Just five minutes later Chase saw the school, an older building but well-kept, and beside it was a rambling two-story home. He was certain they were headed straight for it, and he was right.

They were well on their way to the front door when a male voice said, "Hello, stranger."

Rusty turned with a smile. "Hi, Papa."

Coming from the direction of the school, Clayton Taggart covered the distance in just a few strides and took his daughter in his arms. Rusty's own arms went around his neck, and for long moments they just held each other. Again Chase felt an undefined emotion, but not knowing what to do with it, swiftly disregarded the strange feeling.

"How are you?" he said, holding her at arm's length.

"I'm fine. I wasn't sure I'd ever make it here, but I'm fine."

"What happened?"

"I got sick," she told him and pulled a face.

"You do look a little drawn. Is everything else all right — the children were placed, and that all went well?"

"Yes to everything. I wish you could have seen how happy they were. And this," Rusty had not forgotten, "is Mr. Chase McCandles. He saw us to Kurth and then took care of me when I became ill. I would have fallen apart without him."

"It's good to meet you, Chase." Clayton shook his hand. "Thank you for wiring us and seeing to Rusty and the children."

"It was my pleasure, but your daughter is too kind. She handled nearly everything."

Clayton smiled and put an arm back around Rusty.

"Come on in. Clare, Les, and Dana all went into town as soon as school was out, but your mother is inside."

Rusty took the steps ahead of them, her heart beating with anticipation. Clayton opened the front door and ushered them inside.

"Is that you, Clayton?" a voice called from beyond the living room.

"Yes."

The three of them stood still, and a moment later Jackie Taggart entered the room.

"Are you finished at the school?" she asked.

"Yes."

Jackie cocked her head to the side. Eyes

that had been blinded as a teen kept her from seeing her daughter and guest.

"Clayton Taggart, do you have someone with you?" She knew she was being teased.

"Hello, Mother," Rusty said softly, and Jackie's air left her in a rush.

"Oh, Rusty," she cried, hands outstretched. "Oh, Rusty, come to me. Come and let me see you."

Rusty hesitated no more. She swiftly crossed the floor and went into her mother's arms. Jackie's hands moved over her hair, head, shoulders, and back, "seeing" her daughter as she had always done, but Rusty barely noticed. She was back in her mother's arms, the sweet smell of her skin and hair rising up to meet her. Right now nothing else in the world mattered.

17

"She didn't tell you, did she?"

Chase turned to look at his host and found Rusty's father watching him closely.

"No, sir, she didn't."

Clayton smiled gently. "Rusty's mother has been blind since she was 17. It's all our children have ever known. They think little of it."

Chase looked back at the women and said, "How wonderful that she has you and the children." Chase knew that some blind people were put in special homes or institutions, separated from their families.

"How wonderful that we have her," Clayton said softly. Chase glanced at the older man to see that his eyes were intent on his wife and daughter. With Rusty's being 19 years of age, they'd been married for a long time. Clearly, he was still very much in love with her.

"Come and meet my wife," Clayton invited. "Jackie," he spoke as he led the way, "meet Chase McCandles. He brought Rusty home."

Jackie's hand came out. "It's a pleasure to meet you, Mr. McCandles."

"The pleasure is all mine," he told her sincerely, seeing in an instant where Rusty gained her beauty.

"You're tall," she declared with a smile.

"That he is," Clayton confirmed. "I'd say he's right up there with Robert."

"Robert is my uncle," Rusty explained.

"Robert Langley, correct?"

"Yes, that's right. Sammy would have talked about him." Jackie put the connection together.

"I have an appointment to see him in the morning."

"Have you met him before?" Clayton asked.

"No, I'm looking forward to it."

"He's wonderful," Jackie said with a smile and then suggested they all sit down.

The four adults moved farther into the living room and made themselves comfortable. Rusty took a chair by the fireplace where a fire popped and crackled some added warmth into the room. She watched as her parents took the long davenport. Chase slipped into the rocking chair opposite Rusty.

"How was your train trip?"

"Uneventful," Rusty admitted.

"That doesn't say much for your company," her father teased her.

"That's all right," Chase replied with a smile on his face. "Katherine can't remember that I'm with her half the time anyway."

"I'm working on that, Mr. McCandles," she said pertly, a tease in her voice as well. "I forgot you at the train station but not when it was time to introduce you to my father."

"This sounds very interesting," Jackie said.

"I quite agree," Clayton said. "Who's going to share?"

"I'll tell," Rusty jumped in when Chase opened his mouth. "It was never really my fault, you see. Never anything I planned."

"It never is," her mother reminded her.

"That's true," Rusty said good-naturedly.

"But it wasn't that she didn't plan to plan," Chase spoke up now, his eyes sparkling with humor as he watched her.

"That's right," Rusty agreed, her eyes large as she laughed. "It just happens that way from time to time. The children were a little better at it than I was."

"I think I'm confused," Clayton said. "Better than you at what?"

"Better at remembering that Mr. McCandles was with us."

"Oh, Rusty," her mother chuckled, "please don't tell us you kept forgetting Mr. McCandles."

"I'm afraid so."

Her parents laughed at her — Clayton because he could see the look on her face, and Jackie because she knew her so well.

"In light of that, Chase," Clayton said, "we need to thank you again. It sounds as though you would have been justified in leaving Rusty to fend for herself."

"No." Chase was still smiling, his eyes teasing. "After all, when she did remember I was there, she worked very hard to take care of me."

Rusty laughed, her own eyes gleaming with amusement, but before she could find a comeback, her siblings piled in the door.

Fourteen-year-old Dana Taggart passed the bowl of peaches to their guest and smiled shyly when he thanked her. She looked a little like Rusty because of her red hair, but Chase could see she was going to be much taller. Seventeen-year-old Clare, the second oldest in the family, strongly resembled Clayton. Rusty's brother, Leslie, shared more from each parent. He had his father's looks and build but his mother's chestnut hair. Chase wouldn't go so far as to call it the red that Rusty claimed, but it had more rust and gold highlights in it than even Jackie's. To a person, the Taggart children sported various shades of gorgeous blue eyes, although none as purple as Rusty's, and all had mouths ready to smile at any notice.

"What day do you need to head back to Colorado Springs, Mr. McCandles?" Jackie asked.

"Monday."

"Well, you're welcome to stay with us," she said warmly. "We have plenty of room."

"Thank you. If your hospitality didn't tempt me, the food would."

"Clare made dinner tonight," she told him, a small note of mother's pride in her voice.

Chase turned to Clare. "I'm impressed."

"Thank you," she said and smiled at him with such a "Rusty" smile that his eyes immediately went to the woman. She didn't notice, but her sisters did. They shared a look, both dying to get their sister alone to find out if she was in love with this man. They had always known that Rusty would land a handsome one, but neither had guessed he would be so tall and charming.

"I'll do dishes tonight," Rusty offered.

"Since it's my night," Leslie spoke up, "that suits me fine."

"You can help me, Les," she said. "That way I can find out what you've been up to as well as avoid my sisters. I can tell they want to pounce on me."

"We just want to know how you've been," Dana claimed, defending herself and confirming Rusty's suspicions all in one sentence.

"I'm sure you do, but you also want to know if any new young men have joined the church in Manitou."

"Have any?" Clare asked, not able to keep it in.

"As a matter of fact, yes," she said with a smile. "I think you should visit very soon."

Rusty and Clare shared conspiratorial smiles, and the rest of the table stayed tolerably quiet.

"Do you have a sister, Mr. McCandles?" Leslie broke the silence, his voice comical.

"No, I don't."

"Feel free to take one of mine."

Chase laughed, but again his eyes went to Rusty. She was looking right at him.

"If that would make me Quintin's aunt,

I'd take you up on that."

Chase smiled, but there was something serious behind his eyes.

"Who's Quintin?" asked Dana.

"Mr. McCandles' son. He's almost five and an absolute doll."

Both Clare and Dana were dying to ask if Quintin was home with his mother, but they knew better. The meal was finished soon after that, with a promise of dessert later in the evening. Rusty and Leslie began to work on the dishes, and Chase asked Clayton if he could see the school. Knowing Rusty would want time alone with each of her siblings, Jackie diverted the girls from joining Rusty and Leslie in the kitchen by reminding them that they both had reading to do.

Rusty knew exactly what her mother was doing and silently thanked her. With her arms deep in suds, she began to talk with her brother.

"What did you guys do in town?"

"Not much. Mother had a list, and Dana has a crush on Justin Sommerfeldt and was hoping to see him somewhere."

"And you just went along for the ride?"

"I guess."

Something in his voice caught her attention. "Who is she, Les?"

He smiled but didn't give her a straight

answer. "You think you know so much, you tell me."

"All right." Rusty was more than willing to play along. She began to name names, one after another, but came up blank every time.

"Kay Ridgeway. Barb Ridgeway."

"No, and no again." Leslie told her.

"Have I met her?" Rusty was running out of choices.

"Last fall."

"Last fall," she said softly and signed. "I give up, Les. "Who is she?"

"Wilna North."

"The girl who came and lived with Pastor and Mrs. Henley?"

"Yeah."

"I thought she moved away."

"She's back."

Rusty smiled, and not for the first time Leslie knew why he could talk to her. She never teased him if she knew he was serious.

"Does she know you're interested?"

He nodded, a flush coming to his cheeks.

"And is she interested back?"

He ducked his head this time, and Rusty knew he had it bad.

"Well, I hope she sees a good thing when it stares her in the face."

Leslie still didn't reply. He was pleased by his sister's words but wouldn't have admitted it under threat of torture. Beyond that, he wasn't given much of a chance. Clare and Dana joined them a few minutes later.

"Why didn't you tell us you'd met Chase McCandles, Rusty?" Clare instantly wanted to know.

"Yes, Rusty," Dana added. "He's not the type of man you forget to put into your letters."

"I'm out of here," Leslie declared. The dishes were almost done anyway, so the girls let him leave. Dana picked up the drying towel, and Clare sat on the edge of the table.

"Come on now, Rusty," the older of the sisters urged. "Tell all."

"There isn't much to tell," she declared honestly. "I've known Mr. McCandles for only a week. He escorted me to a placement in Kurth and then saw me home. That's about all there is to it."

"How did you meet his son?"

"I got sick and I ended up staying at his home."

The sisters took a moment to compute this.

"What's it like?"

"His home? Very beautiful. He has a large staff, and I was well taken care of."

"Did you meet his wife?"

"She died a few years ago."

"He watches you, Rusty," Dana told her, but Rusty shrugged it off with a laugh.

"Oh, Dana, you're such a romantic."

Rusty turned her back and didn't see Clare catch Dana's eye. The older girl shook her head very slightly, and Dana wisely let the matter drop.

"Where is Mother?" Rusty removed her apron and faced her sisters.

"In the living room." Rusty went out without speaking, her sisters forgotten. Her sisters, however, did not forget about her. They didn't talk about it, but both knew something was going on, even if Rusty herself had no idea.

18

"Is that you, Rusty?" Jackie asked as soon as her daughter came into the living room. Someone watching might have been surprised, but for Jackie, recognition of her husband and children's footsteps was nothing new.

"Yes, I thought I'd join you."

"I'd love it." Rusty sat down on the davenport close to her mother. For a time they were silent.

"How are you, dear?"

"I'm fine, Mother."

"Should I be worried about you?"

"No. It's been an interesting week though. I was horribly ill on Tuesday — such a bad headache — but I'm sure I'm all right now."

"I'm glad. Do you think you're completely over it?"

"Not quite. I'm still a little tired, but I know I can rest up here."

"Good."

They sat quietly for a moment before Jackie commented, "I have the impression that Mr. McCandles is something of a challenge to you."

Rusty smiled. "He likes to have his own way. Something I don't let him forget."

"Had you met him before he escorted you and the children?"

"No."

"Well, you've certainly hit it off quickly."

"We have, haven't we? At first I thought him rather aloof, but now I find he's really quite easy to talk to."

Jackie thought about how sick Rusty had been and was thankful that Mr. McCandles had been there. She visualized her being sick on the train and swiftly forgot to give thanks. As worry started to inch its way in the door, Jackie began to pray. *I've been giving my children to You for more than 19 years, Lord, and I'm still guilty of taking them back. It's so much harder now that Rusty is away, but Your hand is in Manitou and Colorado Springs as well. Help my lack of faith.*

"You've grown quiet."

"I was just thinking about your being sick and praying for you."

"I can use it."

"Anything in particular?"

"I think I'm such a know-it-all, Mother," Rusty admitted. "I see something that I think should change, and that's the end of it. I want Rusty's way, and Rusty's way alone."

Jackie nodded with understanding. "Was it something you can share with me?"

"I'll feel I'm gossiping."

"Well, don't tell me then, but you know I'll pray."

"Thank you."

Again they fell silent, Jackie doing as she said, praying for her daughter, and Rusty trying to commit Quintin McCandles to the Lord. She had not thought about him constantly, but Leslie's comment about sisters made her long for more in Quintin's life.

And you think you're the perfect choice, Rusty. You think you're the person he needs. Rusty's heart sighed. *I've been so selfish, Lord, that I didn't even want to pray that You would bring another wife into Mr. McCandles' life. I'm sorry I acted that way. Please bring someone to him who will love him and Quintin, a woman who knows You so she can bring fun and joy to both of their lives.*

"It's going to be so much fun to have you here," Jackie said after a few moments.

Rusty blinked at her. "What did you say?"

"Just that it's going to be fun to have you home for a few days."

"Oh, yes," Rusty replied inanely, shaking her head.

"Did I tell you that Sammy wired us and said to be sure and take a whole week off, no matter what day you arrived?"

"No, you didn't. That's wonderful."

"We thought so too. She just wants to know what day they should look for you."

"All right. I'll be sure to cable back tomorrow."

The women fell silent then, a warm, comfortable silence that lasted until the rest of the family joined them.

"So what were the Davidsons like?" Leslie wished to know.

"Very kind, and so excited to have those children. I didn't think Lizzy would manage it, but they both stayed."

"We prayed for you every night," Clare told her sister. Rusty thanked her.

"Did they have room for both of you to stay at their home?" Jackie wished to know.

"Yes. The ranch house is very spacious with many bedrooms." As Rusty said this, she remembered the way Jessie had mistaken them for a married couple. She looked up to find Chase's eyes on her and smiled, knowing his mind was on the same scene.

"About how many head of cattle would you say he runs?" This came from Clayton.

"He told me 2500," Chase filled in. "It's a very nice spread and although he didn't say so, he probably has the largest herd in the area."

The conversation went on in this vein for more than an hour. It was a lazy sort of evening with everyone sharing at one time or another. Leslie was very interested in Chase's line of work, and the older man graciously answered his questions and asked some of his own. The family as a whole got to know Chase McCandles a little bit better, and in return he found himself very impressed with Rusty's family.

"You look tired," Clayton suddenly said to his oldest daughter. To his eye it was easy to see she'd been ill.

"I am. I think I'll go to bed."

"I'll walk up with you," Jackie offered. "Mr. McCandles, do you know which room is yours?"

"Yes, Dana showed me."

"Good. If you need something, please find one of us."

"Thank you, I'll do that."

Clare and Dana joined their mother and sister as they went upstairs, and although tired, Clayton stayed with Leslie, who had a few more questions for Chase. The men talked for another 20 minutes and then took the stairs together. Chase found his bed very comfortable and was asleep in minutes. Clayton found his wife awake and with much on her mind.

"Clayton?" Jackie's voice was low as her husband slipped into bed beside her.

"Right here," Clayton said softly as he moved close to her.

"Are we alone?"

Jackie felt her husband chuckle as he said, "Who else would be in here?"

Jackie raised up on one elbow and reached for Clayton's face. It was what she had always done, satisfying a need to "see" him whenever she felt passionate or frightened about something.

"What is it, love?"

"Clayton, does Chase McCandles know he's in love with Rusty?" she asked him softly.

Jackie suddenly found herself crushed in her husband's embrace. He held her close, turning to his side so he could cuddle her against his chest. Jackie wrapped her arms around him and held him right back. They were quiet for a time.

"What are you hearing?" It was a familiar question to her, one she had heard all their married life. She depended on his eyes, and he often depended on her ears.

"No one calls her Katherine, and when he says it, or addresses her for any reason, he sounds like you when you talk to me."

She felt his chest lift on a sigh.

"Talk to me, Clayton," she begged. "Tell me what you've seen."

Clayton pressed his lips to her brow. "He watches her almost constantly. I would say he's fascinated, but I don't think he would label it love."

"Does Rusty see it?"

"Yes and no. She doesn't have love on her mind either, yet she cares for him. I think she's under the impression that he sees her as a little sister. It's almost as if she wants there to be more, but something is holding her back."

"Maybe he does see her as a little sister. That would stop any woman."

"Maybe."

For a moment Jackie thought about the evening. "She's certainly not afraid to tease him or tell him what she's thinking."

"She's rarely afraid to tell anyone what she's thinking." Clayton's voice was dry.

"True. Do you honestly think she could

be in love and not know it?"

"Yes," Clayton admitted, and they both fell silent.

Jackie well remembered the way she fell for Clayton when they first met. It was months, more than a year, before he returned that love. He had viewed her as a sister, and because of that she felt she couldn't say a word about her feelings.

"Is this going to keep you awake tonight?" Clayton asked Jackie.

"I don't think so. Do you think we should say anything to her?"

"No, we'll just stay quiet and watchful. If we say anything, it might cause Rusty to put a wall up between them. She's always been so careful not to give a wrong impression. Our saying something would probably cause her to back off so swiftly that he would think he'd been struck by lightning. That's not fair to either of them."

"I don't suppose it matters all that much." It was Jackie's turn to sigh. "After all, he's headed back to Colorado Springs on Monday, and she's going to the orphanage later in the week." Jackie felt Clayton's chest shake with laughter and said, "What did I miss?"

"I think you're forgetting how close Manitou is to Colorado Springs. If our Mr.

McCandles wants to see Rusty, he can do so with little effort."

"But that would be obvious," Jackie pointed out, "and if he isn't even aware of the way he feels, I don't think visiting her, at least not without a specific reason, will even come to mind."

She had a very good point, and Clayton took a few minutes to think it over. It was while he was still thinking that he felt Jackie relax against him. He was thankful that the possibility of Chase's loving Rusty was not going to keep her awake. Not so for Clayton. This was a new experience for Rusty's father, and he lay staring into the darkness and praying about it for some time.

19

"What time is your appointment?" Rusty asked Chase over breakfast. Clayton and the others had gone off on various pursuits. Only Rusty, Jackie, and Chase were in the kitchen.

"Ten o'clock. Can you refresh my memory as to which bank it is?"

"I can do one better than that. I can show you. I have to go uptown anyway."

"Now, that's an offer I can't refuse. Are you also free to join me for lunch at the hotel?"

Rusty dimpled at him. "Only if you can make it for three. Mother and I are going shopping."

"I would consider it an honor to escort both of you."

"Escort us where?" Jackie asked. She was

in the kitchen with them but had been intent on her reading and heard only the last part.

"Mr. McCandles is taking us to lunch."

"How nice." Jackie smiled much like her daughter.

"Katherine is going to show me the bank I need, and I'm returning the favor."

"I think we got the better end of the deal, Rusty. Mr. McCandles doesn't know how much we can eat."

Chase smiled. "If your appetite is anything like your daughter's, Mrs. Taggart, I'll not worry."

Jackie laughed and Rusty groaned.

"Are you blushing, Rusty?" her mother asked.

"I'll never tell," Rusty told her and bent over her breakfast plate.

Chase studied Rusty's face. "No blush there," he reported.

"How is Rusty wearing her hair today, Mr. McCandles?"

"Down on her shoulders," he told her. He'd never seen it any other way and wondered at the question.

"Then Rusty is the only one who knows."

Chase made no comment to this cryptic statement, but he did catch Rusty checking the sides of her hair, presumably to see if her ears were covered. The visitor from Colorado Springs knew in an instant that he had discovered a family secret but decided against saying any- thing.

Rusty was just as happy to let the subject drop. She rose just a few minutes later and started on the dishes.

"It's a pleasure to meet you, Mr. McCandles." Robert Langley shook Chase's hand and offered him one of the chairs in his office.

"Thank you, sir. I assure you the honor is mine. I've been trying to get up here for several months. Your niece's plans to travel home gave me the push I needed."

"How is Cat?"

"She's doing well. She and her mother pointed out your front door, and I dropped them off at Squire's Department Store."

"My wife had plans to shop today. I hope they run into each other."

"Katherine told her mother she had plans to track down her Aunt Eddie, no matter what. Is that your wife?"

"Yes, it is," Robert answered with a smile, not just because of Chase's words, but also because he had used Rusty's real name. He suddenly wondered at the relationship between the two. However, that was not the reason Chase McCandles had come to see him. He pushed thoughts of family from his mind, and the two men got down to business.

"This fabric is so soft," Jackie said. "Is this the blue one?"

"No, it's a dark purple."

"Perfect," she said with satisfaction.

"Perfect for what, Mother?" Rusty asked again. "I can't help you if you don't tell me what we're doing."

"It's a secret, Rusty. Ask me again and I'll tell you the same."

"But I won't tell anyone."

"It's a secret for you."

"Well," the younger woman spoke with complete sincerity, "in that case, I won't tell anyone I know."

Jackie laughed but still shook her head. They continued to gather goods — lace, more fabric, buttons, a small piece of silk — until Rusty had no idea what her mother could be making.

Jackie didn't do all the stitching herself, but for a woman who hadn't been able to see for more than 20 years, she still had remarkable taste. If she was making a dress, Rusty knew it would be a beauty. She also knew she would be able to figure the style out when her mother had the saleswoman cut the yards. Rusty, however, hadn't planned on being sent across the store.

"Who will carry this for you?" Rusty protested.

"You can carry it, but you can't come back until it's all wrapped up. Now, off with you."

"You're thoroughly enjoying yourself, aren't you?"

"Yes, I am. I don't have you home much anymore, and your father has given me permission to be as extravagant as I want. How are your shoes, by the way?"

"I just bought a pair."

"Good. Now you go look at gloves. I'll see to this yardage."

This time Rusty was obedient. She had just pulled on her first pair of gloves when a familiar voice spoke.

"Rusty Taggart! When did you get into town?"

"Gary!" Rusty turned with a hug for Garrett Buchanan. "How are you?"

"Just great. How about yourself?"

"I'm doing fine. How is Avril?" Rusty inquired about his wife.

"She's fine; in fact, she's the reason I'm in here. It's her birthday next week."

"Tell her I said happy birthday. How are the kids?"

"Adam and Zach are at school, and Wesley

misses them terribly. The baby isn't much fun for him at this point."

"What did you name your new little one?"

"Peter."

"That's right, I remember now. How about your folks?"

"They're on a trip to Denver right now with the Harringtons."

"How fun! They do that every year, don't they?"

"Yes. For more years than I can remember."

"And I hear that congratulations are in order for Wyatt. I thought he would be a bachelor forever."

Garrett smiled. "He thought so too, but then Grace Harrington returned from that teaching position back East, and he was smitten. All the folks are ecstatic, and we're having the time of our lives watching him in action. He's been walking into walls and staring into space for three months."

Rusty laughed. "Poor Wyatt. You must tease him without mercy."

"Of course I do," Garrett said without repentance. "I well remember what I put up with when I met Avril."

"Well," Rusty tipped her head way back to meet his eyes, "all I can say is that Wyatt is blessed among men. Grace is the sweetest girl in the world, and her grades in school were the envy of us all. I've missed her terribly since she went away. We said we would keep in touch, but we've both failed miserably."

"Have Katie and Roz learned that you're in town?" Garrett asked, referring to his sisters.

"I wrote to Kate, but I haven't seen anyone. I'm going to let them know at church tomorrow that we're having a small gathering Monday night."

"Well, I hope you have a good stay. How's work at the orphanage?"

Rusty beamed at him. "I love it."

Garrett smiled in return. Rusty's love for children was well known.

Jackie chose the moment to look for her daughter. She had a few words with Garrett, also sending Avril greetings, and the two women left Garrett to his shopping.

"Is it time for lunch?"

"Not quite. Hungry?" Rusty inquired.

"A little. How do you suppose Mr. McCandles is getting along with Robert?"

"I think with their identical heads for business, probably just fine."

The women had walked to the door and headed down the boardwalk. Jackie had told the clerk at Squire's that they would return for their package.

"Do you suppose that Mr. McCandles is looking for financing for a new venture?"

"I couldn't say, but if I had to hazard a guess, I'd say no. There might be a new venture, as you put it, but it doesn't seem to me that he has any pressing financial needs."

Jackie nodded, not needing to know more. Beyond that, she wanted a moment of quiet to mull over the tone in her daughter's voice. Had she been matter-of-fact, or was there a slight tone of resignation? Rusty informed her mother a few moments later that Mr. McCandles was coming toward them. Jackie had been given sufficient time to think about Rusty's tone, but she couldn't reach any conclusion.

20

"That was delicious," Jackie told Chase. "Thank you very much, Mr. McCandles."

Lunch was over. The three of them were on the street standing next to the buggy Chase had rented early that morning.

"I'm glad you enjoyed it," he told her. "May I help you into the buggy?"

"You've been so kind, Mr. McCandles, but in truth, Rusty and I are going to see my sister."

"I'd be happy to take you," he offered, but saw in an instant that they were hesitant.

"It was not our intention to take up your whole day, Mr. McCandles," Rusty finally explained. "We've had our time in town, but you might want to do some shopping of your own."

"Shopping?" He said the word as if he'd never heard it before.

"Yes. We have some lovely shops here in Boulder."

"I have no doubt, but what would I shop for?" He was still at sea.

"Well," Rusty replied matter-of-factly, "I thought you might be interested in a gift for Quintin or for some of your staff."

He looked so surprised that Rusty wished she had kept her mouth shut. For just a short time she'd managed to forget what a distant relationship he had with his son. The thought caused a moment of deep regret to fill her. They could have brought Quintin with them, but never before this moment had she thought of it.

"You think I should take something to Quintin?" Chase asked, seeing very swiftly that for some reason he had saddened her.

Hearing his tone, Jackie had to swallow a smile. He was trying his best to please Rusty, and the older Taggart would have bet that he had no idea how he sounded.

"I just think it would be nice," Rusty said softly, her eyes on his.

Chase was still searching his mind for why his response had upset her. Still confused, he said, "I'm not certain he would enjoy a gift."

Rusty's tone changed in an instant. "He's a four-year-old boy, Mr. McCandles. I can't think of a toy in which he wouldn't delight!" There was no missing her mood. This time she was outraged.

"Are you terribly busy for the next few hours, Mr. McCandles?" Jackie inserted tactfully.

"No, Mrs. Taggart, I'm not. As a matter of fact, I have no plans at all."

"I can't guarantee that we won't be somewhat silly and giggly, but if you'd like to go with us to my sister's, Rusty could help you find something for your young son when we come back through town."

"I have no wish to intrude on your time," he said sincerely.

"You won't," she graciously told him. "My sister would love to meet you. Rusty and I were concerned only about your own plans, but now that we know you are free, we'd be honored if you would join us."

Chase inclined his head. "Thank you, Mrs. Taggart." He then assisted the older woman into the coach. As soon as she was settled, he turned back to Rusty.

"I'm sorry I upset you."

Rusty bit her lip. She hated being so transparent.

"I'm the one who needs to apologize. It's

really none of my business what you do."

Her comment bothered Chase. He honestly cared what she thought but knew she would find it odd if he told her that.

"I think that women are more sensitive to the needs of children than men are," he said rather slowly. "I didn't find you intrusive or bossy. Indeed, I strongly value your advice, especially where Quintin is concerned."

His words did a great deal for her heart. Chase saw the pleasure in Rusty's eyes and felt an unexplainable contentment at having pleased her. He sent a smile in her direction, offered her a hand, and helped her onto the seat in the buggy. She thanked him quietly, but he didn't answer. Even after he joined them and picked up the reins, he could still feel Rusty's small hand within his own.

"For heaven's sake, Rusty," Patsy Langley, Rusty's cousin, said, her young eyes huge. "He's gorgeous!"

"Who? Mr. McCandles?"

"Of course! Who else could I mean?"

Rusty laughed. She and Patsy were in the kitchen where Rusty was getting a glass of water. Fifteen-year-old Patsy had not joined her siblings as they went to work at the church cleanup day because she was just getting over a spring cold.

"What did Clare and Dana say when they saw him?"

"About the same, I guess."

"You act like you haven't even noticed," the younger girl accused.

Rusty stared at her. She *had* noticed that Chase McCandles was nice-looking. She'd even told him so. But she couldn't look at him without seeing Quintin, and that put a damper on her view. How could a man be so charming and caring of others, and yet not know his son existed?

"Rusty, are you all right?"

"Yes," she mentally shook her head. Now was not the time to examine her feelings for the handsome Chase McCandles. "I was just thinking," she added but did not explain. She got her drink and then returned to the living room, her cousin in tow. The other adults were still talking. Rusty and Patsy sat down in the midst of a story they never found tiring.

"And Clayton had no idea that you lived here?" Chase asked.

"That's right," Jackie clarified. "Robert and Eddie had brought me here from Georgetown, and we all thought that Clayton was in Denver."

"He had been," Eddie inserted, "until just before we saw him. With no children, Robert and I were not involved in school activities. We had heard that a new schoolteacher had been hired but never heard the name."

"But it turned out to be Clayton?"

"Yes." Jackie picked up the story again, her voice soft with remembrance. "I had lied to him in a letter and told him I'd fallen for someone else. You can imagine how surprised he was to see me. Not only was I not involved with someone else, I was blind. Robert hired him to tutor me, and the fun really began."

It didn't take more than a heartbeat for Chase to see that it hadn't been fun at all.

"Actually," Eddie said, "it was fun as soon as Jackie came to Christ and let Clayton get close to her. He never stopped loving her, not in all that time did his feelings fade."

Chase smiled. Even he could recognize a romantic story when he heard one. And he had seen the end of the story as well. He'd watched Clayton and Jackie Taggart together. They were clearly as much in love today as they had been all those years ago.

"Thank you for telling me," Chase said graciously.

"I think Eddie should tell her story," Jackie said with a smile. "Our Mr. Langley, a most successful banker, actually got a wrong address and lost his heart in the process."

Eddie laughed in delight.

"Now this sounds interesting," Chase coaxed. "I must admit you have piqued my curiosity."

"It's not as complicated as Clayton and Jackie's story, but it was fun. I was having tea at my aunt's, and this handsome man knocked on the door. He had the wrong address. We looked at each other and, well, let's just say he never made his appointment."

Patsy beamed at her mother, and Eddie smiled tenderly at her. "Now, 23 years and five children later . . ." She let the sentence hang.

Chase turned to Patsy as well. She was a lovely young woman with eyes as blue as her mother's.

"Are you the youngest?"

"No, that would be Bethany."

"And she is —" Chase asked.

"Thirteen," Patsy supplied. "Bobby is the oldest, and he just turned 20, then Marty is 18, and Christian is 17."

"Three boys and two girls. Sounds like fun."

"It usually is, but Chris is a horrible tease, and Beth falls for his jokes every time."

"And you never do," Eddie said quietly.

Patsy dimpled. "Only some of the time."

"Chris is a tease," Rusty confirmed, "but

then so is Bobby. Remember when he had us convinced that he'd seen a ghost, and that it kept showing up outside each night?"

"Yes." Patsy was indignant. "And it turned out to be Les! My hair stood on end for a week."

Rusty laughed. "Clare and Dana were sad that they'd missed the whole charade, but I don't think they knew how eerie he looked with that white paint on his face."

"I can't remember how you saw him, Rusty," Jackie said to her daughter.

"He scared me out of my wits when he snuck back into the house while I was in the kitchen getting a snack."

"Oh, that's right. Your father tried to scold him but was laughing too hard."

Listening to them banter back and forth, Chase thought how special it would be to have siblings and cousins near. He did have a few cousins, but they were all in the Midwest. And now for the first time he wondered what family Quintin would have. Chase had no plans to remarry and no siblings. Without forethought, his eyes swung to Rusty. The successful entrepreneur suddenly knew that if he could meet a woman like Katherine Taggart, he would be strongly tempted to marry again.

Eddie chose that moment to ask Chase a

question. His train of thought was interrupted, so he was never given a chance to
ask himself why he thought he needed a
woman like Rusty and not Rusty herself.

"Does he have a toy train?" Rusty asked.
"I don't know."
Rusty bit her tongue. If Mr. McCandles
said "I don't know" one more time, Rusty
thought she might become violent. They had
left the Langleys more than an hour ago, and
even taken Jackie home before attempting to
shop, but they were no further along in their
endeavor. Rusty was becoming more frus-
trated by the moment. She knew Chase was
not involved in his son's life, and she knew
they shared little, but unreasonable as it was,
she still expected him to know what toys the
child had.
"Did *you* notice if he had a train?" Chase
asked Rusty.
She shook her head. "We spent most of
the day out-of-doors and then reading his
books. I did notice that he doesn't have any
little stuffed animals — you know, something
to cuddle at night."
Rusty didn't go on as she might because
Chase was already shaking his head.
"My wife didn't want Quintin to become
attached to toys. She thought that people

238

were more important. I have given Mrs. Harding instructions about switching Quintin's toys often."

Rusty could have wept but told herself not to break down. Her emotions hovered right under the surface, but she knew she must keep calm and think clearly on this shopping trip.

"I understand your wife's viewpoint, Mr. McCandles," Rusty replied kindly, for indeed this belief was not new to her. "I think that in many cases that approach can be wise, but Quintin's mother is gone, and you travel often. I can't help but wonder if a little cuddle toy isn't just what he needs."

Chase's eyes had been on the items on the shelves, but they now swung to Rusty. Carla had been adamant on the subject, but of course that was when Quintin was very young. What would she say now? What type of mother would she be now?

"Have I said something out of line, Mr. McCandles?"

"No." Barely aware of the way she looked right back at him, he realized how odd his behavior must seem. "No, you haven't. I was just thinking."

Chase reached for a tiny figure of a bear. It was very cute but made of porcelain. While he weighed it in his hands, Rusty handed him a stuffed dog. He looked up at her in surprise.

"It's no fun sleeping with a bear that feels like a lump of glass," she explained. "The dog is cuddly."

Chase couldn't stop his smile. She was being fierce again. She was doing an admirable job hiding it, but the bantam rooster in her was coming out. Chase replaced the bear and held the dog in both hands.

"This doesn't really look like a dog."

"Tell me about the last gift you took to Quintin," Rusty requested softly.

Chase shrugged. "I don't think I ever have."

"In that case, the last thing on his mind will be whether this toy really looks like a dog." That was when Rusty spotted another plush toy — a bear. His face was very grumpy, but he was cute nonetheless. She handed it to Chase.

"I think this one might be better. He'll remind Quintin of his father."

Chase looked down into the scowling face and tried not to smile. She was being downright insulting, but he still wanted to laugh. And the bear *was* cute.

"I'll take the bear," he said at last, his voice dry as he gave as good as he got. "And not because of my sour moods. It will remind me of how many times I got frowned at during this shopping trip."

Now it was Rusty's turn to hide a smile. She stayed in the aisle with the toys while Chase turned for the front counter. There were a few more items of interest to her. She looked them over, but her heart was not on the toys. She meandered to the end of the row, and from there she could see Chase as he paid the proprietor.

If her cousin and sisters were any indication, Chase McCandles should be the man of her dreams. Rusty stood watching him, her heart in a muddle. He was leaving Monday, and she would probably never see him again. She couldn't tell right now if she was pleased about that or not. No one heard her soft sigh. By the time Chase joined her, she managed to school her features and cover the myriad emotions inside.

21

"How was your meeting with Robert?"

"It went very well, thank you. There's a piece of land I'm looking at," Chase explained to Clayton after dinner that night. "I have houses in mind right now, but I'm open to other suggestions. Your brother-in-law knows the man who owns the tract and thinks he'll be interested in selling."

"Are you thinking of moving there yourself?"

"No, and it's strictly speculation at this point. To tell you the truth, I'm in no hurry. I've also met very briefly with a land agent in town. He's looking into the matter for me."

"But Robert was open to financing this for you?"

Chase hesitated but then explained. "Actually, I wasn't seeing Robert about financing. I'd heard that he owned the land. He's the one who put me in touch with the agent."

"That's great," Clayton said sincerely. "I hope it will bring you into our area more often."

"I could live with that. Boulder is a beautiful city."

"I quite agree with you." Clayton glanced toward the window and commented on how dark it was getting. He reached for the lantern that sat next to them on the kitchen table and turned it higher.

"I think Jackie is in the living room. Shall we join her?"

"Certainly."

They moved to that room to find it dark. There was a tiny bit of light coming from the window in the front door, but it was quite dim. Jackie's lone figure could be made out on the sofa.

"How come you're sitting here in the dark?" Clayton asked as soon as he set the lantern down. Both men watched her smile and set her book aside.

"Is it dark already? I can't say that I noticed."

Clayton dropped a kiss onto her head before lighting the lamps and stoking the fire. He joined her on the sofa, and Chase took the rocking chair.

"Where are the kids?"

"I think Rusty and Clare are talking in Clare's room, and Dana said something about a report on India."

"What about Les?"

"Didn't he tell us he was headed to Pastor's house?"

"Oh, that's right."

"Did you need him?"

"No, but I wish he could hear this. Chase and I were just talking about the land he's interested in."

"Where is the land, Mr. McCandles?" Jackie asked.

Chase explained the location and his present plans. Jackie and Clayton had many more questions, and Chase, having clearly thought it all out, had an answer for nearly every one.

"I've never felt like this in my life, Rusty," her sister Clare admitted to her. "I want to get out and see things. We go to Denver every year, and of course we visit Grandmother and Grandfather in Georgetown, but I just feel so empty inside." Tears filled the younger girl's eyes. "Even Manitou would be a change of pace. I'm kind of jealous of you."

"What exactly are you looking for, Clare?"

Rusty asked kindly.

"Just people, I guess. I'm studying my Bible right now more than ever, and I think the Lord has really helped me with my tongue and attitude, and that has helped me get closer to more people at school this year. Mother and Papa have both noticed, but the more I study, the more I long for something else. We're studying India right now in geography, and I want to go there. I want to touch the sand and feel the heat of the day. I want to see the people and experience their life."

"Maybe that's what you're supposed to do, Clare," Rusty said simply. "Maybe that's where God wants you. If you're sinning in your discontentment, then you know that can't be from God, but maybe this restlessness is to help you let go of home because you're not supposed to stay here forever."

"You're the second person to say that to me," Clare admitted quietly.

"Who was the first?"

"Papa."

Rusty nodded and smiled. "I'm so glad you talked to him, Clare. He's got such a huge heart. I know he cries every time I leave — Mother wrote and told me so — but he's never tried to hold me back. When I had a heart to go and be with those children, he wrote to Paddy and Sammy immediately. And now this. I wouldn't be too surprised if Papa hasn't talked with Pastor Henley already to see if he knows anyone in India with whom you could correspond."

"Do you really think so, Rusty? Would he do that?"

"That's just what he would do. If I were you, I'd bring it up again, ask him if he has any suggestions for you. After all, you're finished with school next month. Mother and Papa both know you'll be needing something to do."

"I'm supposed to work for Mrs. Wood this summer." The 17-year-old was clearly not thrilled with the prospect.

"Mrs. Helen Wood?"

"Yes, I was going to write and tell you, but I just never did."

"How did that come about?"

"She broke her leg this winter and is still off her feet. Her live-in housekeeper is leaving this summer for two whole months, and she needs someone to come in during the day. There was an announcement at church, and without even taking time to think, I volunteered."

Rusty smiled and then laughed in delight.

"I don't think it's funny, Rusty. She's in

her seventies, and I'm dreading the whole thing."

"Oh, Clare." Her sister grabbed her hand. "God is so good. Don't you know who she is? Don't you remember anything about this woman? She came and talked to us in school one time."

Clare frowned in concentration and then shook her head no.

"Helen Wood has been all over the world," Rusty said with soft excitement. "If you've a yearning to travel to India, I wouldn't be at all surprised if she's been there."

"Are you serious, Rusty?"

"Yes," her sister told her with a huge smile. "God knew just where you needed to be, Clare Melissa Taggart. I don't know what she's like now, but at one time I thought Helen Wood was the most exciting person I'd ever known."

Clare looked like she could laugh and cry all at the same time. She hugged Rusty and then jumped to her feet.

"I've got to tell Dana."

"Okay," Rusty said on a laugh, finding Clare's excitement contagious. "I'm going to head downstairs. You and Dana should come pretty soon. This is Mr. McCandles' last night."

"Okay," Clare called breathlessly as she

dashed from the room. Rusty followed until she reached the stairway and then joined the adults in the living room. It wasn't more than ten minutes before Dana and Clare came as well. Business talk was put aside long enough for Clare to tell her parents what Rusty had said about Mrs. Wood. Her father confirmed the facts and added a few of his own. By the time Leslie joined them and they had decided on a board game to play, Clare was floating on a cloud.

The train station was routinely busy for early on a Monday morning. Chase stood still, waiting for his call to board, his ticket tucked safely into the pocket of his shirt. It was hard to believe the weekend was over. He was a little tired after three late nights with the family, but you wouldn't have known it by looking at him. He was freshly shaved and bathed and already thinking about the journey home. The only one up early that morning had been Clayton, but he had still managed to put a filling meal into his guest.

It was a little chilly, so Chase moved around some, not wanting his feet to get cold. That was when he spotted her. Coming toward him at a breakneck speed was Rusty. Her hair was slightly wild around her face, and her eyes were sleepy, but they lit up when she saw him.

"I thought I might have missed you," she said breathlessly, a full smile in place as she stepped in front of him. "I meant to get up and tell you goodbye and to thank you one last time for everything you've done."

"You're welcome," he said graciously. "Especially considering how late we all retired."

"Well," Rusty replied, at her logical best, "you were up just as late, but you still managed to get up."

"This is true," he said seriously and smiled at her.

"Will you tell Quintin I said hello?"

"I certainly will."

Rusty opened her mouth to say something but then shut it again.

"Was there something else?" Chase had been watching her closely.

"Yes," she admitted, "but it's presumptuous on my part."

"I doubt if you'll offend me."

Rusty bit her lip.

Chase's brows rose in question, his eyes holding hers. Rusty's comment finally came out in a whisper.

"I just hope you won't take the bear away from him."

Chase nodded, his face understanding. "I've thought a lot about that, Katherine, and I have to tell you honestly that I do plan to tell Mrs. Harding that Quintin is to keep this bear, but because he's never been allowed to form attachments to toys, I'm not sure he'll warm up to it."

Rusty nodded. She had not thought of this. Her heart beat a little slower now with sadness, but she worked at not showing this to Mr. McCandles. That was no way to say goodbye to anyone.

"Well, we tried," she said at last, her smile forced but back in place.

"I'll be sure to tell him that we chose the gift together. He'll enjoy knowing that."

"But won't that diminish some of the specialness of your taking him a gift?"

"I don't think so," he spoke sincerely. Chase might have gone on in an effort to convince her, but his train was called.

"That's your train, isn't it?"

"Yes, it is. Thank you for coming to see me off, Katherine."

"Thank you for coming," she said right back. With that she stuck out her hand, and Chase shook it without thinking. He made himself turn and walk away right then, wondering if he should have followed his heart and given her a hug. He boarded the train and sat by the window so he could look out. She was still standing where he'd left her. When she found him at the window, he waved and noticed that she made no move to leave.

The young men gathered around her in the alley flashed through his mind again. The train jerked into motion, and Chase glanced one more time to see Rusty wave again. She was out of sight just seconds later, and by the time the train picked up speed, he had convinced himself that the only reason he felt regret about leaving was because he still thought he could have done a better job taking care of her. With this firmly rooted in his mind, Chase reached for the newspaper he had purchased and settled in for the ride.

"Did you get there in time?" Clayton asked his daughter the minute she came back in the door.

"Yes. We talked for a few minutes, and then his train was called."

Clayton watched as she poured herself a cup of coffee and joined him across the table. Clayton put his paper aside and smiled at her.

"Sorry to see him go?"

"A little, and I don't know why."

"Well, you care for him, don't you?"

"Yes, but we barely know each other."

"Sometimes it's like that, Rusty," Clayton said softly. "Instant attraction. It certainly was between your mother and me."

"You're starting to sound like Dana."

"What did she have to say?"

Rusty rolled her eyes. "As if we hadn't stayed up late enough as it was, after the game last night she tells me she has to talk to me."

"And?"

"According to Dana, I *am* going to marry the man."

"Well, considering the fact that Dana is not prescient, I don't think you need to worry about it. But why do you find her suggestion so outrageous?"

Rusty cocked her head to one side and listed the reasons on her fingers. "For one thing he lives in Springs and I live in Manitou. He's older than I am. He's a businessman who travels a good deal and has a son he barely knows. I have no idea what I feel right now, and most importantly, I can see that he's not interested in me at all."

"Now there you're wrong, Rusty."

The coffee cup stopped on the way to Rusty's mouth. "What do you mean? Has he spoken to you?"

"He didn't have to."

She set the cup back down and looked at her father.

"Don't misunderstand me, honey. I'm not saying he's getting ready to propose, but Chase McCandles is very interested in you. He's not the first man certainly, but he is the first man whom you seem interested in as well."

Rusty stared down at the table. She was interested, but right now she was having a hard time recognizing Mr. McCandles' interest. He was kind and very caring, but she didn't see that as romantic fascination. And if her father did, what had he seen? She was about to ask him when he had a question for her.

"Can you tell me what you meant when you said he doesn't know his son?"

Rusty sighed. "It's true. He has this huge home and a full staff, including a nanny for Quintin, but he simply doesn't know him. They don't talk, they don't hug, they don't do anything together that has meaning. Mr. McCandles doesn't know what toys his son has and doesn't seem to want to know." Again she sighed. "I am interested in him, but I think I'm angry at myself for caring about a man who could have so little regard for his child."

"Does he see it, Rusty? What you described to me — is Chase aware of it?"

"I don't think so. I would love to show him what a lovable little boy he has, but it's not my place."

Clayton's hand suddenly covered Rusty's. "I know you, Rusty. I know you well. And I'm going to say something you must heed. I don't know if God has a future for you and Chase, but you must not become interested in the man because you love the little boy. That's not fair to any of you. If ever you find yourself at the receiving end of Chase McCandles' attentions, and you accept them, you must do so out of love for him, not because you want to rescue Quintin."

Rusty nodded. Her father did know her well. She didn't think she'd go so far as to enter into a loveless marriage, but she was very vulnerable where Quintin McCandles was concerned.

"Have I upset you?"

"No, but you've certainly given me a lot to think about." She paused and met her father's gaze. "How would you and Mother feel if I did care for Mr. McCandles?"

"We both like him very much, Rusty, and we know he took very good care of you, but by your own admission there are some things missing. I would welcome your getting to know him better, and if at all possible, your mother's and my spending more time with him."

"We're talking like it's a done deal," Rusty said, her chest feeling oddly tight. "As I said, I have no idea what I feel, and I have only yours and Dana's opinion that he's even interested."

"Be that as it may, Rusty, this is the time to talk about these issues, not when emotions have taken over and your heart feels as though it's over the moon."

That was yet another good point, and for the moment it was the last one. Leslie wandered into the kitchen a few minutes later and started on his breakfast. Jackie came next and was eventually followed by Clare and Dana. They ate breakfast amid much fun, but another school day was about to begin and before long everyone was off at full speed.

22

Colorado Springs

Chase sank into his chair and looked at the stack of mail on his desk. He'd been gone only two business days, but it had certainly mounted up. After reaching for his business case and setting it on the desk, he flipped the latch, and the first thing he saw was the bear. He smiled at the sight of it and went immediately to find Mrs. Whitley. She was in the kitchen.

"Do you know where Quintin is?" he asked of the older woman.

"I believe he and Mrs. Harding are on a walk, sir."

Chase nodded. "Please send him to me when he returns."

"Yes, sir."

Chase returned to his office and went to work on his correspondence. He had accomplished much when he heard the sound of Quintin's voice and the patter of little feet. Preparing himself to have Quintin stop in the doorway, Chase was surprised when the little boy shot directly into his office, his eyes alight with surprise. Chase watched in confusion as the younger McCandles looked around the office and then at his father.

"Where is she?" Quintin asked, his formality with his father dropping away from him for the first time in his life.

"Where is who, Quintin?"

"Miss Taggart. Where is she?" His little head turned as he looked for her again, and he turned a smiling face to his father, as though waiting for the surprise to end.

"Miss Taggart isn't here, Quintin," Chase said kindly. "She's at her home in Boulder."

Quintin frowned a little. "I found a new nest," the little boy explained. "She has to see my nest. When is she coming?"

"She's not, Quintin," Chase continued gently. "From Boulder she's going back to the orphanage where she works."

"She's not coming?"

"No, Quintin, I'm sorry you thought she was."

The little boy could have been made of

stone, so frozen became his stance, but it didn't last. Chase watched in amazement as tears filled his son's eyes. Numb with shock, he stared when Quintin dropped his face into his hands and sobbed. He was speaking now as well, but Chase caught little of it. A moment later Mrs. Harding carefully put her head around the corner. She looked at her small charge, who was still crying into his hands, and then at Chase, who looked back at her helplessly.

"What is it, Quintin?" Mrs. Harding asked in a voice that was gentler than usual.

"She's not here," he managed. "She didn't come back, and I can't show her —"

Again Mrs. Harding looked to Chase. "Is he talking about Miss Taggart?"

"Yes."

Mrs. Harding nodded, her face exhibiting no surprise. "Shall I take him, Mr. McCandles?"

"Yes, I guess you'd better." His voice still reflected his shock. He watched as Mrs. Harding led his son away and then sat completely still, his eyes on the spot where Quintin had been standing. He had certainly seen that Quintin had become attached to their guest, but never had he expected this.

After a few minutes Chase sat back in his chair. On doing so his eyes caught sight of the stuffed bear. He picked it up and looked into its grumpy face. His lids slid shut on the memory of Katherine, and he knew why Quintin cried. She was so fun, so special, and she made everyone with her feel special. Chase looked down at the toy again, but the bear blurred as Quintin's face jumped starkly back into his mind. He had to do something for his little son, but at the moment he didn't know what.

Boulder

As Rusty had hoped, the house was packed to the rafters on Monday night. Armed with snacks of every kind, more than 30 young people showed up for an evening of fellowship, laughter, and food, but no one minded the noise or lack of space. They were too busy enjoying themselves.

Pastor and Beryl Henley came with Wilna North, and Leslie blushed the whole evening. They sat near each other, but no one saw them speak to one another. Justin Sommerfeldt came, and although Dana showed no outward signs of interest, Rusty remembered what Leslie had said.

Rusty acted as hostess, and in doing so was able to catch up with lots of news. She had a great talk with Katie and Roz Buchanan, as well as a long visit with Pastor and Mrs. Henley. They were all very glad to see her and thrilled with how much she was enjoying her work.

The guests cleared out by ten o'clock, and both Jackie and Rusty voted to leave the cleanup for the morning.

"Thank you for a wonderful evening," Rusty said to her parents before going to her own room.

"You're welcome. Did you see everyone you hoped to see?"

"All but Grace Harrington, but we plan to go to lunch this week."

"Now I wonder what the two of you will discuss, since nothing exciting ever happens in your lives," Clayton said, his voice dry.

Rusty laughed. "Yes, I wonder too. Goodnight, Papa. Goodnight, Mother."

"Goodnight, dear," they bid her and moved down the hall. They were in bed just a short time later, both agreeing that the days until she went back to Manitou were going to pass swiftly. They would surely miss her, but after her departure it was certainly going to be quiet.

Clare thought she might be sick. She had never been so nervous in her life. When her father had first told her that she had an appointment to see Mrs. Wood, she'd been delirious with happiness, a happiness that only increased when Rusty said she would go with her, especially since she was leaving for Manitou in two days. Now they were walking toward the large mansion that sat on Pine Street, and Clare was literally shaking with nerves. She had to force herself not to reach for Rusty's hand.

You're a big girl now, Clare, you can do this. She's not going to eat you.

"What if she's not home?" Clare suddenly asked, her voice as breathless as she felt.

Rusty laughed. "Her leg is broken, Clare. She's housebound. Besides, you have an appointment."

"Oh, that's right."

Rusty laughed again, but then her tone turned compassionate. "Oh, Clare. You have no color in your face. Let's slow down so you can calm yourself a little."

Clare was thankful for the suggestion. The girls slowed their walk to a near crawl, and the younger Taggart tried to breathe deeply. She had taken her sister's advice and checked back with her father, thinking she needed to remind him how much she wanted to travel. She had been wrong. He had needed no such reminder and told her that he was working on the matter. Not two hours later he'd come to tell her she was to meet with Mrs. Wood that week, and that the lady had very close friends in India. Now it was happening. She was on her way to meet her summer employer. Just two weeks ago she would have been pleased to have Mrs. Wood find her unsuitable. Today she wanted to make the very best impression.

"This is the place," Rusty said, and Clare looked up in surprise. How had they arrived so swiftly? "Are you ready, Clare?"

"I think so. How do I look?"

"You look lovely," Rusty said sincerely and stepped back a little. She wanted her sister to take the lead. Clare did not disappoint her. The younger girl took a deep breath before starting up the walk and knocking on the front door. This done, Clare had to force her hands to her side. It was a relief when the door was answered swiftly.

"Miss Taggart?" A smiling woman with gray hair cascading down her back opened the door for them.

"Yes. I'm Clare Taggart, and this is my sister Katherine."

"Come in," she welcomed them warmly. "I'm Thelma Hepplewhite. I keep the house running for Mrs. Wood. She's very eager to meet you."

"I'm eager to meet her too. I hope I'll be able to help."

"You'll do just fine." Thelma was walking now, leading the way. "Her demands are few. Before she got hurt, there were days when I accused her of paying me to keep her company."

Clare smiled and glanced at Rusty, who was smiling as well. Thelma had taken them through the house, past elegantly furnished rooms to a closed-in glass sunroom at the rear of the house. Mrs. Wood was comfortably ensconced in a chair, a book in her lap and a letter in her hand.

"Miss Taggart is here, Helen."

"Oh, good," she exclaimed as she put the letter down. "I'm so glad to see you and terribly put out that I couldn't come to the door myself. Come in and sit with me."

The Taggart girls took chairs, and Clare made an introduction.

"It's good to meet you, Mrs. Wood. I'm Clare Taggart, and this is my sister Katherine."

"It's wonderful to meet you both. I hope you know that I prayed you here," she told them seriously. "I can tell you right now that it wasn't in my plans to break this leg, but that's what happened and that's why I need you, Clare Taggart. All winter Thelma has been planning to take two months off. I was going to be here on my own, but as you can see," she gestured to the leg that was propped up on a tapestried ottoman, "that's impossible."

"So you prayed for someone to come," Clare guessed with a smile.

"I certainly did, and here you are!" The old eyes surveyed her kindly. "You're younger than Thelma. I may want you to stay and replace her."

Thelma, who was headed back into the room with a tray of refreshments, had a good laugh.

"Do you mean I should have slammed the door in Miss Taggart's face?" she asked as she settled the tray on a table. "I wish I'd known."

Clare and Rusty laughed at the banter between the two, and that was just the beginning. They spent the next three hours talking, first in the sunroom and then over a delicious lunch. Clare would start the day after school let out and stay on for the following nine weeks. Several ladies came in weekly to clean and cook, so Clare's duties would be mostly fetching and toting — menial tasks, but Mrs. Wood had a heart of gold, and Clare knew she wouldn't mind a bit.

It was hard to leave, but at last it was time. Rusty didn't think she was going to be able to keep her sister on the ground. By the time they arrived home, Clare was so excited she could hardly speak.

"Oh, Mother," Clare began from the first minute they walked through the door. Disjointed and excited words poured out of her. "I wish you could have been — I mean, you should have . . . India! We talked and . . . her home is wonderful and she's just like, that is, she's wonderful too, and I —" Clare had to stop, and Jackie laughed at her daughter's enthusiasm.

"I prayed for you the whole time, Clare," Jackie said, her eyes and voice full of joy. "I just knew God would make it special. When do you start?"

"The day after school is out. I can hardly, that is, oh, Mother, it was wonderful."

Clare had finally run out of energy. She dropped into a chair in the front room, laid her head back, and stared at the ceiling.

"I think she's out of steam," Rusty said.

"I'll bet she is," Jackie said compassionately. "It's a good thing you and I are making dinner tonight, Rusty."

Conversation quieted then, Rusty filling in details that Clare had missed. All was calm until Dana tore in the door from school. It had killed her that Clare had been allowed to miss school for the interview, but only because she knew she would have to wait to hear the outcome. Seeing her, Clare was off again. Jackie and Rusty voted to leave them on their own and escape to the quiet of the kitchen to get dinner underway.

23

Rusty settled back against the train seat and sighed. Hearing it, her companion turned questioning eyes to her.

"Don't mind me, Papa," she said, having correctly interpreted her father's look. "I'm just tired."

"But you do want to return to the orphanage?" Clayton asked, needing to be sure.

Rusty's eyes shone. "Oh, yes. I miss the children so much, especially my cousins. But I didn't sleep very well last night, and then Mother and I were both awake so early. It was wonderful to have that extra time with her, but now it's catching up."

"Why didn't you sleep well?"

"I don't know — just lots of things on my mind."

She didn't elaborate, so Clayton stayed

quiet and prayed, making himself let go of his oldest child.

She's Yours, Lord. She always has been. I forget and try to take her from You, but she's never been mine. I ask that You keep her safe, but I do so in Your will. I thank You for whatever You have for Rusty. You love her more than I do. I thank You that she's such a special person, and that You put her into our family. We are all blessed by her life.

Help her to keep her emotions in check as she returns to work now. Help her not to grow angry at the injustices she sees, but to see Your hand in all and trust You completely for those children.

Rusty interrupted her father's prayer with a question about when they would arrive but then went back to her view out the window. Clayton had brought a newspaper that he now opened, but at one point he glanced over to see such a look of pain on Rusty's face that he was startled. He folded the paper quietly and waited, his eyes still on her profile. The look passed, but Clayton was not about to ignore it.

"Are you all right?" he asked softly.

Rusty looked up at him. "I was thinking about Quintin."

Clayton didn't need to hear any more. There was little that pained his daughter more than a child in distress. Clayton was not much different.

"I have much for which to thank God, Papa, specifically for Quintin, I mean — but I still want more for him. I try to concentrate on the fact that he's well taken care of and kept from harm — that's certainly more than I can say for a lot of the orphans who come to us — but I still want him to have more."

"I understand, Rusty, but I think you do him a great disservice by comparing him to an orphan. Mr. McCandles would be very offended."

Rusty's brow lowered. "He should be."

Clayton couldn't stop his smile. Without warning, he pictured his daughter married to Chase McCandles and knew nothing but peace.

"Am I being laughed at?" Rusty had caught his look.

"No, but I do find it amusing that with all due respect you call the man *Mr.* McCandles, but you don't hesitate to tell him exactly what you think."

Rusty's lopsided smile was self-disparaging. She *was* outspoken where Quintin's father was concerned, but she'd never come right out and told him what she thought of the whole situation. She hadn't thought it was her place.

"I need to say one other thing, Rusty,"

Clayton ventured. Rusty looked at him. "If you've witnessed sins in Chase's life, such as neglect of his son, you can ask God to intervene. God wants more for Quintin than even you do. Ask God to help Chase see how much his son needs him. You may never know the answer, but you will still have done your job by faithfully praying. That's all God requires of you in this situation."

Rusty nodded. "Thank you, Papa. I'd forgotten how good it was to travel with you."

"I didn't get much time with you. This will give us a good visit."

Rusty smiled but then her eyes wandered to the distance. "I'll probably never see him again," she said thoughtfully.

"Quintin or Mr. McCandles?"

Rusty shrugged. "Both, I guess."

Clayton didn't reply, but he couldn't have disagreed more. He wouldn't go so far as to agree with Dana that Rusty was going to marry the man, but he felt quite certain that if Chase McCandles had anything to say about it, Rusty would see him again.

Manitou

Sammy O'Brien stopped short when her brother-in-law walked in the front door of the orphanage. She had been on her way to hug Rusty, who had preceded him, but was so surprised by Clayton's presence that she hesitated before a huge smile covered her face.

"Clay!" she said warmly. "What a wonderful surprise."

"Isn't it though!" he agreed as he covered the distance between them. "I didn't get enough time with Rusty so I thought I'd see her back."

"I'm glad you did."

They shared a hug before Sammy asked, "Jackie and the kids are all right?"

"Yes."

"How long can you stay?"

"I need to leave in the morning."

Sammy's eyes moved to her niece. "Chase's cable said you were ill; are you all right now?"

"Yes."

"I forgot to hug you." At times Sammy could be all business, but once Rusty was in her arms, she held on for some time and would not let go. Paddy came in on them during this time.

"Well, this is a surprise," he laughed as he shook Clayton's hand with delight.

"Welcome home, Rusty." He also greeted his niece with a hug and had it warmly returned.

"How are you feeling?"

"Back to my old self."

"I wanted to board a train and come and get you when Chase said you had been sick, but I knew he would take care of you," Paddy confided as he hugged her again and then turned to Clayton.

"Is everything okay in Boulder?"

"Yes, everything is great."

Paddy turned back to Rusty. "How are the Parks children?"

"The placement went very well, but things fell apart with the train when we got to Makepeace."

"And that's where you got sick."

"Yes."

One of the other workers needed Paddy just then, so with a brief word to the group about dinner being in an hour, he went on his way. Sammy also had some jobs to do. Rusty and Clayton made their way to the private apartment to be thronged by the younger O'Briens.

"Mother said you placed Lizzy and Thomas," Renny said to his older cousin. They were sitting very close on the sofa, Rusty's head bent close to Renny's smaller one. Rusty was one of his favorite cousins. Although older, she was more his size and

272

always kind in the bargain.

"Yes. They live with the Davidsons now in Kurth."

"The Davidsons?"

"That's right. They own a cattle ranch."

"What was it like?"

"Very nice. Lots of cows and acres of land. They have a big house with a nice downstairs and a great front porch. Both kids have their own rooms upstairs."

Renny fell silent then, and Rusty wondered if she hadn't made him sad. There were times when they all forgot to be thankful. Renny and Nolan were both very happy boys, but if they did fall into bad attitudes, it was usually over having to share a bedroom with their sister and cousin.

"Have you had a sleepover in the boys' room lately?" Rusty asked, keeping her voice very casual.

"No."

"Why not?"

"It's been a long time because last time I got scared and cried."

"That was months ago. I think you should try it again. I could even sit with you if you'd like."

Renny frowned. "The boys would say I was a baby."

"Well, are you still afraid to sleep in there?"

"I never was."

Rusty leaned forward to better see his face. "Then why did you cry?"

"I had a bad dream."

"I didn't know that, Renny," Rusty frowned, "but if that's the case, why haven't you asked to go back?"

"Because Mother was angry that Papa had to go and get me, and she said not to ask to do that again anytime soon."

"It's been a long time, Renny. I think you should check with her again. Something tells me she didn't understand. I think if you talked to her, she would be sorry she made you feel so bad."

"I don't know."

Rusty shifted and pulled the little boy to his feet. "Go on now, find her and tell her all about it."

He hesitated for only a moment before making his way to the kitchen where his mother and sister were working on the dishes. Nolan was reading at the table, and Paddy had taken Clayton to see some repairs he had made in one of the rooms. It took a moment for Renny to get out what he needed to say, but his mother was swift to catch on and just as swift to make things right between them. She told Renny that she would set up a sleepover for him in the boys' dorm for the very next weekend. She then told him it was bedtime.

He went off without a word, a smile on his face. Once he was in bed, his mother bent over him to kiss him goodnight.

"Will Papa come to kiss me too?"

"Yes. I'll ask him to kiss you even if you've fallen asleep."

"I didn't kiss Rusty."

"Shall I ask her to come in?"

Renny didn't even try to cover his yawn. "No, I guess not, but she talked to me and well —" He looked sleepily up at his mother.

"I'll tell her you appreciated it, shall I?"

He nodded. "Thank you, Mother."

Sammy kissed him again, went out, and shut the door. She found Nolan and Eileen in the living room with Rusty. She sat down and listened.

"She was feeling rather down about having to work for Mrs. Wood."

"So what did you say to her?"

"I told her that Mrs. Wood had traveled all over the world, and that might be just what God wants her to do."

"Where would she like to go?" Nolan asked.

"She's most interested in India."

"India?" Eileen's eyes were huge.

"Yes."

"They have elephants there."

"So I've heard, but she's interested in the people, not the elephants."

"Did Mrs. Wood say she would take her?"

"No, Nolan, it wasn't like that. Mrs. Wood is older now, and she's through traveling, but she has a good friend living in Delhi. She's going to write to her and send Clare's address."

Eileen sighed. "That's so exciting. I wish I could see India. Did you hear that, Mother? Isn't it exciting?"

"It certainly is. How did Clare come to work for Mrs. Wood?"

"Mrs. Wood broke her leg, and her live-in help can't be with her all summer. Pastor Henley announced one Sunday that she needed someone, and Clare volunteered."

"So Clare will live there?"

"No, she'll just go during the day. Mrs. Wood has a relative who lives with her, a niece I believe; she'll keep an eye on her during the night."

"How is everyone else at home?" Sammy wanted to know.

Rusty was filling her in when the men returned. Paddy told Nolan and Eileen that they needed to head for bed. Rusty volunteered to do the honors with the older children, and before she could return, Sammy gave Clayton the third degree.

24

"Is my sister really okay?"

"Yes, Sammy, absolutely. Why the concern?"

"There was just something on your face earlier," she said, staring at him, "that made me think she was on your mind."

Clayton looked right back at her.

"What did she think of Chase McCandles?"

Clayton slowly smiled. "I don't know how you two do it, Sam, but you seem to know what my wife's thinking even if you can't see her."

Sammy smiled when she heard Paddy chuckle. "So tell me, what did she think of him?" Her voice had dropped, and Clayton's did as well.

"She liked him, but more than that, she

thinks he's in love with Rusty."

As he might have expected, Sammy did nothing. She nodded and her eyes were thoughtful before she said, "He probably couldn't help himself. I haven't been to Briarly in a long time, but Chase's life is very calm and well-ordered. Rusty must seem a little bit like a flower in the desert. Does Rusty share his feelings?"

"Don't get ahead of them, Sammy," Paddy put in. "I don't think that's what Clay is saying."

"You're right about that. Neither one of them knows a thing except a little bit of attraction."

Sammy was opening her mouth to comment on that when Rusty joined them. She sat on the sofa next to her father and looked across at Paddy.

"Glad to be back?" he asked with a smile.

"More than I can say. I've missed the children."

"They've asked for you daily, and Pastor Brad wanted to know what Sunday you would be back to take the little ones."

Rusty smiled. There was a special time for the children who came to church each Sunday, and twice a month Rusty caught the lesson and sang songs with them. She loved the time, and the children adored her.

"I'll go see him tomorrow afternoon," she said before having to cover a huge yawn. "I know I just got back, but if no one objects, right now I'm going to bed."

"That sounds like a good idea." Sammy rose to do the same, and out of respect the men rose with them.

Rusty kissed everyone goodnight and made her way from the room. Sammy kissed Paddy because she knew she would be asleep before he came to bed. She then hugged Clayton and told him to plan on a filling breakfast the next morning.

As soon as the women left, the men sat back down. Just as Sammy suspected, Paddy did not immediately join her. Although a little apart in age, Paddy and Clayton had grown up together in the same town, their fathers both being mine surveyors. Feeling they had much to catch up on, the two men talked into the wee hours of the morning. It was very late when they decided to call it quits. Rather than take the spare room upstairs that he and Jackie usually slept in when they visited, Clayton opted to stretch out on the sitting room davenport. Making his way silently to bed, Paddy knew that as good as it was to see his brother-in-law, daylight would come all too soon.

★ ★ ★

Rusty saw her father off the next day, feeling so pleased that he'd made the trip with her. She had not, however, been kidding about wanting to get back to work. She returned to the orphanage and immediately sought out the children.

"I think, Charity Wilkinson, that you have grown two whole inches while I was away."

The shy three-year-old would not look up at Rusty, but she smiled at the floor and kept her hand tucked into Rusty's.

"I have to go to town for something, Charity. I'm going right after lunch. Would you like to come?"

Charity looked up then but shook her head no.

"You're sure?"

"I'm sure," she replied, bold enough to answer this time. This was one point on which she did not want to be misunderstood. Charity didn't like to go outside unless she was forced. She'd been delivered to the orphanage before her first birthday and had grown too attached to her room and bed. She ventured out for Sunday mornings with all the other children and into the huge yard when ordered to do so, but whenever the children were given free play and their choice of activity, Charity would be found indoors,

281

happy to draw or look at the pictures of a book. When she was told she must spend some time in the yard, she did not run and jump with the other children but walked slowly around, her face thoughtful and just a little apprehensive. The only time she ran was when the children were given permission to return indoors; indeed, she was usually the first in line.

"I'll ask you again sometime, shall I?" Rusty said, and noting that her little heart seemed relieved, watched the girl nod. They had shared this conversation before. Rusty pressed a kiss to her small, soft brow and opened the book they were going to read together. The subject of going to town was dropped.

Colorado Springs

"Chase!"

Just coming from the barber shop, Chase turned at the sound of his name and saw his pastor, Jeremy Radke, coming up the street.

"Pastor Radke, how are you?"

"Just great. Are you free for a cup of coffee?"

"Sure."

The men continued up the street to the hotel and went inside to find a seat. The waiter brought them steaming mugs and left them in peace.

"I've missed seeing you the last few weeks. How have you been?"

"I've been fine. I escorted one of the orphanage workers and two children to a placement."

"This would be the orphanage you support in Manitou?"

"Yes. The placement went very well, but on the way home, the woman got sick. She was at Briarly for a few days, but I felt it was important to take her home myself."

"Is she all right now?"

"She was when I left her at her parents' home in Boulder. She's probably back in Manitou now."

"Will you be going over to see her?"

"I don't think so," Chase told him, but wondered at the disappointment that filled him. He would have welcomed a reason to visit the orphanage; it had been a very long time since he'd been there. But why did he have to wait for a reason to visit? Before he could form an answer, Pastor Radke spoke again, and although Chase listened, his mind was only half on the conversation. It wasn't long before they finished their coffee and went their separate ways.

Chase arrived home and slowly walked in

the front door of Briarly. His mind was busy going over the question Pastor had asked him about going to Manitou. He never made it out of the front entryway but just stood thinking. That was when the older McCandles heard Quintin's voice coming from behind the closed door of the breakfast room. Since arriving home from Boulder, Chase could not see or hear Quintin without thinking of Rusty. It was probably the toy bear. As soon as the little boy had learned that she'd picked it out, he hadn't let it out of his sight. For a few days he'd pined for Rusty so seriously that they feared he would become ill. Then Chase remembered the bear. Quintin was doing better now, but Mrs. Harding reported that he still spoke of Miss Taggart every day.

Eventually Chase moved into his office, but his mind was still full of Quintin, Rusty, and the Fountain Creek Orphanage.

Manitou

As soon as lunch was over and the children were settled into their afternoon activities, Rusty, true to her word, left for the church. It was not far, just several blocks further into town. The day was lovely. In early May, spring was just coming to life in Manitou.

Although it was a bit cool, Rusty did not cover her uniform, which comprised a dark navy skirt and crisp white blouse. Anyone who saw her made an immediate connection to the orphanage.

Just minutes later, Rusty was knocking on the parsonage door. It didn't take long to open, and when it did, Rusty was immediately hugged.

"I'm so glad you're back!" Tibby Reed, the pastor's oldest daughter, nearly dragged Rusty inside. "It feels like you've been gone for months. How was the placement?"

"Wonderful," Rusty said sincerely as they took seats in the living room. "You should have seen this couple, Tibby. Their hearts were in their eyes every time they looked at Lizzy and Thomas."

"And the kids — they were happy?"

"Very. It couldn't have gone better."

"And how was Mr. McCans?"

"McCandles," Rusty corrected. "He was very kind. He took wonderful care of us."

"Easy to travel with?"

"Yes. Very accommodating."

"I prayed for you."

"Thank you."

"But I prayed for me more," she admitted, and Rusty had to laugh.

"Why?"

"Because I had to fill in with the kids while you were gone. I love helping you — you know that — but being the teacher makes my stomach ache."

Rusty shook her head good-naturedly. "That's why I'm here. Uncle Paddy said your father wanted to know when I would be back."

"Well, he's not home right now, but I'll tell him you're back in town. It's not our turn tomorrow, but I'm sure we'll be on for next week."

"Sounds good. I wish I could stay and visit, but I really should get back. How go the wedding plans?"

Rusty stood, and Tibby saw her to the door. Tibby filled her in on the latest concerning the upcoming nuptials, and the young women agreed to meet that week to go over the lesson for the children. Tibby had a way of brightening everyone's day, and Rusty was cheered by the few moments they spent together. She walked back to the orphanage, a wide smile on her face.

25

Colorado Springs

It was late in May, nearly June, when Mrs. Harding received the letter. Spring had finally stopped teasing the residents of the Rocky Mountains and arrived in full. Color seemed to be in every corner of the world. The lawns and gardens of Briarly were once again a showplace. It was here that Quintin's nanny opened her letter, and here where she sat, her small charge playing quietly beside her, and stared at nothing for a short time.

"Mrs. Harding?"

"Yes, Quintin?"

Mrs. Harding wondered at what her expression must have been when Quintin only stared at her, a worried crease between his small brows.

"I was just thinking, Quintin," she said, smiling to reassure him. She watched his eyes drop to the letter in her hand. He was too bright not to notice, but she knew he would never ask. "You're not cold, are you?"

Quintin's eyes returned to hers. He shook his head in denial and went back to the sketch-pad in his hand. It was a normal enough question to get his mind off of his nanny and also give Mrs. Harding a moment more to think. Indeed, a moment was all she needed. She folded the letter carefully and returned it to the envelope. This very evening she would speak with Mr. McCandles about the contents.

As the drawing room darkened, Chase turned the lantern a little higher and continued to read. He was enjoying a novel by Rudyard Kipling and was quite lost in thought when someone cleared her throat. Chase looked up to see Mrs. Whitley at the edge of the room, her back to the front hall.

"Will you be needing anything else tonight, sir?"

"I don't think so, Mrs. Whitley. Thank you."

"I'll say goodnight then."

"Goodnight."

Chase would have gone back to his book,

but he was sitting so that he could see the stairway. Mrs. Harding was coming down, and as Chase watched, she came and stood almost exactly where Mrs. Whitley had been.

"I'm sorry to disturb your evening, sir, but I wondered if I might have a word with you."

"Of course." Chase was immediately on his feet. He waited for Quintin's nanny to make herself comfortable on the sofa and resumed his seat.

"Is Quintin well?"

"Very well, sir. We had a good day. He enjoys being out without his coat and hat."

"Good." Silence fell between them for a moment, and Chase thought she looked a bit strained. He waited, wondering if he should question her but deciding she would speak to him when she was ready.

"Quintin is a very special little boy, Mr. McCandles, and I enjoy him immensely."

Chase nodded. He suspected there was a "but" in there somewhere, but he wasn't going to assume.

"I've been with him for more than three years now, and I can't imagine life without him. But to tell you the truth, I feel a need to take a few months off. The idea has come to mind over the past several months, but I've not felt an urgency to pursue the matter."

"But you do now?"

"Yes. You see, Mr. McCandles, I've had a letter from my sister." She looked pleased without smiling. "She's going to be married." She actually smiled now as though she couldn't help herself. "She's a woman in her forties and going to be married for the first time."

Chase smiled as well. "Congratulations are in order."

"Yes. She wrote to tell me, certainly, but also to ask if there was any way I might attend."

"By all means." Chase didn't need to think twice. "I wouldn't want you to miss it."

"I appreciate that, sir, but you see my sister lives in Charleston, South Carolina, where I grew up. My hope is that I'll not only be able to attend the wedding, but to take the entire summer off. She doesn't marry until early July, but if at all possible, I would wish to leave as soon as possible in June and not return until early September."

His expression open, Chase nodded but didn't speak. He was not hesitating over her request to go so much as the immediate question of what he would do with his son.

"I realize I've given you little warning, sir, and if you can't work it out, I will stay. But you've always been a fair employer, and I felt free at least to ask you."

"Of course, Mrs. Harding. I'm glad you did. Please plan on going. I'll begin work immediately on finding someone to come in for the summer."

"If I may be so bold to suggest someone, sir . . ."

"Absolutely. I would welcome any names you could give me."

"I don't know if Miss Taggart's contract with the orphanage is flexible, but Quintin speaks of her every day. I feel they would do very well together."

Chase didn't comment, but his mind was moving like a steam locomotive. He was once again seeing Quintin in his office, his face buried in his hands and sobbing. At the time he'd asked himself what he could do for the child. Did he now have an answer?

"I think that Miss Taggart is a wonderful suggestion, Mrs. Harding, and I thank you. If things don't proceed smoothly, however, what would be the latest date you could leave and still be there for your sister's wedding?"

"Train travel continues to improve yearly," she said thoughtfully. "And the wedding is on Saturday, July 3. Barring delays, I think a week ahead of that time would be more than sufficient."

"I'll do all that I can to have you on that

train in time, Mrs. Harding," Chase told her. He was thoughtful for a moment, his eyes wandering across the room and then back to her. "I'll be leaving in the morning for Manitou. Miss Taggart would be my first choice for Quintin, so I'll see to that before I discuss any other possibilities with you. I haven't visited the orphanage in some time, so don't expect me back until Monday or Tuesday."

"Very good, sir. Should I compile a list of other names for you, or do you feel quite confident?"

"I think Miss Taggart will come if she is able, but as you said, I've got to keep in mind her obligation to the orphanage. Go ahead and put together a list of names, and I'll let you know as soon as I return whether I need them."

"I'll do that, sir. Was there anything else?"

"No, thank you, Mrs. Harding."

That lady stood, and Chase came to his feet as well. He watched as she smiled.

"Thank you, Mr. McCandles. I look forward to telling my sister the good news. She'll be very pleased."

"I'm glad, Mrs. Harding," Chase said and meant it. "You deserve some time off."

"Thank you, sir. I shall wait until your plans are a bit more settled before saying anything to Quintin."

"I think that's wise. As I said, I'll know more after the weekend."

"Very well. Goodnight, sir."

"Goodnight, Mrs. Harding."

Chase stayed on his feet until she was out of the room, but even after dropping back into the overstuffed chair, he didn't pick up his book. His mind ran with thoughts of Quintin and Rusty and the one day they'd had together. He wasn't so much worried about whether or not Rusty would come to Colorado Springs — somehow he thought that would work out. His main worry was what Quintin would do when it was time for her to leave again.

Manitou

"Do I look big to you?" Rusty Taggart asked the children from her place on the chair. There was a mixture of answers throughout the large room at the church. The younger children naturally thought her larger than the older ones did.

"Okay," she said as she stepped down and turned to Tibby. "Let's have Aunt Tibby stand on the chair. She's taller than I am. Let's see how big she is when she's on the chair." Rusty stood to one side while her partner stepped up.

"She's pretty tall, isn't she?" Rusty spoke to the group of 30 children again, but she could see that they still weren't impressed. Rusty's mind was racing with what to do next when Chase McCandles stepped into the back of the room. Praying that he would forgive her, she spoke.

"Children, a friend of mine has just come in, and I would like you to meet him."

Following her gaze, nearly every little head turned toward the door. "Mr. McCandles, would you be so kind as to come up front and meet the children?"

Chase recovered from his surprise as he walked toward Rusty, but there was no covering the amusement on his face when he arrived. Rusty smiled at him and told herself not to laugh.

"Children, I would like you to meet Mr. McCandles. Will you please say hello?" She waited until they obeyed and then turned back to Chase.

"Mr. McCandles, would you please tell the children how tall you are?"

"I'm somewhere between 6′1″ and 6′2″," he spoke seriously.

"That's tall, isn't it?" Rusty asked of the children. They all nodded, eyes wide as they stared up at this towering stranger. "Now, what if I ask Mr. McCandles to step onto the chair?"

Chase did so without being asked and found it very satisfying to look into the faces of the awed children below him.

"Isn't he *tall?*" Rusty asked with enthusiasm. "But do you know what?" She waited for Chase to step down and melt into the background with Tibby so that all the children's eyes would come back to her. "He's not as tall as Goliath was. I tell you, he's not. Goliath was *huge.*" Rusty's eyes matched the word, and her arms were spread wide as she tried to make the children see. "But big as Goliath was, God was still taking care of Israel. Whom did He send?"

"David," the children shouted.

"That's right. David knew that God would take care of Israel. The soldiers didn't believe that, but David did. Now who can tell me what happened?"

Hands went up all over, and Rusty called on a little boy near the front. He stood and did a wonderful job of finishing the story, leaving out little detail.

"Thank you, Carlos. You did a great job. Were the rest of you listening? I hope so, because this is not a story that Aunt Rusty made up and told to Carlos." She held up her Bible. This story is right out of God's Word, so we know it's true, and we also know that God wants us to learn something from it.

"Let's all sit still now," she said, taking a moment to restore order. "I'm going to tell you something." Rusty's voice dropped, and the children quieted to hear her. "I have giants in my own life." She watched their eyes grow big again. "Not giant people, but giant sins like selfishness and fear. Do any of you ever have those?" Many hands went up, and she knew she still had their attention. "But do you know who is bigger than all my giant sins?" She watched heads nod. "That's right. God is. Isn't that wonderful? When I'm afraid, I can look in the Bible and be reminded that God is bigger than my fear when He says He'll never leave me or forsake me."

"I get afraid," a little girl called from the front.

"Yes, Vicky, I do too."

Others spoke up then, and Rusty knew she'd kept them long enough.

"Okay, let's stay quiet for just a moment longer and say our verse again. After that, Aunt Tibby is going to sing another song with you, and then it will be time for church."

Rusty reached for the large sign on which she'd printed the verse and listened as the children did very well. Tibby was right on hand leading the children in a final song.

The women had a cookie for each child, and all but the littlest ones understood that they were to line up to get theirs and then proceed to the door. Ten minutes later the room was empty. Children had met their parents, older siblings, and even orphanage workers at the door. All was quiet. Rusty turned to look at Chase McCandles, a wide smile coming to her mouth.

"Welcome to Manitou, Mr. McCandles."

"Thank you." He bowed formally, his eyes alight with laughter. "I must admit that I've never been welcomed quite that way."

Rusty laughed a little. "Thank you for helping out," she said seriously. "The children were very impressed."

"It was my pleasure, but I can't help wondering what you would have done had I not shown up at the door."

"I was working on that when I spotted you," Rusty admitted, "and then there you were. Didn't it feel good to be impulsive?"

Chase laughed, and Rusty motioned to Tibby, caught her arm, and pulled her close.

"Mr. McCandles, I'd like you to meet a very good friend of mine, Miss Tibby Reed."

"How do you do." Tibby smiled at him and put her hand out.

"Very well, thank you, Miss Reed. If you'll

allow me to compliment you, you sing beautifully."

"Thank you." Tibby dimpled with pleasure. "Oh, Mr. McCandles," she glanced behind Chase and continued, "this is my fiancé, Scott Thorstad."

"Hello, Scott." Chase turned, his hand out.

"It's good to meet you, sir." The men shook hands, and with that the strains of the organ could be heard coming from the sanctuary.

"Oh, goodness," Tibby exclaimed. "We're going to be late." She began to gather her things before she took Scott's arm and they moved toward the door. Rusty picked up her own Bible and teaching bag. Chase fell into step beside her.

"Are you in town for business or pleasure?" Rusty asked kindly.

"Business."

"Will you have a chance to see Paddy?"

"Yes. I hope to find him after the service."

They stopped talking as they neared the doors of the sanctuary. There was a nearly empty pew at the rear, and Rusty slipped into it as the congregation stood. Chase joined her as she expected he would, but not until she noticed several women turning to observe them did she realize she might have some explaining to do.

26

"I can tell I've shocked you."

"Yes, you have, Chase, but not for the reason you might suspect. You see we're all terribly attached to Rusty. I've never thought about her leaving, so it's hard to imagine life around here without her."

The businessman nodded. "I'll understand if you'd rather I didn't ask her, Paddy. She's my first choice, so I haven't even checked with anyone else."

Even as he said the words, Chase dreaded Padriac O'Brien's answer. Maybe if he hadn't seen Rusty again, he could have taken a no, but seeing her with those children and then talking to her, albeit briefly, made him sure she was the perfect woman to come and take care of Quintin.

Chase didn't know that Paddy was very

aware of Quintin's situation. One night Rusty had confided in him. Paddy had known that things were not ideal, but until Rusty explained the situation, he hadn't been completely aware of how little time Chase spent with his son. Other facts now chased through his mind. As much as Rusty brought to her job every day, the orphanage staff had many fine workers. It didn't sound as if Quintin McCandles had anyone.

"I think it only fair that you ask her, Chase. I can tell her what you have in mind or let you explain, but if she wants to work for you this summer, I think that's fine."

Since Chase had prepared himself to be disappointed, Paddy surprised him. For a moment he just sat there. "Thank you," he said at last. "When would be a good time to talk with her?"

"This afternoon — she's on duty until 5:00. I can tell her that you would like to speak with her when she's through."

"Okay."

"Do you want me to tell her the reason you're here, or will you explain that she's released from her duties for as long as you need her?"

Chase frowned in concentration. He didn't like the sound of that. "I don't want Katherine to think that she doesn't have a choice. I wouldn't want her to come if she didn't want to."

You have no idea how she feels about your son, Chase. She'll come. She won't be able to say no, Paddy was thinking. What he said out loud was far different. "I'll talk to her. I won't try to speak for you, but I'll explain to her that the choice is completely up to her."

"Thank you, Paddy."

"You're welcome," he said warmly. "Will you be in town long enough to have a tour of the orphanage tomorrow?"

"Yes, that was my plan. I told my house-keeper I wouldn't be returning until Monday or Tuesday."

"Good. Can you plan on having dinner with us tomorrow night?"

"I would enjoy that."

Paddy stood. "I'll tell Sammy. She'll be pleased."

The men parted company then, and Paddy tracked down his wife. She was certain to be pleased about seeing Chase, but as for the chance of Rusty leaving, she was not going to be overjoyed.

"Oh, Uncle Paddy" was all Rusty could say for several seconds.

"You don't have to do this, Rusty."

"That's just it, Paddy. I would love to, but I can't imagine not being here with you all summer. And . . ." she paused and sat there.

"And?"

"I don't know how I would do in that house."

"The house? I don't understand."

"I'm not sure I can explain, but neither do I think I'm the person he's really looking for."

Paddy nodded. "Are you even interested in hearing what Chase has to say?"

"Yes. I think if he's come all this way I should at least hear him out."

"All right. Do you understand where Sammy and I stand on this?"

"I think so. What did Sammy say?"

"That she'll miss you, but she understands."

"You talk as though it's all set."

Paddy cocked his head to the side, his expression gentle. "We both know the way you feel about Quintin McCandles, Rusty. Sometimes I think your tender heart is going to be the death of you."

Rusty's smile was lopsided. "You're probably right about that."

Paddy stood. "I'll tell Chase that you're ready to see him."

"All right. Does he expect an answer right away?"

"I don't know. That's something you'll have to ask him."

Rusty nodded and tried not to let her mind drift too far, but she wasn't very successful. Her thoughts were miles away when Chase stepped into Paddy's office. He stood for a moment and watched her, knowing she was unaware of his presence. He cleared his throat quietly and watched her start.

"Oh, you're here. I didn't see you."

"You looked lost in thought."

"I guess I was."

Rusty stayed in the seat in front of Paddy's desk and watched as he took the chair next to hers. She shifted slightly until they almost faced each other.

"Did Paddy fill you in?"

"Just a little. I take it Mrs. Harding is ill."

"Not at all. Her sister is to be married next month, and she would like to attend the wedding. She's wanted some time off for several months, and now this has given her the impetus to make the trip back East."

"How long does she plan to be gone?"

"She'd like to leave in early June and be away until the beginning of September."

Her face thoughtful, Rusty nodded but did not speak again.

"You must have questions," Chase began. "I'd be happy to explain anything you wish to know."

Rusty's head went to one side. "As a matter of fact, Mr. McCandles, my hesitation is not over questions I'd like to ask of you. I'm asking myself if I could actually be a servant in your home."

The word "servant" caused Chase's blood to run cold. That was *not* the way he viewed Rusty Taggart and never would be.

"I don't know if I'm comfortable with the word 'servant,'" Chase said, keeping his voice even. "Or even 'nanny.' I guess I would look at you as Quintin's companion. You would certainly be welcome at all meals and family functions." If pressed, Chase couldn't have named any actual family functions, but he had to make his point. He noted, however, that Rusty still did not look at ease.

"Was there anything else I could tell you?"

"No," she said. "I'm not worried about what I know, Mr. McCandles, so much as what you *don't* know."

"Concerning?"

"Concerning me and my style of doing things."

His expression told her she had lost him. Her voice was very gentle when she continued. "Here at the orphanage we have to have rules, but you live in a home, Mr. McCandles. I would want to act in your home the way I do in my own."

"Why do you think I would object to that?"

Rusty barely kept the shock from her face. *Why do I think you'd object? Because I've been there. I've seen the structured way Quintin is being raised. It's not for me, and it shouldn't be for your son either.*

"You want to say something, but you're hesitating."

Rusty hadn't realized how closely he'd been watching her.

"Yes, I do," she admitted. "I'm not doing a good job of explaining this. I'm sorry."

"It's all right, Katherine. You can tell me."

She sighed, knowing in an instant that she must leave Quintin out of this. "It's nothing personal, Mr. McCandles, but I can't work under the kind of structure you have in your home. As I said, here at the orphanage we have to have rules to survive, but I would be miserable with those kind of limitations in your home — in any home. I know I would."

Chase nodded. "Now it is my turn to apologize. I'm not asking you to come and be Mrs. Harding. I want you to come with your own style and ideas."

Rusty was shaking her head. "You don't know what you're saying, Mr. McCandles."

"Yes, I do," he said firmly.

"Hide and seek all over the house," she tested him.

"That's fine."

"Forts under the dining room table," she tried again.

"Fine."

"Towers made from books in the library. No particular schedule or focus."

"All right."

Rusty eyed him. Did he really mean it? Had she really made herself clear? This was the way she had grown up. It had been wonderful, but it was not the sedate environment to which he had become accustomed.

"It won't always be quiet," she felt a need to remind him.

"No one is going to complain. I know better than to worry that you would let anything happen to Quintin, and nothing else concerns me. The house is yours to do with as you like."

Rusty licked her lips. Could he mean it? If she could do with Quintin all summer what they'd been able to do in one day, it would be one of the greatest summers of her life. She reminded Mr. McCandles of that day.

"Do you recall the day Quintin and I had together?"

"Very well."

"It could very well be like that day *every* day, Mr. McCandles. Muddy boots and late to lunch."

Chase shrugged. "So far, Katherine, you haven't said anything I can't live with. Not to mention knowing that Quintin will love it."

If you know Quintin will love it, why hasn't he had that all along? The question came out of nowhere, and Rusty knew she was going to have to watch her thoughts. He was asking her to come and be with his son, not give a critique on his past performance.

"When do you need your answer, Mr. McCandles?"

"I'm leaving here Tuesday afternoon, but I don't want you to feel pressured. If you still don't know what you want to do when I'm ready to leave, you can get word to me later. If that's the case, I'll begin interviewing nannies when I arrive home, but you're my first choice, so I won't hire anyone until I hear from you."

Rusty nodded. "And if I took the job, when would you need me?"

"Mrs. Harding would like to leave as early as possible. The first of June is this Tuesday, so I think anytime the following week would work for her."

"Does Quintin know you've asked me?"

"No, he knows nothing of our plans. Mrs. Harding and I decided that she would tell him when things were a little more settled."

Rusty's mind wandered to the little boy in question. She could still see him at the front door of Briarly. Had he thought of her after that or had he gone back to his own world without a qualm? Rusty knew better than to ask. The answer might tempt her to handle her decision on emotions, and she couldn't do that. She needed to do some level-headed thinking right now.

"I don't think it fair that I leave you hanging on this subject, Mr. McCandles." Her voice was all business. "I'll have your answer by the time you leave Tuesday. Is there somewhere I can reach you?"

"I'll be here for dinner tomorrow night, and beyond that I'm staying at the Jarvis House. If you'd like, I'll stop back here on my way to the train station."

"Very well. I'll plan on that, thank you."

"Was there anything else you wished to know?"

Rusty shook her head. "I don't think so, although . . ." Rusty had a thought. "Your staff is very warm and kind, but when I was last there, I was a guest. Will they welcome someone new working in your home?"

"They were very impressed with you. I have no doubt that you'll all get along splendidly."

Again Rusty nodded, but another thought had come to mind. "I just remembered, two of my friends are getting married this summer. If I come to Briarly, would I be able to take time off to return here to Manitou and Boulder?"

"Absolutely. Just let me know your plans as soon as you know them."

"And my family. Where in Colorado Springs would my parents stay if they wanted to visit me?"

He blinked in surprise. "They would stay at Briarly for as long as they'd like."

"Oh." Rusty felt slightly taken aback at his matter-of-fact tone. Again her head cocked to one side. "I would be working for you, wouldn't I, Mr. McCandles? Right now I'm beginning to think I'd be a glorified houseguest."

"You would have a salary, Katherine, and days off to do with as you choose. I would naturally depend on you to take care of Quintin, but if you come, I would want you to see Briarly as your home for the summer. If there is anything we can do to make you more comfortable, or if Quintin needs something, you have only to ask. If you don't like the way the furniture is arranged in your room, you can change it. If your friends or family want to visit, they will be more than welcome. Have I made myself clear?"

"Yes. Thank you."

Rusty had a lot to think about indeed. The job sounded like a dream come true, but knowing very well how things were between Quintin and his father, she needed to be cautious about dreaming. That alone was enough to make her pause over getting involved. She would seek counsel with Paddy and Sammy, and she would pray.

Watching her face, Chase knew that she needed to be alone. It had been foolish of him to believe that if Paddy could spare her, Rusty would automatically agree to come. He could tell she wanted to, but there was also something holding her back. By the time he and Rusty parted, Chase assumed he would indeed be headed home to interview nannies.

27

"Do you wish someone would just tell you what to do?" Sammy asked of Rusty much later that day. Rusty smiled.

"No, I guess not. I keep asking myself, what's the worst thing that can happen?"

"And what do you come up with?"

Rusty shrugged. "That I'll be miserable and have to tell Mr. McCandles that I can't stay."

"Said like that, it doesn't sound bad at all," Paddy put in, "but it might be harder than you think."

"In that case," Rusty replied logically, "I'd have to ask myself what would be harder: staying on or telling Mr. McCandles that I have to leave. I'm not being naïve — saying goodbye to Quintin would be horrible — but I've tried to view all the options to see if I can make this work."

Paddy nodded. For having had only about three hours to think it over, Rusty had certainly come up with many possibilities.

"I am worried about one thing, Rusty."

Rusty had been looking at nothing in particular. She now centered on her aunt.

"You can't go in there with a mind to 'fix' things between Chase and Quintin." Sammy's voice was gentle but to the point.

"As much as the relationship bothers you, you can't have that attitude or plan."

"I honestly wasn't planning to do that, Sammy, but that doesn't mean it wouldn't have come to mind. Thank you."

The three of them fell silent, but the silence didn't last. Rusty had made up her mind.

"I'm going to go," she said softly. "I'll miss everyone here, but I think I should do this. Thank you, Uncle Paddy, for giving me this opportunity."

"You're welcome. We'll miss you too. Our loss is Quintin McCandles' gain."

Rusty smiled at the compliment. "Mr. McCandles told me he'll be coming to dinner tomorrow night."

Sammy nodded in affirmation. "Six o'clock."

"In that case, I'll tell him then." She fell

silent again and just thought about Quintin. She wanted to see him again and was certain they would have a wonderful time together.

"What will you do about the children's church schedule?" Paddy asked.

"I'll talk with Pastor tomorrow. That will still give me time to reconsider if it puts him in a spot. I know Tibby is going to faint."

"What day will you leave?" Sammy asked.

Rusty looked at her uncle. "What works for you?"

"Did he say anytime during the week of the seventh?"

"Yes."

"I think later would be better than earlier. Maybe Thursday or even Friday."

"Okay."

No one spoke for several minutes. Rusty was praying, still thanking God for this opportunity and asking for His help to do the job and be the person Quintin needed. At one point she glanced up to find Sammy's eyes on her.

"I'll miss you, Rusty" was all she said, but it was enough to send them both into tears.

Colorado Springs

Mrs. Whitley lost track of Quintin for several minutes, but she need not have worried.

313

Standing straight as a soldier, he was still in front of the window in the vestibule, his eyes on the front drive. She knew whom he was waiting for. The wise housekeeper suspected that the woman arriving was his favorite person in the world.

Mrs. Harding had been gone since the day before. It had been decided that she would be away before Miss Taggart arrived. Quintin had known of the plans only since the beginning of the week, but Mrs. Whitley couldn't help but ask herself if Mrs. Harding might not be hurt by Quintin's buoyant mood. The staff had never seen him so happy. He hadn't even cried at the prospect of not seeing Mrs. Harding for the entire summer. Of course time was a vague thing to a five-year-old, but Mrs. Whitley knew there was more to it than that.

The housekeeper was turning away from Quintin's vigil when Mr. McCandles wandered by. He'd been doing a bit of pacing and worrying himself. Chase was thinking about his last conversation with Rusty. He'd been very pleased to know that she was coming.

"That's great," he had said at least twice. "I'll come and get you. What day will you be finished there?"

"I don't need you to come," she'd told

him, "but thank you."

Chase had already been shaking his head. "I'll come for you; just tell me the day."

Rusty's chin had instantly gone in the air. "I'm not sure what day," she said, her eyes challenging him. "But I will get there on my own."

Chase opened his mouth to set her straight, but she cut back in.

"Mr. McCandles, I'll come over to Briarly on my own, and when I need to travel to Boulder or back here to Manitou, I'll also do that on my own. And that's my final word on the subject."

He hadn't been happy about her decision, and she knew it, but she never gave any hint of backing down. He'd had no choice but to let the matter drop. Chase now wished he had pushed the point and gone for her anyway.

Why, Chase? he found himself asking. *Why do you need to bring her here — so you won't have to worry? You shouldn't be worrying anyway. Is God in control or not?*

With this reminder, he turned, and leaving his son at the window, went back to his office. Quite sadly, it never occurred to him to speak to the boy or initiate any type of interchange. He didn't even notice that Quintin held his bear snugly in his arms.

Rusty stepped onto the platform and immediately hailed a porter. The porter, a young man with a preference for redheads, was happy to be of service to this petite woman with the determined glint in her lovely lavender eyes.

"I have a trunk," Rusty told the gawking porter. Not even she could miss his interest. "And I'll need a hack. Are you able to see to those things for me?"

"I certainly am," he told her with a smile. He was tempted to ask if the trunk meant she would be in town for a while, but the question remained inside of him for fear that she would report him to his superior. "If you'll come with me to the station and point out your trunk, I'll get right to it."

"Thank you."

The porter smiled at her and made light conversation as he got her trunk and saw her settled into a waiting carriage, but other than tipping him fairly and thanking him for his time, Rusty had nothing else to say. Indeed, she didn't look at him again. Had she done so, she would have seen the huge lift of his eyebrows when she told the hack driver that her destination was Briarly.

Quintin McCandles couldn't breathe. His

little chest rose but would not fall. She was here. Miss Taggart was in the front of the house, stepping lightly down from the carriage and smiling at the driver who had helped her. He had to tell someone. He had to let someone know! His little legs turned and he moved to the hallway, but it was empty. Panic was filling his breast when Mrs. Whitley came down the stairs. One look at the mute appeal on his face and her heart wrung with tenderness.

"Is she here, Quintin?"

All he could do was nod.

"I'll let her in, shall I?"

Again Quintin could only manage a nod, but as he did so the door opened. Mr. Whitley, the footman, carriage driver, and general handyman, had opened it. Quintin watched as he stepped back and then she was there.

Miss Taggart was the most wonderful person he'd ever known, and now she was coming in the front door. Every time he held his bear, he thought of her and tried not to cry, but he wouldn't merely have to think of her any longer.

He couldn't move. He wanted to run to her, but his legs wouldn't work. There was no need. The moment Rusty spotted him, she dashed across the vestibule, under the ornate archway, and into the foyer to scoop him up into her arms. Quintin's arms went around her. He heard her say his name, but he couldn't reply. His little face was buried in her neck, and he thought she smelled like flowers. A moment later he felt his feet touch the floor, and when he raised his head, he found her kneeling in front of him and smiling into his face. "Hello, Quintin McCandles."

"Hello, Miss Taggart," he said, feeling all at once shy.

"Now that," she declared, "is the first thing we must correct. My name is Aunt Rusty. Can you remember that?"

"Yes."

"And that's what you'll call me, do you understand?"

"Yes."

"How have you been?" She smiled at how much he wanted to please her.

"Very well, thank you."

"Is Mrs. Harding still here?"

"No. She left yesterday."

"And what did you do today to have fun?"

"I watched you come."

Rusty smiled. She didn't need an interpreter for that one. She was also relieved. It was not going to be a painful transition, at least not today. When she began suggesting things that he'd never done in his life, he was certain to panic, but for today he was glad to see her.

"Would you like to come and help me unpack?"

"I believe Mrs. Whitley planned on seeing to that."

Rusty looked up at the sound of Chase's voice and stood to full height, taking Quintin's hand without thought. Chase was glad she'd just now seen him. He'd come to the hallway in time to see her enfold Quintin in her arms. The scene had so touched him that if he'd been required to speak prior to that moment, he would have been at a painful loss.

"Hello, Mr. McCandles," Rusty acknowledged graciously.

"Hello, Katherine. How was your trip?"

"It was fine," she said, her eyes sparkling.

"Uneventful?"

Rusty laughed. "Very."

"I'm glad to hear it." Rusty watched as he turned to Mrs. Whitley. Rusty had smiled at her when she came in but otherwise had been wholly taken up with Quintin.

"Mrs. Whitley, has Miss Taggart met the rest of the staff?"

"I don't believe all of them, sir. Would you like me to see to it?"

"Please." He turned back to Rusty. "Mrs. Whitley is prepared to see to Quintin for the remainder of the day if you care to rest."

"Thank you," Rusty said, her gaze encompassing both of them, "but the trip just wasn't that taxing. I had hoped that Quintin and I could do some things."

"As you wish." Chase was at his most gracious. "If there is anything you need, please don't hesitate to ask."

"Thank you, Mr. McCandles," Rusty said to him. She then turned to Briarly's housekeeper. Mrs. Whitley was swift to respond.

"Miss Taggart, I don't believe you've met my husband." She indicated the man who had helped her after she'd paid the carriage driver. Marshall Whitley was fair-haired like his wife, with a quick smile and ready-to-please eyes. He'd come in to stand quietly in the background, his hat in his hand. Rusty went right over and shook his hand.

"Hello, Mr. Whitley. Thank you for taking care of my trunk."

"You're welcome, Miss Taggart. I'll just see that it gets upstairs to your room."

"Thank you. Are you going to lead the way?" Rusty asked Quintin.

He nodded. "You're in the same room."

Rusty's eyes grew with enthusiasm. "How nice. That's a beautiful room."

320

"My room is across the landing."

"We can visit each other." Her voice had dropped to a conspiratorial tone.

As usual, he nodded yes to everything she said. Rusty started toward the stairs. Just two steps later, Quintin took the lead. He went ahead of her, talking all the way.

Watching them, Chase suddenly knew why children were so drawn to her. She never said things to children and then looked to other adults with a teasing glint in her eye. Her conversations with children were strictly for them. What a special gift she had.

Chase returned to his office, a great peace filling his heart. He wouldn't think about the end of the summer when she had to go away, or how Quintin might take it. Right now he determined to be thankful that she had come for this time. As God's Word reminded him, tomorrow had enough worries of its own. Right now he would focus on today and give thanks.

28

"Can you tell me what this flower is?" Rusty asked of Quintin just three hours later. She was unpacked and settled, and they were off on what Rusty termed an "adventure."

"I think those are Shooting Stars."

"I think you're right. They're so wonderful, and the gardens here are so beautiful, Quintin. Don't you love them?"

He nodded but his eyes didn't drift to the flowers. As she had been since arriving, Rusty was keenly aware of his adoration. She'd been praying all morning that she would be very careful with this child's heart, and she did so again right now. He was so impressionable and sweet. Already she felt blessed to have him love her as he did.

"Well, now, I think that we can go inside for a while. Was Mrs. Harding reading a particular book to you?"

"We just finished one. She didn't start another because we ran out of time."

"So we get to pick one ourselves?"

Again the familiar nod.

"Well, let's go." She held out her hand. "I can't wait."

Just minutes later they were in the library, and Rusty was pulling books from the shelf in no particular order. She placed them on the library table, the room's only piece of furniture, and continued to pull some more. Watching her, Quintin felt alarmed. Mrs. Harding *never* let him choose from that many books. Rusty was intent on her task, so it took her a moment to notice his face.

"Quintin, what is it?"

"It's too much."

Rusty looked at the pile of books on the table and back at the little boy. "You think I chose too many books?"

"We're not supposed to."

Rusty knew right then that she could not listen to that for the rest of the summer. She glanced around and spotted Mr. McCandles across the drawing room. He was at his desk, head bent over his task.

"Come with me, will you please, Quintin?" Rusty took his hand and led the way toward Chase's office. The doors were open, and he saw them approaching. He began to stand, but Rusty stopped him.

"Please don't get up, Mr. McCandles. We just have a question." With that she looked to Quintin. "Quintin, will you please ask your father about the books?"

He looked as if she'd just asked him to spit on the carpet. He glanced at her and then at his father, his face frozen with surprise. Rusty took over.

"Quintin and I would like to know if there are some books in the library that we should not touch, or if you would rather we looked at only a few at a time?"

Chase shook his head. "All the books can be touched, and you may read or look at as many as you like."

"We can take them down from the shelves?"

"Certainly."

Rusty looked down to her side.

"Did you hear that, Quintin?"

"Yes."

"We can pick any books we want, and as many as we want," she reiterated.

He nodded, and she watched his little chest rise and fall with relief. Rusty smiled at him.

"Quintin, will you do me a favor and go back into the library and look at the books on the table? Take out anything that looks fun to read and put it in a separate stack. I'll join you in a minute."

He walked away to do as she bid. Rusty watched him move out of earshot and then turned back to Quintin's father.

"Did you mean it when you said I should come to you for anything I need, Mr. McCandles?"

"Absolutely," Chase answered without hesitation. He had come to his feet now but was still behind the desk.

"I'm feeling in something of a quandary," she admitted. "I took you quite literally when you said I should come with my own style and way of doing things, but as you can see, it's not that simple. The quandary comes as I realize that Mrs. Harding will be returning. I can't tell Quintin to forget all her rules, but by my actions I'll be saying just that. If you don't mind that we look at as many books as we wish, then this must be her rule. From the one other day Quintin and I spent together, I know she has many. What would you like me to do?"

Chase nodded. The reason Rusty had hesitated over coming was clear to him for the first time. He had determined just hours ago, however, that he was not going to look to the end of the summer.

"I'll speak with Quintin."

Rusty was surprised by this but very pleased. She stood to one side and then held her place. Halfway across the drawing room, Chase looked back at her.

"I want you with me, Katherine," he told her, and Rusty joined him without comment. "Quintin," his father spoke as soon as he entered the book-lined room. "I have something I need to tell you."

Rusty tried to ignore the painful way the child came to attention to listen to what her employer was saying.

"Mrs. Harding took good care of you, Quintin, and she did so in the way she thought was best. She had rules for you, and that was fine. Miss Taggart is here —"

"Aunt Rusty," Rusty boldly corrected him, and after only a glance at her, he started over.

"Aunt Rusty is going to have her own rules. When Mrs. Harding comes back she'll have her rules, but for now — for this summer — you are to do as Aunt Rusty instructs you. Do I make myself clear?"

"Yes, sir."

"What if we get dirty?" Rusty asked, and this time he didn't even glance at her.

"You can get dirty," Chase told his son.

"What if we don't do things on schedule?"

"You're to follow Aunt Rusty's schedule

of doing things, which means you might not go to the reading room on certain days or even eat at the set time. Is all of this clear to you, Quintin, or shall I explain something again?"

"Yes, sir — I mean, no, sir."

"Very good. I know I can trust you to be a good boy for Aunt Rusty and do as she says. She'll take good care of you."

"Yes, sir." Some of the rigidity left his posture when Chase placed a hand on his shoulder. Rusty was waiting with a smile when the little boy looked at her.

"Did you find a book you like?"

"Not yet."

"Well, we'll keep looking. Be sure to thank your father for coming in to talk to us."

"Thank you, sir."

"You're welcome. I'm glad I could help."

Rusty now smiled at Chase. "Thank you," she said softly. "I hope I won't disappoint you."

"Such a thing has never entered my mind."

Rusty gave him another grateful smile and stood aside as he went on his way. She turned her attention to Quintin and in no time at all they had found a book and replaced all the others. With only a small amount of coaxing, she talked Quintin into lying beneath the library table and starting their book there. It was going to take some time, but she was going to give him what she termed a "normal" summer. She knew they were well on their way when she looked over at one point to find his eyes on her.

"Do we want to be done with this book for the day?" Rusty asked, her hand going up to tenderly cup his cheek.

"No, but I'm hungry."

"I'm hungry too. Shall we ask Mrs. Whitley if we can eat in here under the table?"

"Yes," he said simply, his eyes alight with joy. He hadn't even hesitated. Rusty knew they were making progress.

Rusty came slowly down the stairs, not too tired, but feeling that she'd worked hard and done well. Quintin had been bathed, read to, and prayed with. He was now sound asleep. Tempting as it was to seek her own rest, something occurred to her as she was putting him to bed. She knew she wouldn't sleep until she checked into it. As she hoped, Mr. McCandles was still downstairs.

"I'm sorry to bother you, Mr. McCandles," Rusty said, standing at the doorway of the drawing room and watching her employer rise from one of the deep chairs —

the very one she'd slept in during her last visit to the McCandles home.

"It's no bother at all. Please be seated." Rusty complied, and he asked, "How did the first day go?"

"Very well, I think. Quintin is so delightful, but I'm just a little concerned about being so far from him during the night. The upstairs landing is so large, and our rooms are across from each other. His room sits at such an angle that I can't see him in his bed. I'm more than willing to sleep with my door open, or if you would like, I could sleep on the floor of his room."

"I appreciate your offer, Katherine, but I don't think you need to do that, at least not while I'm home. Quintin's room is the nursery, so I have a door that leads from my room into his. I'll just start sleeping with that door open. I'll come for you should he need you."

Rusty nodded, looking relieved. It was clear that she was on the verge of thanking him and rising from her chair, but for reasons Chase never thought to examine too closely, he didn't want that. He stopped her with a question.

"Did it help for me to speak with Quintin?"

"Yes, thank you very much. He has moments when he looks at me uncertainly, but since you spoke with him he has stopped saying, 'We can't do that.' And of course, that is what I hoped for."

Chase frowned. "I guess I've been remiss in not keeping a little closer eye on the way Mrs. Harding does things, but she told me she was strict, and that was the reason I hired her."

Rusty's head went to one side. She spoke with no censure in her tone, only curiosity. "Was there some reason you especially wanted someone who would be strict?"

"Yes. I feel that I was allowed to run altogether too wild when I was young. I wanted better for Quintin."

"And do you feel that you've accomplished that?"

Her question gave him pause, not because he caught any underlying message in her tone or face, but because he didn't think anyone would ask that unless that person thought he hadn't been completely successful. He was on the verge of asking her about her question when Mrs. Whitley came to the door.

"Will that be all for the night, sir?"

"Yes, Mrs. Whitley. Unless Miss Taggart wishes something."

"No, thank you," Rusty said as she rose.

"I'm tired and ready to turn in, but thank you for offering."

"You're very welcome. I hope you sleep well."

"Thank you."

With that Rusty bid one housekeeper and her employer goodnight. She made her way up the stairs, her mind still on the conversation with Chase. He had said he might have been remiss where Mrs. Harding was concerned. Rusty saw that as a hopeful sign. Maybe given enough time, time to see Quintin laughing and happy, he would want that for him all year and not just for the summer.

Down in the drawing room Chase eventually went back to his book, but like Rusty, the conversation stayed on his mind. Had he failed where Quintin was concerned? He simply didn't know. He hadn't answered Rusty's last question or been able to ask any more of his own. Was he relieved or not? He found himself with yet one more question for which he didn't have an answer.

"Mrs. Whit," as Rusty had come to call her, "if anyone is looking for us, Quintin and I will be in town."

Melinda Whitley took this announcement in stride, forcing herself not to look in Cook's direction, but she was not as calm as she appeared. Nearly a week of living with Rusty Taggart had taught her many things, but she was still not beyond surprises.

"Is Whit taking you, Rusty?" the older woman felt free to ask. She used Rusty's nickname also, since Quintin's summer companion had insisted upon familiar names as soon as she'd met all the staff.

"No, I found a pony trap in the stable, and Quintin and I get along famously with Dobbins, so we're going to give it a try. We'll be gone only a few hours."

"Just a few hours," Quintin echoed from her side. He was already a different boy in her care.

"Would you mind if I asked Whit to take you in the carriage?" Mrs. Whitley tried again. "I know he wouldn't mind."

Rusty shook her head and said with a smile, "Please don't. I might need a little help with the trap, but Quintin and I want to go for a ride on our own."

Mrs. Whitley sighed, but she had to smile. There was a time when she'd had Rusty's energy, but never was she so imaginative. It was something to see.

"All right. I'll ask him to check on you. When did you want to leave?"

"As soon as we can get the trap ready.

We're off to see to it now."

Cook and Mrs. Whitley watched as Rusty and Quintin pilfered cookies from the pan on the table, called a thank you, and nearly skipped out the door. In something of a state of shock, the housekeeper finally looked at Cook. That woman's voice brought her back to earth.

"Melinda, you'd better get Whit."

"Oh, yes." Mrs. Whitley sprang into action, all the while hoping that something would be wrong with the pony trap. She knew after the first weekend that she couldn't run to Mr. McCandles every time Rusty did something out of the ordinary, but right now she was strongly tempted to seek him out. Thankfully there was no need; her husband was nearby and saw to everything.

Within 20 minutes he had them ready to go, and under his watchful eyes he was able to report back to the kitchen that Rusty did know what she was doing. Whit had also been able to get an approximate time of return out of her and added that if she wasn't back within three hours, he would come looking for her. Knowing Rusty would never do anything to bring harm to Quintin, and barring the unforeseen, the staff knew they would have to force themselves to rest. It was sure to be a long afternoon.

29

Chase McCandles was standing at the window of an upstairs bedroom when he spotted the pony trap carrying Rusty and his son. Certain his eyes were playing tricks on him, he blinked and did a double take, but it was all too real. He hit the stairs at a full run and arrived in the kitchen to find Cook and the Whitleys. He wasted no time in small talk.

"Where are Katherine and Quintin?" he asked, his breathing labored.

"On their way to town," Mrs. Whitley answered honestly.

"In the trap?"

"Yes, sir."

"Saddle my horse, Whit."

"I'm on my way, sir."

Chase didn't even watch him leave. He turned right back to Mrs. Whitley.

"Did they say where they were going?"

"Just into town, sir — I believe for lunch. Whit told Rusty that he would come looking for her if she wasn't back in the time she said."

"How long was that?"

"Three hours."

Chase shook his head but didn't speak. He knew she was impetuous, but this had never occurred to him. Anything could happen to a pony cart. The thought of Quintin being harmed was more than he could take. He knew he might be overreacting, but he wasn't going to turn back now.

"I'm sorry, sir," Mrs. Whitley was saying, feeling she'd failed when she let Rusty go. "I know that Rusty would never do anything to harm Quintin, and Whit worked with her and said she handles the reins very well, but I'm sorry, sir."

"It's all right." Chase was calmed by her words. She was right, of course. Rusty would not be foolhardy. "I'll just see how they're doing and go with them into town. Don't look for us anytime soon. We'll come right back only if there's a problem."

"Very well, sir. I hope everything is all right."

Chase had the very same hope as he thanked her, slipped into the coat Cook had fetched for him, and moved out the door. Moments later he was in Shelby's saddle, headed toward town at a full gallop and praying all the while that Rusty and Quintin were safe, but also that he would keep his head in this new situation.

"Quin! Do you see that bird?" Rusty exclaimed, bringing the trap to a stop in the middle of the road. The little boy gasped as he followed her pointing finger.

"He was big!" he exclaimed, and both of them looked over the small lake they were passing. The bird was winging his way toward a copse of trees on the other side, and the two travelers watched in delight and awe.

"What type do you suppose it was?" Rusty asked with a genuine desire to know.

"It looked like a prairie falcon," Quintin said with confidence. "I wish I had my book."

"We'll have to check when we get home. Wouldn't it be fun to see the nest and eggs? Do you suppose the eggs are large too?"

"They might be. The book will have that too. Mrs. Harding always found that for me."

Rusty sighed. It was such a special treat. "I'm so thankful we were able to see that bird. God makes such wonderful creatures, doesn't He, Quin?"

"Like birds," he agreed.

"Yes, indeed."

Rusty slapped the pony's reins and they were off again. Briarly was not far from the main streets of town, but they were not quite there when Chase caught up to them. He rode up easily, looking more as if he were out for a ride than searching for them. When Rusty realized who it was, she brought the trap to a stop.

"Well, Quin, look who's joined us. Hello, Mr. McCandles."

"Hello." He spoke calmly enough, but Rusty caught a look in his eye as he swung down from the saddle. "I thought I might join you."

"Certainly," she said, but some of the delight had left her. Had she done something wrong? Had he gotten bad news? Rusty knew she would have to wait to find out, but she was rather uncomfortable about the direction of her thoughts.

"We were just going into town to have lunch and do a little shopping," she explained, her voice somewhat subdued. "Won't it be nice to have your father join us, Quin?"

The little boy nodded but didn't comment.

He was still preoccupied with the possibility of seeing more birds. Rusty kept her eyes on her employer, but he said nothing else until he'd pulled himself back up into Shelby's saddle and they had started down the road.

"Where were you planning to eat?" he asked Rusty over the clip-clop of the hooves.

"I'm not sure. Can you make a recommendation?" She was still feeling uncertain.

Chase nodded. "I think the Antlers Hotel."

"Have you been there, Quin?" Rusty tried to keep things light for him.

"No. Aunt Rusty, what will we eat?"

"What are you hungry for?"

Quintin only looked at her.

"Not sure?" she pressed him.

He shook his head no, and Rusty let it drop. Thinking he might not be hungry for lunch just yet, she considered that they might look around town first. She said as much to Chase.

"Whatever you want to do is fine. There's a small livery near the hotel," he directed her. "When we get near that block, we'll stop and leave the horses there."

Rusty stared up at his profile for a moment, but his look gave nothing away. It never occurred to her how it might feel to have Chase McCandles coldly angry with

338

her. She was learning swiftly that she didn't like it at all. They made the rest of the journey in silence.

Once in town, Rusty swiftly saw the livery and directed the pony to the open double doors. She had never personally left an animal at the livery, but she'd watched others do it and hoped it would be as easy as it seemed and not too costly. Unaware that Chase had already handed Shelby's reins to the young man who approached, she was surprised when he was almost instantly at her side, his hand coming out to help her alight. He reached for Quintin the moment Rusty was on the ground, and the little boy moved away from the horse and toward his companion as soon as his father set him down. Chase stepped over to have a word with the stableboy, and a moment later they started down the street. Rusty wasn't given time to take care of any of it.

As they walked along she tried to be calm, but it wasn't working. The day was going to be ruined if she didn't find out what was bothering him. Very aware of Quintin's small hand within her own, she kept her voice light as she addressed his father.

"Is everything all right, Mr. McCandles?"

"Yes," he said without hesitation, but Rusty was not convinced.

"You're going to think me fanciful," she tried again, her voice calm and even, "but I almost had the impression that you'd gotten word from my family and needed to find me."

For the first time Chase really looked at her. Her face was pale, and her eyes were sober and vulnerable. He came to a stop, and she naturally stopped with him.

"I've had no word from your family or bad news of any kind. I'm sorry you were frightened about that. I might have overreacted by coming after you," he began hesitantly, his eyes going down to Quintin at one point. "But I was concerned when I saw you in the trap. Ponies can be unpredictable."

"I thought you were angry," Rusty said softly.

"No," Chase assured her truthfully. "It was not my intention to ruin your outing, but I must admit that I never dreamed you'd drive into town on your own."

Rusty nodded. She could explain all of her reasons to him, but now was not the time.

"Will you be home this evening, sir — possibly reading in the drawing room?"

"That is my plan," he said, his eyes saying more than his words.

Rusty smiled at him as if he'd just suggested an outing. She looked down at

Quintin, who had been staring up at both of them the whole time.

"Well, now, Quin, what sounds good to you? Shall we eat or do a little shopping?"

"I'm hungry."

"Very well. Was it the Antlers Hotel, Mr. McCandles?"

"Yes, they have wonderful food. Shall I show you?" he offered.

"Please."

They weren't far from the front door of the hotel, and with Chase accompanying them, they were almost immediately seated in the dining room. As a waiter brought them menus, Rusty's complete attention was on Quintin as she tried to help him decide.

"Let's see. They have chicken. Do you want chicken?"

He stared at her as he'd been doing since she first mentioned eating out.

"No? Okay, how about pork? Do you like pork, Quin?"

Again he just looked at her.

Rusty went back to the menu, read some more, and then turned again to Quintin. She was somewhat flummoxed when she saw that tears had gathered in his eyes.

"Quin." Her voice was soft and gentle, the menu put aside. "What is it, sweetheart?"

He stared at her, tears welling just at his

lids but not spilling.

"Did Mrs. Harding never bring you here?" Rusty tried again.

He shook his head no, still looking miserable.

Chase watched all of this in silence but then spoke.

"Tell me, Quintin, where did you eat lunch when you came to the reading room with Mrs. Harding?"

Quintin began to get out of his chair, but Rusty stopped him with a hand to his arm.

"You can tell your father from your seat, Quin."

He looked at her in misery.

"We ate at Mrs. Reynolds'," he said just before he broke down. "I don't want to eat paper." With that he began to cry in earnest.

Rusty looked to her boss. "Is Mrs. Reynolds' a business or a private home?"

"A private home. She and Mrs. Harding are friends."

Understanding hit Rusty before it did Chase. She moved her chair close and put an arm around him.

"It's all right, Quin. He's never eaten out before, has he, Mr. McCandles?"

"I don't know," Chase admitted, and Rusty felt angry enough to shout at him. Just looking at her, Chase could tell she was upset with his answer, but she didn't pursue the matter. Indeed, Rusty knew well that now was not the time. She turned her attention to the little boy in her arms.

"It's all right, love. Let me tell you how it works."

The waiter chose that moment to return. "Is everything all right, ma'am?"

"Oh, thank you for asking. Do you have chocolate milk?"

"Certainly, ma'am, or hot cocoa."

"I think the chocolate milk. I would also like you to bring the fried chicken with all the trimmings."

"For one, ma'am?"

"For now, yes, thank you, but we'll also want to see the dessert tray when we are finished."

"Certainly. And you, sir?" He turned to Chase.

"I'll order later as well."

"The first thing we must do," Rusty spoke as soon as the waiter left their table, "is dry your face." A soft white handkerchief came from up her sleeve, and just a minute later she had Quintin dry and somewhat calmer. "The next thing we must do is talk about eating in a restaurant." She had cupped his small face in her equally small hands and made sure that he was looking directly at her.

"We don't eat paper, Quintin James McCandles," she said with a kind smile. "The papers that are given to us are called menus, and we read them to see what foods the restaurant serves. Do you know what I ordered for you?"

He shook his head no.

"I ordered chicken and chocolate milk. Doesn't that sound wonderful?"

"Yes."

"I think so too. I just might have the same. And when we're all finished with our meal, we can have dessert!"

He nodded, his breath coming with only a small shudder. Rusty smiled into his eyes and waited for him to smile in return.

"Even though you can't read, Quin," she said next, reaching back toward her plate, "I want you to look at this menu. I'll look over your shoulder and make certain I want to order the chicken, but you just study the words."

Rusty placed the large menu card in his hands and then bent so she could see it from his side. All the foods described sounded very tempting, but Rusty's mind was only half on the words.

You have no right to grow angry with him, Rusty. You knew the situation when you came.

Grow up and stop being surprised by how little he knows about his son!

With this little pep talk, Rusty sat back in her chair. In truth the chicken did sound good to her, and she was getting a headache trying to read the small, curly letters. She hoped the waiter would return soon so she could order a cup of coffee.

"Are you still going to have the chicken?"

Until that moment she had not been aware of Chase's scrutiny.

"Yes, I am. What did you decide?"

I've decided that we need to talk about more than your coming into town today, but I don't know how to go about it. Aloud he said, "I'm going with the chicken too." He set his menu aside. "What plans did you have for after lunch? Are you shopping for something in particular?"

"No, just a little browsing. My sister's birthday is next month, but other than that I don't have anything on my list."

"If Quintin needs something, I hope you'll get it for him. I'm not sure if I told you, but Mrs. Harding saw to his clothing. I have accounts in most of the stores in town, so feel free to shop for whatever he needs. Also, if you find you need something for yourself because of the job, don't hesitate to purchase it."

Rusty nodded, but in truth she didn't have a clue as to what that might be. It was, however, the type of thing she was coming to expect. Chase McCandles was very good at seeing to everyone's needs without having to get involved. He gave orders in the kindest, most gracious way, and everyone rushed to do his bidding. Rusty had never known anyone like him. His care of those who worked for him could not be faulted — she'd seen this before — but it was as if Quintin were invisible.

It was a relief to have Quintin's food arrive. Rusty was able to order her coffee, which took her mind from problems she could not solve. They ate and enjoyed their meal without incident. Afterward, they shopped as planned, and Chase saw them all the way back to Briarly. Anyone looking on would never have guessed at the storm clouds gathering in Rusty's heart.

Quintin's companion knew she was growing more angry with her employer every day and that she must repent of her feelings, but it was not going smoothly. She was fighting God on this issue and spent the rest of the day giving the situation to Him. By the time she put Quintin to bed, she felt at peace. She was able to go to Briarly's drawing room that evening ready to explain to Mr. McCandles why she had gone to town. She did so asking God to help her take any rebuke that might be coming and to remember: As much as she was treated like a family member, she was still an employee of the McCandles house.

30

"I was surprised that you would take the pony trap to town, Katherine." Chase had wasted no time. He had asked Rusty how the remainder of the day had gone and then plunged right into the subject of that afternoon. He was not angry or upset, but he clearly wanted answers.

"I wanted to do it for Quintin."

Chase still didn't get it. "I'm not sure I understand. You didn't seem to have any specific plans. Why did you need to go into town at all?"

"To give Quintin an outing, and I'd have done so on my second day here if I'd realized he'd never eaten in a restaurant."

"But Whit could have taken you; you must realize that."

"Yes, I do, but Quin is terrified of the

horses. I thought that if we started out with Dobbins, who he's more comfortable with, we would have taken a positive first step toward seeing that he had nothing to fear."

It was just as Mrs. Whitley had told him. Rusty would never deliberately do anything to harm Quintin. He didn't think her capable of this much forethought, but all of this had been completely planned out, and all for Quintin's well-being. Without warning, however, he thought of her in the alley in Makepeace.

"Tell me, Katherine, what would you have done if you'd encountered another group of young men? Had you even thought of that?"

"I haven't dwelt on the incident, but yes, I have thought it out. In the first place I would not have taken any short cuts and put myself in an alley, and if someone had tried something anyway, I would have shouted for a policeman. I wonder how bold those men would have been if the eyes of Makepeace had been on them. If something had happened today, I had decided to shout and cause a huge scene."

Chase now saw why she had insisted on coming alone on the train. She was determined not to let the past hold her down.

"Were you not afraid at all?"

"Maybe just a little," she confessed, "but

I'm trying to work with Quintin on his fears. What kind of hypocrite does it make me to tell Quin not to fear the horses when I won't even go into town?"

She had stumped him. He sat and stared at her, at a complete loss as to what to say.

"May I ask *you* something, Mr. McCandles?"

"Yes, of course."

"Did you object to our going to town, going in the pony trap, or both?"

"My biggest fear was the pony trap. I was afraid that you or Quintin might be harmed if something startled that animal and you lost control."

"I won't take it out again," she told him immediately. "I can work with Quin around the animals and still leave them in their stalls."

"Why is it so important that Quintin be comfortable around the horses?"

"Because it's normal," Rusty said before she thought.

Chase blinked at her, and Rusty knew she would have to do some backtracking.

"Normal?" His voice had gotten rather cool.

Rusty knew there was a wise way to word this subject and an unwise way. She opted for the first.

"Maybe 'normal' is the wrong word, Mr. McCandles. I'm sure it makes me sound arrogant, and I honestly don't mean to be. The truth of the matter is, I grew up differently than Quintin is growing up." There was so much Rusty wanted to say, but she stuck to the subject at hand. "I was around horses from the time I was very young, and although I was taught caution, I didn't fear them. Horses, just like stairways and honeybees, are a part of our world. I don't want Quintin to be afraid of any of those things — cautious when he needs to be, but not fearful."

There was so much more to Rusty Taggart than was first apparent. Chase thought he understood that, but now he saw that he'd missed some important elements. The main difference between Rusty and Mrs. Harding suddenly became very clear to him. Mrs. Harding had taught Quintin manners and all that could be learned through books. Rusty was trying to teach Quintin about life — honeybees and restaurants — the unavoidable aspects of living in this world.

"I've prepared myself for any rebuke you feel I need, Mr. McCandles," Rusty spoke when the silence lengthened, her heart trying to be thankful for whatever he might say. "If you think Quintin would do better with someone else, I'll understand if you feel a need to dismiss me."

"No." Chase's head was shaking adamantly. "You're not dismissed. That never occurred to me. I want you to stay on. I even think your using the pony trap is fine, just as long as you stay here at Briarly, and Whit or I know of your plans. I'm very pleased with the way you handle Quintin. Please rest assured on that count."

Rusty took him at his word. Her heart lifted with the knowledge that he was pleased with her performance. She'd spoken with more bravado than she felt. She would never have given him a word of argument if he'd dismissed her, but she would have missed Quintin like her own child.

Watching her, Chase knew that this was the perfect time to ask her why she had been upset with him at the Antlers Hotel, but he couldn't make himself do it. Things were at such a calm right now, and his heart felt light just knowing how much she wanted for Quintin and how far she was willing to go. As with the first night, he could see that she was ready to stand and bid him goodnight. And again, as the first night, something inside of him didn't want that. He stopped her with a question.

"Which sister has a birthday next month?"

It was a remarkably simple question, but

it did the trick. They talked of nothing in particular yet touched on everything for the next hour. When Rusty realized how late it was, she was very apologetic.

"Look at the time!" Rusty came to her feet. "I'm so sorry. I've disrupted your entire evening."

"Not at all. I enjoyed our talk." Indeed, if he could have thought of some other way to hold her, he would have done so, but she was on her way up the stairs just a short time later. Chase Jefferson McCandles, a man very comfortable and accustomed to being on his own, wondered at his own train of thought. Maybe he was more lonely than he realized, but was that possible? How could a person be lonely and not know it? He thought the whole idea ludicrous, but he couldn't quite dismiss it from his mind. He read for a time, but the question governed his thoughts for the rest of the evening. By bedtime he was even asking himself if it might be time to look for another wife. He was still wondering if the idea had merit when he finally drifted off to sleep.

"Come on now," Rusty urged her young charge. "Just pull it off your bed."

Quintin's eyes were saucerlike, but he was doing as he was told.

"Do I fold it?"

"No, I've got my counterpane, and Mrs. Whit gave me two more blankets."

"Why do we need them?"

"For our fort. You can't build a fort without lots of blankets and bedspreads."

He looked completely at sea.

"I'll show you," she said, but he didn't reply, following her in silence as they moved into the upstairs hallway and toward the stairs, yards of cloth trailing in their wake.

They were conquering one room at a time. As the days had passed, Rusty had been showing Quintin that his home was to be lived in, not worshiped. She hadn't used those words, of course, but by her actions it was slowly dawning on him. He had always been at ease in the breakfast room and his own bedroom, but now he was coming and going into the library, touching books, and even leaving things a little out of order. The kitchen was also a place of comfort now, as right along with Rusty he "stole" cookies and asked for food between meals if he was hungry.

They had made splendid headway in the bathroom, splashing the walls and getting suds on the floor, all of which they cleaned up before leaving. Quintin looked forward to bathtime as he never had before. They had even played hide-and-seek in the drawing room twice. In one way this game was the most helpful at teaching him to enjoy his home, since it always spilled over to the rest of the house. Today they were headed into the dining room.

Rusty had never in her life seen a dining room table the size of the one at Briarly. Her brother and sisters would be mad with envy if they could see the fort she was planning to build. They had built forts under their tables at home on almost a weekly basis, but none of them could compare to the size of this one.

"We're going to the dining room?" Quintin asked when Rusty turned right at the bottom of the stairs.

"That's right," she answered in a singsong voice. "We're going to make the best fort in the whole wide world."

"In here?"

"Yes, it's perfect!"

Quintin's look was more than dubious, so Rusty just laughed.

"Now, we'll need to cover both ends of the table and this whole side," she instructed, referring to the side nearest the door, "but we'll leave the other side open so we can look out onto the veranda and the garden. Won't that be great?"

As had been happening for almost two weeks, Rusty's enthusiasm was contagious. In moments Quintin's hesitancy fell away, and he was helping Rusty throw the spreads over the top of the table and position them just right. Moved gently so as not to scratch, the chairs helped hold things in place, and with the aid of a few more blankets, all was in readiness. Rusty scrambled beneath without a word and waited for Quintin to join her.

It took a few seconds, but the look on his face was worth every moment. With the light coming from the French doors off the veranda, Rusty could see she had delighted him yet again. Short as she was, Rusty sat nearly upright, and as soon as she giggled, Quintin flew into her lap.

"I love you, Aunt Rusty."

"Oh, Quin," Rusty breathed. "I love you. Aren't we great fort builders?"

"Yes." He looked around. "It's dark in here." His voice was hushed.

"Yes, it is. Don't you love it?"

He nodded, his eyes big and bright with wonder.

"Now, you go up to my bed and your bed and gather all the pillows you can carry. I'll find the book we're reading and tell Mrs. Whitley that we *must* have lunch in the fort today."

"Okay." He scrambled out and dashed off to do as she bid. It did Rusty a great deal of good to hear him run up the stairs. Such a thing had been utterly forbidden as she was growing up and also at the orphanage, but this situation called for new rules and standards. Moving a bit more sedately, Rusty made her way to the kitchen. As she hoped, she found Cook and Mrs. Whitley.

"Mrs. Whit," she said, "May Quin and I have our lunch under the dining room table today? We don't expect you to wait on us." She always said that. "We'll come and get everything, but we don't want you to outfit the breakfast room when we're not going to be in there."

"That's fine, Rusty," Mrs. Whitley always enjoyed saying. "Cook and I will bring everything to you. Sandwiches might be easiest."

"I think so too, and those short round glasses that won't tip so easily.

"Lemonade?"

"Perfect. With lots of sugar please."

"Cookies or some of the cake?"

"Cookies, so we won't need forks. Oh! Would you please ask Whit to bring the Gramophone to us? I think we need a little music."

"Certainly."

Rusty thanked them as she always did,

making them feel as if they'd made her day, and went on her way. The two older women smiled at each other.

"Have I mentioned that I'm glad she's here?" Cook asked Melinda.

"I think just about every time she comes into the kitchen."

"Did you think it was boring around here before she came?"

"No. We were never out of things to do, but I guess it was pretty quiet."

"You must be speaking of Rusty," Whit said as he came from the small porch off the kitchen. The women laughed at how obvious it was. Melinda took great pleasure in telling her husband that Rusty needed the Gramophone under the dining room table. They laughed all over again at the stunned look on his face.

"Chase, come in!" Pastor Jeremy Radke stood with a smile. "Have a seat."

"Thank you, Pastor."

"What brings you by today?"

"I just thought I'd say hello," Chase replied, but Jeremy thought there might be something on his mind.

"How are things with Rusty and Quintin?"

"Fine," Chase told him, but Jeremy wondered why he wasn't convinced. He'd only been with this church body for two years, and it was taking some time to get to know Chase McCandles. The affluent businessman was a very private individual, and sometimes Jeremy was at a loss as to how to get close to him. Many times Chase had come to him with questions concerning the Scriptures — he was very open to learning — but nothing personal was ever mentioned. He certainly traveled a lot and that made fellowship even harder.

"Well, good. Quintin certainly seems to be enjoying her."

Chase looked at him and wondered how he knew that, but before he could ask him, Jeremy surprised him.

"I'm starting a men's Bible study, Chase. There are four of us right now, and we hope to get started in about three weeks. I'd like it if you could join us." Jeremy could see that his words had stumped him but did not back down. "Right now it looks as though we'll be meeting on Tuesday nights. We're going to study the book of Mark. You think about it, and I'll check back with you."

"All right," Chase finally managed. He wondered if maybe trying the study might not be a good idea; however, he did not commit himself. "Thank you," he said, standing.

Jeremy saw him to the door, and Chase was on his way just a short time later, his mind only half on what the pastor had said. As had become the norm, he was once again thinking of Rusty, and this time Quintin was on his mind as well. Pastor Radke had known that Quintin and his companion were getting along well together, but Chase hadn't checked with Rusty nearly as often as he'd planned. Tonight he would rectify that.

31

As soon as Chase left the church and pastor's office, he posted a letter to a man in Boulder and headed for home. At Briarly he came through the kitchen, and since he had mail for the staff, left it with Cook.

"Are Miss Taggart and Quintin indoors or out today?" he asked of her.

"They're in the dining room, sir," Cook filled in.

Chase thanked her and moved in the direction of his office, planning to say hello on his way past. His mind was still moving back and forth between his son's companion and his conversation with Pastor when he entered the dining room and stopped short. Protruding from what looked like every blanket in the house was a small pair of high-buttoned shoes. The lacy edge of a petticoat and the hem of a dark checked skirt could also be seen. Chase watched as the shoes crossed, uncrossed, and recrossed at the ankle.

Staring in fascination, Chase suddenly realized someone was talking.

"Will you read that part again?"

"The part about the bear?"

"Yes. He's so big."

"Yes, he is! I think he scares me."

Quintin laughed. "I'll protect you."

"You're so brave, Quin. What would I do without you?"

There was more giggling, and the feet disappeared altogether. A moment later, the sound of music drifted out from under the table. Chase's head came up and he stared out across the veranda at absolutely nothing. Some moments passed before he heard a noise behind him. He turned to find Mrs. Whitley standing out in the hall. She was smiling at the stunned look on his face.

"It looks as though you're having fun around here," he said as he joined her and saw the sparkle in her eye.

"If the giggles coming from under that table are any indication, you're right."

"How long have they been under there?"

"Since an hour before lunch."

Chase looked back into the room. "How can she see to read to him?"

"The front is open to the veranda. They've been in and out all day."

Chase shook his head and looked back down at the table.

"You could go under with them," the shrewd housekeeper said.

Chase looked and saw that she was serious, but he didn't respond. Mrs. Whitley made no further comment. Neither did she stay to see what he would decide. Chase watched her walk toward the kitchen and then looked back to the table. Only a moment passed before he turned, went through the drawing room, and into his office. He needed to tell his son that he was leaving for a few days, but that could wait. He opted to spend some time on the papers that showed the land he wanted to develop in Pueblo and not to interrupt them. Since he had to leave the next afternoon, his trip was the more pressing matter at the moment. Just seconds after the plat map was open in front of him, he forgot all about wanting to say hello to Rusty or speak with his son.

"Okay now, put your hands here and pull yourself up." Quintin put his hands on the tree, but he didn't really try to climb. He picked at the bark a little, plucked at a low leaf, and finally dropped his hands.

"I've never climbed a tree," he said, picking up a stick from the ground to fiddle with.

"But wouldn't you like to try?" Rusty asked him. "I'm coming up right behind you."

Quintin looked at her in uncertainty.

"You'll like it," she coaxed him. "You can see for miles. We can pretend we're sailing on the high sea." Rusty watched him carefully. "There might be a nest," she encouraged, but he was having none of it.

Quintin dropped onto his knees and began to write in the dirt and leaves on the ground.

"Quin?"

"I'm hungry."

Rusty saw it for the stall tactic it was but decided to let it go for the moment.

"Let's go get something to eat. We'll come back and climb the tree later."

He seemed a little easier with this suggestion and gladly raced her back to the kitchen door when she challenged him. When she'd first come, his racing gait was nothing short of pathetic, but his stride was lengthening now, and he was holding his own very nicely.

Cook was not at all surprised to see them when they tumbled in through the back door and proclaimed they needed food. She immediately went for the tray that she had learned to keep handy. Without even bothering to wash their hands, they feasted on fruit, nuts, and a tin of crackers. Cook also had ginger water that she kept cool in the pantry. They were just partway through this sumptuous snack when Kimberly, one of Briarly's part-time workers, came in and saw them.

"Oh, there you are, Rusty. Mr. McCandles wants to see Quintin."

"Oh, all right. Thank you, Kimmy." This request was not new to her, so she simply said, "Did you hear that, Quintin? You can go see your father, and then we'll finish our snack."

"All right."

Rusty rose to move from the room, but Quintin held back.

"What is it, Quin?"

"I'm not clean."

Rusty stared at him. He had a little mud on his chin where the ginger water had mixed with the dust, but to Rusty he looked like a typical little boy.

"You're fine," she said at last.

"My face and hands aren't clean," he reiterated, his eyes growing worried.

"Quintin." Her voice was very gentle, but she was not going to panic as he was. "Your father wants to see you. He won't care how you look. Come now."

He followed, but his eyes had taken on the panicked look she'd seen whenever they broke the old rules. Rusty led the way to the drawing room, but she had to stop twice and wait for him. Once they had covered half the distance of the long, elegant room, Rusty stopped.

"I'll wait for you in the library, Quin. Just come for me when you're through." Rusty thought this was the end of it, but she was wrong. She began to turn in the direction of the library, but Quintin stood stock still. At that point Rusty wished she had washed him. It seemed so silly when they were going right back out, but at the moment Rusty wished she'd taken a rag to him in the kitchen. She knelt down in front of Quintin and tried to explain.

"Do you remember that day your father told you we could get dirty? We were right in the library, and he said not to worry about it."

Quintin was miserable. He couldn't even nod and agree with her. Young as he was, he well remembered this as one of Mrs. Harding's firmest rules. *You must be on your best behavior and look your best when your father calls you into his office.* Now Aunt Rusty was telling him none of it mattered. What should he do?

Neither Rusty nor Quintin was aware that Chase had been watching them. He'd seen them start across the room, and he'd watched as Rusty knelt on the floor. His son looked very upset, and he debated whether to get involved. He knew that Rusty's authority was of little use if he as the parent undermined her. When they continued to talk in the middle of the drawing room, however, he felt he had to step in.

Rusty heard him approach, and rather than stand to her feet, she only sat back on her heels and remained on the floor. Chase grabbed an ottoman, brought it over close, and sat on it.

"Is everything all right?" Chase asked of Rusty, but she immediately looked to Quintin.

"Do you want to tell your father, Quin?"

He shook his head, tears coming to his eyes. Rusty's heart broke. What a horrible, painful way to grow up. Such fear, and without purpose. Rusty sighed, this time not caring who heard. She spoke with her eyes still on the younger McCandles.

"He was afraid to come to you with a dirty face and hands."

"It's all right, Quintin," his father said in his usual, quiet way. He felt very moved by his son's upset and by what he saw in Rusty's face. She looked shaken. "I understand that you're playing," he continued kindly.

"Mrs. Harding —" Quintin began but stopped, his hands wringing together with frustration.

"Is that what Mrs. Harding expected, Quintin," his father pressed him, "that your hands must be clean when I sent for you?"

He nodded, still miserable. When he sniffed loudly, Chase produced a large white handkerchief. He didn't help his son wipe his face or blow his nose, but when Quintin was through he put the cloth back in his pocket as a matter of course.

"You don't need to clean up when I call you into my office, Quintin. And today I can tell you right here what I need."

Hearing this, Rusty began to rise.

"Please don't go, Katherine. You'll need to hear this too." He waited until she had settled back on her heels. "I'm going out of town on business tomorrow, Quintin. I have plans to be gone a few days, but if it's more than that, I'll send word."

Quintin nodded, his eyes still looking as though he thought he were in trouble. Rusty could hardly stand it. She couldn't look at Quintin or his father. It was a relief when Chase stood, presumably to return to his office.

"Plans for the afternoon?" he asked of Rusty, who knew it was time to come to her feet. Chase's hand was there to assist her, and she thanked him, unaware of the way her face showed all her emotions.

"Yes," she tried to sound as normal as possible. "I think we might read for a time, or maybe we'll draw."

Chase nodded. Something was very wrong. Rusty had only glanced at him, but he could still see that she was completely distraught over something. He was strongly tempted to speak with her immediately, but reminding himself that he needed to seek her out that evening anyway, he held off.

"Well, don't let me stop you," he said, knowing Rusty would not feel free to go without his leave.

"Thank you," she said briefly before they moved off with Rusty leading the way to the kitchen. Rusty's emotions threatened to overwhelm her, and she thought it would be a blessing if Quintin just wanted to finish his snack and draw for a time. Cook had left things just as they were, and for the space of several minutes, Rusty thought she would get her wish.

"I thought we were going to climb the tree," Quintin said between bites of pear.

Rusty shook her head. She wouldn't have

tried to coerce him for the world. "You don't want to Quin, and I don't want to force you." Her voice was gentle. She didn't want him to feel any guilt.

"But you said there might be a bird's nest."

"That's true, there might be. Would you like me to climb up and look?"

"You'll do that?"

"I certainly will," Rusty was able to tell him with a smile. At the moment she wanted to lay the world at his feet.

"What if you fall?"

"I won't fall. I've been climbing trees since I was just a little girl."

Quintin gazed at her in awe. They finished the snack moments later.

"Well, Quin, what's it to be? Drawing, reading, or tree climbing?"

"Tree climbing."

"Okay, let's go."

Rusty was tired, but she wouldn't have denied him for the world. They thanked Cook and headed back outside. Some of Rusty's fatigue fell away as she watched Quintin's excitement. He climbed into the tree with her even after finding that it didn't have a nest. Rusty chose to put the earlier experience behind her and be thankful for all that God had done so far. In doing this, their trek into the woods turned out to be a wonderful adventure.

The evening was passing swiftly when Chase climbed the stairs. He hadn't seen Rusty the rest of the day, and for some reason he felt compelled to speak with her before she retired. It wasn't at all unusual for her to come down and get something cold to drink after she'd put Quintin to bed, but tonight she hadn't done that. Chase speculated about what he'd seen in her face earlier but still had no answers.

He gained the top of the stairs, ready to knock on her doorjamb, but he heard voices from the nursery. He went to Quintin's door and entered. Both Rusty and Quintin were sitting on his son's bed, their backs against the headboard. Rusty's hands were folded on a closed book in her lap.

"Hello," Rusty said.

"Hello. I thought you might have retired."

"We're just talking."

To Chase's eyes they both looked very tired, but he didn't comment.

"Did you need something?" Rusty asked.

"Just to speak with you when you have a chance."

She nodded. "Will you be in the drawing room?"

"Yes. Come at your leisure."

"All right."

"What happened then?" Quintin asked when his father left.

"Well, Zacchaeus ran ahead of the crowd and climbed into a tree. He knew that Jesus was going to come that way, so he waited, and sure enough, Jesus stopped right under the tree, looked up, and spoke to him. Jesus even told Zacchaeus that He wanted to have a meal with him. The two ate together, and Zacchaeus' life was changed forever. He saw that he was a sinner and needed Jesus Christ to forgive him."

"Why is that your favorite Bible story?"

"Well, I love all the stories about Jesus, but I especially like Zacchaeus because he's short like me."

"My father is tall. He could have seen Jesus."

"Yes, he is. You'll have to tell him that."

The look that Rusty had become accustomed to seeing at the mention of Chase McCandles now covered Quintin's face. Was it yearning or indifference? She honestly couldn't tell. What did this little boy think of his father? Did he know him well enough to have any opinion about him?

"I think you'd better sleep now, Quin," Rusty suggested. If she didn't rein in her thoughts on this subject, she'd be sorry.

"Are you going downstairs?"

"Yes. Will you be all right?"

"I think so."

"If you need anything, just come to the drawing room."

As had become their custom, Quintin now stood on the bed so Rusty could give him a long hug. She rocked him from side to side as her arms held him close.

"I love you, Quin."

"I love you, Aunt Rusty."

"Sleep well, Quin," she said as she kissed his small cheek. He scrambled into bed and waited while she tucked the covers close. This was the way Clayton Taggart had always put his children to bed. Rusty's father would have wrestled Quintin a little and snuggled him again, but Rusty only leaned down so they could rub noses. Quintin smiled up into her eyes. Rusty exited but left the door open. Her mind was busy, but her movements were serene. Indeed, her feet made almost no noise as she moved to the stairs.

32

After leaving Rusty and Quintin on their own, Chase found his usual chair in the drawing room, the one that let him see the stairs and foyer. He hadn't been looking for her, but because he was expecting her, he came to his feet the moment he saw Rusty descending. She smiled kindly when she saw him, but to his eyes Quintin's caregiver still looked tired. He determined not to keep her long.

"Would you like anything? I'm sure Mrs. Whitley is still in the kitchen."

"Thank you, no. I'm fine." Chase nodded and took his seat. "I wanted to speak with you about Quintin. How do you feel he's doing?"

"Very well. He climbed a tree today, and it was his idea to go and see Dobbins."

"Have you taken the cart around the grounds yet?"

"Yesterday. I thought we might be noisy, so we tried to stay away from your office windows."

Why such a statement would bother Chase, he wasn't certain, but it did. Was it her tone or just the fact that he would have enjoyed seeing them come past the window? For a moment he was incapable of responding. As the silence lengthened, Rusty shifted in her seat, drawing Chase's attention back to her. He had the impression that she was ready to make her excuses and head upstairs for the night, but Chase had one more thought on his mind. "I saw Pastor Radke today," he said suddenly. "He commented to me that you and Quintin seemed to be getting along well."

Tired as she was, Rusty smiled. "I'm glad he noticed. Quintin and I have been by to see him a couple of times. He always has a kind word. And Quin genuinely seems to enjoy him."

Chase was surprised that Rusty and Quintin would visit their pastor, so much so that he had no immediate reply. Again he was silent for so long that Rusty thought they were finished.

"Was there anything else, Mr. McCandles?"

"No." Chase shook his head and then cordially asked, "Unless there was something you wanted to discuss with me."

Rusty looked at him, at least 20 things coming to mind, but only shook her head no.

Chase nodded, but he knew very well that she had things she wanted to say. Had she not looked so weary he might have pushed the point.

"I'll say goodnight now, and if I don't talk to you again, have a good trip, Mr. McCandles."

"Thank you. Goodnight, Katherine."

A study in courtesy, Chase came smoothly to his feet and remained standing until Rusty was well out of the room. He sat down again but felt immediately restless and stood up. He wasn't scheduled to leave for Pueblo until the following afternoon, but it wasn't that easy to find an audience with Rusty when she was taken up with Quintin's care.

Chase suddenly caught himself and stopped pacing. He debated going back into his office to work, but that was not a habit he wanted to fall into. He stood now in the huge bay window on the east side of the drawing room, his eyes roaming over the spring landscape.

I have no idea what to do, Lord. I have the uncomfortable impression that Katherine wishes she'd never taken the job. I knew how good she would be — I've never seen Quintin so happy — but I can't shake the feeling that she wishes she'd never come. Should I say that outright? Should I come right out and ask her? The staff all enjoy her, I can see that, so it must be Quintin or me, or possibly both of us.

Chase had no answers. It wasn't enough for him that the job got done. If Rusty was disturbed, he wanted to know. Chase turned to look back at the sofa where she had been sitting. She had looked so tired. Although there were things he needed to prepare, his train didn't leave until two o'clock the next day. He would keep an eye on things over breakfast and as the morning passed. If anything seemed amiss, he would talk to Rusty on the spot. The plan gave him rest, and when he sought his bed and opened his Bible, he felt at peace. He read for more than an hour and slept as soon as he turned down the lantern.

Rusty woke slowly and stretched. She had slept so soundly that her hip ached where she had lain on it most of the night. It took a moment to get her eyes fully open, and when she did, she reached for her Bible. The morning was chilly, so she rolled off her painful hip and onto the other and sank down beneath the covers to read in the book of Ephesians. She silently studied Paul's prayer in the third chapter.

For this cause I bow my knees unto the Father of our Lord Jesus Christ, of whom the whole family in heaven and earth is named, that he would grant you, according to the riches of his glory, to be strengthened with might by his Spirit in the inner man; that Christ may dwell in your hearts by faith; that ye, being rooted and grounded in love, may be able to comprehend, with all saints, what is the breadth, and length, and depth, and height, and to know the love of Christ, which passeth knowledge, that ye might be filled with all the fullness of God.

Here Rusty had a note in her Bible. It simply said:

"Filled with all the fullness of God."
That as much as God is, we will be
like Him.

Rusty mulled the words over in her mind and then read them again. "Filled with all the fullness of God" was a line of Scripture that captivated her. The fullness of God was an awesome thing, almost too much to take in. But Paul had prayed it for the believers in Ephesus, and this told Rusty that it was something to be attained.

Rusty read on: *Now unto him who is able to do exceedingly abundantly above all that we ask or think, according to the power that worketh in us.* Rusty closed her eyes to think about what she had just read. Not many seconds passed before she began to pray.

I might be overwhelmed in trying to learn what Your fullness is, Lord, but You're able to do more than I can even ask of You. Thank You for the prayer in chapter one, Father. Thank You for this reminder that I must never forget what You did for me. Thank You for dying for me and then coming from the dead to conquer death forever. Thank You for bestowing on me all the riches of heaven. Such riches are not without responsibility, Lord, so please help me to stand strong and keep going even when I don't want to.

Rusty lay still and thought about what she'd just asked. She had never dreamed how hard it would be to live in this house. She thought back to her brief conversation with Chase the night before. He knew something was wrong — she could tell by the way he watched her — but she still believed it wasn't her place to give advice.

So what is my place? she asked the Lord.

Without having to think very long, she had her answer. *I'm here to take care of Quintin. That's all. If I see things that go against Your Word, Lord, then I can ask You to intervene.* Her mind resolved, she got out of bed in order to clean up and dress.

Rusty felt her heart lighten. She had a job to do, and she was going to do it to the best of her ability. Quintin McCandles would be the recipient of her faithfulness, and that was impetus enough to keep Rusty going.

Will I ever have my own child, Lord? Every year I see children leave or, like this summer, I commit my heart and then have to walk away. Will You remember me, Lord, when You think of motherhood? Will You please remember how much I want children of my own?

"Aunt Rusty," a small voice sounded just outside Rusty's door. She was dressed, although her hair wasn't combed, but she did not go to the door. She waited for Quintin to open it just a crack and then dashed around the bed and into the closet. She knew Quintin saw her from the delighted giggles that followed her across the room.

"I saw you, Aunt Rusty. You can't hide from me."

But hide she did, and it was a few minutes before Quintin found her behind the dresses in her walk-in closet.

"I see your shoe," he cried triumphantly, and with that Rusty came rushing at him. He squealed and tried to run, but she was too fast. She grabbed him with a triumphant cry and ran out to toss him onto the bed. A wrestling match ensued, lasting until they were both laughing too hard to move.

"I've got to finish getting dressed," Rusty said, her voice still breathless. "It's time for breakfast."

"I'll wait for you."

"All right. I just need to do something with my hair." She scooted off the bed and made for the mirror.

"Put it on top," Quintin recommended, and Rusty turned to him, confusion lowering her brow.

"On top?"

"Yes, like in the picture."

"Oh, all right."

As Rusty's hands began to gather and brush, she remembered the small photo album she had brought along. It showed all of her family, including a very formal picture of her with her siblings. It was for this photo that she had piled her hair atop her head. This was not something she usually did unless it got very warm, but to please Quintin she went to work.

"You missed some," he offered, having

come close to advise her.

"I'll get it," she assured him. "How's that?" Rusty finally turned to present herself and Quintin smiled.

"I like it."

"Thank you. Now, help me make the bed, and we'll get something to eat. Did you make your bed?"

"I think so."

"Well, did you or didn't you?"

"I tried."

"I think I'll check for myself," Rusty decided, her voice quiet but firm.

"I'd better go try again."

Rusty shook her head when he dashed from the room. She finished the bed on her own and then sought him out.

"Well, now, this is nice, Quin. I can tell that you tried hard."

He smoothed one more wrinkle and looked very pleased.

"Shall we go down?"

He skipped over to take her hand, and just a few moments later they were entering the breakfast room. Chase was already in attendance.

"Good morning," Rusty said to him, smiling.

"Good morning," Quintin echoed her.

"Good morning to both of you," Chase

replied in his usual quiet way. But he was feeling anything but quiet inside. It hadn't occurred to him how different Rusty might look with her hair up, but the change in her was dramatic. The effect was heightened by the pale blue blouse, which sported a high collar around her neck. She looked very lovely and mature, and right now, thankfully unaware of the way Chase stared.

"Doesn't that smell good, Quin? I'm hungry."

"You're always hungry, Aunt Rusty."

The remark swiftly grabbed Chase's attention away from Rusty's appearance. He thought such a remark to be impertinent, but his son's companion obviously didn't agree.

"I am always hungry, aren't I, Quin?" Her voice revealed no affront.

"It's because you don't clean your plate," Quintin explained.

Chase waited for Rusty to correct his son, but a reprimand never came. Instead she took what she wanted from the buffet and made her way to the table.

"No, I don't," she agreed good-naturedly. "I get distracted, but I'm always satisfied."

Rusty and Quintin had finished filling their plates, their backs to the room's other occupant. When they took their seats at the table, Rusty saw very swiftly that her employer's attention was not on his food or paper, but she didn't comment. She bowed with Quintin, said a prayer of thanks for the two of them, and then picked up her fork.

"I took too much eggs."

"Did you, Quin?" Rusty was glad to have something else to think about. "Just finish what you can and next time take less. You can always go back for more."

"Do you want some?"

"No, thank you, dear. I took only what I needed."

Rusty went back to her food, but not before she glanced at Chase. He was not staring at them anymore, but something told her that he would seek her out before leaving town. Rusty guessed correctly. As the trio finished their meal, Chase sent Quintin to the kitchen on his own and asked to see Rusty in his office. He spoke to her without shutting the door or taking a seat.

"I'm a little concerned with how familiar Quintin has become with you. I find him impertinent when he tells you that you're always hungry."

All the color drained from Rusty's face. She felt as if he'd just thrown ice water on her. "I'm sorry, sir," she said with soft sincerity. "I forget my position here — as one of your employees, that is. I'm sorry I've been too familiar with Quintin."

"Katherine, I was not speaking of *your* behavior but of Quintin's."

Rusty swallowed past a dry throat and frowned in confusion. Chase could see that he'd lost her.

"Do you not find it rather personal when he tells you that you don't finish what's on your plate?" he asked.

"Yes," she said slowly, "I guess I do find it personal, but I don't find it offensive. If I could be so bold as to ask, sir, if Quintin can't be informal and at ease with me, with whom can he get close?"

Chase visibly started. He opened his mouth and shut it again. He didn't have an answer.

"I'm sorry, sir." Rusty felt immediate regret. "I shouldn't have said that. You've asked me not to be too familiar with Quintin. In the future I'll do my best to remember." Rusty fell silent, waiting to be dismissed. She tried to ignore the painful squeezing sensation around her heart, but she was all too aware of it.

Chase couldn't believe what she'd just asked him. With startling clarity he remembered the teasing and laughter around the Taggarts' table in Boulder. Chase knew in an instant that it was time to find a wife. His son couldn't grow up as lonely as he had. He had to have some siblings, but in the meantime . . .

Chase realized that Rusty was still standing in front of him. Her eyes looked large enough to swallow her whole face, and until that moment Chase didn't realize how much his words must have hurt her. He tried to make amends.

"I think I'd like us to forget about this conversation, Katherine. You're right, Quintin doesn't have anyone with whom to laugh and joke. In the future, I'll leave his manners and choice of words to your discretion."

"All right." Rusty was relieved, although she still felt somewhat bruised. "I feel that I should tell you, Mr. McCandles, that Quintin is always polite. He thanks me for reading to him and for helping him with his shoes. I've yet to find him disrespectful. Mrs. Harding did a very thorough job."

Chase nodded, but no words came.

"Was that all, sir?" Rusty finally asked.

Chase looked down into her pale face and felt a sudden need to stay home. It was too late to cancel his appointment, but he wouldn't stay any longer than absolutely necessary.

"Yes, that's all, Katherine. Please send Quintin to me. I'm going to leave earlier than I'd planned, but I'll be home no later than Thursday."

"Yes, sir."

Rusty slipped away, and Chase looked after her with regret. She was doing a great job, and he'd made her feel like she'd failed. For some reason his eyes lingered on the back of her slender neck as she made her way through the drawing room. She seemed so vulnerable to him that he felt an ache inside.

I didn't even tell her how nice her hair looks. His thoughts were cut off when Quintin came into view. His words to the little boy were brief, and just minutes after he spoke to him, Chase headed out the door for the train station. His only thought was to get to Pueblo and return home as swiftly as possible.

33

Rusty received two very welcome letters on Thursday. The remainder of Tuesday had been hard as she'd tried not to take Chase's words personally; he had been on her mind off and on all day. Rusty kept reminding herself that he had only been concerned about his son, but she was surprised by how much the conversation had affected her. Wednesday had been almost as bad as the scene had been on her mind all that day as well.

For a time on Tuesday she felt a barrier between her and Quintin, and wondered if she was doing anything right, but by lunchtime she was back on firm ground. She had a job to do, and she would do it! It didn't come with a lot of praise, but she would still work hard. On this day Rusty also discovered something else: Quintin McCandles needed a little time on his own. She was not tiring of him, but she was beginning to see that this child was never alone.

Starting that very day — one hour after lunch — she would ask Quintin to find something to do on his own. When she first told him of the plan, he stared at her, but then understanding dawned and he wandered off to play on the veranda, seemingly quite content. Rusty hung around in the background for a few minutes to see if he would do well, but she left him on his own when she saw that he would not wander into danger.

He did splendidly on Tuesday and even better Wednesday. Now Thursday had come, and she had just told him it was time for his free play. Quintin headed onto the veranda for the third day in a row, and Rusty went into the drawing room to read her letters. One was from Tibby, and the other from Grace Harrington. Rusty had known the date for Tibby's wedding since before she left, so with hopes that Grace would have a date for her as well, she opened that letter first.

We have a date! were Grace's opening words. *August 14. Please tell me you'll be here, Rusty. You know I'm planning on your standing up with us as a bridesmaid. Melissa has already picked out a dress pattern she likes and is ecstatic to show it to you. Write as soon as you can and tell me what you think.*

The letter went on about Grace's wedding plans, but Rusty took only half of it in. She was thinking that she must tell her employer which dates she needed to be away. Now that she knew both, she would write them down and put them on his desk. Rusty took care of this on the stationery in her room. Tibby's date was in July, and Grace's wedding was planned for five weeks later. Rusty had just placed the message on Chase's desk when she turned and found him coming across the drawing room.

"Oh, Mr. McCandles!" Rusty tried not to act as awkward as she felt. She didn't know if she should say "Welcome home" or not. She opted to stick to business. "I was just putting some dates on your desk — the days I need to be gone for my friends' weddings."

"All right." His manner was slightly aloof, and Rusty felt guilty for having gone into his private office. Irritated with herself for feeling that way, she decided to slip away and leave him alone. However, his voice stopped her.

"Katherine, will you please send Quintin to me?"

It was on the tip of her tongue to assure him she would, but a spark of anger ignited inside of her, and she did nothing to ignore it. She walked completely out of the room but then turned and went right back in.

"Why do you always do that?"

Chase looked up in surprise. He had gone around to the chair behind his desk but paused, the paper in his hand ignored.

"Do what?"

"Send for Quintin. Why don't you ever go to him?"

Chase looked at her patiently. "This is a large home, Katherine. I don't have time to run around and look for my son."

Anger exploded in Rusty's brain. "That's more than obvious," she gritted out. "Anyone living here could attest to the fact that you don't have time for your son."

In shock, Chase stared at her for a moment before indignation leapt into his eyes. Even then Rusty did not back down. Chase came out from behind the desk, but Rusty stood her ground. They glared at one another for several seconds, both breathing hard.

"I believe you're out of line, Miss Taggart," Chase managed, sounding calmer than he felt.

"If you don't like it, fire me!" Rusty shot back, not calm at all.

"You're fired."

"I'll pack my bags," she said without missing a beat, her voice rising slightly, "but not before I've had my say. You just made the biggest mistake of your life. No, I'm wrong," she said with a downward slash of her hand. "You just made the biggest mistake of Quintin's life. *I'm* the only human he knows." With that she turned to storm across the room.

"*What* is that supposed to mean?" Chase's voice cracked like thunder as he followed her.

Rusty turned back so fast that her hair fanned out behind her. They were now in the middle of the drawing room, both red in the face with emotion.

"I'll tell you," she said ruthlessly. "If you and your wife had wanted a little wind-up toy, it could have been purchased with a lot less trouble and expense at the general store in town!"

"How dare you!" Chase exploded, well and truly furious, but Rusty was not intimidated.

"How dare *I*? How dare *you* for having a child you don't care about!"

"And what, may I ask, makes *you* an authority on child-raising, *Miss* Taggart?"

"I don't need to be an authority. I just need to have eyes!"

"Well, *open them,* and you'll see the way I

love and provide for my son!"

"Is that what you call it?" Her eyes were huge with shock. "Where I come from we have a different term!"

Chase was opening his mouth to retort when he caught movement out of the corner of his eye. Quintin was standing in the doorway between the hall and the drawing room. Rusty followed his eyes and saw him as well.

"Come in, Quintin," she commanded none-too-gently. Chase looked at her in shock, but she didn't notice. She went on before he could tell her to stop.

"Your father and I are having an argument. Did you know that people argue, Quintin? I am angry at him, and he's angry at me. We might be sorry for some of the things we've said, but right now we're very upset!"

The little boy looked between them, his face ashen. He surprised both adults when he looked to his father and asked, "Are you going to hit Aunt Rusty?"

"No, Quintin," Chase replied, his voice returning to its normal quiet. "I would never hit your Aunt Rusty. Not for any reason would I do such a thing."

Hearing the calm in his voice, Rusty came to her senses so swiftly that she thought her heart would burst. *Rusty Taggart, what have*

393

you done? Telling herself not to burst into tears, she took a deep breath and tried to calm the wild beating of her heart.

"Come here, Quintin," she said softly and held out her hand. Seeing her behave normally again, the little boy came without hesitation. Rusty went to the long davenport, sat down, and lifted Quintin onto her lap. She was somewhat aware that Chase had taken one of the chairs.

"Tell me something, Quin. Did you and Mrs. Harding ever start a book that you weren't able to finish?"

"I don't think so."

"Well, even though you haven't done that, you do understand that it could happen, don't you? You might be reading a book that you like very much, but for some reason you must put it back on the shelf and not finish it or get it out again?"

The little boy nodded.

"Sometimes it's like that with people too," Rusty continued.

"Don't do this."

The words came so softly that Rusty almost missed them. Quintin's eyes were still on her face, so she knew he had missed his father's plea. She swallowed and brushed the hair from Quintin's brow, thankful that she could at least apologize before she had to go.

"I'm going to need to explain this to you later, Quin. Your father and I still need to talk."

"Are you going to fight again?"

"No, we're not." Rusty's shame was huge. "But we do need to talk. Will you go into the kitchen or back to the veranda? Maybe Cook has a snack for you."

"All right."

Quintin slid off her lap and started toward the door that would take him to the front hall and then the kitchen. He worriedly glanced back on his way through the portal, but Rusty was watching and smiling at him. He left with a smile of his own.

Rusty was at a complete loss. She could feel Chase's eyes on her but couldn't bring herself to look at him. She'd been so angry and out of line.

"I didn't mean it when I said you were fired," Chase said softly, his eyes never leaving her face. "I only said that to see what you would do. I'm sorry."

Rusty shook her head, not wanting him to apologize. She deserved all he had said and more, and for that reason she still couldn't lift her eyes to his. Standing suddenly, she walked to the bay window. Chase followed right behind her.

"I can't do this anymore," she said, barely holding her tears. "I can't do this, and I should have told you."

"Katherine." Chase's voice was lower than usual. His hands were on her upper arms, and he turned her to face him. He held her in front of him, and she looked up to meet his gaze with wide, tear-filled eyes.

"He's so precious, and you don't even know he's here." Her voice was just above a whisper. "I don't know how you can stand not touching him. Have you ever smelled his hair and skin after he's had a bath, or had him look you in the eye and say, 'I love you, Papa'? He doesn't even know you, Mr. McCandles." Rusty shook her head. Every ounce of helplessness she'd felt came bubbling to the surface.

"Whatever it is that keeps you so busy — this house, the staff, whatever — I wish you would get rid of it. Sell this expensive home, dismiss the staff, and move into a small apartment in town so you have time to be a father to that child. I see more than 30 little boys every day who would die to have a father. Quintin has one, but what good does it do? All the nice clothing, food, and surroundings aren't worth a thing unless Quintin knows you love him."

The tears spilled over then, and Chase's

heart broke for more than one reason. Without permission he pulled Rusty into his arms and just held her. He'd seen this on her face for days now and not known what it was. His father had not had a hand in his rearing, and his mother had been ill for much of his childhood. He'd been raised by a nanny. It had never occurred to him to do it any other way. Was Quintin really in so much need of him? Was his life truly missing so much?

Without warning, Clayton Taggart came to mind. There was such warmth and caring between that man and his family. Chase hadn't shared any kind of depth with his father until a year before he died. He didn't know when he'd thought to have that type of relationship with his own son. Maybe that was the problem. He hadn't thought about it at all.

Chase removed one arm now, reached for his handkerchief, and pressed it into Rusty's hands. He put a hand to her back and gently propelled her to the sofa.

"Sit here, Katherine."

She complied, and he sat on the edge of the cushion, his body turned so he could look at her. He waited until she was a little more in control of herself and then began to speak.

"You've been upset about something since you arrived, and I haven't known how to ask you what was wrong."

Rusty looked up at him and tried not to sniff, the handkerchief balled in her hand.

"This was what you were talking about when you said you'd been raised differently; I see that now."

"I'm so sorry for the things I said." Rusty had to stop him. "You told me I was out of line, and I just kept on. You did the right thing in firing me."

"You're not fired," Chase said firmly. "If you tried to leave us, I think I would block the door."

They fell silent for several moments. Rusty used the handkerchief again and tried not to cry. This was no easy task. The pain and confusion was almost too much for her.

"Tell me about your childhood, Katherine."

Rusty blinked at him. "My childhood?"

"Yes. Tell me what it was like growing up with your father."

"I don't know where to start," she hedged. Chase would not let her off that easily.

"You said you were raised differently. What did you mean by that?"

Rusty bit her lip. Should she do this?

"Why are you hesitating?"

"Don't you see how wrong I was, Mr. McCandles? It's not my place to tell you how to raise your child."

Chase's eyes moved to the distance. He thought she was the perfect person to tell him. He would have to go about this another way. His eyes suddenly swung back and pinned her to the seat.

"If you could have anything for Quintin, what would it be?"

Rusty's brows rose.

"If you need to think about it, that's fine."

This was easier said than done. For a moment Rusty's mind was blank. She nearly laughed, however, when the most obvious thing came to mind.

"Go ahead," Chase urged. He'd been watching her closely.

"I wish his mother were still alive," she said simply. "I know how I feel about my mother, and I wish he could have a mother as loving as mine."

"What else?"

"I know what you're doing," she accused.

"Just tell me." His voice was quite firm, and Rusty obeyed, albeit quietly.

"I wish you would play with him." Rusty made herself meet his eyes. "I wish you would tickle him and chase him through the house. I wish you would take him up in Shelby's saddle and ride for miles. I wish you would read your Bible to him and tuck him in at night, eat dinner with him, and take him to town for haircuts and shopping."

"Your father did all of this?"

Rusty nodded. "My mother was blind, Mr. McCandles. She wasn't completely helpless by any means. She did a lot for us, but my father probably did more with us than would have been the norm. I know that the situations are not identical, but that's the way I was raised. That's the way it was with Clayton Taggart. He wasn't perfect, but he had time for us. We understood how deep his love for Christ was and how we meant everything to him."

Chase's eyes closed. How could he have been so unaware?

"Are you all right?" Rusty asked.

Chase looked at her. "I've never told Quintin a Bible story. I know Mrs. Harding reads the Bible to him, but I don't know what he knows."

Rusty nodded. "He can recite many stories, but I don't think he's taken anything to heart. That is, I don't think he's made any kind of personal commitment."

Chase nodded, and this time his silence lasted for quite some time.

"I should go," Rusty said when the time lengthened. She suddenly found her jaw captured in one of his large hands.

"You're not fired."

"I didn't mean that. I only meant I should go check on Quin."

"Oh," Chase said, but didn't drop his hand. "We are settled on this, are we not, Katherine? You know that I want you to stay, and you plan to stay, don't you?"

"Yes, but I'm afraid that I've ruined things forever. You'll not trust me and —"

Chase was shaking his head. "Things will be different now, but not because I don't trust you." He dropped his hand and stared at her. "Why don't you go and put a cool cloth on your eyes? I'll go check on Quintin."

"All right," Rusty said quietly, trying to hide her surprise.

Chase waited for her to stand and precede him from the room. Rusty naturally took the stairs to her bedroom, but not before she took note of the fact that her employer went right past the stairs toward the kitchen. Rusty finished climbing the stairs with her heart in her throat. She didn't know what the final outcome would be, but she knew with a certainty that she would never forget this day.

34

"Quintin," Chase called as soon as he saw his son at the kitchen table. "Are you finished with your snack?"

"Yes, sir," Quintin answered quietly, wondering if he was in trouble.

"Will you go for a walk with me?"

The little boy was utterly stunned. He knew better than to question or argue, but his eyes kept darting past his father to the doorway. It was impossible for Chase to miss.

"Aunt Rusty went up to her room for a little while," he told him quietly. "I think she'll be down later."

Quintin stared up at his father and watched as he started toward the door. The little boy followed, his eyes watchful. Chase opened the door and stood aside for

Quintin to go out.

When the door was shut, the women in the kitchen looked at one another. It had been impossible not to hear the shouting from the other room, and then Quintin had come into the kitchen on his own. It was anyone's guess as to whether or not Rusty still worked at Briarly, but more confusing than that was Chase McCandles coming to take his son for a walk. Dozens of questions swarmed the women's minds, but neither said a word.

Chase was many feet taller than his son, so once outside he shortened his steps and started toward the garden. Quintin fell in beside him, and for some moments no one spoke. Chase searched for something to say to this little person whom he barely knew, and then he caught sight of the woods. He remembered that Quintin and Rusty visited there almost daily.

"Did you come to the woods this morning with Aunt Rusty?"

"Yes, sir."

"What did you do?"

Quintin tried to stop and stand at attention to report to his father, but his father kept walking. He dashed ahead and tried again, but his father changed positions once more.

Wondering at his odd gait, Chase came to a stop and stared down at him. The older McCandles' heart sank when Quintin stopped like a little toy soldier and began to speak in a monotone voice. Rusty's words about a wind-up toy came swiftly back to him. Chase interrupted his son.

"Why don't you tell me while we walk, Quintin. Can you do that?"

"Oh, all right." He sounded slightly confused. "We went to the woods."

"What did you see?"

"Trees and a dead bird."

"A dead bird? Was it a baby?"

"No. It was big, like a mother bird."

"Will you show it to me?"

Quintin nodded affably and led the way from the garden. Chase stared down at his small head and felt something tear at his heart. *He's all I have, Lord, but I've never told him. He's so precious to me, but to him I'm just "sir." How could I have been so blind? How can I make this up to him? Will he even want anything to do with me? I need a miracle here, Lord — in his heart as well as my own.*

"It's here," Quintin pointed out as Chase cried to control his heart. "Right here under this tree."

"Oh, yes," Chase returned as he squatted down to look. "It is a big bird, a —" Chase

404

had been on the verge of naming it but stopped. "What is this bird, Quintin?"

"It's a starling," he said confidently. "We didn't see a nest, but then we couldn't look very high."

Chase began to move among the trees, his height giving him a firm advantage among the low branches. He searched for several minutes before finding a possibility.

"Here, Quintin, look at this one."

Quintin came over and without thought Chase swung him up into his arms.

"Do you see it?" Chase stood so Quintin could look over the tree branch and into the nest. "Is this the one?"

"It might be," Quintin said after he'd looked at it carefully. "I need to check my book."

Chase looked back into the nest and made a few more comments. He knew a little about birds and took a moment to point something out to his son about the way the twigs were laid in the nest. He glanced back to see if Quintin was understanding, but he found the younger McCandles watching him, not the nest. Chase was so overcome by emotion that he felt a sting behind his eyes.

"Thank you for showing me the bird, Quintin," he said quietly.

"We're up high."

Chase could only smile, his heart melting into a puddle when Quintin smiled in return. Just a moment later, however, Chase began to feel awkward and gently lowered Quintin to the ground. The little boy looked up at him, clearly waiting for the next order. Chase was at a complete loss.

"Do you suppose Aunt Rusty is downstairs now?" he tried, wondering why his voice sounded so strained.

"I don't know. Was she coming to the woods too?"

"I don't think so. Maybe we should go and check on her."

"All right."

Quintin didn't notice that anything was amiss with his father. In truth, he knew Chase McCandles so slightly that anything his father did was new to him. Quintin walked back toward the house, seemingly without a care in the world. Chase was not quite so at ease.

What does Katherine find to do all day with my son? She never seems to be at a loss. But he had no answers and prayed only that she would be down from her room and ready to take Quintin, or at least help him to know what to do. His sigh was very quiet. No one had to tell Chase that he still had a lot to learn.

★ ★ ★

"I didn't know. I had no idea! I can't believe his face. Did you watch his expression?"

Rusty nodded, a smile coming to her lips, but Chase didn't see it. It was much later that day. The three of them had eaten dinner together, and Chase had volunteered to help with Quintin's bath. He then read him a story. But as with the nest, Quintin's eyes had been on his father, not the book.

Now Quintin was asleep, and Chase was pacing in the drawing room downstairs, too excited to sit down. He had asked Rusty to come down so he could speak to her, but he only talked to himself and paced.

"What do you have planned for tomorrow?" Chase asked suddenly, turning to her.

Rusty shrugged. "I don't usually plan too far in advance. Was there something you wanted to do?"

"That's just it. I don't know." With that, Chase stood and stared at her, his expression revealing that he expected her to produce a day's plan at a moment's notice.

Rusty started to laugh. She didn't want to but she couldn't help herself.

"What did I miss?" His hands had gone to his hips, and he tried to look indignant.

Still chuckling, Rusty tried to explain. "You don't do anything in half measures, do

407

you? You want to get to know Quintin, and you want to do it *now*. It's like a piece of land you've spotted and want to buy. You want the deal settled by sundown!"

Chase dropped into a chair and tried to frown at her. Rusty had never seen him so dramatic. She couldn't keep the smile from her face.

"You're still laughing at me."

"I can't help myself. I never realized before how intense and driven you could be, but I shouldn't be surprised."

"Why is that?"

"All of this." Rusty's head moved as she looked around the elegant, expensively furnished room. "You don't come by things this nice by sitting on your hands."

"As a matter of fact, this was my parents' home. I grew up here."

Rusty's eyes widened. "I had no idea."

It was Chase's turn to look around the room. "I've taken it all for granted, but now that I think about it, it was a great house to grow up in."

"It must have been." Rusty studied the bay window. The surroundings were so lovely. "Did you tell me at one time that your mother lives in Texas?"

"Yes. That's why I live here at Briarly." Chase stared at her for a moment. She knew nothing about him. She'd come in to take care of Quintin and asked no questions. He felt a sudden need to explain.

"I was as spoiled as any child could be," Chase began again. "My mother was ill for most of my childhood, and my father was very preoccupied with her health and his business opportunities. I was raised by a series of nannies who basically gave me anything I wanted to keep me out of trouble. My mother had tuberculosis and was at a special care facility here in the city. I was allowed to see her only once a month. She had no idea how I was growing up, and when she came home, I was 16 and already very set in my ways. Not for some months did I understand how my actions and attitudes were breaking her heart, but I came to Christ and enjoyed a wonderful relationship with my mother. When she asked me to go to school in the East, I agreed.

"My father passed away while I was home one summer, and I thought my mother would curl up and die. I was wrong. She took on much of my father's business dealings and threw herself into a life she hadn't had since she'd become ill.

"It was during that time that she hired a secretary, a young woman who had grown up at the Fountain Creek Orphanage. Her name was Carla Bensen, and my mother talked of her in every letter. When I finished school and returned home, I knew it was my mother's greatest wish that Carla and I be married.

"It wasn't a love match," he admitted, "but we cared for each other, and I think we were happy. We lived in a small house here in town, and I began to work with my mother. No one could have predicted what came next. A man from Texas visited church one Sunday. He and Mother took one look at each other and fell in love. I remember the shock I felt the first time I saw him put his arm around her, but then I also remember the shine in her eyes that hadn't been there since my father died.

"It wasn't long before they were married and she moved to Texas with him. My father's business dealings, this house — everything — was handed over to Carla and me. Quintin was born, and as with my mother's second marriage, it never occurred to me that anything might happen to my wife. But a nasty virus came through the area. Carla was struck down. At first she couldn't walk, and then she couldn't breathe. One month she was healthy and active, and the next month we had her funeral."

"I'm so sorry," Rusty said softly. "I'm also

sorry if it hurt you to speak of it."

"It's all right, Katherine. It feels good to talk about that time of my life and to look back on the way God took care of me. My only real ache is for Quintin. He needs a mother."

Rusty nodded, feeling suddenly awkward. Chase seemed to be out of things to say, and as Rusty thought was proper, she rose to say goodnight. It was best that she not forget she was employed here.

"I'll say goodnight now," she said softly.

Chase came to his feet, the feeling of disappointment now familiar to him. He said goodnight as well, but before she could get too far, he called her name.

"Katherine?"

Rusty stopped on the first step of the stairs and turned back. Chase came and stood right in front of her, their eyes much more level with her up a step.

"Have I thanked you for today? Have I told you how well you're doing?"

Rusty shook her head no.

"Then I will now. Thank you for everything. Thank you for today and for working so hard with Quintin. You're right. He's a special little person."

Rusty smiled but felt a strong need to repeat herself. "I'm glad you're pleased, Mr.

McCandles. And please accept my apology again over shouting at you."

"Of course. I hope in the future you'll come to me as soon as you see a problem. Don't wait until you're angry, Katherine. Come to me right away."

"I'll do that. Goodnight, Mr. McCandles."

"Goodnight." Chase said these last words very softly. He watched her go up the stairs, but even when she was out of sight he didn't move.

It's just the emotion of the day, he told himself. *That's all. A passing thing. Just ignore it, and it will go away.* The words were all well and good, but they didn't work. More than anything Chase McCandles wanted to take Rusty Taggart in his arms and kiss her. As he looked into her eyes, the thought had come on him so suddenly that he'd almost acted on it. He had teased Rusty in the past about her impetuous nature, but he had been strongly tempted to take a page from her book.

With a firm resolve, he walked into his office. He had achieved almost nothing today in his paperwork, and right now he needed a diversion. He naively thought that work would do the trick. It would be the next day before he knew differently.

35

"I think we should go out to lunch today," Rusty said to Quintin as he watched her do her hair. He had asked her to put it up again, and wanting to please him, she obliged. "What do you think, Quin? If Whit can take us, would you like to eat out?"

"Yes, I would."

"Good." Rusty crossed her eyes in the mirror at him, and Quintin laughed.

"Can I have chicken and dessert?"

"*May* I have chicken, and, yes, you may. We'll see about dessert after we get there."

"What will you have?"

"Oh, I think I'll just eat the menu."

"Aunt Rusty." His tone was indulgent.

"Yes," she insisted, her eyes big. "I'll use

a little salt. It should be just delicious."

He fell backward onto the bed now, and Rusty had to scoot him off since she'd already made it up.

"Is your bed made?"

"Yes, but it's not flat like yours."

"That's all right, as long as you did your best. Come here, Quin. Let me do something with your hair." He stood patiently as she worked. "I think a haircut is in order today too. Mrs. Harding always saw to that, didn't she?"

"Um hum." He was busy making faces at himself in the mirror.

"Where did she take you, Quin?"

Quintin was too busy looking down his throat to answer.

"Quintin McCandles, listen to me. Where did Mrs. Harding take you for your haircuts?"

"Into town."

"Well, that's a big help. Maybe Whit knows."

"Or Rick. He came one time."

"All right. Let's go get breakfast and see if anyone is free to take us to town today."

"Why can't we take Dobbins?"

"Your father is afraid that he'll get spooked and run off with us."

"Is he going to read to me tonight?"

"Your father? I don't know. Would you like him to?"

They were at the bottom of the stairs now, and Quintin only nodded, a small smile on his face.

"You could ask him if he plans on it," Rusty suggested.

They were in the breakfast room just a moment later, but to their surprise, Mr. McCandles was not there. His newspaper was at his place, but it didn't look as if he had eaten. Rusty went ahead and got Quintin settled with his plate before slipping into the kitchen to see if she could locate Whit.

"Good morning, Cook. Do you know if Whit is around?"

"Good morning, Rusty. I believe he's in the stable. Did you need him?"

"I have a question for him. Quintin is having breakfast, so I'll just pop out and ask him."

"Or I can tell him you want him. He talked as though he'd be right back."

"Oh, all right. Thank you." Rusty returned to the breakfast room and to her surprise and pleasure found Chase. He was talking to Quintin. Rusty stood very still so as not to disturb them.

"I found something I thought you might like," Chase was saying. He took a small box from his pocket and placed it next to Quintin.

"Should I open it?"

"Yes, you should. It's yours to keep."

Quintin opened the box, and his little mouth opened in surprise.

"Can you get it out?" Chase asked him.

Quintin pulled on the chain and out came a miniature pocket watch. The little boy stared at it in awe.

"My father gave that to me when I was five," Chase explained. "I know you were five last month, so this is late, but I still wanted you to have it."

"It's so small."

"Yes, and it still tells time. You'll take good care of it, won't you?"

He could only nod.

At that moment, Chase noticed Rusty. He came swiftly to his feet, and she felt free to enter.

"I hope I'm not interrupting."

"Not at all. I was just giving something to Quintin."

Rusty looked down at the little boy, but his complete attention was on the pocket watch. She looked at Chase and found his eyes on her. Something in his face arrested Rusty's attention. She realized not for the first time that the events of the previous day had to have been upsetting. Her employer looked very vulnerable to her right now. It seemed a little too familiar, but Rusty had to question him.

"Are you all right, Mr. McCandles?" she asked softly.

No, I'm not, he said in his mind. *This feeling was supposed to stay behind with yesterday, but it didn't, and now I don't know what to do.*

"Mr. McCandles?"

"I'm sorry," he covered smoothly, "my thoughts wandered." He cleared his throat. "I realized this morning that I don't know what plans you have for Quintin today."

"A haircut," Rusty told him. "If Whit can take us to town. We also thought it would be fun to go to lunch, but I think the haircut is more important."

Chase nodded. "I have some work that should take just a few hours, and then I could see you to town."

"Oh, thank you."

Rusty dished up her food and sat at the table. She leaned over Quintin's shoulder and looked at the watch he still had in his hand.

"Isn't it nice, Quin? Did you remember to say thank you?"

"Thank you," Quintin said immediately.

Rusty watched as the little boy went right

back to the watch. Rusty could see that he wasn't going to eat a thing. The last thing she wanted to do was interfere, but she still had a job to do.

"I'll tell you what, Quin. We'll put the watch right here in the box where you can see it while you finish your breakfast."

"Okay," he agreed absently.

Rusty exchanged glances with Chase.

"It looks like you've made someone's day," Rusty said softly.

"I think so too," Chase agreed with her, but he wasn't just thinking of his son.

I wasn't prepared for the way it would feel to have her here every day, Lord. She's sweet and sensitive, and when I don't see her, I miss her. I've asked You if it's time to seek another wife, and right here . . .

Chase caught the direction of his thoughts before they could roam too far. Right now his heart couldn't take it. He also knew he would make them both miserable if he didn't handle the situation wisely. If she knew what he was feeling, she'd be overwhelmed. She would most certainly quit on the spot, and he knew he couldn't handle that. He had to keep things light or talk of business. Rusty couldn't possibly know of his change in feelings, and it simply wasn't fair to try to court her without warning.

"I found the dates you left for me on my desk," Chase said, his voice mild.

"Oh good. Are those going to work out all right?"

"They'll be fine. Whose wedding is first?"

"Tibby's. I shouldn't be gone for more than the weekend. In August, however, I'll probably need a little more time. I had a sudden thought this morning. I wondered if it would be possible to take someone with me when I go to Boulder." Rusty's eyes darted down to the little boy with the pocket watch and then back to Chase. As she had hoped, Quintin missed the whole thing.

Rusty watched Chase's brows rise and could tell he liked the idea.

"That would be the August date?"

"Yes. I think he would have a wonderful time with my family."

Chase nodded; he was sure of the fact. However, he said only, "I'll think about it and get back to you."

They finished the meal in relative quiet, and it wasn't long before Chase excused himself and went to work. He was striving desperately for a balance. Early that morning as he'd shaved and dressed, he had been tempted to seek out Quintin and spend the whole day with him, but before he even left his room, he knew that was going too far. He still had business matters to see to, and there would be time later to get to know his son a little better.

Added to this was a deep desire to spend more time with Rusty as well. His new awareness of her could have come at a better time, but he knew he was going to have to find ways to deal with it. A protectiveness toward both of them swelled up so swiftly inside of him that for a moment he sat at his desk and did nothing.

I'm going to lose my mind if I go on this way, Lord. Either I trust You to take care of them or I don't. Chase was tempted to tell God that he would feel at ease if he only knew how Rusty would welcome his overtures, but he knew better. Trusting meant having a "no matter what" attitude. It wasn't always going to be easy, but he was willing to try. Without warning, Chase remembered the Bible study that Pastor Radke had invited him to join and knew very clearly in his heart that he should. He would talk to the pastor the next time he saw him. Chase spent a few minutes in prayer and then threw himself into his paperwork. It did the trick. Before he knew it, the morning had flown by.

"Are you having dessert, Quin? They

have chocolate cake."

The little boy shook his head and said honestly, "I'm too full."

"I'm full too," Rusty agreed. She took another sip of her coffee and watched as Mr. McCandles returned to the table. They were dining at the Clausen House, and he had spotted someone with whom he needed to speak and left them for a moment.

"How about dessert?" he asked of Rusty and his son.

Rusty was on the verge of telling him they were too full, but she'd been trying not to talk too much so father and son would have a chance to get to know each other.

"Quintin?" his father pressed.

"I'm full."

"Oh, all right. How about you, Katherine?"

"None for me, thank you."

"Well then, I guess it's off to the barber."

As he'd been doing since they left Briarly, Chase took charge. Rusty had no qualms over this. In some ways it was nice to have someone else take responsibility. She didn't know that Chase had not been ready to leave the papers he'd been working on, and in order to stay focused on the needs of his son, he was being rather stern with himself. In turn, he was a bit stern with Rusty and Quintin.

The barbershop was not far from the restaurant. The threesome walked the distance, and other than Rusty telling Quintin not to lag behind, they didn't speak. All this ended at the barber's door. When Chase began to walk through the door, Rusty asked, "Were you going to see to Quintin's haircut, Mr. McCandles?"

"Yes, I'd planned on it," he said simply.

"I think I'll just go across the street to the dry goods store then," she felt free to say. "I'll check back in a while to see if you're finished."

Chase's gaze turned somewhat fierce, and he looked across the street toward her destination. He was being overly protective again, like the day he wanted to come for her when she started the job. Rusty wondered for just an instant if he expected to see bandits loitering in front of the store and nearly laughed out loud at the thought. Instead, she checked to see if she'd heard him correctly.

"You did say you would see to Quintin's haircut, didn't you, Mr. McCandles?"

"Yes." He looked at her now.

"Then I'll see you in a little while."

"I'll walk you across the street."

"No, you won't."

The words were said softly, but there was no missing the command in Rusty's voice. Chase turned eyes on her that dared her to challenge him, and Rusty did just that. With eyes holding his, she said, "I'll see you later." She then stepped off the boardwalk.

"Katherine," Chase called in a voice she could not ignore. She turned back and found him larger than ever since she was standing in the street and he was still on the walk. "You will be in the dry goods store and nowhere else. Do I make myself clear?"

"Very clear." Her tone was tolerant.

"Quintin and I will come to you when we are finished. You will not leave there until we come."

This time Rusty only looked at him, very aware Quintin was watching the whole scene. She thought Chase was being ridiculous and wanted to tell him so, but she knew that now was not the time. He spoke before she could say a word one way or the other.

"Those are your choices — into the barber shop with us, or to the general store and stay there."

Rusty gave up. It really wasn't worth the fight. "I'll be in the general store," Rusty said quietly. She moved off and didn't look back, but she could feel Chase's eyes on her all the way across.

★ ★ ★

Rusty had not been in this particular dry goods store and found it to be wonderful. They had a huge selection of fabric, patterns she'd never seen before, and scores of notions. She was examining some tiny fans when one of the store clerks approached.

"Those are just in."

"Oh, are they?" Rusty replied to the nice young man. "What are they for?"

"You put them in your hair."

"Your hair?" Rusty's brows winged upward.

"Yes. May I show you?"

"Oh, all right." Rusty found nothing offensive about his manner, and since she'd piled her hair atop her head this day, she could barely feel his fingers as they pushed two little fans into the fat coil of hair. Chase came in as he was finishing, his height letting him spot Rusty immediately, and although he said nothing, his eyes followed the young man's actions and attention like a hawk watching its prey.

"Now," he said kindly, "if you'll take the hand mirror." He gave it to Rusty. "I'll adjust the counter mirror so you can see." He worked efficiently, and in just a moment Rusty had a view. "What do you think?"

Rusty smiled. "I think it looks wonderful. What do you think, Quintin? Will my sister like these for her birthday?"

"For her hair?" the little boy smiled up at her.

"Yes," Rusty smiled back, completely blind to how lovely she looked. "*Your* hair looks nice," she took a moment to say to Quintin. Then she turned back to the man behind the counter. "I'll take these," she said.

"All right. Will you be wearing them?"

"No, I'd like them wrapped." Rusty began to reach for the combs, but the man's voice stopped her.

"Here, let me help you."

Not wanting to tear her hair down, Rusty turned a little to oblige. She didn't look at Chase right then, or she'd have seen that he was as stiff as a poker. Moments later the young clerk saw them to the door, and they made their way out of the store, combs in hand.

"He was nice," Rusty commented, not having seen anything amiss.

"I'm surprised he didn't follow you up the street."

Rusty stared at her employer. "You really

are a worrier, aren't you?"

Chase looked down at her. "I don't know what you're talking about," he said and meant it.

"Mother hens never do," Rusty said with a smile.

Chase couldn't believe what he was hearing. She made it sound as if this was *his* problem. The man's actions had been completely improper! His voice told of his exasperation.

"If we'd stayed any longer, Katherine, I think he would have proposed."

As she had wanted to do in front of the barbershop, Rusty laughed. Not a light, small laugh, but a Rusty laugh: full and loud.

Chase, who had not meant to be funny at all, was having a hard time seeing the joke, but Rusty couldn't stop. She chuckled all the way back to the carriage and even some on the ride home. Between bouts of laughter, she asked Quintin all about his trip to the barber. Listening to him, Chase could not stay in a poor humor. Rusty noticed that her employer's mood lightened, and by the time the carriage pulled up in front of Briarly, she felt free to question him.

"Are you angry with me?"

"No. Are you angry with me?"

"No, but I think you're too protective."

Chase nodded and didn't deny it. He'd been telling himself the same thing, all the while realizing it wasn't at all easy to change.

They made their way inside, and Mrs. Whitley met them in the front hall. She made over Quintin's hair for a moment and then turned to Rusty.

"Rusty, you have visitors. They're waiting for you in the drawing room."

"Oh, thank you, Mrs. Whit." Rusty's voice was calm enough, but she turned to exchange a look with Chase. He only lifted his brows and shrugged.

Rusty looked back toward the drawing room but for some reason didn't move.

"Do you want me to come with you?" Chase's voice came softly to her ears, and she immediately turned.

"Would you?"

"Certainly."

Although she felt a bit apprehensive, Rusty led the way. There was nothing to fear. She stepped into the drawing room and laughed in delight. A moment later she was in Clayton Taggart's warm embrace.

36

"I wondered why you never answered my last letter," Rusty said to both Clayton and Jackie, a huge smile on her face. They were on the sofa, and Rusty and Chase had taken two of the overstuffed chairs. "How long have you been planning this?"

"Since before you were last home," her mother answered. "You said in your first letter to us that your family and friends would be welcome here, so we kept our plans even though you weren't at the orphanage."

"I'm so glad you did," Rusty said softly. Indeed, it was wonderful to see them. "How long can you stay?"

"Until Monday."

"Good. Oh, Mother." Rusty's voice was suddenly excited. "Has Papa described this room to you?"

"Yes," Jackie said fervently. "The bay window sounds marvelous."

"It's gorgeous," Rusty assured her. "It gives so much light to this room. I'll have to take you into the gardens outside too. They're beautiful."

"Well, now," Clayton broke in as soon as Rusty paused. "Whom do we have here?"

Both Chase and Rusty looked toward the two people who had just walked in the door and found Quintin with Mrs. Whitley.

"I'm sorry to bother you," she offered, her eyes going back and forth between Rusty and her employer, "but Quintin wants to know if he should have his free play now."

A free play period was something new to Chase, so he looked to Rusty. Rusty was looking right back.

"You don't mind if he joins us, do you, Mr. McCandles?"

"Not at all," Chase replied happily. He felt awful that he'd forgotten his son so swiftly.

"Come here, Quin." Rusty held out a hand. Quintin came right to her, and Rusty lifted him into her lap. "Quintin McCandles, I would like to introduce you to my parents, Mr. and Mrs. Taggart."

"Hello, Quintin," Clayton and Jackie both said.

"Hello," he said softly.

"How old are you, Quintin?" Clayton asked. He was practically on the edge of his chair, his eyes intent on this beautiful child.

"I'm five."

"You're a very big boy."

He glanced up at Rusty at that remark, and she smiled at him.

"Can you tell my parents what we did today?" she suggested.

Quintin moved to stand on the floor, and this time Rusty let him.

"We ate chicken, but we didn't have dessert."

"Chicken," Jackie interjected. "That's my favorite."

"I have a watch," Quintin couldn't help but say. The lovely gift had not been far from his thoughts all day.

"You do?" Clayton asked. "May we see it?"

Quintin went right over to the sofa and carefully withdrew the watch from his pocket.

"Well, would you look at that." Clayton was impressed. "May I hold it in my hand, Quintin?"

Quintin handed the watch over without a qualm. Clayton studied it and then passed it into Jackie's hand.

"It's a miniature," she said softly. "This is wonderful, Quintin. Was it a gift?"

The little boy nodded. "From my father. It was his."

"It's so small and perfect," Jackie said, still "seeing" it in the palm of her hand. "You must be so happy to have it."

As she had been doing off and on since they'd sat down, Rusty glanced from Quintin and her parents to Chase and once again found his eyes on her. His gaze was a bit intense, and not for the first time Rusty wondered if she'd done something wrong.

It was so different here. At the orphanage her duties were well-delineated, but at Briarly so much was left up to the moment and day. And now with Mr. McCandles' change toward his son, she felt even more uncertain than she had before. When should she step in, and when should she hold back? Then there was the scene in town. She had all but defied him outside the barbershop.

"I think," Jackie mentioned quietly, "that I would like to freshen up a bit."

"You and Papa can take my room, Mother," Rusty immediately offered. "I'll sleep in Quintin's."

"The guest room is all made up," Chase quietly put in. "I think your parents will be quite comfortable in there, Katherine."

431

"Oh, all right." Rusty had a sudden idea. "Quintin, would you mind showing my parents where the guest room is? I'll come along in a few minutes."

"Yes, Aunt Rusty."

"Thank you, Chase," Clayton said as they stood.

"Yes, thank you, Mr. McCandles," Jackie added.

Chase had also come to his feet. "You're welcome. If you need anything at all, you need only ask."

Thankfully Chase did not miss the significance of Rusty's orders to his son, and as Quintin led Jackie and Clayton from the room, he hung back with Quintin's companion. She watched her parents leave with their small escort and turned to find Chase's eyes on her once again.

"Is everything all right, Katherine?"

"I think so."

"Did you need something?"

"Only to ask you a question."

Chase gestured with his hand and indicated one end of the davenport. He took the chair nearest her after she'd seated herself.

"Mr. McCandles, may I assume that you'll tell me if something is wrong; that is, if you're not pleased with me or my performance?"

"Absolutely," he said without a moment's hesitation. "Has something made you think I was unhappy?"

Rusty moved her hands restlessly, clearly uncomfortable with mentioning what was on her mind. She was grateful when Chase understood.

"Is it because I stared at you just now, or because of what happened in town?"

"A little of both, I guess," she said softly, eyes on her lap, feeling very embarrassed.

She had turned her head just enough so that Chase was given a perfect view of her right ear. It was as bright as a cherry. The conversation in Boulder, the one with Rusty and her mother, came flooding back to him. The temptation to say something very warm and personal to her right now was strong, but he pushed it away.

"I owe you an apology, Katherine," Chase began instead, and Rusty looked at him. "I'm simply horrible when it comes to telling someone they've done well. I'm more than willing to point out mistakes, but my inner attitude of 'no news is good news' doesn't help anyone know when I'm pleased. You're doing a wonderful job. I'm delighted with the changes I see in Quintin and the way you've helped me."

Rusty nodded, pleased that he was not

upset with her, but there was more. "And our words in town —" she began, "are you upset with me over that?"

"I'm not upset with you, but I still don't know how I feel about it," Chase admitted. "You seem comfortable wandering around town at will. For the most part it's very safe, but I'm just not sure you're as cautious as you need to be."

"I'm not completely without fear, Mr. McCandles, but I can't let it control me. Too many times in my life I've been afraid of things, and I wanted to do better this time. I want to stand up to anyone who might threaten me and not cower in fear."

Rusty found Chase sitting next to her almost before she saw him move.

"Please tell me you're not going to do that, Katherine. Please tell me it's just a thought and not a plan. Please tell me you'll yell for the police as you said you would."

He was very close, his head bent so he could speak directly into her face. She met his eyes and wondered why she never noticed what a dark brown they were.

"Katherine?"

"It's not a plan," she said, pulling her mind back to the present subject. "And I would never do anything foolish, but I do wonder how I could do better than I did in Makepeace."

"Katherine," Chase returned, working to keep his voice calm, "my imagination does crazy things when you make statements like that. I picture you walking into some alley, just to take on anyone who might be loitering there."

"I wouldn't do that," Rusty said calmly.

Chase sighed. He still hadn't scared her, which in truth is what he'd hoped to do. He admitted as much and watched Rusty's chin go into the air. It looked as if they were headed into another battle.

"You were trying to scare me?" She was outraged.

With one long finger, Chase pushed Rusty's chin back into place. He then addressed her with maddening calm.

"You have a very nice chin, Miss Taggart, and you can point it at me anytime you like, but before we start shouting at each other, will you please tell me you understand the severity of this issue? By your own admission you tend to be impulsive, so will you please tell me you're not going to take it into your head to confront the next man who acts improperly toward you."

"All right," she agreed, still sounding as if

435

she was searching for another method. "If I decide to stand up to someone, I'll make sure you know."

"That's not exactly what I meant," Chase replied, realizing what he had said.

"Well, it's the best I can do." The stubborn look was back on her face.

"No, it isn't," Chase argued. "You can tell me you're not going to do this at all."

"Are we headed into another huge fight?"

"No, but I want to make sure you don't end up helpless in an alley again."

Rusty stopped. The word "helpless" got her attention like nothing else could. She had been utterly powerless with her back against that building and those men in front of her, and it was not something she wanted to repeat.

"I won't do anything rash."

"Thank you." Chase sat back, knowing she was good as her word. He also had to lighten this conversation — talks with Rusty that went along this vein were going to result in someone's heart failure: his.

"I'm relieved," he added. "For a minute there, I thought I was going to have to resort to blackmail."

Since he'd moved back from the edge of the davenport and was sitting right next to her, Rusty had to turn in the seat to see his face more fully. He was looking very pleased with himself.

"Blackmail? What would you use?"

"Oh, just a little information about a certain woman whose ears turn red when she's embarrassed."

Rusty smiled. "You wouldn't."

"I would." He shook his head in mock severity. "I wouldn't have any choice. A man has to do what he has to do."

Rusty bit her lip to keep from laughing. "You're shameful," she finally accused.

"Not at all. Like I said, I wouldn't have a choice."

"In that case, I'll just have to wear my hair down for the rest of the summer."

"Now, that would be a shame."

The warmth and extra softness of his voice made Rusty stop and study him. Chase looked right back. It was the first time Rusty saw it: interest — pure, straightforward interest that Chase McCandles did nothing to hide. Emotions surged through the small redhead, who found she couldn't speak; neither could she look away. Not knowing if he'd moved too swiftly or not, Chase was just as silent.

It was some minutes before Rusty could find her voice to tell Chase that she had to check on Quintin. If she had looked panicked, he would never have let her go, but the sweet smile she gave him before she left the room did his heart a world of good.

"This is the bed," Quintin told Rusty's parents, his little face very serious. "And this is the mirror." Quintin pointed to the large mirror over the dresser.

"Thank you," Clayton smiled down at him. "It was nice of you to help us find things. Do you ever come in here and look out the window, Quintin? You can see a long way."

The little boy joined Clayton at the lacy curtains.

"That's town. That's Colorado Springs."

"It looks nice. Do you go there often?"

He nodded. "With Aunt Rusty and sometimes my father."

"That must be fun."

Quintin fell silent then, and Clayton knew he needed rescuing. "Thank you for showing us, Quintin."

"You're welcome. I have to find Aunt Rusty now."

"All right. We'll see you later."

Clayton waited for him to walk out the door and then closed it softly.

"Oh, Clayton," Jackie breathed as soon as they were alone. She had parked herself by the footboard of the bed until Clayton could give her the layout of the room. "If he's half as darling as he sounds, Rusty must be in love with him."

"He is very cute," Clayton told her without hesitation. "And I'm sure you're right. I'm half in love with him, and I just got here."

"Tell me, Clay." There was a catch in Jackie's voice. "Was I just hearing the voice of my first grandchild?"

Clayton came to her, wrapping his arms tightly around her. He bent close to her ear and said, "Yes."

"Oh, Clayton," she cried as her husband held her.

"Did you hear anything this time?"

"Not yet." She sniffed and felt for her hankie. Clayton found it for her. "Tell me what you saw."

"He can't keep his eyes off of her. It's more obvious than it was in Boulder, and now she looks back at him. I was open to being wrong until Quintin came in and Rusty held him in her lap. I could see that Chase's heart had gone into his eyes. He could hardly look away."

"Do you think Rusty realizes?"

"I'm not certain. Something tells me the relationship between Chase and Quintin is better, and that's going to go a long way in getting Rusty's attention."

Jackie took a deep breath. "I knew when she moved to Manitou that we wouldn't be around to watch something like this happen, but it's so hard not to be here, Clayton."

"Yes, it is, but I can tell you she looks wonderful, and we know from her letters that she's thinking well and trying to deal with the surprises that come up. What else can we ask for?"

"You're right. Instead of being thankful that we're here now, I'm complaining about not having her all the time!"

Clayton pressed a kiss to her forehead, but Jackie lifted her face. Clayton was more than happy to oblige, and several more minutes passed before either one remembered that Jackie still needed to know the layout of the room.

37

"Did you get my letter?" Clayton quietly asked of Chase soon after dinner that night.

"Something this week? No, I didn't."

Clayton frowned. "I must have mailed it too late."

"Was there something you needed?"

"I don't want to presume upon your hospitality, Chase."

"I sincerely doubt that will be a problem."

Clayton nodded. "I wrote to Paddy to let him know that we would be here. I'm hoping he will bring Sammy over to surprise Jackie, but I'm afraid you'll feel like we've invaded."

"On the contrary, I've been trying to get Paddy and Sammy to visit for months. I hope they come and bring all the kids."

"Great. If they don't, we'll go ahead and make time to stop there on Monday before

441

we go north. It means getting home later and spending less time with them, but Jackie hasn't seen Sammy for months."

"Well, I hope they come, and I assure you they are welcome. I'll inform Mrs. Whitley so she can prepare Mrs. Harding's room."

"They may not come, Chase. I don't want your staff to go to a lot of trouble."

"My housekeeper, Mrs. Whitley, will not feel that way. It's usually pretty quiet around here, and I know she likes company."

"All right. I can also let Rusty know. She's always willing to help out."

It had not been Clayton's intention to play games with Chase, to look for some sort of reaction or set him up in any way, but the look that crossed the younger man's face at the mention of his daughter's name was unmistakable — something was going on.

"I think Katherine and your wife are settled in the drawing room with coffee, Mr. Taggart," Chase said in a softer-than-usual voice. "Could I have a private moment with you?"

"Certainly."

Chase led the way from the dining room. The night was cool but comfortable, and he guided Clayton onto the veranda and out toward the gardens.

"You're pleased with Rusty's work,

Chase?" Clayton asked almost immediately.

"Yes, I am. Quintin is having the time of his life. Until Katherine came I didn't realize that I'd been remiss on my son's behalf." The knowledge of this was still so new that Chase paused a moment. "Mrs. Harding meant well," Chase continued slowly, not wanting to sound unkind or cast blame. As Rusty had reminded him, *he* was Quintin's father. "However, she never taught Quintin about life. Katherine is seeing to that, and her influence has been invaluable."

"That's great." Clayton felt proud of his daughter. "Rusty must have told me, but I can't remember — when do you expect Mrs. Harding back?"

Chase paused for a long time. The men were still walking, but Chase hadn't said a word.

"I don't want to ignore your question, Mr. Taggart, but could I ask one of you?"

"Of course."

Chase came to a stop. This was not a question he could ask while casually strolling along. "Would you object to my getting to know your daughter on a personal level?"

"No," Clayton replied without hesitation, "but I can't make assumptions where my daughter is concerned. Rusty's approval must follow my own."

"Of course. To be honest, I haven't spoken to her about this. I wanted to take more time — and when I did, I was going to ask her if she wanted me to check with you, but since you're here, I thought it might be all right to question you in person."

"I'm glad you felt free to do so, but I'm going to be direct with you, Chase. I feel there's no other way. Do you have marriage in mind?"

Chase took a deep breath, wanting to be wholly honest. "I'd be lying if I said I haven't thought of it, but at the moment I only want to know if Katherine would welcome my suit. I don't care for the thought that she might believe I'm just trying to secure a mother for Quintin, so I feel I must move carefully. Alongside of that is the complication of her living here. The last thing I want to do is make us an object of gossip."

Clayton couldn't have been more pleased with the man's reasoning. It was good to know that Rusty was in such careful hands.

"I appreciate that, Chase. Rusty's not been so sheltered that she wouldn't understand empty gossip, but your testimonies could be at stake. You'll keep us informed?"

"Yes, you can count on that. Does Rusty

know that you've invited Paddy and the family?"

"No, but she likes surprises, and in no time she'll have some fun ideas in mind."

"That I can imagine. At times I laugh at your daughter's spontaneous nature, but I must admit there are moments when she scares me to death."

Clayton laughed. "She's been like that from the time she was a child. Her sister Clare was different. If Clare had seen that a pot was going to boil over on the stove, she'd have come for her mother or me. Rusty would simply remove the pot. It's so clear in Rusty's mind: If you see something that needs doing, you do it. At the same time you wonder why you never got the job done before."

"That just about describes her," Chase said with a shake of his head.

"Come now, Chase," Clayton teased him. "You wouldn't want to be bored."

The younger man smiled wryly. "I don't know. Every once in a while, I'd welcome a little boredom."

Clayton could only laugh.

"Your father told me you look well."

"Did he?" Rusty said with a smile. "I'm glad."

"You must be enjoying the work."

"Oh, Mother, Quintin is such a sweet little guy. He stares at your face when you read to him. He's more interested in the person holding him than in the book. The eyes he turned on his father tonight were enough to melt my heart."

"I can tell. I wish you could have heard him show us the room. He took the job so seriously. Am I right that things seem to be better between Mr. McCandles and his son?"

"Yes. Mr. McCandles is trying so hard." Rusty paused. "We had a huge fight. I was out of line, but he was very forgiving."

"But you think it helped."

"Yes, I do. Wrong as I was to attack him, he wasn't aware of what he'd been doing. As I said, he's forgiven me for the way I spoke to him, but he's also taken things to heart and is trying."

"You must be so pleased."

"Yes, I am," Rusty said softly as snatches from the day came back to her. Quintin was special, but then so was Mr. McCandles. Rusty was more drawn to him all the time. Even when she was angry with him, she somehow wanted to protect and help him. Anyone meeting him would not see him as a man in need of help, but Rusty wouldn't have agreed.

"You've fallen quiet."

"Just thinking."

"About Mr. McCandles?"

"Yes."

"Is your heart being affected in all of this, Rusty?"

"I think it is, Mother. I'm not sure how I feel about that."

"Shall I tell you how I feel?"

"Oh, please do."

"I don't think you should fight this, Rusty, even if it means letting yourself fall in love."

"Oh, Mother."

"Come here, dear." Jackie needed her oldest child closer. "Come so I can see you."

They had been side by side on the davenport, but Rusty moved until Jackie could put an arm around her. Jackie spoke again once she'd pulled Rusty close and cradled her cheek with her free hand.

"Did I frighten you?"

"No, but it's a little shocking when someone so perfectly speaks my thoughts."

"What did I say?"

"That I'm afraid to let myself fall in love with him. It's the truth, Mother."

"Why does it frighten you?"

"Because I'm afraid he won't love me in return. But worse than that, I'm still afraid he might not be a good father. I couldn't stand that."

Jackie pulled Rusty's head down close and rested her cheek on the top of her head. *What do I say, Father? I can't promise her that Mr. McCandles will love her, although I suspect he already does. I can't tell her just to throw caution to the wind; she must think clearly on this. They haven't known each other very long. Help me to be wise and careful with my words. I fell for Clayton so swiftly, but it was years before we had each other. Help me, Lord, and help Rusty to know her heart but never to forget Yours.*

"We are never to worry, Rusty," Jackie said softly. "That's a much easier thing to say than to practice, but God is firm on this subject: Worry is a sin. If you are fretting about your feelings or whether he'll be a good father, you must confess your lack of trust. God has so much better for us than we ever do for ourselves, and His yoke and burden are light. Did that make sense?"

"Perfect sense. Thank you." Rusty paused again. "How would you feel about Mr. McCandles in the family, Mother?"

"If you love him, and you both want to build your relationship and family in Christ, I think it would be wonderful."

Rusty sighed, a huge load lifting from her

heart. For some reason she needed her mother's permission; and not just her permission, but her approval with God's standard behind it. She knew if she kept this in mind she could not go wrong.

"You're feeling better already, aren't you?"

"Yes. I needed to hear those words."

Jackie pressed a kiss to her brow. "I'm glad, but I must be honest with you and tell you that your hairpins are putting a hole in my cheek."

Rusty sat up with a surprised laugh. Jackie joined her. By the time the men gained the drawing room, the women were both flushed with giggles that were aided by fatigue. They knew it was time to head to bed when neither of them could explain why they were laughing. Clayton and Chase let them go. Rusty walked with her mother upstairs where they talked a little more, but both women were sound asleep when the men finally called it a day and came upstairs themselves.

Saturday morning started with the O'Briens' arrival. All the McCandles and Taggarts were gathered in the breakfast room when Mrs. Whitley told Chase privately that he had visitors. Just seconds later he was hugging Sammy and putting his finger up to silence the children. With a sparkle

449

of delight in his eyes, Chase led the way under the arch, into the hallway, and finally into the breakfast room.

Jackie's head turned at the sound. She could tell that several people had entered the breakfast room, but for a moment no one spoke. There was a small giggle, but Jackie didn't think it was Quintin. This only added to her curiosity.

"Hello, Jackie."

Jackie's face split with a huge smile. "Hello, Sammy. I've had a feeling Clayton's been up to something. Are you all here?"

"Yes, we are," Paddy answered as they surged en masse to hug and greet one another. What followed was a scene of complete confusion punctuated with laughter and giggles. Quintin met everyone, a smile on his face, but then sought Rusty's lap as a refuge. It wasn't often that he saw this many people in Briarly, let alone in the breakfast room.

"Renny." From her corner of the table, Jackie was almost through "seeing" everyone. She spoke with her hands on the little boy's shoulders. "You're so tall. I wouldn't have known you."

"Aunt Jackie," he said seriously, "we studied about Louis Braille in school. Do you know who he is?"

"I certainly do. I've shown you my Bible and some of my books, haven't I?"

He nodded before remembering. "Yes, I've seen them. He made those, didn't he?"

"Well, he made the method of the raised dots so I could read them."

"He was blind too," Renny informed her.

Jackie smiled and hugged him again. "Thank you for telling me, Renny. I'm so glad you studied him, and I'm so thankful for the method he developed." She sat back in her seat a little and just listened to the words around her.

"I'm so pleased that you got my letter," Clayton was saying. "How long can you stay?"

"Until tomorrow night."

"Good!" Chase declared, echoing everyone's thoughts.

It was just the start of a full day of laughter and fun. The group had a complete tour of the house, stable, and grounds, and then loaded into every carriage that Chase owned and went for a long drive and outing. They missed lunch, but came back in the late afternoon and had an early dinner. Then they played games until it was time to turn in.

More laughter ensued at bedtime as everyone found a place to sleep. Rusty gave her bed up for Paddy and Sammy and bunked in with Quintin. Her cousins took Mrs. Harding's room.

In the morning there was a line for the bathroom, but at last they were all ready and even arrived for church on time. It was not a huge congregation or church building, so it wasn't hard to take up an entire pew. Pastor Radke was relaxed and fun, and Rusty felt her heart swell with pleasure when he asked Chase to introduce his guests.

"This is Clayton and Jackie Taggart, Katherine's parents. They live in Boulder. And Mrs. Taggart's sister and family. It's been awhile since they've been here, so I'll refresh your memory. This is Padriac, Samantha, Eileen, Nolan, and Renny O'Brien from Manitou."

"You're with the orphanage that Chase supports, is that right, Mr. O'Brien?"

"That's right."

"We pray for you often. Would you mind giving us a rundown on the work there?"

"I'd be happy to," Paddy agreed and took the next few minutes to do so. He gave the present number of children at the orphanage, as well as the present number of staff, and then closed with these words, "Please know that God is honoring your prayers on our behalf. Some children Rusty placed just this spring, a boy and a girl, visited us with their new parents last week. They're doing so well with their new family that the parents are interested in two more children. God is doing great and mighty things, and we thank you for remembering us."

"Thank you, Mr. O'Brien," Pastor Radke said sincerely. And with that the service was underway. As with most Sundays, it was a special time of praise and nourishment from God's Word for Rusty, but her mind was also on something else, or rather someone else, this morning. She finally had a moment with that someone when they were all back at Briarly for lunch.

"I didn't know," Rusty whispered so softly to Chase that he had to bend down. Everyone else had gone inside, but Rusty lingered without in order to have a moment alone with her employer. Chase didn't mind. She looked beautiful in the new dress her mother had had made for her, the very one they had chosen the fabric for on Rusty's last trip home.

"I didn't know you were a benefactor at Fountain Creek." She was still speaking very softly, and Chase stayed bent over to hear her, his eyes on her face.

"Does that bother you?" His voice was quiet too.

"No, I just didn't know." She was afraid she might become emotional, but she still had to say it. "You make it possible for those children to have a home, and well, all this time," she shook her head. "I just didn't know." Rusty ran out of words. For a moment she looked into his face and then suddenly shifted just enough to tenderly kiss his cheek. Chase's brows rose in question, and Rusty dropped her eyes.

"I think you're wonderful," she told him by way of explanation and began to turn toward the house. Chase stopped her with a hand to her arm.

"Thank you," he said when she let her eyes meet his.

Seeing how pleased he was, Rusty was glad she'd said something. She smiled a lavender blaze at him, but Chase didn't detain her any longer. However, he thought about the kiss off and on for the rest of the day.

"It's been a wonderful weekend," Clayton said to Rusty as they took a stroll around the property.

"Yes, it has. You and Mother can surprise me anytime you like."

Clayton only smiled.

"What train are you taking?"

454

"The ten o'clock. We'll get in a little later, but it's nice not having to rush around this morning."

"Please hug my sisters and brother for me."

"I'll do that. They'll have a hundred questions for me."

"Well, tell them I'm doing fine and that they all could write a little more often."

Clayton laughed. "I'll tell them, but Clare for one is so busy at Mrs. Wood's, you probably won't hear a thing."

"She told me in her last *brief* letter that she loves it, and that Mrs. Wood said to tell me hello."

"She does love it, and Mrs. Wood is a gem. Clare hasn't heard from anyone overseas yet, but her enthusiasm mounts daily."

"I'm so happy for her."

"She'll be happy for you too," Clayton said calmly.

"Over what?"

Clay only glanced at the house and then back at his daughter, who looked content.

"I'm leading with my head, Papa, just like you told me, so don't give Clare any news yet."

Clayton smiled at her. It was foolish to take Rusty Taggart for granted. Her innocent eyes and impetuous nature made her seem overly protected and naive, but beneath that head of dark red curls was a hardworking mind.

"I will tell Clare and your other siblings that you're doing fine, because it's very true."

Rusty's smile was warm. "Thank you, Papa."

With Clayton's arm around her shoulder, the two strolled back toward the house to join Jackie, Chase, and Quintin in the breakfast room. Rusty felt no sadness when Briarly's coach took them away an hour later. It had been a wonderful weekend, and her heart was so thankful that there wasn't room for tears.

38

Two weekends later, near the middle of July, Rusty returned to Manitou for Tibby's wedding, and her absence proved to be an enlightening time for everyone. Chase thoroughly enjoyed his time with Quintin and found his heart did erratic things when the little boy sought him out over Mrs. Whitley, or when he climbed into his lap and called him Papa, as Rusty had begun to refer to him. But still Chase recognized that something was missing, or rather, someone.

Chase had not wanted to pursue things with Rusty too swiftly after the Taggarts had gone home, but the way he missed Rusty on this weekend could not be ignored. He thought about her constantly, and when Quintin asked about her almost as much, he knew it was time to speak with her. Easier to think about than act upon. Just exactly what was he going to say to her — I want to court you? How do you feel about me? Have you ever pictured yourself married to a widower with a child? All those things seemed so contrived. He lost a great deal of sleep over the weekend, but to his surprise the decision was partially taken out of his hands.

Rusty's train had brought her back to Briarly on Sunday night, so Monday morning brought business as usual. Whit had made an early run into town and kindly stopped at the post office on the way back. Normally he would have placed the mail on Chase's desk, but he spotted him in the breakfast room and delivered his correspondence there. On the top of the pile was a personal letter.

"She's not coming back." The words were out of Chase's mouth before he remembered that he was not in his office. He lowered the paper to find both Rusty and Quintin staring at him.

"I beg your pardon?" Rusty said politely.

"She's —" Chase began, but then his eyes darted to Quintin and he shut his mouth. Rusty assumed that he wished to speak to her privately.

"Are you almost finished, Quin?"

"I have to drink my juice."

"All right. When you're through, will you

please run upstairs and check to see if you made your bed?"

"You already checked."

"Oh, did I? Well then, when you're finished you can wait for me on the veranda."

The little boy nodded, but he was in no hurry to leave. Completely oblivious to anyone else in the room, he sipped his juice as if he had all day. Rusty's eyes went to her employer and found him looking very amused. They shared a small smile before Rusty went back to her breakfast and Chase read more of the letter. At least five more minutes passed before Quintin asked to be excused.

"Yes, you may," Rusty told him and helped him move his chair to leave. She watched as he skipped off but noticed that he turned in the wrong direction. Rusty stood and went to the door.

"Quin," she called to him. "I thought you were going to be on the veranda."

"I am," he stopped and said to her, "but I have to thank Cook."

Rusty smiled at him. "I'll find you wherever you end up."

"All right."

With that Rusty stepped back into the breakfast room and took the chair immediately to Chase's right.

"Did you need me, sir?"

"Yes, thank you," Chase said calmly, thinking it was an odd time for him to wish she would call him Chase. "I've had a letter from Mrs. Harding. She's to be married in a few weeks' time and will not be returning."

Rusty's mouth opened in a most un-feminine way, and Chase chuckled at the sight.

"That's just the way I felt when I read this letter." He lifted the paper.

Rusty still could not laugh; she could only think of Quintin.

"Do you think Quintin will be terribly upset?"

Chase's brows rose. "I don't think he'll be upset at all."

Rusty looked taken aback.

"I can see that I've shocked you, Katherine, but the truth of the matter is, I don't believe he's given her a thought since you arrived."

Rusty was at a complete loss. Was that possible? She then remembered the first day she and Quintin had spent together many weeks ago. Yes, it was possible. A child who had been under that much rule would cherish his freedom indeed.

"What will you do?" Rusty finally asked quietly.

"Two options come to mind," Chase said without elaborating.

Rusty knew better than to question him. After all, it wasn't her business — but she did need to tell him that she understood how Mrs. Harding's departure could affect the situation.

"I'll understand if you don't need me to stay the entire summer, Mr. McCandles. I know this changes our original plans."

Chase studied her and said simply, "That all depends on which option I take. If I hire another companion for Quintin, you're right — I won't need you to stay. If I take the other option, however, I'll need you very much."

It took Rusty a very brief time to catch his meaning. When she did, she could only stare. She licked her lips and tried to say something. A second later she froze and watched her employer reach up and tuck her hair behind her left ear. He smiled, and she knew it was bright red. Rusty swiftly raised her hand to bring the hair back out, but Chase caught it and held her hand in his own.

"Have I horrified you, Katherine?"

"No," she said softly, "I'm just so surprised. That is," she hesitated as a heartsinking thought struck. "Oh, I see."

"What do you see?"

"You need a mother for Quintin."

"You're not even close," he told her in no uncertain terms. "This is not about a mother for Quintin. Is that clear to you?"

"I think so." She was trying to get used to the idea in such a short time.

"But?" he prompted her.

Rusty saw no choice but to be honest. "If that's the case, it's even more of a surprise."

"Why is that?" Chase had to know.

"Aunt Rusty?" Quintin chose that moment to look for her, and Rusty realized they'd been talking for quite some time. She pulled her hand from Chase's hold, and he let her go. But before she could speak to him or rise, Chase called his son over.

"Come here, Quintin."

The little boy came right to his father, and Chase lifted him into his lap.

"Mrs. Harding has written me a letter," Chase wasted no time in saying. "She's going to be married this summer to a man in South Carolina. She won't be coming back to us."

Quintin looked up at his father and then over to Rusty. He looked back at Chase.

"Is Aunt Rusty going to stay with me?"

"That's what we're talking about right now. No decision has been made for the present, but I wanted you to know about

Mrs. Harding. Won't getting married be nice for her?"

"Do I know that man?"

"No," Chase replied, picking up the letter. "He's a man she's known for years but hasn't seen for quite a while. They're going to be married on July 31."

"I think you should marry Aunt Rusty," Quintin said without even looking at the woman. Chase wisely didn't look at her either.

"Do you?"

"Yes. She could stay with me."

Chase tenderly smoothed his son's hair but didn't comment or question him further.

"I think I'll go upstairs for a few minutes," Rusty said, her voice breathless.

Chase wanted to stop her but, seeing how pale she was, wisely didn't.

"I'll see you in a little bit, Quin," Rusty said softly.

She made for the door, the sound of Chase's voice in her ears as he gave instructions to Quintin. She did not expect Chase to stop her before she could gain the second stair.

"Can we talk tonight?" he asked, both his hand and eyes holding her.

"Yes."

"Have I ruined your day?"

"No."

"But you're upset."

"I don't know what I am," Rusty admitted, telling herself not to cry.

Chase's thumb stroked the back of her hand, and Rusty's eyes softened.

"Please give me time, Mr. McCandles."

Chase smiled. "I'll give you all the time in the world if you'll just call me Chase."

Rusty sighed, her heart needing this lighter subject. "Chase Jefferson McCandles."

"It's rather a mouthful, isn't it?"

"I think it's easier than Katherine Alexa Taggart."

Chase relaxed. Her voice was back to normal, and he felt he could at least let go of her hand.

"Quintin and I will go on a walk in the woods or to the stable. Will you come down when you're up to it and join us?"

"Yes."

"And we'll talk tonight."

"All right. Thank you."

He had no choice but to let her go, although it was the last thing he wanted to do. She still looked shaken. He comforted himself with the knowledge that they could have an uninterrupted conversation after dinner that evening. What he didn't know was that

Rusty would not join them in the woods before Quintin would need to come back to the house for a personal need or that his mother and stepfather would show up just as he and his son were headed back outside.

"Oh, Quintin," Nan Capland said for the fifth time. "You've grown so much, and Grandma is so proud of you. Look at him, Cap," she said to her husband, whose full name was John Charles Capland III. That man grinned at the little boy in their midst but didn't speak.

Quintin smiled up at his grandmother before saying, "I have a watch."

"You do?"

"I think you'll recognize it," Chase put in. He sat across from them on an overstuffed chair, one that would give him a view of the stairs.

Nan looked surprised by this until Quintin pulled the watch from his pocket and held it out for inspection.

"Oh, Quintin, you have the watch! Do you know how proud your father was of this watch? He loved it, and he gave it to you."

Nan looked across to smile at her son, but his attention was focused on the door. He stood a moment later, excused himself, and went to the hall.

"My mother and stepfather are here," Chase told Rusty, who had just gained the bottom step.

"Oh." Rusty's eyes grew large.

Outside of her family, Briarly had not had company since she'd come. She hated to presume. "Would you like me to go to Manitou for a few days and give you some time alone with them?"

Chase blinked at her, looking slightly shocked. "Do you know how much trouble I would be in if Quintin's companion didn't meet my mother?" He shuddered theatrically.

His actions and voice were so dramatic that Rusty laughed her normal, loud laugh and had to slap her hand over her mouth. Chase smiled hugely at her. Just a moment later she heard Quintin's voice.

"Aunt Rusty, Aunt Rusty," he cried, dashing into the foyer. "Come and meet Grandma. She's here to see me!"

Rusty fell in with his enthusiasm without a moment's hesitation, allowing him to take her hand and lead her to the drawing room. She didn't count on Quintin's breach of manners.

"This is Aunt Rusty," Quintin said as soon as he entered the room. Although she knew he was excited, Rusty nonetheless felt embarrassed when her small charge interrupted the man and woman who were speaking to each other. It grew worse when Cap came to his feet but Nan just sat still and stared at her as if she'd had the shock of her life.

"Hello," Rusty said. She was smiling but feeling terribly awkward.

"Please allow me to make the introductions," Chase broke in as he stepped beside her. Rusty turned grateful eyes to him. "Miss Katherine Taggart, please allow me to introduce my mother, Nan Capland, and her husband, John Capland."

Nan recovered herself and stood, a gracious smile coming to her face.

"How lovely to meet you, Katherine. I can already see that Quintin is very blessed to have you."

Rusty smiled. "It's a pleasure to meet both of you, and please call me Rusty."

"Join us, Katherine." Chase indicated the nearest chair and waited until she sat down.

"I need to find my bear," Quintin said, coming close to his companion. "I need to show Grandma my bear."

"All right. I think it must be in your room."

Quintin turned to charge from the drawing room, but a very soft word from Rusty stopped him.

"Quintin."

He spun and caught her look.

"Oh, okay." He turned to the other adults. "Please excuse me now," he said to the room at large, and still in an obvious hurry, he turned, moving much more slowly to walk from the room.

Rusty watched him take the stairs at breakneck speed, but he didn't look back so she could catch his eye. When she turned around, the other three adults were watching her. Her ears felt on fire. She was thankful she'd worn her hair down.

"I'm sorry," she said softly and sincerely, her eyes telling of her shame. "You must wonder how Mr. McCandles could have ever hired anyone so ill-equipped to care for Quintin. I've let much of his good training go by the wayside. I hope you won't hold it against him. It's all my fault."

Chase was on the verge of going to her. He couldn't stand to see her upset over something that needed no apology. But his mother jumped in ahead of him.

"We weren't thinking that at all, Rusty," she said softly. "I've never seen my grandson so happy. In light of that, I don't care if he runs from the room or never remembers to thank me."

Rusty smiled at her. "You're too kind, Mrs. Capland."

"Not at all," she spoke bracingly. "I only spoke the truth."

"How long will you be here, Mother?" Chase realized he'd not asked. He also thought Rusty needed to be rescued with a change in subject.

"Until you throw us out," she returned with her standard reply.

Chase frowned. "I just realized how early in the day it is. When did your train get in?"

"Last night," Cap answered. "It was late so we stayed in town."

Mrs. Whitley came to the door of the drawing room and spoke to Chase.

"Lunch in the dining room today, sir?"

"Please."

"And at the regular time?"

"I think so. What are your plans, Cap?"

"We haven't scheduled a thing."

Chase turned back to his invaluable housekeeper. "That will be fine, thank you."

On the heels of Mrs. Whitley's departure, Quintin arrived with his bear. For the next hour Nan and Cap were wholly taken up with the little boy, and that suited Rusty, who needed time to think. Had Chase McCandles all but proposed to her earlier? Rusty was beginning to doubt her own sanity. She'd gone upstairs to try to make sense of it all but ended up sitting on her bed and staring off into space. She knew that this was not the way to deal with her confusion, but she felt overwhelmed.

It was even more of a relief when lunch was called over an hour later, and served in the elegant dining room. Rusty's time and attention were taken up with Quintin's needs during the meal. The other adults seemed sensitive to this, and little conversation came her way. However, she had the distinct impression that it was going to be a long day.

39

"Where did you find that girl?" Nan asked her son the next afternoon. She had tracked him down in his office.

Chase came to his feet until his mother sat down in one of the office chairs. "She's the young woman I escorted from the orphanage, the one who placed the children I wrote you about."

"Please don't let her get away, Chase. She's so special, and I can see that Quintin adores her."

He smiled. "If I have anything to say about it, she'll not be going anywhere."

Childish laughter coming through an open window caused them both to move to the windows behind Chase's desk. They watched Cap, Rusty, and Quintin in the garden. The little boy was talking to his step-grandfather, and Rusty was down on her knees gathering blooms into her hand. As they watched, Nan's husband leaned down to kiss Quintin's forehead before starting toward the veranda.

"In the office," Nan called to him when they heard the door. Cap was with them a moment later.

"You looked as though you were having fun," Nan told him as she went up on her toes to kiss his cheek. Cap put an arm around her waist.

"I was. I thought Quintin was good with bird names, but he can name all the flowers too."

"He's remarkably intelligent," his grandmother proclaimed in complete sincerity. "I've always known it."

Cap smiled down at her but then looked at Chase and asked, "How smart is his father?"

Chase laughed. "Something tells me I can't win with that question, no matter what I say."

"That's not true," Cap went on. "You just have to tell me you're going to marry that little girl, and I'll call you brilliant."

"I've just been telling him the same thing," Nan put in. "Do you hear that, Chase? Cap and I agree, so you know it's the right thing."

"Thank you," he said dryly. "Should I check with the lovely lady herself or just tell her we've all agreed."

The older two were full of merriment, but Chase knew they were serious about Rusty. *He* was serious, but finding time to talk to the woman in question was proving to be a chore. His mother and stepfather were talking now and moving toward the drawing room. Chase returned to the window. Rusty and Quintin were still in the garden. The afternoon sun bounced off Rusty's hair, giving her a red halo, and Chase's eyes were riveted to her. He watched Quintin go down on his knees beside her and then slip an arm around her neck. Rusty turned and kissed his small cheek, and Quintin just stood holding her close with his arm.

Why didn't I find it strange that Mrs. Harding never touched Quintin? Why didn't I notice? Chase asked of the Lord, but he knew the answer. He was too wrapped up in his business to see anything. Chase's eyes now went to his desk. Things were not getting done as they should be, and that brought more questions. Should he sell off some of his properties, all of which he managed himself, or hire a manager?

Chase turned away from the window just

then, or he would have seen Rusty and Quintin leave their flowers and wander toward the woods. It was hot in the garden, and Rusty had forgotten her bonnet. She was hoping to escape even more sunburn by moving to the cool of the trees.

"Are you sad, Aunt Rusty?" Quintin surprised her by asking. She hadn't even been aware of scrutiny.

"No, Quin, I'm not. Why did you ask?"

"Your face looks sad."

"I was just thinking."

"About marrying my papa?"

Rusty stared at him. Could he actually know about that, or was he remembering his own suggestion to his father the day before? And what did Rusty say now, since she *had* been thinking about marriage to Chase McCandles?

"Sometimes it's best to let someone be private with her thoughts, Quin. So if you don't mind, I don't think I'll tell you right now."

The rebuke was given gently, but Quintin got the point. He nodded and looked toward the trees, but before he could ask if Rusty wanted to climb one, he remembered his grandmother. With Aunt Rusty to play with, he had actually forgotten she was there.

"Can I go see my grandma now?"

"*May* I," Rusty corrected, "and yes, I think that would be fine. Would you like me to come?"

"Yes, please."

Rusty escorted him to the house and waited until he had gone through to the drawing room. She listened as Nan greeted him with enthusiasm and then made her way to the kitchen. Rick was at the table working over a bowl of green beans. Rusty washed her hands and joined him. They had become friends over the past weeks, and although Rusty suspected he was a bit taken with her, he now visited with her with very few blushes and stares.

"You look sad today," Rick said after just a few seconds.

"Quin just said the same thing to me. I must be too wrapped up in myself. Tell me what you did today in school, Rick, and take my mind off me."

He shrugged. "It was the same as always."

"What's your favorite subject?"

"History, but we didn't do much with that today." The young man stared at her. It wasn't polite to tell a lady that her nose was sunburned or that her burned nose and freckles made her look about ten years old, but that was what he was thinking. Her youthful look also added to the sadness in her eyes, and Rick wished he could think of a way to make her laugh. Rusty's laugh was the best he'd ever heard.

"This is a quiet crew," Cook remarked as she came up from the cellar and spotted the two bean-snappers.

Rusty smiled at her and didn't comment, but it did get her to thinking. She *was* being quiet. Why was that? The reason hit her swiftly. She never had a day off, at least not a full day, and she was tired. She'd been at Briarly for more than a month and not had a full day off. She'd been back to Manitou the previous weekend for the wedding, but that had been anything but restful. Her mind made up, her hands began to move faster. Rusty swiftly helped Rick finish the bowl of beans and then walked to the office. As she had hoped, the drawing room was empty, but Chase was behind his desk.

"May I bother you for a moment?"

"No bother at all." Chase had come to his feet and waited for her to enter. Rusty took a seat and began when he sat back down.

"I know I was just away for the weekend, but I was wondering if I could possibly have tomorrow off."

"That would be fine," Chase didn't hesitate to respond, but then he just sat still and looked at her. "Something is bothering you. Can you tell me what it is?"

Rusty shook her head. "Everyone has been asking me that. I think I'm just tired. It's very hard to find rest and time alone when you live in the same house you work in." Rusty stopped talking and looked at him.

Chase worried about her. She did look tired, but something else was amiss. "Take tomorrow off," Chase told her. "Rest. Do whatever you like. Quintin and I will manage just fine. We may take the day off ourselves and spend it with my mother and Cap."

"Thank you," Rusty said gratefully and stood. "I'll plan on that."

"You worked in the garden without your bonnet, didn't you?" Chase asked. His voice was light, but Rusty felt very self-conscious, almost rebuked.

"Yes." She managed a strained smile, her hand going to her nose as she turned away. "I'd better find Quintin." She had to get out. If she stayed she would cry.

"All right," Chase said, not catching the dismay in her eyes. "I told Mrs. Whitley to plan on dinner for the five of us again. I want you and Quintin to join us."

"Yes, we'll do that," Rusty agreed, glad to be back on a business basis. She said good-bye and slipped away to find her charge. Her heart hurt so badly that she thought it might kill her, but now was not the time to dwell on that. She would work hard at her job the whole summer if she had to, but as far as marriage to Chase McCandles went, Rusty's confused heart told her that it would never work.

"Actually," Cap explained to Rusty after dinner that night, "I'm one of the few men in Texas who doesn't run cattle. My father did, but I had no interest, so my brother owns and operates the family ranch. I enjoy work with less dust and travel, so I bought into a boot factory."

"A boot factory?" Rusty had not been expecting that.

Cap grinned. "Cowboys must have their boots, and the best part about it is that it allows me to have more time with Nan."

"How wonderful for you," Rusty said and meant it. She smiled at him and thought how blessed they were. Cap clearly adored his second wife, and if Nan's eyes were any indication, she was as much in love today as she had been when they met.

"Cap," Nan spoke up, "Did we bring that picture of the ranch? I was going to show it to Quintin and forgot all about it. It's the Capland Ranch, taken from the water tower on the edge of the property," Nan explained to Rusty.

"I think we brought it," her husband said. "It should be in the case."

"I'll go get it."

Quintin was already in bed for the night, so he would have to see it later, but Nan wanted Rusty to see it now. She rose to find it, and Cap went on with his story. Nan, however, did not come back. Some time passed, and Cap decided to check on her. Rusty watched him walk from the room and then looked to Chase. As had been the case all evening, he was watching her.

"I want you to be my wife," he said softly, his eyes watching her intently.

Rusty's air left her in a rush. There was no longer any reason to wonder or imagine. Chase had laid his cards on the table for Rusty to see. She had no idea what she was going to say. Intent on framing a reply, her mouth opened but no words came. A moment passed, and just as she thought she had the words, she heard movement on the stairs. Cap and Nan were returning.

"Here it is," Nan cried triumphantly. "This is the house. I think Cap told you his brother and family live there now." She handed a large daguerreotype to Rusty and bent over her shoulder to explain. Rusty took in only half of it.

She had had such dreams. Her parents had warned her from early on to lead with her head and not her heart where romance was concerned, but what girl didn't dream of sweet words and courtship? Mr. McCandles' proposal sounded like a business arrangement. How would she tell him? What should she do? Rusty was so tired of asking herself that question that she ached.

"I think you're tired, Rusty," Nan's voice suddenly came very gently to her ears.

"I'm sorry." Rusty realized Nan had been speaking to her and she hadn't heard a thing.

"There's no need. Cap's daughters and daughter-in-law have little ones. The work you do with Quintin is exhausting. I'm glad you're taking the day off tomorrow."

"You're very kind, Mrs. Capland."

"I'm also wise enough to see that you need to be rescued. Go to bed, Rusty."

Rusty smiled at her, a wide, genuine smile. "I believe I will." With that she stood. The men came to their feet as Rusty bid everyone goodnight. Chase announced that he would walk her upstairs. Rusty didn't comment. She was too tired to care one way or the other.

As it was, Chase said not a word. He walked Rusty up the stairs and to her door where she turned and looked up at him. A moment later he bent his head and kissed her softly on the mouth.

"I haven't said I would marry you." Surprised as she was, Rusty felt the need to remind him.

"I must be more aware of that than anyone, Katherine."

"Then why the kiss?"

Chase's eyes traversed her face, as if memorizing every detail. "Before you stands a man who's desperate to show you that he's not trying to secure a mother for his child."

Rusty sadly shook her head.

"Why can't you believe that, Katherine?"

Her hands moved helplessly; she saw no help for it but to tell him. "I don't think you even find me attractive," she said softly. "Maybe when I wear my hair up, but that's not very often. Sometimes you seem exasperated with my ideas, and I think you see me as something of a child. I couldn't live in a marriage like that, a marriage of convenience so you'll have a live-in nanny for Quintin. I want children of my own, lots of them.

"I also think you must find me a very shallow person, but I'm not. I give much more thought to things than you think I do. I haven't seen much of the world, but I'm not the foolish little girl you imagine. I'm a woman, capable and willing to work hard. It's true that I make mistakes and look on life as an adventure, but just because I have the heart of a child when I play with one doesn't mean that I'm a child myself."

"Oh, Katherine," Chase whispered — he'd never known such pain.

"It's all right." She knew she needed to release him before he could say another word. "I understand. I would never hold you to your proposal. You just didn't realize that you felt that way. I'll work as long as you need me to this summer, but I won't mention any of this again. You can still count on me to work hard and put this behind us."

Chase was too stunned to move or he'd have taken her in his arms. This was all his fault, and he knew it. He should have made time to talk with her the day he received Mrs. Harding's letter, but he didn't do it, and now she thought this.

"I love you, Katherine," he said softly.

Rusty stared at him.

"And it's all my fault that you don't know that. I haven't talked with you. I haven't been the same since I stood at the train station and looked up to see you coming toward me with the Parks children."

Rusty couldn't believe what she was hearing.

"I should have told my mother when she arrived that the timing was terrible, and that I needed to be alone with you. She and Cap would have understood. We could have left Quintin with them and gone into town for the day or even taken the train to Manitou, anything that would have given us time so I could do this properly."

Rusty was still speechless.

"You see, this has nothing to do with Mrs. Harding. I was trying to figure out how I would word the letter to her when I wrote to tell her I wouldn't need her anymore: I'd found a woman to love and marry. I asked your father when they were here that weekend if he would object to my approaching you. He told me that he approved as long as you did, but I didn't want to rush you."

Rusty licked her lips. She could hardly breathe.

"I know you're tired, and I didn't plan to overwhelm you tonight as I have, but will you tell me one thing?"

Rusty nodded yes.

"Are you open to hearing more from me on this subject, or do you wish to tell me right now that you never want marriage mentioned between us again?"

Again Rusty licked her lips. "A real marriage?"

"Oh, yes," His voice had grown even softer. "With *many* children."

"You love me?" She had to make sure she'd heard him right.

"So very much."

It was all too huge. She couldn't take it in, but she had to tell him that she did want to hear more.

"On Thursday," Chase said slowly, "after you've had your day off, could we talk of this?"

He had rescued her. Rusty could have sobbed with relief but didn't. She said only, "I would like that."

"I need to let you rest now."

Rusty nodded. It was very true.

"Goodnight, sweet Katherine. Please don't be upset about this. Just rest, and we'll talk soon."

"All right. Goodnight."

Rusty was in a state of shock as she readied for bed. She didn't remember entering the room or shutting the door. She went through the motions of bedtime preparation without thought or emotion. Once beneath the covers she felt she could cry herself to sleep, but it didn't happen. Rusty lay there dry-eyed until she couldn't hold her eyes open any longer, and then slept for the next 11 hours.

40

Not surprisingly, Chase McCandles was the first thought on Rusty's mind the next morning. *He loves me,* she thought in amazement. *It doesn't take every problem away, but he does love me. I could see it in his eyes. I thought this was about Quintin, and I know it is, but its not just about Quintin. Thank You, Lord. Thank You for loving me so much. Thank You for putting Chase and Quintin into my life.*

Rusty lay in bed and tried to take it in. She was not the giddy type, but this made her want to be with Clare and Dana so she could whisper the news to them, have her sisters hug her, and then giggle like little girls again.

I think he's so special, Lord. I love the way he tries with Quintin. Some mornings I can see he's preoccupied, wanting to read the paper, but I've seen him force his attention to his son and try to get into his world. He doesn't always remember to do that, but he tries. He doesn't talk enough, Lord. He doesn't tell me what he's thinking, and I think he takes his responsibility for me a little too seriously, but I could love this man with all my heart.

I don't know what he does, not really. I haven't felt it was my place to ask. I assume he owns property and such — I guess he did tell me that — but I don't really know where all of this came from or how it all works. Rusty felt better just having said this, but there was more. She talked to the Lord for close to an hour before she fell asleep again.

Downstairs and all over Briarly it was very quiet. Chase had let everyone know that Rusty needed rest. Chase, however, did not bank on accomplishing so little. His mother and Cap had taken Quintin out for the day. He was free to get as much done as he needed, but all he could do was stare out the window and think about the previous night. Rusty had looked him in the eye and told him he didn't know his own heart, but that she would never hold it against him. Chase had all he could do not to weep.

I wouldn't let myself overwhelm her, and now I've taken it too far the other way. I thought she might be able to tell by the way I look at her, but that's not working. Well, things are going to change, Katherine Alexa Taggart. You'll doubt my feelings no more.

Chase caught movement from the corner of his eye. He looked over and watched Melinda Whitley come across the drawing room toward him. She stopped at his open door.

"It's coming on to lunch, sir, and Cook says Rusty hasn't been down at all. Should I check on her?"

You think I'm a child.

"No," Chase said softly even as he heard Rusty's voice in his mind. "She'll come down when she needs something."

Mrs. Whitley nodded, but she looked miserable.

"She would not thank us for babying her," Chase said gently, as much for himself as for the housekeeper.

The woman sighed. "You're right, of course, but there's just something so young and vulnerable about her."

Chase couldn't disagree with her, but Rusty had been partially right in her description last night. While they were in Kurth he had determined not to baby her by telling her to eat her food, but somewhere along the way he started to treat her as a child. He had never considered her shallow, but at times he did treat her as an underling and not an equal. It was true that she didn't always do what he would choose, but what made him the expert?

"How long do I wait, sir?" Melinda's voice cut back into his thoughts.

"To see if she needs something? All day. As tired as she was, she might just need to sleep. She'll come down when she's ready. We'll wait on her to come to us."

"But what if she's become sick in the night and can't get out of bed?" It was the first time the woman had ever argued with him, and Chase thought she might have a point.

"All right," Chase put his hand up, "but that's all. You may check to make sure she's still alive, but no more. If she needs something, she'll ask for it. You know she's never hesitated before."

"Thank you, sir," she said with great relief.

Chase watched her walk away. It had passed through his mind that the staff might have to make some adjustments if Rusty became mistress of Briarly, but the thought had been foolish. He'd never once considered how heartbroken the staff would be to have her leave at the end of the summer. He looked forward to the day when he could tell them that she never had to leave again.

Rusty descended the stairs that evening

feeling as though she'd been given a new lease on life. She'd slept for most of the day. Mrs. Whitley had come to check on her just as she was headed down the hall for a bath. Rusty had been very honest when she said she hadn't needed anything to eat. Mrs. Whitley graciously took her at her word, and as soon as Rusty finished her bath, she had gone back to bed and fallen right back to sleep. Once she woke, she slowly did her hair and nails, studied her Bible, wrote a few letters, and even dressed at a snail's pace.

She was finally hungry. Realizing that she might not have been planned on for dinner, she was prepared to eat in the kitchen. She hit the bottom of the stairs and headed that way. Having seen her from the drawing room, Chase caught her while she was still in the hall.

"Welcome back," he said softly from behind her.

Rusty turned, slightly startled. Chase came to stand in front of her and she self-consciously stepped back against the wall. He just kept coming until his hand was on the wall above her head and his face was bent down to speak to her.

"Were you able to rest?"

"Yes, thank you." Rusty's voice was soft and a bit breathless. He'd come so close, and she was awfully glad to see him, but the things she was feeling were very new to her.

"Would you like to join us for dinner?"

"I was going to eat in the kitchen and not disrupt things."

"We haven't started, and Mrs. Whitley set a place for you just in case."

"Oh. All right."

She would have pushed away from the wall to join him then, but Chase didn't move.

"I missed you today," he told her.

"I thought of you a lot," she admitted.

"Good thoughts?"

"I think so."

Chase couldn't help himself. He reached with two fingers and pulled at one of the springy curls at her temple.

"This hair of yours really has a mind of its own."

"Especially after I wash it."

Chase's brows rose in amusement. "I'd forgotten that you were a lady of leisure today."

Rusty sighed. "It was difficult, but someone had to make the sacrifice."

Chase pushed away from the wall and held his arm out for her. Rusty took it and found that she was glad her ears were covered. All embarrassment faded, however, when she walked to the door of the dining room.

Quintin was just coming from the drawing room, and a moment later he charged toward her. Rusty scooped him into her arms and held him close. Quintin's arms went around her neck, and he buried his face in her hair.

"I missed you today," Rusty said softly.

Quintin pulled back enough to look at her. "I missed you too. We had chicken, and I wanted to bring you some, but Grandma said it wasn't a good idea."

"How sweet of you to think of me, though."

Quintin pushed his face forward so they could rub noses. Rusty turned when Nan and Cap came to join the group. Setting Quintin back on his feet, she greeted them.

"I'm hungry," Cap proclaimed when the amenities were out of the way. Rusty had to agree with him. She hadn't felt a twinge all afternoon, but now she felt hollow. It was wonderful that she didn't have long to wait. Mrs. Whitley and Rick began bringing bowls of food to the table just moments later. Chase seated Rusty and then bent over and whispered into her ear.

"That was quite a greeting Quintin received. I'll have to learn his secret."

Rusty took no time to catch his meaning and looked at him with amused eyes.

"It's just one of those things you can get

491

away with when you're five."

Chase's hand lingered on her shoulder as he moved away, and Rusty thought he looked very pleased with himself. She wasn't feeling too poorly herself. They ate the meal in high spirits, and for the first time since the Caplands had arrived, Rusty felt rested and able to relax with them.

"Tell me, Rusty," Nan invited, "do you have siblings?"

"Yes. Two sisters and a brother. They all live at home with my parents in Boulder."

"So you are the oldest?"

"Yes. Clare is next, then Les and Dana."

"How fun. I always wished for at least one brother or sister for Chase. Has Chase told you I was gone for much of his childhood?"

"Yes, he told me a little. It must have been hard."

Nan shook her head. "At times I thought I would die of loneliness. I knew that someone else was raising my child and that I couldn't be home when my husband needed me. I felt I'd been set free when I finally came back to Briarly."

"What is your home like now?"

That was all Nan needed. In the next minutes Rusty went on to learn that Cap had built a beautiful home for them just a year after they were married. Aspects of it were similar to Briarly, and Rusty could see that it was Nan's delight.

"We attend a small church in Austin, and rather than have a midweek service at the church, we meet in our front room. We've always tried to use our home for the Lord, and He has blessed us time and again. Cap has a Bible study with two young men on Sunday nights, and I've started a weekly tea for some ladies who don't live too far from us. Nothing spiritual has come of it yet, but I'm hopeful."

"Katherine, tell them about your ministry with the children at the church in Manitou," Chase encouraged her.

"Oh, certainly. On Sundays we have a special children's service 45 minutes before the regular service begins. There are several teaching teams, and I'm a part of one of them."

"Who does the teaching?" Cap wished to know.

"On my team, I teach and my partner does the music."

"How old are the children?"

"The age span is anywhere from four to ten."

"That's marvelous," Nan exclaimed.

"You should see her in action." Chase couldn't disguise the pride in his voice.

"She's able to keep 40 children hanging on her every word."

"They're good kids," Rusty said, and everyone could see that she meant it. She didn't really see herself as anything special. However, Cap and Nan looked to Chase, who was watching Rusty, before exchanging a warm, knowing glance.

"Coffee in the drawing room, Mrs. Whitley, if you please," Chase directed when she came to check on them.

"Right away, sir, or a little later?"

"Later is fine, I think, or whenever you have time."

"Very well, sir."

Soon after that, Cap, Nan, Chase, Rusty, and Quintin moved from the dining room to settle in the drawing room. Chase suggested an exception for Quintin, allowing him to come back and join the adults when he was ready for bed. Cap read a story to him while they all listened.

The adults started talking when he finished the story, and while no one was looking, Quintin fell sound asleep in Cap's arms. They left him alone until they all turned in, whereupon Nan and Cap did the honors of tucking their sleeping grandson into bed.

Thinking back on what a restful day and

fun evening it had been, Rusty was certain she would not sleep. However, she slept within minutes of turning down the lantern.

41

Rusty scooted past Chase's chair and under his desk and then sat still. She could still hear Quintin counting in the drawing room, knowing that any moment he would give up and come searching.

"37, 38, 39, 30-ten."

Rusty heard a long pause.

"50! Ready or not, here I come!"

She could hear him moving around, but there was no tenseness in her. He would *never* find her in here. She almost wished she'd brought a book to read. Sitting quite comfortably beneath the wood desk, Rusty let her thoughts roam. It was for this reason that the sound of sudden footsteps and the sight of adult, trouser-clad legs made her gasp. One moment there was nothing, and the next moment the chair was moved completely out of the way and Chase was standing just inches from her. He'd obviously heard the gasp since he cautiously stepped back and slowly bent to see her.

"Hello," he said with soft uncertainty.

"I thought you went to town," she whispered at him.

"I'm back. What are you doing?"

"Hiding from Quin," she replied, still speaking in a stage whisper. "He's figured out all my other hiding places, so I had to find someplace new, and you were gone — well, I thought you were gone. Anyway, this seemed like the perfect place."

Chase smiled, thinking she looked adorable. Her hair was in her face, and her eyes were huge. He didn't know many adults who could fit so easily under his desk.

"You could just forget I'm here."

Chase's look was comical. "Trust me when I tell you I couldn't do that."

Rusty laughed softly, and a second later she heard Quintin's voice and watched Chase stand.

"Is Aunt Rusty hiding in here?" the little boy asked.

Chase hesitated. "Is it cheating if I tell you?"

"Oh, I don't know. I can't find her."

"Where have you looked?"

"Everywhere!" He sounded dismayed. "We're not supposed to go outside."

He looked so forlorn that Chase had to help him. "Have you searched here in the office?"

"No."

"Well, I guess you could look in here." Chase felt a small fist hit the top of his shoe, but he didn't move.

"Aunt Rusty!" Quintin shouted just a moment later as he scrambled past his father's legs to get to her. Rusty laughed as he climbed beneath the desk and tried to sit in her lap. Chase followed him down to the floor, actually stretching out on his side to talk with them.

"You told him!" Rusty accused.

"I felt sorry for him."

"You should feel sorry for me. Do you know the places he can hide? My hair and dress always manage to hang out, and he finds me every time."

For all the scowls being sent his way, Chase could only smile. She was marvelous when she was fierce.

"What was I supposed to do?"

"Ask him if he was ready to give up. That way I can come out, and he doesn't have to know where I hid. Then I can use this place again."

"That wouldn't have worked."

"Yes, it would," she insisted. "Next time I wouldn't make a sound. You wouldn't even know that I was here."

The look he sent her caused her to lower her eyes.

"Don't you think Aunt Rusty is pretty, Quintin?" he asked his son.

Quintin smiled at Rusty.

"He's being silly, isn't he?" Rusty asked Quintin in order to cover her embarrassment. She wouldn't look at Chase but felt him reach up and tuck her hair behind her ear.

"Mmm, very pretty indeed."

Rusty still wouldn't look at him, and Quintin, thinking this a great game, just laughed. Rusty fixed the hair over her ear, but Chase pushed it back again and caught her hand.

"Quintin?" Mrs. Whitley's voice carried into the drawing room; she was clearly looking for him.

"You'd better go see what she wants," his father told him.

Chase looked back to Rusty when the small McCandles went on his way. He stared at her a moment and then stood to his feet. When Rusty crawled from beneath the desk, he gave her a hand up. He propped himself on the edge of the desk and waited for her to push the hair from her face before speaking.

"This is going to be a challenge."

"What's that?"

"Courting you. I didn't court my first wife at all, and now I'm trying to get to know you while having to share you with my five-year-old son."

Rusty could only stare at him.

"Not to mention the fact that you can't go on living here."

This was news to Rusty, so she didn't respond.

"Unless, of course," Chase said, only half-kidding, "we were married this weekend. Then you could live here."

Rusty decided to go with the wry humor she heard in his voice. Her chin went into the air as she teased back.

"I'm not certain that I can marry a man who tells my opponent where I'm hiding. Where I grew up that was a pretty serious offense."

"I was way off when I asked Quintin if you were pretty," Chase returned seriously. "Pretty doesn't come close to describing how lovely you are."

Rusty's heart swelled. She had worried about what he thought of her. The admiration she saw in his eyes went a long way in her heart.

"Have dinner with me tonight," Chase said suddenly.

Rusty blinked. They had dinner together almost every night.

"In town. Just the two of us."

Rusty felt a rush of excitement go through her but still said, "Quintin."

"Something tells me Mrs. Whitley or my mother would be thrilled to take care of him."

"All right. Shall I check with them?"

"I'll take care of it. You just be ready to leave at 6:30, and wear that lavender dress with the purple trim."

Rusty's mouth opened.

"What did I say?"

"I don't know." He had flabbergasted her. "I just didn't think you noticed anything about me, and now in one morning you say I'm pretty and that I am to wear a certain dress."

Chase laughed — not at Rusty — but at himself. He *had* done a good job of keeping his feelings to himself. The truth was that he noticed everything about her.

"Why is that funny?" She sounded so uncertain that Chase sobered in a moment.

"It's not, Katherine, not really. I was

laughing at myself, not you." He looked at her for a moment. "Did you honestly think I didn't find you attractive?"

Rusty bit her lip.

"Tell me, Katherine," he urged softly.

She couldn't look at him but still managed to say, "It's just little remarks about my curly hair having a mind of its own, or my nose being burned because I forgot my bonnet. You say things like that, and I just assume they're distasteful to you."

"Katherine," he said and waited for her to look at him. "Nothing could be further from the truth."

She nodded, but he wasn't certain she was persuaded. He was sure she was not reassured when she said only, "I'd better get back to work. Are Mr. and Mrs. Capland around today?"

"As far as I know," he said slowly. He was going to have to let the other subject drop and take time to show how very lovely he found her; telling her wasn't enough. "My mother and Cap plan to leave Saturday to spend some time in the mountains. They might come back here on their way home."

Rusty nodded. "I'm glad I was able to meet them."

"They're quite taken with you."

This was good news to Rusty, but she

didn't stay or ask what they had said. Mrs. Whitley had asked Quintin to put his puzzle away so she could mend the rug in his room. Rusty found him there still gathering all the pieces. She knelt down to help him but could feel how distracted she was. Tonight she was going out with Chase. Tonight they could talk and be alone. The day was sure to last forever.

"How's this?" Chase asked of Rusty as he waited for her to slip into the booth.

"Fine. Thank you."

Rusty had half-expected something to prevent them from going out, but it didn't happen. Quintin was with his grandmother, and she was out with Chase McCandles — just the two of them — with the whole evening waiting to be explored.

"How hungry are you?"

"Not very," Rusty had to admit. She had not eaten since lunch, but her stomach felt jittery and nervous. What if he learned that she was not the woman he wanted after all? Rusty's eyes left her menu to study the man across the table. His gaze was still on the food list, but she stared at him so long that he finally looked up.

"Did you decide?"

"No."

Chase put his menu down. "What is it, Katherine?"

"We don't know each other very well, do we?"

Chase was well able to understand her hesitancy and said, "And you're naturally wondering what type of man has asked you to be his wife."

"No, I'm wondering if you'll want me after you get to know me."

Chase looked at her for a moment. This conversation was somehow familiar. At last he remembered.

"If I could give you any advice right now, it would be for you to take care of yourself and not me. Do you remember when I asked you to come work with Quintin?"

"Of course."

"I don't remember your asking me any questions. You were more worried about my response to you. You can't do that this time, Katherine. You've got to make sure that I'm the man with whom you can spend the rest of your life. Does that make sense?"

"Yes. I'm still just getting used to the whole idea."

"Then don't let me rush you. I might be tempted to do that since I'm a little further along in my feelings, but just tell me, and I'll give you time, as much as you need."

"Thank you," Rusty said simply, but then her head cocked to one side. "I don't really know what you do. I know you make investments and such, but I'm not exactly sure what that entails."

"I do make investments, but mostly I own a lot of property. If I see a piece of land that I think would develop well, I buy it and build on it."

"That's why you need to travel."

"Yes, and that's one of the reasons I'm looking into selling off some of those properties or hiring a manager. I can't keep up with all of it and be home as much as I want."

Rusty was thrilled to hear that he was committed to being home more, but she also wondered what it would be like to have the kind of money he had at her disposal.

"What are you thinking?"

"I was just letting my mind wander. What would I do if I had money to invest?"

"What would you do?"

She didn't have to think long. "I'd see if I could buy that large piece of land by the pond."

"What would you do with it?"

Rusty smiled. "Put up an orphanage."

Chase did not smile back. "I already own that land," he said softly.

Rusty's brows flew upward.

"And it never once occurred to me to put an orphanage on it," Chase admitted.

His voice was so thoughtful, so stunned, that Rusty felt she needed to remain silent. The silence lasted until the waiter returned. They asked him to wait and take their order. When he left, the conversation didn't go back to land and investments, but Rusty could tell she'd said something that would make Chase think.

Nearly two hours later, as they were leaving the restaurant with plans to walk through town, Rusty remembered something Chase had said while they were standing in his office.

"Do you want me to look for another place to live?" she now offered.

"I've already started looking into that. I can't imagine you not living at Briarly, but I think it's for the best. The space between us will also help me give you the time you need."

"All right. Maybe I should ask around at church."

"That's a good idea. I know of a couple of women who live together; maybe they would have room for you to join them. I'll introduce them to you on Sunday."

"I could also live with a family who needs help with their children," Rusty suggested in complete sincerity.

Chase smiled. This one was special; his heart had told him that all along. He knew he would never find another like her. The orphanage came to his mind again. It was a fascinating idea. He praised God that Rusty had suggested it. He praised God for her. He glanced beside him now and caught sight of her lovely profile. They hadn't been touching, but he reached for her hand.

"Does that bother you?"

"No," Rusty said, but she could hardly breathe. He made her feel so cherished and special.

I think I love this man, Lord. I wasn't planning on it, but I realize now that he hasn't been far from my thoughts in weeks. Help me to go slowly with this. Help me to enjoy it, to be thankful and wise.

"Are you all right?" Chase suddenly asked, seeing how intense her face had become.

Rusty looked at him and smiled. "I'm just fine."

Chase smiled right back at her before tucking her arm in his and slowing his stride just a little more. It was going to be a wonderful evening.

42

Chase led the way up the center aisle of the church but then stood politely aside so that Rusty and Quintin could precede him. Once in the pew Quintin snuggled happily between his father and Rusty. He had been quite sad when Cap and his grandmother had left the day before, but his father had reminded him to be thankful for the time he'd had with them. He was now back to his cheerful self. His hand went into the folds of Rusty's skirt as he moved especially close to her.

Rusty lovingly touched his little knee, letting her eyes scan the other pews and her mind wander. Not for the first time she noticed how many children there were. Quintin was just one of three or four dozen. She found herself wishing there was a program for them here as there was in Manitou —

not a time to replace church, but to have a Bible story and time of singing a little more on their level. Rusty's brow lowered. She had no way of knowing if there were many biblically qualified teachers, but Colorado Springs Bible Church certainly had enough people to set up several teams of teachers.

"That's quite a look." Chase's quiet voice was softer than usual. He had an arm along the back of the pew behind Quintin's head. His hand lay lightly against Rusty's back. She glanced up to find him watching her and felt horrible for her thoughts.

"I'm being difficult," she whispered back. "I always think I have the answer to everything."

Chase's brow rose. "You don't strike me as being extremely opinionated, Katherine."

Rusty shook her head in self-accusation. "I can be impossible. Right now I'm sitting here thinking that this church needs a children's program like the one in Manitou. What arrogance on my part! I don't know these people well enough to know if any of them meet the Bible's standards for teachers. Even I know that you don't set up a program before you have obedient workers."

"It's an experience knowing you, did you realize that?" Chase surprised her by asking, his eyes tender.

"Why is that?"

"Well, I couldn't agree with you more that godly workers have to be found before committees or programs are instituted, but the whole idea of a children's church time never occurred to me. I've even attended yours and still didn't think of it for this church."

"Well, at least you're not a know-it-all."

"You're too hard on yourself," he said gently. "But it wouldn't hurt to talk to the elders. They might be thinking along the same line." Chase managed to get these words in before the song leader stepped behind the pulpit and asked them to rise. Their eyes locked for a few seconds before Chase opened the hymnal.

Rusty thought about his words. *He might be right,* she said to the Lord, *but it's all in my attitude. Instead of looking around and praying for a children's class, I'm critical. Instead of asking You to prepare hearts so that this church could have a great children's program, I'm scowling at innocent people and making judgments. Instead of finding out the path the leaders are on, I'm making my own.*

As Rusty sang and prepared her heart for the sermon, Chase was doing a little praying of his own. *She has ideas that challenge me. Sometimes I think my world is small. She has such a different outlook. My view has been busi-*

ness, and hers has been children. I know you need godly businessmen here on the earth, Lord, but something tells me that Katherine's dreams and focus have a much more eternal reach.

Chase forced his mind onto the sermon and was pleased that he did. As he had been for the past few weeks, Pastor Radke was in 1 Corinthians, and Chase was convicted by what he heard. At times his walk with the Lord was inconsistent. He prayed that he would have a no-matter-what attitude of obedience seven days a week.

With that in mind, Chase remembered his words to Clayton Taggart. He must honor Rusty and their relationship and move her out of the house before their courtship went much further. He was praying about how to go about it when Darcey Lackland, the church organist, walked up for the closing song.

Darcey wasn't elderly by any stretch of the imagination, but she was a widow, all her children grown and gone. She lived alone in a comfortable home downtown. Chase remembered that he'd taken care of the sale of some property for her several years earlier, and they had gotten along very well. He decided to approach her at once.

"I need to speak to someone," Chase told Rusty when the congregation was dismissed.

"All right. Quin and I can visit. Do you want to find us, or should we come for you?"

"I'll find you."

The last strains of the postlude were just ending when Chase reached the front. Darcey spotted him immediately and came off the bench with a smile.

"Well, Chase McCandles, how are you?"

"I'm well, Mrs. Lackland. How about yourself?"

"Can't complain," she said with a smile. "You look like a man with a mission."

"As a matter of fact, I am. I have a business proposition for you."

"This sounds interesting."

The two sat in the front pew to talk, and although Chase could see that he had surprised the organist, she was not against the idea of giving up one of the bedrooms in her home. She liked her privacy, she explained, and Chase was able to reassure her that Rusty would be at Briarly nearly every day. He offered her a generous monthly amount that made her brows rise, and even insisted when she tried to protest.

"When would you need her to come?"

"The sooner the better."

Darcey eyed him. "Like that, is it?"

Chase looked pleased without smiling. "Yes. It's not going to be as easy or convenient to have her away from Briarly, or as much fun for that matter, but it's the best thing right now."

"May I let you know in a week?"

"Absolutely. I haven't checked with anyone else. I will, though — ask around a little bit more. That way you won't feel pressured."

"Please don't," Darcey replied quickly. "I can all but give you a yes right now, but I tend to do things too swiftly. By making myself think about this for a week, I'll know if I've done the right thing."

"That's fine. Would you like to meet Katherine?"

"I believe I would. Who knows, she might take an instant disliking to me."

Chase laughed, remembering all at once how fun this woman was. Five minutes later, Rusty thought so too. Chase introduced them and then explained the plan. Rusty wasted no time learning whether Darcey had grandchildren, and with that they were off. She heard all about their ages and personalities. As fascinating as Rusty was to watch, Chase's eyes were on Darcey as the women spoke. Her smile was nonstop, and he felt confident that the older woman's forthcoming answer would be in the affirmative.

Rusty enjoyed herself as well. She had

wondered where she would end up in all of this, but there was no need to worry. By the time they said their goodbyes and walked to the waiting carriage, she was floating on a cloud.

"I forgot to check with her about the cost," Rusty commented as she stopped and looked back to find her.

"I'll be taking care of it," Chase told her and turned to help her into the carriage.

"All right. I guess adjusting my salary would be just as easy."

"I won't need to do that."

Rusty wasn't very comfortable with Chase spending more money, but she didn't question him right then. Back at Briarly, however, Quintin said his pants made his legs itch and asked if he could go right to his room. Rusty gave him leave, but she did not step down from the carriage herself.

"I don't know much about the way the well-to-do live," she began quietly, "but I do know that they don't keep their money by giving all of it away."

"You're talking about the salary."

"Yes. You already pay me a generous amount. If you're going to pay for my room, then I think you should cut my pay or let me pay Mrs. Lackland out of the salary I get now."

Chase didn't answer her. He sat next to her in the carriage, his arm along the seat back, and stared into her eyes.

"Have I told you that your eyes are beautiful?" he said suddenly.

"I'm not sure."

"I'm not trying to distract you, by the way. We can talk about the salary for as long as you like, but I didn't want to forget to tell you that I think your eyes are beautiful."

"I hated the color when I was a child," Rusty admitted.

"Why?" Chase asked gently, wishing he could have seen her as a little girl.

"People stared, and one of the other girls at school was cruel about them. She and I eventually became friends, but for a few years she hated me."

"Jealousy?"

"I think so. Her home was a mess. Her father yelled a lot. Our teacher was wonderful — everyone loved him — and of course he was my father."

"When did you begin to love children?"

"When an abandoned baby was left at our door."

Chase blinked at her. "What did you do?"

Rusty smiled. "We kept her. It's Dana."

Chase's mouth dropped open. "I had no

idea. I mean, she even has red hair like you and Les."

Rusty smiled. "Amazing, isn't it? No one even remembers that she wasn't born to my parents. It's as though she's always been there."

"No wonder you're so special."

Rusty smiled. "That was a nice thing to say."

"I meant it. And it's also the reason I want to take care of your room with Darcey Lackland, as well as leave your salary where it's been." He paused and stared at her again, his hand coming up to caress her cheek. "If you really aren't comfortable with it, I'll do what you want, but if you haven't caught on yet, Katherine, I do things differently where you're concerned. I always have, even before I realized I loved you."

"How can I possibly refuse an offer like that?"

Chase smiled. "You can't, just as I hoped you wouldn't." This time he leaned down and kissed her cheek. "Ready for some lunch?"

"Yes, I am. Quintin never came back. I wonder if he got out of his pants."

Chase helped her to the ground and offered to see to Quintin. He left the carriage for Whit.

The afternoon was spent in idle pursuits. Rusty and Quintin put a puzzle together, and Chase fell asleep on the davenport while reading a book. They walked in the woods and talked a little of the future; Rusty knew her heart was falling fast. It was bedtime before it hit her that this was probably her last week at Briarly, at least for a time. She closed her eyes and tried to fall asleep quickly — anything to block out the pain of leaving for who knew how long.

Tuesday morning found Rusty and Quintin on the floor of the drawing room, newspapers spread in front of them, working on small dolls they had made from sticks and pieces of cloth. They had two families completed, including grandparents, a dog, and one horse.

"This is your mother, Aunt Rusty," Quintin said seriously.

"Thank you, Quin. I'll put her with my father. Now, does your family have the dog or the horse?"

Before he could answer, Chase wandered through. He took a seat on the nearest ottoman, and Quintin explained to him all about the families. The little boy stumbled a little as he got to the mother of his own family — he didn't have a name for her — but he went on to tell the dog's name, and Chase praised him warmly before saying he had to get back to work. He stood and moved away after a smile to Rusty, and the two dollmakers went back to their play.

"I wish our dolls had hair, Aunt Rusty."

"Oh, Quin, what a good idea! We could use some of my hair."

"Really?" The little boy's eyes were round with excitement. "Could we really?"

"Of course. It's a great idea. Do you know where my little sewing scissors are?"

"Katherine, I would have a word with you," Chase spoke, very suddenly back at her side.

He was roundly ignored.

"In your little sewing box in your closet?" Quintin questioned.

"That's right. Now you mustn't run or even walk fast once you have them in your hand."

"Katherine." Chase's voice came through again, but the woman in question had eyes only for Quintin.

"I'll find some glue and —" Rusty cut off when Chase stepped directly in front of her. Bending low, he brought her to her feet.

"If you'll excuse us for just a moment, Quintin, I must have a word with Aunt Rusty."

Without waiting for an answer, Chase pulled Rusty through the drawing room, into his office, and shut the doors. Quintin dropped back to his knees next to the newspaper but did not pick up his dolls. His eyes were on the glass doors that led to his father's office and the man and woman inside.

43

"You will not do this," Chase told Rusty firmly, his voice very low. He bent over her in an attempt to make himself understood. "You will not cut your hair."

"It won't be very much," she explained as if he hadn't spoken.

"You will not, Katherine, and I mean it."

"It's perfect. I don't know why I didn't think of it before."

"You're not listening to me," Chase tried again. "You will not cut your beautiful hair."

"Chase," Rusty said gently, putting her hand on his chest. "It's such a good idea, and Quin will be so pleased."

Her hand, her huge eyes, and the softness of her voice all worked to stop him in his tracks. This was who she was. This was the woman he'd fallen for. She did not leave things undone, not even stick-doll making. Chase's chest rose on a huge sigh, and for a moment his eyes closed. He opened them again and found her still staring up at him. Chase stared helplessly back. Carla had been so mild. She'd been steady and quiet and very predictable. Never once had she hid under his desk. With Rusty he never knew what was going to happen from one day to the next, yet he loved her with all his heart.

"Chase?" She spoke his name with soft uncertainty.

"I told myself if you ever called me Chase, I would kiss you."

Rusty smiled and glanced out the door. Quintin was just where they'd left him, his eyes on their every move. Rusty looked back at the man with her.

"We have an audience in the other room."

Chase didn't even bother to glance toward the door.

"He'll have to get used to the sight," he whispered and lowered his head to tenderly brush her lips with his own. It was brief, but oh so sweet, and when he raised his head, he smiled warmly into her eyes. Not able to refrain from touching her, he tenderly cupped her jaw and let his thumb stroke over her cheek. For an instant Rusty's eyes closed. He made her feel so warm and cherished.

She looked up at him, her eyes saying the words before she could utter them.

"This isn't the place I would have chosen to tell you," she whispered softly, "but I love you, Chase McCandles."

"This place is fine," he said, his voice low, his eyes drilling into hers. "I'll hear those words anytime you want to say them."

Rusty couldn't speak. Her heart was too full. He was the one. She had led with her head, and now her heart had followed. He was the one she could share her life with. They stood close for a moment, not speaking, just looking at each other. It was some moments before Rusty forced her mind back to the little boy in the next room.

"I need to get back to Quin."

"Is the hair issue settled?"

Rusty nodded her head. "Yes. I won't cut it if you don't want me to, but I just need a little. The dolls are so small." He could see that her creative mind was working again. "Actually, I was hoping to get some of yours too."

Chase's head went back as he laughed.

"You could spare some, Chase," she said matter-of-factly. "Just a little off the neckline. I would be so careful."

Chase was ready to kiss her again, but both adults caught movement through the glass doors. After hearing his father's laugh, Quintin had come close, his little face a mix of anticipation and anxiety. Chase beckoned to him with one hand and he came in with a smile. Chase lifted him on one arm and put the other one around Rusty.

"Are we going to cut Aunt Rusty's hair now?"

"Yes," his father said, having reconsidered. "Just a little." He looked down at the woman who had been an unending source of surprise and delight. "It looks as though I'll lose some of my own too."

This news was naturally met with rave reviews from his son, and Rusty beamed at him before leading the way into the drawing room for haircuts and to finish the dolls. Chase never did go back to work. When everyone got hungry, he suggested a picnic lunch.

They were off in the open carriage less than an hour later, the picnic basket tucked safely in the back. Chase didn't tell Rusty where they were headed, but he stopped the horses by the pond, and they walked to the field where Rusty wanted her orphanage. For the next four hours they caught grasshoppers, ran, played hide-and-seek in the trees, rested on the blanket, and ate the picnic Cook had prepared.

When Quintin ran out of steam, he lay

next to his father, and Chase put his arm around him. Rusty was gathering the last of the lunch when Chase began to share.

"This day, the hot weather and stillness, reminds me of the summer I came to Christ." Rusty looked over at him, but his eyes were on the horizon.

"I was 16 when my mother came home and so self-centered that I couldn't even see it. I'll never forget that summer. My mother had been home only a few months and was doing well, but for as much as I'd missed her when she was gone, I didn't want to spend any time with her. Each morning she read her Bible out loud at the breakfast table, but I just wanted to get away — away from her and away from Briarly."

Chase looked over at Quintin and saw that he had fallen asleep. He continued his story for Rusty.

"My mother was so gentle and kind, but I just wanted to run from her. My father was all business and gruff, and for some reason that was easier to take. Then it happened. One Sunday morning I announced that I didn't want to go to church. I don't even know where my father was right then, probably on a business trip. My mother and I had a huge fight. I tried to walk out on her, but she followed me right to the stable. I saddled my horse and would have ridden away, but I looked over and saw that she was crying.

"I couldn't look away. It somehow broke my heart. She began to speak, and for the first time I listened. 'All those years I prayed to return to you,' she said. 'All those years I begged God to let me come home to you, but now I wish I hadn't. I wish I'd died in that sanitarium. No amount of pain there could ever compare to the pain I feel here at Briarly.'

"I couldn't believe my ears. She said those words and just walked back to the house. I was stunned. She told me not long after that that she regretted her words almost immediately, but on that day God used them to get my attention. I unsaddled my horse, and when my mother left for church, I was in the carriage with her. I didn't speak of it, and neither did she, but from that day forward I determined never to make her cry again.

"The weeks that followed weren't easy. I went to church when I didn't want to and made myself sit and listen to the Bible reading when I wanted to be anywhere else, but I stayed. Then one day God opened my heart. My mother was reading in Luke about Lazarus and the rich man, and I realized that I was a hell-bound sinner. She looked over and found tears in my eyes and simply asked me if I was finally ready.

"All I could do was nod my head. Sitting right in the breakfast room, I bowed my head and repented. I told God that I needed the salvation that only His Son could provide. I confessed my need for a Savior and believed in Jesus Christ." Chase sighed with the sweet remembrance. "To say the least, I was a changed person after that." He looked at Rusty and found her eyes filled with tears.

"Thank you for telling me," she whispered.

Chase reached for her hand. "Thank *you* for breaking into my routine Christianity and making me aware that my son needed a father."

Rusty only smiled at him, too emotional to speak. Quintin was still asleep, but Chase looked down at his little face.

"Not until right before my father's death did I even know if he believed in Christ. He said he did, but he didn't lead an exemplary life. I want better for Quintin. I love the verse in 1 Timothy 4, I think it's verse 16, where Paul warns Timothy. He says, 'Take heed unto thyself and unto thy doctrine; continue in them; for in doing this thou shalt both save thyself and them that hear.' God's promises encompass tomorrow. And not just the day after today, but all the tomorrows yet to come, so I can claim that verse for Quintin and me. If I am faithful, he'll hear and know that he must turn to Christ not only for his salvation, but every day for the rest of his life."

"Thank you, Chase. Thank you for reminding me that God never gives up."

Chase smiled at her and gave her hand a small squeeze. They continued to talk until Quintin woke up and then made their way back to Briarly.

It was Rusty's idea of a perfect afternoon. By the time she returned to Briarly, she was extremely tired but also very peaceful. Word had come from Darcey Lackland that Rusty was more than welcome to move in. Knowing it to be the wisest thing, Chase arranged for her to go the next day. Both Rusty and Quintin cried, but by Saturday night she was comfortably situated in town. It helped Quintin to see what her new room and home looked like, and also to know that they were going to pick her up for church the very next morning.

As she had done Friday night, she fell into bed and slept instantly. Things had been a little too busy in the past few days. Her last thoughts had been that things would probably slow down now. She had completely forgotten that it was almost time to return to Boulder for the next wedding.

44

Boulder

Quintin McCandles' eyes were huge as he disembarked from the train, his hand snugly held by his father's. Rusty had walked ahead of them and turned to smile at him.

"This is my hometown, Quin. This is Boulder."

All the little boy could do was nod. Although he was a bit tired from the trip, he was also excited. Rusty exchanged a smile with Chase. It had been so fun to watch him on his first train trip. They had come north for Grace Harrington and Wyatt Buchanan's wedding. Rusty was in the wedding party and had wanted all along to bring Quintin to meet all of her family. Chase had impressed her to no end when he asked if he could join them and didn't insist on it. Since Rusty couldn't see enough of the man, she was more than happy to oblige. It was wonderful living at Mrs. Lackland's, but she didn't see as much of Chase and Quintin and missed them terribly.

"Shall we be off?" Chase asked, taking charge. "Are you up for the walk, Katherine?"

"Yes, I am."

"How about you, Quin? Can you walk a few blocks?"

"I think so. What is that barrel over there, Papa?"

They didn't leave the train station as swiftly as they expected — Quintin had a dozen questions. When they did arrive at the Taggart home, everyone was in attendance. Rusty was thronged, and when it was time for her siblings to meet Quintin, they fell in love with him.

Rusty performed the introductions. "This is Dana. She's my youngest sister. And this is Clare. She's just a little younger than I am. Les," she said, pointing to the young man who stood next to his father, "is my brother."

Quintin nodded, his eyes going to all of them but then quite naturally straying back to Rusty's brother. It wasn't hard to read his mind. If Leslie Taggart was as much fun as his father and Clayton Taggart were, they could have a good time.

"Mother, have you decided where we're all going to sleep?"

"Mr. McCandles will have the same room as last time," Jackie replied, "and I thought you might want to decide where you want Quintin. He can be in with his father, with Les, or with you. Wherever you think best."

"I think he should come to my room," Les put in. "We'll have a great time."

"What do you think, Quin?" Chase asked him. "Do you want to stay in Les' room with him?"

Quintin nodded shyly, but he also looked very pleased. Rusty watched as Leslie led his small roommate up the stairs. It was certain to be the start of a wonderful week together.

McKay Harrington's heart felt like it was going to burst as he walked his oldest daughter down the center aisle of the church. His wife, Callie, was in the front pew, and when McKay saw the tears standing in her eyes, they almost started his own.

Wyatt Buchanan, as fine a Christian young man as McKay could ever hope to meet, stood down front. His heart swelled again when he thought of the way Wyatt and Grace loved each other. If their marriage was anything like the one God had blessed between him and Callie, they would find no greater joy.

McKay handed Grace over to Wyatt, giving her cheek a quick kiss before moving to stand with Callie. Her hand sought his immediately, and he turned to smile into her eyes. Across the aisle from them stood Travis and Rebecca Buchanan, parents of the groom. Rebecca was in no better shape as far as tears went, and she spent the whole service with a hankie to her face. The four adults were extremely close, and having their children joined in marriage was more wonderful than they could have ever dreamed.

Standing up with the happy couple were friends and family. Wyatt's best man was his brother, Garrett. The two groomsmen were Grace's brother, Daniel, and Wyatt's friend, Tom Bacher. Grace's sister, Melissa, was her maid of honor, and standing up with her were Rusty and Wyatt's sister, Katie.

The other siblings, Roz Buchanan, Bart Harrington, and Andrea Harrington, all had jobs at the reception that was to be held immediately after the wedding. During the ceremony they sat with their parents.

Chase sat with Quintin and Rusty's parents, about halfway back on the bride's side.

He didn't know when he'd felt like this. He remembered his wedding with Carla. It had been a very small, private affair, but that had not been the difference. The difference had been what Chase witnessed in the groom's eyes. Wyatt Buchanan was a man in love. Chase had cared for Carla — he had cared very much — but those feelings had never approached the depth and intensity for the woman he now loved.

Chase had been able to write to Mrs. Harding with genuine best wishes, as well as tell her that he and Rusty had formed a strong attachment. The words had sounded stilted as he reread them, and he realized what a private person he was where others were concerned. With Rusty he could talk about any subject, but it wasn't like that with many other people in his life.

Now as Chase watched Rusty stand up front, lovely in a peach-colored gown, her hair piled atop her head, he couldn't help but wonder when their own wedding would take place. They often talked of the future, shared their dreams and desires, but Chase hadn't actually come right out and asked Rusty to marry him. She loved him, he knew that, but he was enjoying with Rusty what he'd never had with Carla: a true courtship. It was wonderful to get to know her a little more every day and to dream of the time when they would be man and wife.

The wedding ended while Chase was still lost in his musings. He realized with a start that he'd heard little of the ceremony. Clayton must have figured that out, since the older man asked him what he thought and smiled at him with a mischievous glint in his eye. Chase smiled in return, knowing he'd been caught out.

"Papa," Quintin touched his father's hand just then, "I have to be excused."

"All right." Chase scooped him up onto one arm and made for the door, thankful the ceremony was over.

"Did Aunt Rusty get married today?" Quintin asked his father after he'd used the private facilities.

"No, Grace Harrington, a friend of hers, did."

"Oh. Who was the man?" Quintin asked as they walked back to join the other guests.

"The man who got married was another friend. His name is Wyatt Buchanan."

Quintin nodded, and Chase stopped him with a hand to his shoulder. He bent down in front of him and spoke into his face.

"Are you worried about something, Quin?"

"No, I just want to see Aunt Rusty."

Chase nodded. "I do too, but it might be a little while before she's free to be with us. Will you be okay until then?"

He nodded, and Chase leaned close to press a kiss to his brow. Quintin reached up with both hands, his face very serious. He held his father's cheeks in his small hands and tilted Chase's head down so he could kiss his forehead. Chase laughed.

"Oh, Quin, you do my heart good."

"My heart is good too," he said, and Chase laughed again.

The little boy gladly took his father's hand so they could head into the reception. Chase spotted Clayton and Jackie and moved to join them. Before he could get that far, Dana commandeered Quintin and took him off to play.

"How did the bride look?" Jackie asked, and Chase listened as Clayton described her. "And Rusty?"

Clayton laughed. "I could tell you, but I couldn't do half the job Chase could."

"I thought it was you, Mr. McCandles," she commented.

"How did you know?"

"Well, I knew it was someone tall, and I thought I caught a faint scent of bayberry. I know from being in your home that that would be you."

"Amazing," Chase said and meant it.

Jackie smiled. It wasn't amazing to her, just the facts. "So are you going to tell me? How does my daughter look today?"

"Beautiful," he said softly, and Jackie could tell by his voice that he was no longer looking down at her. She was right. His height making it easy, Chase was staring across the room to where Rusty stood with the other attendants. She spotted him after just a few minutes and smiled when her eyes met his. Someone was waiting to speak to her, so she had no choice but to look away. However, she glanced back whenever possible and often caught Chase's eyes on her. Just as soon as she was able, she escaped to his side.

"Hello," she said softly as she tucked her arm into his. "What did you think of the wedding?"

"Yes, tell us, Chase," Clayton teased. "How did you like it?"

Chase laughed.

"Have I missed a private joke?" Rusty wanted to know.

"I'll never tell," Clayton vowed.

Rusty laughed but looked confused. It was hours later before they had a few moments alone, and she could ask him.

"Your father is a tease," Chase told her, pushing a stray curl from her cheek. "He could tell that I was more interested in a certain redheaded bridesmaid than in the bride herself."

Rusty dimpled at him. The wedding had been wonderful, but she had missed some of it as well, asking herself when it would be her turn. She sensed this was Chase's distraction but didn't mention it.

They were rarely alone in the days that followed, but what they lacked in privacy, they made up for in fun. Quintin followed Leslie around like a puppy, and one day even went with Clare to Mrs. Wood's house.

All too soon it was time to return to Colorado Springs. Rusty did so with a mix of feelings: happy to be going back to her routine and time alone with Chase and Quintin, but also sad because she loved to be with her family. As the train pulled from the station, Rusty knew she would miss them, but she also wondered more seriously than ever before if it might not be time to start a family of her own. She said nothing to Chase, but the thought lingered in her mind all the way home.

Colorado Springs

Chase, Rusty, and Quintin had been home for less than 24 hours when Chase tracked her down. She had arrived on time that morning but had not seen him. Now she was on the veranda reading a story to Quintin. Chase listened for a time and then wandered off. Rusty had the impression that he wanted to talk, but when she paused and started to close the book, Chase shook his head. This went on for the rest of the day. Chase would seek her out, but if she was busy with Quintin, he would let them be. At nearly the dinner hour, he finally found her alone in the drawing room.

"Are you all right?" she asked without hesitation.

"I have to know," he said softly. "I thought I could wait, give it more time, but I have to know for certain, from your own lips, if you're going to marry me."

Rusty nodded, remembering all her thoughts and prayers from just the day before. She had wondered when he was going to ask but would never have brought it up herself.

"Can you give me about 20 minutes?" she asked.

"Certainly. Is there something I can do?"

"I just need to speak with Quin."

"All right. Do you want me to find him?"

"Would you, please?"

Chase rose to get his son, and Rusty en-

537

joyed a few minutes alone. She had had such a wonderful time with her family. She'd made time to talk to everyone, but her mother had asked a question of her that had stopped her in her tracks. The way Rusty cared for Quintin, she was surprised that she'd overlooked this. She hadn't been able to say anything for a time but had ended up thanking her mother and giving her a great hug.

A few minutes later, Chase returned, Quintin on his back. He deposited the little boy onto the davenport and started on his way.

"You can stay if you'd like," Rusty said softly to him.

Chase nodded and sat down across from her.

"Come here, Quin." Rusty patted her lap. Quintin was more than happy to comply. "Do you know that I love you, Quintin James McCandles?"

"I love you too, Aunt Rusty. We love each other."

"Yes, we do, and I'm so glad. Tell me, Quin, have you thought about my leaving, you know, at the end of the summer like we planned?"

"Yes. I don't like it. It makes me sad," he said with quiet respect.

"What if I stayed here and married your papa? Do you think you would like that?"

"Stay for always?" He made sure he understood.

"That's right."

Quintin nodded, his face open and sweet. "I think you should," he said simply. "I would like it." Rusty smiled at him but then noticed his frown of concentration.

"Are you still Aunt Rusty?"

"You mean, what should you call me?"

Quintin nodded.

"I think you can call me whatever you like, but more important than that, Quintin, is that I know for certain that you would be all right. I love your father, but I wouldn't want to stay and marry him unless you thought it was a very good idea."

"I think it is. Would you still live at Mrs. Lackland's?"

"No. I would live here. Is that all right with you too?"

"Would you still play with me?"

"I would play with you every day," she said softly. "You would be my own little boy."

"Like a mother?"

"That's right."

The smile that crossed his face was too much for Rusty. She wrapped her arms around him and held him close. Her eyes went to the man across the room from them, and she smiled.

"I love you," Chase mouthed the words very softly.

Rusty's smile was tender. "Do you have your answer?" she asked quietly.

Chase nodded, knowing that the evening would seem long until they could be alone. Weeks ago he had chosen a ring for her, and tonight he could present it. Suddenly he saw her again. She was coming from downtown Colorado Springs, the Parks children in hand. He had confessed to Rusty that he hadn't been the same since. Now watching her hold his son, knowing she would be the best mother in the world — not to mention the most loving wife — he wanted to tell her again. He didn't know if he could find the words to explain to her what had happened on that day, but he would find a way. If it took the next 50 years, he would show Katherine Alexa Taggart that she was in his heart to stay.

Epilogue

Colorado Springs
April 1911 — nearly 14 years later

Chase stood back and waited for Rusty to precede him through the front door of Briarly. Quintin, now close to 19 years of age, came behind her, as did four of his siblings: Ethan, a tall boy of 13 years; Alisa, who was 10 ½, also tall like her father but redheaded; Simon, another redhead, who had turned 8 his last birthday; and 6-year-old Jordan, whose smile was infectious. Leah and Marcus, ages 4 and almost 2, had been sharing a cold and had not accompanied the rest of the family to the orphanage.

Chase thanked the children for going with them and reminded them not to make noise before finding out if Marcus was sleeping.

He then followed Rusty, who had gone into the drawing room to sit down. Chase sat across the room and eyed her, his gaze taking in her shape first and then studying her face.

"I hope you're ready to have this baby," he said in the quiet way she had always known from him.

She was ready but still asked, "Why?"

"Because I would say you have less than 24 hours."

Rusty smiled. "Thank you, Dr. McCandles."

Chase grinned back at her. "You may laugh all you want, Katherine, but I've seen you do this six times. You're going to have that baby very soon."

"What is it you see?" she asked, honestly curious.

Chase shrugged. "Your walk changes. And you sit very carefully. I didn't notice it until you were moving among the children at the orphanage today, but it's there, and every time I see it, you present me with another child within 24 hours."

Rusty's eyes were skeptical, but she still smiled at him.

"You were wonderful with those children today," Chase complimented her, knowing she was not convinced about the baby's coming so soon.

"Thank you," Rusty said softly. Her dream had come true. For over ten years the Prairie Lake Orphanage had been operating in the field where Rusty had first imagined it. The facility was able to house 48 children and 20 staff members or potential parents.

"They were certainly excited about that picture of Clare on the elephant," Rusty commented. "I'm glad you remembered to take it."

"That's all Alisa can talk about," Chase said. "She prays for her aunt Clare every night but then asks God if she can join her in India."

"Who knows?" Rusty said, even as she tried to stay open to the idea. It was one thing to have her sister go to the mission field; her own child was a little harder to grasp. "I have to remember that they're not mine, Chase."

"I know what you mean." His thoughts were moving along the same line. "I also need to watch that I don't put the cart before the horse. She is but ten."

Rusty smiled. For a moment she had forgotten that as well. She let her eyes drift shut and wondered if Chase might be right. She didn't tire easily when pregnant, until it came down to the last few weeks. Right now she was bone weary. She'd have drifted off to sleep if Leah had not come looking for her just then. Sniffles or not, Rusty welcomed her youngest daughter into her lap and held her close. Marcus was close on his sister's heels and threw himself at Chase the moment he spotted him. The children's favorite toy was their father.

"I didn't get to go today," Leah reminded her mother.

"I know." Rusty was compassionate as she smoothed her dark hair. "But we didn't want any of the children to get a cold."

"Marcus didn't cry," Leah also informed them, her four-year-old mind happy to change subjects that swiftly.

"Good boy," his father said to him. "Did you take a long nap?"

Marcus, whose vocabulary was limited, said only, "Nap."

The older children had been busy at various pursuits, but as Chase and Rusty told their youngest two children about the trip to the orphanage, the others slowly made their way to the drawing room, all wanting something to eat. It wasn't long until dinner, but Chase said they could have a small snack.

Rusty rose to do the honors, and after making sure she was all right, Chase told his wife he had some work to do in the office. Rusty was a little hungry herself, so she ate with the children and then agreed to accompany Simon and Jordan to the stable.

"Quin," she asked the son who now towered over her. "Will you keep an eye on Marky?"

"Sure. Where is Leah going to be?"

"With Alisa. She said they're going upstairs to work on a present for Marky's birthday next month."

"Mother," Quintin teased her with a glint in his eyes, so much like Chase that it was frightening, "he'll hear you."

Rusty laughed and looked down at her youngest. Marcus was still working on his crackers and milk, showing little interest in the conversation.

"I suppose I'll have to wash his face too." Quintin sounded much more aggrieved than he felt.

"I'll do it," Cook said good-naturedly. Marcus McCandles, with his dark hair and huge dark eyes, had quite easily captured her heart.

Seeing that all was in order, Rusty thanked Cook and Quintin alike before exiting through the kitchen door, the boys in tow. Halfway to the stable, Ethan caught up with them. He usually had his head in a book, but he needed to discuss his latest theory. His mother was always the first to hear. Ethan was fascinated with airplanes and air travel of any kind. He always had a new idea he was working to perfect.

Rusty listened with half an ear, not because she didn't care but because Jordan was having a hard time remembering that he couldn't climb into the stalls. She had to reprimand him twice.

The second time she finished warning him, she said, "That's the end of it, Jordy." She did not shout, but he got the message. "Once more and you're to the house and in your room."

"Yes, Mother," he said, and went to join Simon, who was sitting in the open touring car their father had owned for several months. Chase let them sit in the front seats if they were very careful.

The interchange over, Rusty watched him walk away and thought she might find a bench to sit on. She was on the verge of asking Ethan to find her one when she suddenly found herself feeling quite sick. If she opened her mouth, she thought she might lose her snack. Rusty was relieved when it passed swiftly.

In the midst of Rusty's discomfort, Ethan decided to draw out his latest design and with a swift goodbye darted back toward the house. He had been gone for only ten minutes when Rusty's first pain hit. She put a hand on the stable door to steady herself. Chase's words came back to her. If she hadn't been in so much pain, she would have laughed.

"Boys," she called to them when she could, "we need to go in now."

"We just got here," Jordan protested.

Rusty's brows went in the air, and he immediately remembered his attitude.

"Yes, Mother."

Simon had come down without comment and caught his mother's hand as soon as he was near. Jordan took her other side, and the three of them walked back to the house.

"I can't wait to drive that car, Mother," Simon said wistfully. "I wish I could now."

"I know, Simon. Doesn't it sometimes feel like time stands still?"

The eight-year-old smiled up at her, and Rusty bent to kiss him. Jordan was next. A very affectionate child, he reached up to hug his mother while telling her he loved her. Rusty smiled into his eyes. With energy to spare, Simon and Jordan raced the rest of the way, and Rusty finished the distance in relative comfort. She sought out Chase immediately. He was still at his desk.

"Chase."

"I knew this would happen." Still in his

chair, he held the news article in his hand.

"You were right," Rusty said quietly.

"Oh, did I already tell you about this?" Chase went on. "The whole thing folded. I knew when I read about it that it was a poor investment. I'm just thankful we didn't get involved."

"Chase, you were right."

When she repeated her statement for the second time, Chase really looked at her. He wasn't long in catching on. He came around the desk immediately, the paper and everything else forgotten. He hugged Rusty and asked, "Have you had pains?"

"Only one, but I wish I hadn't eaten that snack with the children."

Chase gently kissed her, his hand dropping to the swell at her waist.

"Do you want to go upstairs?"

"Not yet. I just wanted you to know."

He smiled tenderly down at her, not even a hint of *I told you so* in his attitude as he brushed his hand down the back of her hair and kissed her brow.

"Why don't you sit down?"

Rusty shook her head. "I want to keep moving as long as I can."

"Okay, but as quickly as things happened last time, don't you think I should send for the doctor?"

"I don't think that will happen again," Rusty replied, but feeling rather uncomfortable just minutes later, she changed her mind and decided to head up to her room. Chase carried her, and for a moment he sat on the side of the bed and held her in his lap. Surprisingly, none of the children noticed them. They talked quietly about nothing in particular until Rusty had another contraction.

"That felt like the real thing," she said when she could breathe.

"I'm sending for the doctor."

This time Rusty didn't argue.

Quintin lay sprawled on the floor of the upstairs landing, a book open in front of him. The other children were settled in bed, all having prayed for their mother and the new baby. Mrs. Whitley had come and gone from the room several times. The doctor had come a few hours earlier. However, things had not progressed as swiftly as they had hoped.

For a moment Quintin thought about Katherine Alexa McCandles. She wasn't his biological mother, but for all the love she'd shown him, she could have been. He would never forget the day she donned a long, lacy dress and married his father. True to her word, she still played with him, read to him every day, and never once let him forget that he was loved. He'd only grown closer to his father as the months passed, and when they had started presenting him with siblings, the fun and joy increased. It was like a dream come true.

Quintin suddenly found himself very emotional and forced his mind to concentrate on the book in front of him. It worked for a time, but he often glanced toward the closed portal and prayed. It was during one of these times that he heard the small cry. As young as Marcus was, Quintin had forgotten what a wonderful sound that was. His eyes slid shut, and a relieved smile crossed his mouth.

"Thank You, Lord," he breathed. "Please be with both of them. Please take care of my mother."

His soft prayer was interrupted just minutes later when his father suddenly opened the door. Quintin was pushing to his feet when Chase said, "A girl, Quin. You have another sister."

Quintin smiled as his father hugged him. "How's Mother?"

"Come in and see."

Quintin didn't need to be asked twice. He walked swiftly into the room and right to his mother's side.

"Oh, Quin," Rusty smiled up at him. She was flushed and tired, but also delighted. "A girl — did your father tell you?"

"Yes. Michelle, isn't it?"

"That's right. Michelle for a girl and Clayton for a boy."

"Michelle McCandles. That's nice."

"Have you seen her?"

He hadn't. Michelle was still being cleaned up and checked over by the doctor and Mrs. Whitley, but it wasn't long before Chase had her in his arms and moved to show Quintin. Quintin watched as her face scrunched up, but she didn't actually cry.

"She's wonderful," he said and turned to smile at his mother. "I'm glad it's a girl."

Rusty smiled back at him and kissed his cheek when he bent over her.

The next few hours were spent settling in. Quintin took himself off to bed, proclaiming that this business of delivering babies was exhausting work. Rusty had a good laugh before the room emptied of all but Chase, giving her a chance to nurse the baby to sleep and fall asleep herself.

Chase ended up with Michelle in his arms, not yet ready to put her into the cradle. He sat on the bed, his back propped against the footboard, and looked down into her sleeping face. It didn't matter how many God gave them, Chase thought they were all miraculous. He was on the verge of putting the baby to bed when he found Rusty's eyes on him.

"I think you're wonderful," she told him as she did so often.

Chase's eyes locked with hers for a moment. He then stood and gently settled the newborn in her bed. He joined Rusty, sitting beside her on the edge of the mattress.

"Why am I wonderful?"

Rusty reached for his hand, not sure she could express herself. "You just are. You take such good care of us, and no matter how many children we have, you love them all."

Chase kissed her. "Since most of them look like their mother, that's not at all hard to do."

It was such a romantic thing to say, but then she'd learned early on that this was what she could expect from him. Chase McCandles loved his God, his wife, and his children with his whole heart. Through the years he had taught Rusty so much. They had grown in the Lord and closer to each other with every passing day.

"Coming to bed now?" Rusty asked.

"Yes."

Chase joined her a few minutes later. Rusty let a huge sigh escape when her head was finally pillowed on Chase's shoulder.

"Why the sigh?" he asked.

"Eight children, Chase. Can you believe it?"

"Yes, I can, but even if I were having trouble, I would need only to walk around the landing and look into each door."

Rusty laughed. "A long time ago I asked God to remember me when He thought of motherhood."

"I didn't know that." Chase came up on one elbow to look down into her face.

"It's true." Rusty brushed the hair from his brow. "I worked with children at the orphanage and even with Quin, and I wondered when I would have children of my own."

Chase smiled. "Now Quintin is your own, plus seven besides. God certainly did remember you, didn't He, Katherine?"

"Yes, He did, but that's no surprise at all, is it?"

"No surprise at all," he echoed softly, a smile in his voice. "No surprise at all."

The employees of Thorndike Press hope you have enjoyed this Large Print book. All our Large Print titles are designed for easy reading, and all our books are made to last. Other Thorndike Press Large Print books are available at your library, through selected bookstores, or directly from us.

For information about titles, please call:

(800) 257-5157

To share your comments, please write: